DATE DUE

AS TIME GOES BY

AS TIME GOES BY

TED ALLBEURY

Hodder & Stoughton

Copyright © 1994 by Ted Allbeury

First published in 1994 by Hodder and Stoughton,
a division of Hodder Headline plc

The author thanks Editions Raoul Breton for permission to quote
from Charles Trenet's song, 'J'ai ta main'.

'La Petite Tonkinoise' is reprinted by permission of Boosey &
Hawkes Music Publishers Ltd. English words by Eustace Ponsonby.
© Copyright 1906 by Hawkes & Son (London) Ltd.

The right of Ted Allbeury to be identified as the Author of the
Work has been asserted by him in accordance with the Copyright,
Designs and Patents Act 1988.

10 9 8 7 6 5 4 3 2 1

British Library Cataloguing in Publication Data

Allbeury, Ted
As Time Goes By
I. Title
823.914 [F]

ISBN: 0 450 60439 X

Typeset by Phoenix Typesetting, Ilkley, West Yorkshire

Printed and bound in Great Britain by Mackays, Chatham, Kent

Hodder and Stoughton Ltd
A division of Hodder Headline plc
338 Euston Road
London NW1 3BH

CHAPTER 1

A lot of people seemed to find it surprising, even incredible, that a man could bring up two girls, but it had seemed simple enough to him in the doing. The nanny had stayed on after Jenny died, he was reasonably well-off and he worked at home. And he had never tried to be a mother as well as a father. It had meant dodging a few issues that were essentially feminine but between Nanny Freeman and school they seemed to have filled the gaps all right. To him it had seemed all quite simple and straightforward. He loved his two daughters and taking care of them was, in his fortunate circumstances, a pleasure not a burden.

Victoria was thirteen. Very pretty. Blonde and leggy, with a temperament and character very like Jenny's. Pauline was dark and beautiful, calm and slightly aloof. At eighteen she seemed to have more common sense than he had himself. No doubts about herself or how life should be lived. She seemed to have inner strength rather than the bounce and enthusiasm of young Tory. He sometimes had to look away when one of her gestures was too like Jenny to be ignored.

He had found that while time didn't heal all wounds, it was possible to keep the memories of Jenny under control for most of the time. But there were odd things – a song, a place, Chanel No. 5, Le Figaro on a news-stand or a smell of bluebells in a wood – and she was there as if she had never been away. Sometimes, late at night when he was tired and perhaps uncertain about some film-script that he was writing, his low spirits could dissolve into depression at the thoughts that came surging back. So real that his mind started going over camera angles, lighting and dialogue as if it were some film that he was working on.

If his memories could have been only of that lovely happy-go-lucky girl and their days of wine and roses, they would have been welcome. But, inevitably, his thoughts were of the two years of deterioration and *those last months of doomed failure when love and caring were not enough. But he had kept all that from the girls. It had meant letting Jenny become a vague background figure. Not mentioning her birthday, their wedding anniversary or even the date of her death.*

The past closes quickly behind young children and he had done his best to keep the door tightly closed. When they were older and more mature, perhaps he could tell them how it had been. Unfair to the dead but beneficial for the living. He was never sure that this was the right way to deal with the problem and sometimes he had the fear that some day he would be proved wrong and a lot of birds would come flying back home to roost.

The birds started flying home the following Christmas when Pauline was unpacking from her first term at college. He was sitting with her in her room, chatting as she put her clothes in drawers and her books on the shelves. She had not responded very enthusiastically as they talked, and finally she sat on her bed facing him, her big eyes looking at him intently.

'Tell me about Moma.'

'What about her, sweetie?'

'Everything.'

'Is something worrying you?'

'Yes.'

'What? Tell me.'

'Was Moma a drunk?'

'What on earth made you ask that?'

'A reporter from a newspaper phoned me at college and said he wanted to interview me. He came down and showed me some old newspaper cuttings about Moma. He said he was doing a piece about forgotten heroines of World War Two. He said he'd contacted you and you'd refused to see him.' She paused. 'One of the newspaper cuttings was about her death. It implied that she'd died of drink and drugs.'

'What did you say to him – the reporter?'

'The same as you. I told him to go to hell.'

'Reporters are used to that. I can't imagine he just went.'

She smiled wryly. 'I opened the window and shouted for somebody to find one of the college servants as I was being pestered by a man.' She shrugged. 'He left before one of the porters arrived.'

'Have you told Tory about this?'

'*No.*'

'*Why not?*'

'*I wanted to talk to you first.*'

'*Was that because you thought that the newspaper cuttings were true?*'

She smiled wryly, '*I'm not sure.*'

'*How about we leave it until tomorrow and I'll talk to you both about it?*'

'*Whatever you want.*'

'*Let's do that. We'll go out for lunch and come back home and talk.*' *He paused.* '*Meanwhile, I want to say something to you. Don't ever judge people by their appearance or what other people say about them. Other people could be gossips or liars, mistaken or even intentionally mischievous. Your Moma was beautiful, brave, honest and . . . well, I'll try to tell you about her tomorrow. Now let's have a glass of champagne to celebrate us being back together again.*'

He tried to sleep that night but failed, and about 2 a.m. he got up and went to his study with a cup of tea. He turned on the gas fire and sat in his old leather chair. He may be a film-script writer but this time he was in the wrong film. People were tired of hearing about the war, and the girls were no exception. They knew more about the Battle of Hastings than they did about World War Two. And that had suited him fine. But there was no way he could give them a fair picture of what happened to Jenny without explaining what the war had been like in Special Operations Executive. And inevitably his mind went back to the Dordogne.

And for some inexplicable reason, thinking of the Dordogne and Baker Street made him think of the club. The Special Forces Club. The girls might get a feel of the atmosphere of the Resistance. And as if that had solved all the problems, he was suddenly tired and slept through until morning in the leather armchair.

It was years since he had been to the club. There were too many memories there. Too many reminders. But Jenny and he had lunched there most Saturdays. Sometimes with a baby in a carry-cot asleep under the bar counter. Carefully watched over by Albert, the barman.

Going there would maybe bring the two worlds together. The Special Forces Club members mainly consisted of old SOE and SAS people with a few from the wilder areas of military intelligence. And if he was lucky it would provide him with some inspiration on how to tell the girls what had happened. He wanted them to have the right picture of their mother. Sooner or later they would hear some snide, weasel version and they had to be armed to confront it. Two months of dying doesn't represent a whole life.

He booked a table for them to lunch that day.

The three of them sat at a table by the tall windows with a bottle of the club Bordeaux, the girls sipping gingerly and, he suspected, really wishing that it was Coke. When Michael signalled to him that their lunch was ready they walked over to the dining room.

They were just by the door when Vi came into the bar and, seeing him, she waved and walked over to them slowly, prodding the carpet with her stick, and breathless when she got to them.

'Harry. My dear. How lovely to see you here. We've all missed you. How are you?'

'I'm fine, Vi, thank you. Let me introduce you to my daughters. This is Victoria and this is Pauline.'

She looked at each in turn and then back at him. Her voice trembled as she said quietly, 'They're so lovely, Harry. She would have loved them so much.'

He saw her try to blink the tears away but she had to put up her hand to smooth her cheeks.

There was a slightly awkward silence and then she said, 'It all seems a long, long time ago, doesn't it? She's so like her, Harry.'

She turned and headed unsteadily for the bar.

They were eating their crème caramel when Pauline said, 'By the way, who was the old bag?'

'What old bag?'

'The one with the blue rinse hair and too much rouge who spoke to you by the door.'

It would have seemed to him a harsh commentary in any circumstances but in that place at that time it was like a physical blow. He felt a quick flush of anger. And then realised that that was unfair. The comment may have been flippant and unkind but it was no more than that. It was made in ignorance.

'She's a club member. She knew your mother very well.'

'Are you cross with me?'

'Why do you say that?'

'You said "your mother" – you usually say "Moma".'

'No, I'm not cross with you. Drink up your coffees and we'll get on our way.'

He'd paid the bill and they went down the stairs slowly, the girls not even glancing at the photographs on the wall. Photographs of the heroes and heroines of the Resistance in France, Holland and Norway.

Half-way down, he stopped them in front of the three photographs grouped together. The photographs of three pretty young women. One smiling, the other two looking rather solemn.

He pointed at the photographs. *'Do you know who they are?'*

The girls looked at the photographs but without any real interest. They exchanged glances and shrugs as they said *'No'* together.

'You should recognise the one on the right. Have a good look.'

Victoria said slowly as she looked at the photograph, *'They're all very pretty. The one on the right reminds me of someone.'*

'Go on.'

'In fact she's very like Pauline,' she said slowly. *'The same eyes, all big and bedroomy, and the same mouth.'* She turned quickly. *'It's Moma, isn't it? It's our Moma.'*

He nodded, smiling. *'Yes. That's Moma. She was about four years older than Pauline is now when that was taken. She'd just finished her training course.'*

'It says underneath, Les Trois Anges – the three angels – why that?'

'It was a joke. They were very close friends. All on the same training course. All three of them were highly rated except for discipline. They were all rather naughty so far as the army's rules and regulations were concerned. That's why they got the nickname, because they always looked so surprised and angelic when they were confronted with their misdeeds.'

'What sort of misdeeds, Daddy?'

'Nothing very bad. They were just a bit wild.'

'Who's the one in the centre?'

'She was Paulette. You were named after her.'

'And the one on the left? The smashing brunette.'

'She was a special friend of Moma's.'

'What's her name?'

'Well, her name then was Violette Daudet. I'll tell you about her some time.'

13

He'd cast the baited hook deliberately for Victoria who could never
wait for anything. She rose so easily.

'Tell us now or you'll just forget.'

'Let's get home and I'll tell you about the three of them.'

He settled them down in his study and looked from one to the other.

'So what do we talk about?'

It was Tory who rose to the bait, as usual.

'Tell us about Moma and how she was when you first knew her.
Where did you meet her?'

CHAPTER 2

He stood leaning on the post-and-rail fence watching Max taking the chestnut over the triple jump again and again. They looked so beautiful in the late afternoon sun. The eager young man with his blond hair flapping and the chestnut mare who was not quite up to international standard but who was so willing. When she'd learned to lift her hocks just another twenty centimetres as she came over she'd be there. Meanwhile it would have to be the big bay who had done it all before and loved the applause. It was far from the house and all he could hear was the sound of the pigeons and the creak of the leather saddle.

It was the first week in October and as warm and balmy as any June day. He turned to look towards the woods. The chestnuts and beeches were still bright green but the oaks were already shedding their leaves. Some instinct told him to savour those coming weeks in case it was all coming to an end. The British and the French had backed down over Hitler's threats and the Czechs were about to be made part of the Third Reich. Siegfried, his eldest son, had been one of the staff officers at the Munich meeting. He sighed as he turned back to look at his younger son. He too would have to go. He had only lasted this long because he was one of the German show-jumping team.

Siegfried had never been a worry. The family name and his enthusiasm had served him well. He looked as if he'd been born to wear a uniform. German through and through. But Max had travelled all over Europe. He had friends everywhere. Paris, London, Rome and Dublin were like second homes to him. As typical a German as Siegfried but not in the same way. Max was a romantic and slightly old-fashioned. He liked foreigners and they obviously liked him. Siegfried had determination but Max had charm. He loved them both but his heart was with Max who was so like his mother.

15

He waved to Max and walked back slowly up the gentle grass slope to the gardens and the house. Schloss Leine was more a mansion than a castle. In England they would have called it Something House despite its size. It had been in the von Bayer family for nearly two hundred years but what had once been an estate incorporating the land covered by two villages was now a farm of just under a thousand hectares, with a staff of sixty people for the house and the farm. Most of them had fathers and grandfathers who had worked for his father and grandfather. He knew them all and cared for them all. He called them by their Christian names and they called him Count Otto.

In England, August 1938 would be remembered by a few people as being the month in which the German army was mobilised. For many more people it was the month in which Len Hutton scored 364 runs against Australia at the Oval Test Match.

For Harry Bailey it was the month in which he had to make his mind up about spending three pounds on a Rudge-Whitworth cycle or going the extra ten shillings for a Raleigh with Sturmey Archer three-speed gears. He finally opted for the Raleigh on the grounds that he'd need the gears to get him up the long steep hill of Victoria Road, the last mile of the journey from Erdington to King Edward's Grammar School, Aston. After all, he was well paid for a 21-year-old junior French master at seven pounds a week. Five pounds a week was a married man's wages in Birmingham at that time and a bowler hat would be worn to mark the status.

Harry Bailey had spent the whole of the summer holidays in France. With fares and keep the seven weeks had cost him just under seventeen pounds. From Ostend he had cycled down to Chartres and then back to Paris and home from Calais. Every hour of his holidays at Christmas, Easter, Whitsun and the summer were spent in France. It had been started when he was only twelve by a school trip to Boulogne, and the whole atmosphere of France and the sound of the beautiful language had possessed him right from the start. Even when spoken in anger or derision the language was like honey on brown bread.

The senior French master was Frank Summers, a quiet, unobtrusive man who was more in love with French grammar than the language itself. He was particularly fond of conditional phrases using subordinate prepositions before or after the principal proposition. But Harry Bailey's classes were made to use the language.

There would be boys who would remember the words of *J'attendrai* for the rest of their lives and others who would always see the cloud of dust as the sheep came down from the hills in Daudet's *Lettres de mon moulin*. Harry Bailey's subsidiary subject was history which seemed to be mainly concerned with Mary Queen of Scots and her relationship with the French Court. There was a touch of Bothwell about Harry Bailey himself.

Harry Bailey's parents found their only child a constant surprise but his status as a schoolmaster at the 'grammar' at twenty-one despite no university degree was enough to make anything tolerable. And there was that framed certificate on the wall by the upright piano, that announced that Harold George Bailey was a 'Licentiate of the Royal College of Preceptors'. They had no idea what a preceptor was or did, or even what a licentiate was, the certificate alone was enough. He had bought his mother a copy of Warwick Deeping's *Sorrell and Son*, and his father an airtight tin of Three Nuns tobacco to celebrate the award.

He liked dancing at the Palais and the Masonic and summer evenings at the Congregational Church tennis club. If it hadn't been for his job and the obsession about France he would have been considered a bit of a lad by his contemporaries. It wasn't that they were against the French business, it was just that they couldn't understand why it should interest him. Harry's other indulgence was membership of the Left Book Club. Two shillings and sixpence a month for the book and a newsletter from Victor Gollancz. Unwrapping those red-covered books was a kind of magic and the contents were amazing. Revelations about Tory MPs and how they used their votes to support arms manufacturers in which they had shares. There were warnings about Hitler and comparisons of earnings in different countries. They left no doubt that socialism and communism were the only way to a civilised future. Harry Bailey absorbed it by a kind of osmosis rather than analytical convictions and it stayed at the back of his mind rather like declining '*mensa*' and bits of Caesar's Gallic wars – just thinking '*Caesar jam adolescens . . .*' brought back the dusty classroom and the worn desk-lid, with his initials carved on it with the others.

Despite the ominous warnings from the Left Book Club books Harry Bailey gave almost no thought to the likelihood of war. That sort of thing was for politicians, not ordinary people.

* * *

Nobody could explain why the agency was called 'Agence Presse Dijon'. Nobody in the firm had any connections with Dijon. Some wag had suggested that it had something to do with Dijon's reputation for fiery mustard. Older members had vague recollections that one of the founder's pretty mistresses was from Dijon. But why pick on her when there had been so many. In fact it had been a mark of recognition to a rich man from Dijon who had made his money in Burgundy wines and the manufacture of motor cycles who had funded the agency for its first five years. His widow had got his money back years ago and by 1938 the agency was doing quite well. It made no profits but that was a matter of intent rather than bad management. Why pay taxes when a trip to survey the current situation in Saigon or Ottawa could level things out to better advantage. The offices had a fine address in the Champs-Elysées but inside they reflected the current management's philosophy of carpets at home rather than at the office. Not that the offices were bad; they were sprawling and untidy, but despite that, the agency was highly respected. It was both non-political and universal. In other words if you wanted an item on suspected scandal at the Foreign Ministry or, alternatively, a fulsome piece on the good works of the Minister himself, then Agence Presse Dijon could supply it. They were totally uncommitted. Rivals said that they were hacks without beliefs. But they were very efficient and successful hacks and Paul-Henri Fleury was their most valuable reporter. He was offered a management job with an increase in salary which he declined, for Paul-Henri lived better than the owners let alone the managers. Paul-Henri always knew which way the wind was blowing, whether it was a political wind or an economic breeze.

Paul-Henri had several other virtues including great charm and an ability to listen. The fact that he was both selfish and unprincipled was not considered a drawback by most journalists in the agency. He knew everybody, and he knew most of their secrets. He was fond of women and got on well with them for short periods. But that perceptive eye and the sharp tongue could be devastating when he was tired of a relationship. He had married only once but that was more than enough. Two massive egos grinding together was painful and Louise now lived her own life. She had felt no need to remarry but she had a constant stream of lovers. As a top entertainer that was *de rigueur*. She sang beautifully. The ballads made popular by the likes of Tino Rossi and Maurice Chevalier. She sometimes claimed that she was the Louise in Chevalier's song. She was still beautiful, but no longer desirable so far as he was concerned.

He had always got on well with his daughter, Paulette. She was lively and pretty and had a good degree, and when she wanted to be a journalist he hadn't hesitated to get her a job at the agency. Nepotism was only one of his perquisites. And it was very French . . . '*faire une fleur par quelqu'un*'. It had been decided that she would serve the agency best as a researcher. History graduates always ended as researchers or schoolteachers.

Paulette Fleury lived with her father in a pleasant apartment within walking distance of the agency. It wasn't that she preferred her father to her mother but her mother's place was constantly full of the hangers-on that performers always attracted. She liked her mother and admired her father, and she had inherited his independent spirit and her mother's dedication. Nothing was impossible to either of them. You decided what to do and you did it without hesitation.

The evenings she spent with her life-long boyfriend, Jacques Lévy, who worked in a merchant bank advising the wealthier clients on their investments. They both liked music. Classical music. Jacques had wanted to be a cellist and for a year had played as a professional with an orchestra. But the pay was not enough to live on and they planned to marry some day.

The Fleurys had a cottage in the Dordogne just outside Brantôme but after the break-up of the marriage it was seldom visited. But Paulette and Jacques used it from time to time when their free time was enough to drive down for a day or so. Life in France in 1938 wasn't bad for the Fleurys and many people like them.

The Campbells had owned the manor house and the estate around it for at least three generations. There was some doubt about ownership before that because in those days part of the estate was in Scotland. Long ago the estate had been measured in thousands of acres, most of it wild and uncultivated. But after 1917 the family had lived, generation after generation, on the estate in Sussex, on the green, rolling hills behind Chichester. But the present generation had followed the father in his peripatetic life at the Foreign Office. For six years their home had been in Berlin and then ten years in Paris at the embassy. Only holidays had been spent at their

English home. It had taken some wire-pulling to achieve such long postings in the same place but the Minister's awareness of Alistair Campbell's talent went hand in hand with the realisation that he was financially and socially completely independent of his salary from the Foreign Office so the family were allowed to be together far more than most diplomats' families could expect. Justice was served in a way because if the usual rules had applied, Alistair Campbell would normally, by 1938, have been an Ambassador instead of First Secretary. He was knighted in the monarch's birthday list in June 1938, 'for services to the Foreign Office'.

Lady Campbell had been a society beauty even among the twenties crowd. Impetuous and self-willed she was not every bachelor's dream, but she had fallen in love with Alistair Campbell the first time she had set eyes on him at a hunt ball near her home in Leicestershire. And she had adored him ever since.

Jenny Campbell was their only child. Restless and impetuous she used up her energies on riding and skiing. A fearless rider to hounds and with a real understanding of horses and ponies.

She was courted by many young men. She flirted with them, went to night-clubs and danced to Carroll Gibbons at the Savoy and Roy Fox at the Kit Kat Club. But that was all it was. MG cars and quick-step lessons at Santos Casani's, and horses. Horses to be trained, ridden and cared for. Because she was bilingual in French and English with a good working knowledge of German she was co-opted onto the committees organising the international equestrian competitions in those countries. The times she most enjoyed were with the Duponts in Paris and at the von Bayers' place near Hanover. The von Bayers had a wonderful string of home-bred showjumpers that were the envy of all European competitors. There the Campbells were treated as part of the family. She would be seeing them at Christmas.

John Crowther had been eighteen years old when he was wounded in the attack by the Canadians and British on Passchendaele Ridge. He lost his sight despite the devotion and care of a nurse in the local hospital. He was too ill to be moved to a military hospital and by the time he could get about despite his blindness there were only a couple more months to go before the Armistice was signed. He was demobilised at Catterick Camp in Yorkshire and the young nurse from Flanders who had looked after him was waiting for him with his parents and a taxi. They were married later that day at the Registrar's Office in Stockport. Their only child, a daughter, was born two years later. John Crowther, despite his blindness, had work as a night telephonist at a Manchester hotel and was fatally injured by a lorry as he walked home in the early hours of a spring morning.

His wife, Marie, was left to bring up her four-year-old daughter, and being an enterprising young woman she got a job as a nurse at a local hospital while the young daughter was cared for by her paternal grandma. It was easier for Marie to talk to her daughter in French and there was nobody else to accommodate and Violette took quite easily to talking French at home and English outside. They were a loving group, the in-laws, Marie, and her daughter, and they got on well together.

Violette grew up in an atmosphere that was almost the same as it would have been in France. She was thrilled by her first trip to meet her mother's parents who had a small farmholding in Normandy that gave them a reasonable living. They loved their young granddaughter and she stayed with them for two long summers and helped them on the farm. It suited her mother to stay in England and when she was courted by the local veterinary surgeon there was all the more reason to stay. They married a year later, just after Violette finished at the local girls' grammar school.

Her stepfather was genuinely fond of her and was an easy-going man, not put out by being excluded when the two females always talked together in French. When Violette came back from her summer with her grandparents she started work as an assistant in her stepfather's small surgery.

It was her French grandparents who offered to keep her and pay her fees at the nearby veterinary college at Rouen.

CHAPTER 3

Otto von Bayer was sitting in his study leafing through the German translation of an American novel that Max had brought back from Berlin. The title seemed strangely apposite: *Vom Winde Verweht*. He checked its English title – *Gone with the Wind*. As someone knocked on the door he called out for them to come in and put the book on the small table beside his armchair and looked at his watch. It was 2 a.m. and August 23, 1939.

As the door opened he saw that it was Siegfried and, to his surprise, he was in uniform, the uniform of a Wehrmacht captain with the crimson stripes on his breeches and crimson piping on his shoulder straps that denoted that he was an officer on the General Staff. He was twenty-eight but he looked much younger as he walked across and bent to kiss his father's cheek before settling in the armchair beside him.

His father smiled. 'I was going to ask you why such a late visit but maybe at this time in the morning it's an early one.'

'I wanted to talk about Max, father.'

'Why? What's happened?'

'We signed a non-aggression pact with the Russians last night.'

Von Bayer was silent for long moments. 'I can't believe it. Was that why Ribbentrop was in Moscow?'

'Yes.'

'But what has this got to do with Max?'

'The pact means that we shall be able to attack Poland without interference from the Soviets. There is a secret protocol that gives some Polish territory to them and we take what we want, including Danzig of course. It's August 23 today, Hitler had planned on launching the operation against the Poles on the 25th. It's been put back to September 1.'

'But what has this got to do with young Max?'

'He must volunteer immediately, not wait to be called up. If he waits he'll just be drafted to some infantry unit. There has been talk about him using his riding for the team to avoid military service.'

'But the authorities told him that that's what they wanted.'

'I know. But it doesn't stop the gossip.' He paused. 'I've talked to friends of mine. If he will come back with me tomorrow, today that is, I can get him posted to the Abwehr. They would value his languages.'

'The Abwehr. Is that Canaris's lot? The so-called spies?'

'Yes.' He smiled. 'The proper description is Intelligence.'

'Is it really necessary to do all this in such a rush?'

'It would be wise, father. We must persuade him.'

'Fair enough. Let him sleep until breakfast then we'll talk to him.' He turned to look at his son. 'Does this mean war?'

'We think not. Hitler thinks the French are too demoralised to do anything and the British lack tanks and planes and artillery. The Russians think they'll both back off once we've taken Poland.'

'But the British have just signed a pact with the Poles to stop any aggression.'

'There's nothing they can do, father. They're too weak and too far away.'

Von Bayer sighed, shaking his head. 'They'll fight, Siegfried. Believe me. The British will fight. The politicians won't want to but the public will. Munich and Berchtesgarten were a humiliation.'

'Don't worry, father, Hitler has called their bluff time and time again, and won everything we wanted. He'll go on winning.'

'Are the Generals with him on all this?'

For long moments Siegfried was silent and then he said quietly, 'Let's say – they aren't going to oppose him. They've learned their lessons in the last few years.'

The two cycles were leaning against the trunk of a beech tree and down at the edge of the river they sat eating sandwiches and drinking orange juice. It was a hot, sunny day and there was a bottle of wine on the end of a piece of string cooling in the water.

Paulette was sitting with her chin resting on her drawn-up knees as she watched a fish rise near a lily-pad.

'Your father said they might move out of Paris. Do you think they will?'

Jacques smiled. 'You never can tell. He dreams these dreams. Sometimes he talks of living on one of those canal boats. Sometimes it's an apartment on the harbour at Honfleur. Right now it's a cottage in the Var with a hectare of land with a field of sunflowers.'

She laughed softly. 'I like people who dream dreams.'

He smiled. 'Even if they don't ever do anything about them?'

'Yes, of course. At least dreamers think about things.'

'Ah yes. Divine discontent.' He looked at his watch. 'It's time we were starting back. We've got to get things straight at the cottage for your father.'

'He won't be here until ten. There's no hurry.' She paused. 'We must buy some bread in Brantôme on the way back.' She smiled at him. 'Let's drink the wine first.'

'OK.' And he leaned forward pulling the bottle from the stream and wiping it down before he uncorked it and poured the wine into paper cups.

As she sipped the wine she said, 'Do you dream dreams, Jacques?'

He laughed softly. 'Sometimes.'

'What do you dream about?'

'Playing the Elgar concerto with a famous orchestra.' He looked at her. 'Hearing you say you love me and you'll marry me.'

'I love you. You already know that. But I don't want to be like Daddy and Moma – rushing into marriage and then finding you prefer being separate and independent.

He stood up, reaching out his hand to help her to her feet.

As they came out of the baker's by the bridge in Brantôme, the old lady from the sub-Post Office came out, waving to them. They walked towards her and she was panting as she said, 'M'm'selle Fleury. There's a telegram for you from Paris.'

They walked back into the shop with her and she pulled the telegram from the board behind the counter where it was fastened to a cork board with a brass drawing-pin.

The telegram just said – 'Phone the office urgent. Papa.'

They had to walk to the main Post Office to use the telephone and it took almost twenty minutes to get through to Paris. Her father was very brief.

'Come back tonight. Both of you.'

'Aren't you coming down to the cottage?'

'To hell with the cottage. Get in that damn car of yours and get back here.'

'What is it, Papa, tell me?'

'I don't want to talk about it on the phone.'

'Is it something to do with you? Or is it Moma?'

'Neither. Just get back. It's serious. Come straight to the office. I'll be sleeping here if I can get the chance to sleep.'

As she hurried from Jacques's car to the office Paulette turned and waved to him as he drove off. Upstairs at the agency it was almost empty. There was only her father and the teleprinter operator. She looked at her watch. It was 3 a.m. The copy for the morning papers would have gone out before midnight. Her father was talking on the phone at his desk and he waved her over and pointed to the chair beside him. When he hung up he turned to look at her.

'Good journey?'

'No. There was a lot of traffic on the road. Soldiers in trucks and some tanks on transporters.'

'Heading for Paris or going away?'

'To Paris. What's going on?'

'God knows. It's chaos at the Elysée Palace.' He sighed. 'The Germans are going to attack Poland in two days' time. We have a treaty with the Poles to defend them in case of a German attack. Daladier insists that we stick by the treaty. Bonnet says we should back out. So we've got the Foreign Minister opposing the Prime Minister and less than two days to make our minds up.' He paused. 'They've been at loggerheads for weeks. It's unbelievable.'

'What will happen?'

'General Gamelin says the army is ready to fight. The British will stick by the treaty with the Poles. And we'll be dragged in with them because we can't stand aside. We'll be at war with the Germans some day next week.'

'Is this why you wanted me to come back?'

'Part of the reason.'

'What's the other part?'

For a few moments he was silent, then he said quietly, 'The Germans will win. They'll take over this country when they've taken Belgium and Holland.'

'How can you be so sure?'

'Because the top people in this country have been ready to go along with the Germans for the last two years. We're a decadent society, Paulette, and we don't have the will to fight.'

'So?'

'So this time next week life is going to change for all of us. And that includes you and me. It's the end of August now. This time next year the Germans will be in Paris and occupying the whole country. It won't ever be the same again.'

'What are you going to do?'

'I've thought about it for months. The facts are simple. We deserve to lose and the Germans deserve to win. There's nothing I can do to change that.' He sighed as he looked at her face. 'So I'll go along with the Germans and I'll keep my job. I'm a coward, my dear, I'm not ready to die for a bunch of traitors. But you'll have to make up your own mind.'

'What do you think I should do?'

'Work here with me until this time next year. See how things go. Don't go all patriotic. Just stay neutral. Life has to go on.'

Helen Campbell stood with her husband, her arm linked in his as they looked across the placid water of the lake. There was a pair of swans and their grey cygnets, their reflections trembling on the surface of the water as they turned to face the evening breeze.

He had been silent for several minutes and then, shaking his head as if to clear away his thoughts, like a dog coming out of the water, he said, 'Where is Jenny?'

'She's at a party at the Hendersons'.'

'When is she due back from the party?'

'I said no later than midnight. John Henderson is driving her back.'

He sighed deeply and then turned to look at her, putting his hands lightly on her shoulders. 'I love you both so much. Especially you. You've been so patient with me'

She smiled because she knew how low he was. 'We love you too, my dear. Especially me, because you've always been like a rock to me.' She paused and giving in to a fear she wished wasn't there, she said quietly, 'Do you have to go back to London tomorrow?'

'I'm afraid so.'

'And Paris.'

'Yes. But I want you and Jenny to stay here. At least until we see which way things go.'

She sighed. 'Let's go in. It's getting chilly.'

She was happiest when they were all there, daughter, husband and her. In the last few weeks she had gone back to saying her prayers again. Praying for them all, that they would be kept safe and happy. And feeling guilty when she added a postscript that there would be no war. Guilty because her husband was sure that it was a phoney peace and that England should have risked war with the Germans and called Hitler's bluff. In public she said nothing, but in her heart of hearts she would have given Hitler the whole of Europe if it avoided a war that involved her family.

Alistair had phoned her earlier that morning to warn her about Chamberlain's speech to the nation on the radio at 11 a.m. She had asked him if Jenny and the maid should hear it and he had said that he thought they should. If was a piece of history. A speech that would change their lives and the lives of millions of other people.

She had let Jenny sleep late and they had sat in their nighties and dressing gowns. She watched her as they listened to the solemn tones of the Prime Minister.

'. . . I have to tell you that no such undertaking has been received and we are therefore at war with Germany.'

She leaned over and switched off the radio. There was silence for a few moments and then Jenny stood up, yawning and stretching her arms. She turned to look at her mother.

'I'll take Rudi out for a run. He needs the exercise.'

'Take care.'

She smiled. 'Don't worry about me, Moma. I can look after myself.'

She decided that they'd go to church that evening. She needed to be with other people.

As Jenny checked the girth on the chestnut mare it reminded her of Max von Bayer and his chestnut that he was so pleased with. There would be no more international jumping until it was all over. It seemed crazy that she and Max would be on different sides.

When they came back from church that evening she tried to phone him and was told that no calls were being put through to Germany.

As she hung up she wondered if her father might be able to contact him.

As they had no wireless Harry Bailey and his parents had been invited next door to hear the speech. Old man Rogers was sure that it would all be over inside six months. The newspapers said that half the Germans' tanks were fakes. Just cardboard and paint because they were running out of steel.

The next day Harry Bailey had walked his parents to the church hall so they could all be fitted with gas-masks. They were warned that they must take the little cardboard boxes with them wherever they went. There were special gas-masks for babies. As they walked home they saw the first barrage balloon going up from its site in the park. And suddenly they were aware that the country really was at war.

The French government didn't make its declaration of war against the Germans until 5 p.m., six hours after the British announcement. Even as she heard it on the radio, Paulette Fleury was organising two carpenters who were screwing a large cork board to one of the office walls. There was a large-scale map of Europe rolled up on her desk. By midnight it was up on the wall with coloured pins in three rows waiting to mark on the map where the battles were being fought. She still couldn't believe that it was really going to happen.

CHAPTER 4

In the first few weeks after the declaration of war the great fear was of the air raids and the government evacuation scheme was publicised by posters, the much reduced newspapers and the BBC. Well over half a million children were sent from their homes to the countryside, to people they didn't know and who frequently resented them. Their only link with home was an officially printed and franked postcard sent on arrival to parents with nothing more than the child's address.

In the cities Air Raid Wardens were recruited and trained, and the Fire Brigade recruited thousands of men to the Auxiliary Fire Service. In London and several other cities there were occasional air raid warnings but no planes attacked. Slowly the fears abated. But at sea the war was real. The line *Athenia* was sunk on the day war was declared with 1400 passengers and crew on board. Liners carrying evacuee children to Canada and the USA suffered similar fates. U-boats were already assembling in packs in the North Atlantic to be used for hunting down unarmed merchant ships.

The Princesses stayed in Scotland but the King and Queen came back to London. Lonely and homesick children were being brought back home. People were beginning to describe it all as 'the phoney war'.

While men in pubs were singing 'Roll out the barrel' and 'Hang out the washing on the Siegfried Line', mandarins in Whitehall and the Elysée Palace were summarily rebuffing secret peace feelers from Berlin. From time to time the war impinged on civilian morale. The sinking of the Royal Navy's *Royal Oak* by a daring U-boat commander who penetrated the naval defences of Scapa Flow was a shock. However, by Christmas the fate of Germany's star warship

Graf Spee was settled when she was scuttled in Montevideo by her captain after a battle with the Royal Navy in the River Plate.

At Christmas 1939 it was as if the belligerents had all decided to give their civilian populations a break from even the 'phoney war'. But 1940 came in with strict rationing of bacon, sugar and butter in Britain. A month later the Russians invaded Finland and got a bloody nose for their pains. But a second offensive mounted during a peace treaty spelt the final defeat of the Finns.

In France the political bickering went on as usual and in March Paul Reynaud took over from Daladier. A month later the phoney war was over. Germany invaded Norway and Denmark and on May 10, 1940 the Germans invaded Holland, Luxembourg and Belgium. They smashed on through the French defences at Sedan and captured Amiens and Arras. On June 14 they entered Paris.

Paul-Henri and Paulette Fleury had stood on the office balcony and watched the grey-uniformed Wehrmacht goose-stepping arrogantly down the Champs-Elysées. There were small groups of silent people on both sides of the street and the smoke from a burning tyre-factory was sending a dark cloud across the sun. Ordinary people watched the marching Germans but they didn't believe it.

On the country roads of France the Luftwaffe was machine-gunning the thousands of civilian refugees heading south from Paris with their hand-carts and prams piled high with all they had left of their lives and their homes. The police were treating them like gypsies, trying to prevent them from settling in some already overcrowded village. Dead carcasses of horses and cattle lay rotting in the fields and ditches and, as the tide moved on inexorably, the wounded and exhausted died at the side of the roads. The weather was beautiful. Clear blue skies and a blazing sun. And out of the blazing sun the Stukas bombed and gunned without opposition. Even the trial runs of the Luftwaffe in Spanish Guernica had not been so easy and so fruitful.

There were pictures in all the dailies of worn-out British troops being landed from all sorts of craft on the Channel coast after their evacuation from Dunkirk. The War Office gave them passes for a few days' leave to give them time to sort out where to post them. Oddly enough the British public seemed strangely relieved that they were now on their own. Like Winston Churchill had said: 'We shall fight on the beaches, we shall fight on the landing grounds, we shall fight in the fields and in the streets, we shall fight in the hills; we shall never surrender.'

CHAPTER 5

Harry Bailey spent the first week of the school holidays helping his father dig out the hole in the back garden and erect the air raid shelter. Then there were exam papers to mark. His job as a teacher was a reserved occupation so he had not been called up for the services. His few friends who were not in the Forces counted themselves as lucky, but he was uneasy about his sheltered life. There was nothing to stop him from volunteering. Two or three older teachers had left to join the army and there were already reports in the papers of ladies going around handing out white feathers to young men not in uniform. Instinct and inclination told him to join up but he remembered all too well what his father constantly told him – 'Don't go until you have to. They'll come for you soon enough when they want you.'

It was an advertisement in *The Times* that changed his mind. The front page was small ads and personal messages. He had smiled at one of them where a chap was trying to contact 'the girl in the green hat on the 6.15 train to Croydon last Sunday', suggesting that they should meet under the clock at Victoria Station. Just below was an ad that seemed to leap out of the page. It was short and brusque.

> Linguists required for special work
> in the army. No promotion beyond
> lance-corporal. Apply Box 390.

He posted his letter to catch the early evening collection.

Three days later he got a buff envelope enclosing a railway warrant and instructions on attending an interview in London.

The address was in Trafalgar Square at the top of Northumberland Avenue and he felt that there must be some mistake when it turned

35

out to be a barber's shop. But he carried out the instructions and
went inside and asked for Mr Palmer. The man went on cutting his
customer's hair but pointed briefly with his scissors at some bead
curtains and said, 'Go on through there.'

There was an ATS girl in uniform sitting reading the *Daily Mirror*.
She put aside her paper and led him along a short corridor to an iron
fire-escape. He followed her up four flights of stairs and down a long
corridor. She knocked on a door and a voice called out, 'Come in'. She
opened the door and waved Bailey inside to where an army officer sat
at an ancient desk. He pointed to an ancient slatted folding chair.

'Take a pew. It's Bailey, isn't it?'

As he fixed the chair and sat down Harry Bailey nodded, 'Yes,
that's right.'

'Good journey from Birmingham?'

'Not bad.'

'You go from Snow Hill Station or New Street?'

'Snow Hill.'

'Why Snow Hill?'

Bailey shrugged. 'A friendlier station. New Street is for business
people.'

'What made you reply to our advertisement?

'I'm a linguist and it sounded interesting.'

'But you're protected in a reserved occupation. Why give up an
easy billet?'

Bailey shrugged. 'I'll get called up sooner or later and if I wait I'll
probably end up in the infantry, bored to death.'

The questions went on for nearly an hour and then the officer said,
'You'll have a few tests while you're here. First your languages, then
a bit of this psychology stuff and a medical. If you get through those
and you're considered suitable we'll do a check on your background
and you'll come for another interview when we'll tell you whether we
want you or not and what your job in the army would be. OK?'

The officer didn't wait for an answer but stood up and led him to
another office where a sergeant was obviously waiting for him.

There was only a brief chat in German but a long conversation
in French. At the end no comment was made on the assessment
of his proficiency in either language and he was taken to another
room where a man in civilian clothes chatted to him before he
was told to fill in a questionnaire. There was the newly introduced

Rorschach blot and questions such as – 'Who do you like most, your father or your mother?'

There was another casual chat about his views on politics. An elderly lieutenant took over and they talked about French politics and politicians and his views on the French surrender. Some time was spent on his views of the French and their characteristics.

The medical was casual too. Blood pressure, eye tests, lungs, flexing reactions and sample of urine.

It was mid-evening before he got home. He had said nothing to his parents about the reason for his day away or his application. They wouldn't have been obstructive but for some reason he felt slightly embarrassed about what he was doing. It wasn't very *New Statesman* and it wasn't Left Book Club either.

It was a week before he got the second summons to an interview and this time it was relaxed and friendly. Everything had been satisfactory and as from that day he was a private in the Intelligence Corps. To be sent on a three-month basic infantry course so that he knew what soldiering was all about. It seemed that there had been incidents of Intelligence Corps personnel saluting with the wrong hand and not standing to attention when spoken to by an officer. When that was over he would be a lance-corporal and the rather boyish lieutenant told him the old joke about the army calling the Intelligence Corps 'The Eunuchs' because they had no privates. It was the sort of stuff that would have gone down well in the common-room at school. And suddenly, school seemed a long way away and part of another world.

He reported at the guard-room at the barracks of the Royal Sussex Regiment in Chichester a week later. He was issued with battledress and boots, webbing, Lee-Enfield .303 and bayonet, mess kit and drawers, woollen, long.

Apart from the actual training and disciplines he found the army like school. A greater camaraderie perhaps and a cosy feeling of being part of a special rather useful and respected community.

By mid-July the training squad were called on to help with the anti-invasion measures. Long summer days were spent pegging down mile after mile of coiled Dannert wire across the lush, rolling Sussex hills. There were beginning to be dogfights overhead between Messerschmitts and the Spitfires based at Tangmere. Rumour said that the Germans were planning the invasion for the end of August.

The training was mainly foot-drill on the parade ground and weapons training with Lee-Enfields and Bren guns on the firing range. There were route marches through the country lanes around Goodwood and basic map-reading which was beyond the understanding of most of the training squad. They did guard duty twice a week and marched to the Cathedral on Sunday mornings with flags flying and the regimental band playing 'Sussex by the Sea'.

There were plenty of girls to meet. The same girls who giggled at the fence watching them attack the hanging sandbags with 'grim determination' with their bayonets served them tea and doughnuts in the canteen in North Street in the evenings. But the competition for girlfriends was tough. With glamorous fighter pilots down the road at Tangmere and the Royal Navy's long hold on nearby Portsmouth, the soldiers had to sacrifice their sweets ration to get a date.

The passing-out parade of the training squad was inspected by an elderly general from Southern Command, and the Officer Commanding, his staff and the regiment were congratulated on the turn-out and performance of the new recruits who were now adjudged to be fully-fledged soldiers.

Private Harry Bailey was given a forty-eight hour leave pass and travel warrant and instructions to report to the Intelligence Corps depot in Winchester in two days' time.

CHAPTER 6

Harry Bailey's parents had been amazed and proud of their son being promoted so quickly to lance-corporal and his mother had carefully stitched the stripe on each arm of his battledress blouse with her best invisible stitching.

He reported on a Saturday afternoon and was shown to a large hut with double-tiered bunk-beds and standard issue army blankets and pillow. He was one of a squad of twelve new recruits and in case they were under the impression that being members of the Intelligence Corps with green flashes on their blouses made them special, Harry Bailey found himself on the Sunday morning with two other new boys cleaning out the sergeants' toilets. But what was more disturbing was discovering that both the other men were double-firsts from Cambridge and lecturers in Modern Languages at Bristol and Glasgow. He wondered how he would survive against standards like that. As time went by he realised that although either one of them could write a dissertation on medieval French they were typical Brits and didn't actually like speaking the language.

Life at the depot was a strange mixture. The recognition that the new boys were both well-educated and reasonably mature meant a relaxed attitude with the Intelligence training. But the routine non-training staff were ex-Guardsmen who had instituted a disciplinary system that seemed to combine fantasy with stupidity. It was an offence to look an officer in the eye. It was rated as dumb insolence. If the Camp Commandant's office was empty you had to salute his chair. Walking was an offence, all movement had to be at the double. All Guardsmen had to be answered with, 'Yes, trained soldier.'

The training was mainly more advanced work on normal army training. Complex, advanced map-reading, the organisation and administration of the army. The instructor pointed out that they could

39

need this knowledge in the future to obtain goods and services to which they were not entitled. If you knew the rules it was easier to play the games. There were two weeks on motor-cycles at the rough-riding course at Bagshot and a week on the duties of a Field Security Section in the field.

A month later the training squad moved to a luxury hotel in Matlock where the real intelligence training began. Surveillance, and its avoidance, interrogation, penetration of suspect organisations and construction and use of a wide variety of non-standard weapons. Finally there was a week of observation tests and some elementary unarmed combat.

The course was modular so that, for instance, a man who was virtually bilingual but not capable of anything physical could be diverted to do an excellent job at a deep-interrogation centre. He never knew that it was not the end of the course when he left for his new work.

For those who went on to the next stage it meant a two-week stint at a grim base in Scotland where they were taught every kind of self-defence and how to disable or kill your adversary silently.

After this module Harry Bailey was posted to a Field Security Section based in Edinburgh that was responsible for the security of Edinburgh docks and the Atlantic convoy collecting point at Methil, a small port in Fife. He went out daily in a drifter to the boats at anchor in the roads as they waited for the convoy to be assembled. With his little black book of suspects' names and descriptions, he checked all the boats sailing under neutral flags – Greek, Turkish, South American and United States. In the captain's cabin he would check through the crew list and call for men to be questioned when he was suspicious.

It was after one of those trips that his CO was waiting for him on the jetty with a small van. He was an acting-sergeant then and his CO said, 'I'm taking you into Scottish Command. All your kit's in the van.'

He frowned. 'What's it all about?'

'There is somebody waiting to see you. He's taking you back to London for a meeting.'

He shook his head. 'I don't understand. What's going on?'

'They'll tell you themselves.'

'Have I done something wrong?'

'No. Definitely not.'

The man who met him at Scottish Command introduced himself as George Watts. He brushed off questions and they were driven in a staff car to an RAF airfield. Two hours later they landed at Croydon and were taken on to London. They stayed that night at a small hotel in Paddington, sleeping in the same room, and after an early breakfast a staff car came for them and took them to the War Office. Left alone in a small office he was faintly amused to see that it was a Field Security sergeant who stood outside the door.

CHAPTER 7

The man who held out his hand was in his fifties with grey hair and deep lines at the sides of his mouth. And blue eyes that looked at Bailey's face.

He said quietly, 'Sergeant Bailey. Thank you for co-operating.'

When he saw Bailey's involuntary smile he said, 'Why the smile?'

'The co-operating. I didn't have much choice.'

'My name's Fuller. Dickie Fuller. How about we sit down and talk for a bit and then we'll go to my office which is a little more comfortable.'

As Bailey pulled up a chair Fuller said, 'Have you heard of SOE? Special Operations Executive?'

'No.'

'I'm glad to hear that.' He paused. 'We've only just started. Still sorting ourselves out. Our brief from Winston Churchill is, in his own words, "set Europe alight". The first thing we need to do is check out the possibilities for resistance in Europe. France and Holland and maybe Belgium.' He paused to check Bailey's reaction but there was none. 'That means sending people over by boat or plane to reconnoitre. We have the nucleus of several teams. Four, maybe five. Each team consists of two men. The leader has to be a man whose mother-tongue is French. His back-up must be fluent but not necessarily bilingual. We have a man who was brought up in France and lived there most of his life. But he's essentially a civilian. No military experience and not a physical type.' He smiled, briefly. 'We'd like you to be his second-in-command. What do you think?'

'Why me?'

'He asked for you.'

'You mean it's someone I know?'

'Let's say you've met him but you probably don't remember him. But he remembers you.'

'Who is he?'

'You stayed with him last summer and the summer before. He's a teacher, or he was, in Paris . . .'

'You mean Lemaire. Jean Lemaire.'

'That's the man. He came over to England three weeks ago. We've been giving him some training but he'll never be a soldier. He needs someone tough and capable as an assistant. He asked about you.'

'Why?'

Fuller shrugged. 'Who knows. He was obviously impressed.'

'By what?'

'That you would make a good partner and that you cared deeply about France.' He paused. 'Do you want a couple of hours to think it over?'

Bailey shook his head. 'No.'

'Why so quick?'

Bailey smiled and shrugged. 'It sounds interesting.'

'And dangerous.'

'Not if we're only reconnoitring. When can I meet him?'

'I'll take you to see him this afternoon. He's not in London.'

The staff car pulled up on the wide gravelled drive in front of the big house. It was a beautiful summer evening and on the parkland there were long shadows from the trees and there were sheep grazing on the slope down to a lake. But inside the grand house there was the hammering of builders dividing up the big rooms into smaller areas.

There were uniformed Military Police at the entrance to the drive and an MP captain saluted Fuller as they walked inside the house. At a reception desk an ATS girl spoke to Fuller and pointed up the wide staircase.

Jean Lemaire was in a large bedroom still furnished with the owner's antiques and Fuller suggested that it would be more peaceful out in the gardens.

It seemed strange to see Lemaire again and away from his apartment by the school. He was a man of great enthusiasms that ranged from some newly discovered musical delight to the latest painting bought on a visit to the flea-market. He was in his early forties, a great talker who was easily diverted by his students and a great optimist and innovator of new teaching methods. Above all a warm and generous man.

The talk with Fuller had been cautious and disjointed as none of them had much idea of what was to happen next. It was to be Fuller who would decide what training and planning was necessary.

When he told them this he shrugged as he added, 'I feel in a way that I owe you both an apology. As you can see from the work going on we are not yet properly organised.' He smiled wryly. 'My colleagues in London are equally disorganised but we're all working hard to get things on a sound footing.'

Bailey said, 'What training have you got in mind?'

'Parachute training, sabotage and radio. And I'd like you, Harry, to go over the basics of avoiding surveillance with your friend, Jean.' He smiled. 'Better get some rest and we'll get started about six thirty tomorrow morning.'

They had been sent up to the Parachute School at Ringway just outside Manchester and Lemaire had surprised them all. Despite appearances he was a model pupil, ready to do whatever the instructors required and they had both completed the ten-day course without any problems.

Back at what was now christened the Manor House they found that some of the training staff were now installed. In Guildford, the nearest large town, they practised both surveillance and the avoidance of surveillance. There were lectures to all five groups under training on the uniforms and organisation so far as it was known of the German forces and intelligence organisations. Lemaire himself gave a talk on documentation required in both occupied and unoccupied France. They were actively discouraged from talking to the other groups and all members of groups were given code names.

Finally they were sent on a three-week radio operator's course. Bailey was to be Lemaire's radio operator in the field.

It was only after nearly three months' training that they were briefed on their actual operation. And before the briefing started Fuller had told them that this was their last opportunity to decide against carrying on. There would be no recriminations or bad feeling if they decided that it was not for them. Fuller emphasised the dangers and the organisation's inexperience of active operations. Only the seriousness of the war situation warranted them being sent at all.

He told them quite openly that two members of other groups had decided to withdraw and they would be suitably employed in some other role, their honesty and integrity respected.

Both Lemaire and Bailey had no doubts about their capability and Fuller had been obviously relieved. SOE were not looking for gung-ho heroes but for quiet men with the courage and determination to be the pioneers to learn what could be done to harass the Germans and what sort of help they could expect from the local population.

The first talk with Fuller on the actual operation revealed that they would be working from a base in Bergerac. They would be dropped at night and there would be nobody to receive them on landing. It was the first time that Bailey had really understood how primitive the organisation was. During their training time more staff had been assembled and on a brief visit to London they had met senior officers who were obviously highly competent soldiers but with virtually no experience of such operations. It was accepted that there was no ready source of men with experience of 'setting Europe alight'.

The only consolation they had in the briefing was the name and address of a man in Bergerac who was prepared to provide shelter for them for a short time. At the most, two weeks.

Their brief was to cover as wide an area as possible to report on bridges, roads, and railways that were prime strategic targets. To report on the morale of the general population and its attitude to the Germans and to the Vichy government. And lastly and most hazardous, identify possible recruits for a properly organised SOE network. Names of German officers and administrators. Samples of passes and permits and details of local German regulations. Details of military units and their duties. Premises occupied by Germans or used by Germans. And information on people who were openly pro-Vichy or collaborating with the Germans.

The next full moon was in a week's time and Fuller told them to rest and relax. They would be one of SOE's first blind drops into France and would be dropped from a Whitley bomber, the plane they had used in training. They would go from an airstrip just outside Bedford.

There were several people from London to see them take off after a thorough check that they had nothing on them in clothes or possessions that were not genuinely French. It was all very low-key and only Fuller walked out to the plane with them.

Fuller stopped in St Albans on the way back to London and parked near the cathedral. There were lights inside but no people and Fuller was conscious of the noise of his shoes on the tiled floor as he moved to a pew that was in the shadow of one of the arches. It was a long time since he had prayed and he didn't kneel but just sat there with his eyes closed and his head in his hands. He prayed for the two men and the success of their mission but he knew it wasn't that that had driven him into the cathedral. He prayed for forgiveness for sending two men who trusted him on such a hopeless mission. A mission so amateurishly contrived because there was neither time nor experience to make it better. They were the scapegoats who might make it possible in future to be efficient and effective. And with better odds on survival. His only consolation was that at least Baker Street had given them funds enough to cover almost any need including bribery.

He shivered involuntarily as he walked back to his car, and wondered why; it was still September. Only a year since the Germans had attacked Poland. And since then once-proud countries had been ruthlessly and efficiently defeated and occupied.

CHAPTER 8

In the week before the Wehrmacht paraded down the Champs-Elysées, Paris had been seized by what was called '*la grande peur*'. A state of panic that suffused the whole population. A desperate need to escape being 'caught like a rat in a trap in occupied Paris', as Simone de Beauvoir wrote in her diary. But once the Germans arrived it was almost as if they were just an influx of tourists. The big hotels like the Crillon and the Métropole were taken over by the military and a whole team of German officers was engaged in requisitioning buildings that would be occupied, but waiters, cleaners and cooks were now being employed by the Germans.

Thousands of people were suddenly having to take an attitude towards their conquerors. There were no stories of rape or violence, most Germans seemed to be photographing the beauties of Paris, eating at restaurants and looking for things to buy. So most people carried on. A job was a job and from the very first day they were paid at full rates.

By the end of the first week there was only one problem: the shops were running out of luxury goods and almost overnight the black market was born.

After a long interview with one of the Military Governor's senior staff officers, Fleury had written a long piece about the honourable intentions of the occupying forces. The civilian population should carry on with their lives as usual. With the close co-operation of Marshal Pétain as president, the nation would be treated with respect. Co-operation would make things easier for all concerned.

His piece was printed in several newspapers and he was rewarded with a priority press pass to the Military Governor's staff at the Crillon. What he wrote brought relief to many people and

Paul-Henri Fleury was seen by both the Germans and Parisians as a bringer of hope and good news.

He had an office of his own now and she watched him typing on his old Olivetti Lettera, hunting and pecking urgently with two fingers. So assured that he never stopped to read his copy.

She looked at her watch. It was 10 p.m. and she stood up, threading her way through the empty desks, leaning against the open door, waiting for him to notice her. When he did, he smiled.

'You want to go?'

'Yes.'

'Give me five minutes.' He pointed to a brown-paper bag. 'Sugar and butter, my dear. Or shall we go to Mario's place?' He looked at the clock on the wall. 'My God. Better be Mario's. Phone him that we're coming.'

'What do you want to eat?'

'Leave it to him – just say *la cosa di casa.*'

She smiled and went back to her desk. When she had phoned she looked at the map on the wall. The pins hadn't been moved in four weeks. It was as if there wasn't a war.

Mario stood smiling as he refilled their coffee cups. 'And what're you writing for us today, my friend?'

'The prisoners of war. Several thousand are being sent back and the Germans would like a return gesture of Frenchmen volunteering to work in Germany.'

'Making planes to bomb the English, yes?'

'No. Not war work. Our treaty with them doesn't allow that.'

'Maybe they won't fight the English. Just cut off their supplies and leave them to rot.'

Fleury smiled and shrugged. 'Who knows, Mario? Who knows?'

'You do, m'sieur,' he said quietly as he moved away to another table.

As they walked back to the apartment the streets were almost empty. It was warm and the street lights had been back on for two days.

'Have you seen *Maman* at all?'

He laughed. 'Yes. She's got herself a tank colonel. She's much in demand.'

'Did she ask about me?'

He hesitated for only a moment. 'Of course. Sends you her love and all that.'

She knew he was lying but it didn't matter. There was a phone call for him as they walked into the apartment. He put down the paper bag and picked up the phone, silent as he listened. After a few minutes he said, 'Are you sure – quite sure?' He listened for a few more minutes and then hung up. For a moment he stayed with his hand still touching the receiver and then turned to look at her. 'What's the date today?'

'July 3, 1940.'

For a moment he closed his eyes and then he opened them, as he said, 'The British navy have sunk our fleet in North Africa. Over a thousand of our sailors were killed or drowned. Could be more.' He sighed. 'I'll have to go back to the office and do a piece.'

'Who told you about it?'

'The German press officer at the Crillon. I've got a twelve-hour exclusive.'

He was asleep with his head on the keyboard and his arms cradling his typewriter when she went in the next morning. His phone rang but he slept on and she picked it up.

'Agence Dijon.'

'Is Paul-Henri there?'

'Not at the moment. This is his assistant, can I help?'

'Yes. Tell him that the French government are breaking off all relations with the British. If he wants more he can phone me. We want him to help us with our own views on these events.'

'OK. I'll tell him. Who is it speaking?'

'He'll know who to contact.'

She made him black coffee, woke him and gave him the message.

Paul-Henri had taken Paulette and Jacques Lévy to Mario's for a meal and they had walked home together in the fading light. The talk had been about Charles Trenet and Josephine Baker and what was their real appeal. Was it their personalities or their voices? Or was it just the songs themselves?

Back at the apartment Paul-Henri had opened one of his last bottles of Mouton Cadet and Paulette had lit half a dozen candles that gave just enough light to see each other's faces.

51

It was Jacques Lévy who set them off when he put his question to Paul-Henri.

'Why did we lose the war, Paul-Henri?'

Fleury laughed softly and looked down at his glass before replying.

'I suppose in one sentence, because we had become a decadent society.' He paused. 'Perhaps decadent is too important a word. We had become a foolish, irresponsible, unprincipled society. A society that was ruled from the *salons* of titled women.

'Reynaud's mistress was, still is, Hélène de Portes, daughter of a rich contractor who married an aristocrat. Beautiful, ambitious and fancies herself as a manipulator of ministers. Daladier's mistress is la marquise Jeanne de Crussel, daughter of the rich owner of fleets of sardine fishing boats.

'At their tables any night you will find people like Otto Abetz, an influential Nazi, and Geneviève Tabouis, the journalist who claims to know all the deepest secrets. Rich people like Francois de Wendel. These people know everybody who matters and who sleeps with whom.'

'Why do politicians waste time with such people?'

Paul-Henri smiled. 'Because they like having a beautiful young mistress who is also very rich and they find support in their *salons*.' He shrugged. 'The whole population has grown sick of politicians. It doesn't trust them. Neither their promises nor their wisdom. The Germans have encouraged this feeling of *ennui* for years. They knew we wouldn't fight. We want an easy life and the Germans will give us just that. But we'll pay for it, my dears, we'll pay with our souls.'

Paulette said quietly, 'What do you mean? How will we pay?'

'In the coming months you will see the dregs of our nation collaborating with the Germans. Not the gentlemen at the Crillon but the fanatics who made the Nazis into what they are. We'll have black-market millionaires and every kind of corruption. Ordinary people will keep quiet because they are frightened, and things will be done in the name of France that will shame us as we learn what has been done.'

'But you collaborate with them, Papa.'

'You're right, I do.' He shrugged. 'I'm no better than the others. But there's one difference and it's what matters. I don't believe in what they believe. I'm like a smoker who smokes but doesn't inhale.' He sighed. 'We'll be making lots of excuses for ourselves in the next few years.' He shrugged. 'Survival will be everything.'

CHAPTER 9

Alistair Campbell had been one of the last of the embassy's diplomats to leave the building when the orders came from London on June 4. He had taken one last walk around the deserted streets before he was driven to the airport at Le Bourget. He loved the city and he loved France and it had grieved him to see the superficial upper classes virtually welcoming a German victory. But there were others like Malraux and Picasso who would never go along with the Nazis. The Germans would be very proper and *korrekt* at first and then when things were calm they would deal with the Jews and the Communists in their usual way. It was the brilliant, the witty, the rich and the privileged who had destroyed the country, not the ordinary people. At the Arc de Triomphe he stood looking at the grave of the Unknown Warrior. There was a bunch of faded marguerites, their petals lifting in the breeze that came down the Champs-Elysées.

He made no protest when the Ministry of Defence requisitioned the house and they had moved to the flat in Ebury Street. He walked to the Foreign Office every morning no matter what the weather and after helping to sort out the embassy archives he had been given a week's leave.

It was only the second day of his leave when the call came for him to go back for a meeting and he was surprised that the meeting was to be at the Ministry of Economic Warfare. He was to meet a Colonel Latham, who he remembered had paid several visits to the Paris embassy in the last year.

Latham wasn't in uniform, he was wearing a tweed sports jacket and grey flannel trousers.

He held out his hand, smiling. 'Latham. Thanks for giving me your time, Sir Alistair.' He pointed at an armchair. 'Make yourself comfortable.'

Latham settled in the other armchair. 'I always regretted that I was never able to meet you properly on my visits to the embassy in Paris. My contact there was the Third Secretary and the ambassador didn't like our work. Thought we were trouble makers. So he kept us away from his staff.'

'Nichols, the Third Secretary, he was MI6 wasn't he?'

'Yes.' He paused and smiled. 'So was I until I retired. And now they've yanked me back to give them a hand.' He paused. 'You won't have heard of SOE, I expect. Special Operations Executive.'

'No, I'm afraid I haven't.'

'It's one of Winston's babies and right now we're desperately looking for French speakers. I wondered if you would join us.'

'Have you spoken to the FO about it?'

'Yes.' He smiled. 'They're not keen to let you go. Always a good sign in this business.'

'What business is that?'

'Sabotage, training local resistance people. Generally making a bloody nuisance of ourselves to the Germans.'

'Isn't that the job of your people in MI6?'

'Not really. And they're not too happy about SOE. MI6 are gatherers of information, intelligence. And despite what people think, they want a quiet atmosphere to work in. Blowing up bridges and railways only makes things more difficult for them.'

'I'm too long in the tooth to be blowing up anything.'

Latham smiled. 'Fifty-two if the records are correct. But that wasn't what we had in mind.' He paused. 'Could I tell you what we hoped you could do for us?'

'By all means.'

'We want senior people to administer and control our operations. People who know the country concerned. People who are good judges of other people. Their motivations, their weak points and their strong points. These people need special handling. Tolerance and understanding combined with a sense of dedication. Caring for people who are both brave and sometimes foolhardy. Men and women who don't take easily to normal discipline.

'We saw your role as passing judgement on possible recruits and then taking charge of some of their operations in the field.' He smiled.

'A cross between the best kind of parent and a sergeant-major.'

When Latham stopped talking Campbell was silent for several moments and then he said, 'Are you sure I'm what you are looking for?'

'Yes. There would be others who will want to talk to you but there's no doubt we want you. And quickly.'

'Would I be overseas or in the UK?'

'We've got a very untidy spread of offices in the Baker Street area. You would be there most of the time.'

'Where else?'

Latham smiled. 'At your place near Guildford. The Ministry of Defence took it over for a photographic interpretation unit but they needed to be nearer to Henley. So it fell to us. I'm afraid we're making ghastly alterations inside but it'll all be restored when this wretched war is over.' He paused. 'Would you like a couple of days to think it over?'

Campbell shook his head. 'No. When do I start?'

They were having a coffee talking about the film they had just seen, Walt Disney's *Fantasia*.

Helen was full of praise for the film.

'There's never been anything like it. It really is special.' She looked at him. 'You don't agree. Or you weren't listening to me.'

Her husband smiled. 'I changed my job last week. I was thinking about that.'

'What will you be doing?'

'I can't tell you, my love. But I've got petrol coupons for a trip tomorrow. I thought you might like to come with me.'

'Where to?'

'To the house. Our house. The new outfit I'm working for are the ones who've taken it over.'

She looked thoughtful. 'I don't think I could bear seeing all that lovely parquet ruined by hobnailed army boots.'

He laughed. 'It's not that kind of place. There are a few officers but it's mainly civilians.'

'I miss it so much, darling. I really do.'

'Will you come?'

'Yes. Of course I will.'

'I had in mind using young Jenny's MG. It's very economical on petrol.'

'She'll be back later so you can ask her. Can she come too?'

He hesitated for a moment and then shook his head. 'Better not. It's a bit hush-hush.'

He saw the stricken look on her face and he said quickly, 'Mine's just a desk job. Don't fret.'

They stayed only an hour but they took time out to walk down to the lake. She hated what they had done inside the house but Alistair's colleagues had been very charming and when she went up to see what had been Jenny's bedroom she was surprised and grateful that it was just as it had always been. Nobody was using it. And on the staircase they had left the portrait of her that Julius had painted just after she was married.

'What do you think?'

'Not as bad as I expected. Will you be spending much time down here?'

'I don't know. I'm not sure that I want to. At least I can still walk home from Baker Street if the weather's OK.'

She looked up at the clear sky. There were contrails everywhere and she said quietly, 'Is it true what they said in the *Daily Express* this morning. That the RAF shot down ninety German planes yesterday?'

'It was a lot anyway, and there will be more in the next few days. Hitler wants to break our air defences before he invades us.'

'Will they invade?'

'I don't think so. It'll all depend on the RAF.' He paused. 'Is young Jenny back tonight.'

'Yes. But she hates being called "young" Jenny.'

'How's she spending her time these days?'

'She's part-timing at an old people's home.'

'I can't imagine it. Probably treats them like putting old horses out to grass.'

'She's very bored. All that energy with no place to go. Can't you find her something to do?'

'What about translating? Would she do that?'

'You'd better ask her.'

To his surprise she had seemed interested.

'What sort of things would I have to translate?'

'Cables, messages, documents, reports. That sort of thing.'

'I mean what about.'
'I can't tell you until you've been interviewed.'
'Why not?'
'Security.'
'That sounds interesting. Would I be working for you?'
'No. Definitely not.'
'OK. Can you fix for me to have an interview?'
'When?'
'Today. Tomorrow.' She shrugged. 'Soon as you can.'

It was Latham who interviewed her. Her French was perfect and she was bright and intelligent. And she knew France. The only snag that he saw was all that obvious energy brimming over with nowhere to go. He took her on straight away. She would start the following week and would be working at Baker Street, her employer the 'Inter-Services Research Bureau'.

CHAPTER 10

'Is this really his office? I can't believe it.'

Max von Bayer laughed softly. 'He's a very modest man, Siegfried. Not like your friends in Bendlerstrasse.'

Siegfried seemed genuinely shocked. 'But it's incredible. This dog-kennel is the office of the head of German Military Intelligence. Look at it.'

There were a few battered filing cabinets along one wall. An ancient desk with a model of the cruiser *Dresden* and an old camp-bed in the corner by the window that looked out over the Tiergarten. Several non-matching chairs and a threadbare Persian carpet in the centre of the small room.

Siegfried was a major now but in deference to his brother in civilian clothes he was not wearing his uniform.

'We'd better go, the cleaners will be here soon.'

'Where do you want to eat?'

'At the restaurant we went to last time. The one by the cathedral square. I've booked us a table.'

They walked to the ancient elevator which clanked and groaned as it slowly descended. The house at 76/78 Tirpitzufer had been the original building taken over for the Abwehr and the old admiral had refused all offers of better premises or even a refurbishment.

The coffee was *ersatz*, made from acorns, but it was sweet and the cream was real. As Siegfried poured himself a *Schnapps* he said, 'You seem to have raised a bit of a storm with that report of yours.'

'Have you read it?'

'Of course. Why were you so critical?'

'I wasn't critical. I just gave the facts.'

59

'They don't know whether to promote you for your honesty or court-martial you for insolence.'

Max von Bayer shrugged. 'They can do what they like. What I said is true and it's serious.' He looked at his brother. 'There isn't any part of our security and intelligence services capable of putting an agent into England and maintaining him.'

'What about the SD, the Sicherheitsdienst, or the Gestapo?'

'Not a chance. Their eyes have always been turned inwards into Germany.'

'What about your people?'

'It's too late. We've got suitable men but they should have been over there before the war started.'

'You know what's going to happen, don't you?'

'No. Nothing, I expect.'

'And there you're wrong. Your report was shown to Walter Schellenberg at the SD. He's put in an application for you to be transferred to them. Says you're wasted at the Abwehr.'

'I wouldn't make such a move.'

Siegfried shook his head slowly. 'You won't have any choice, my friend. There's a war on and you'll go where you're ordered to go. Anyway, why don't you want to go to the SD?' He grinned and held up his hand. 'No, don't tell me. I'll tell you why. The Abwehr are gentlemen and the SD are toughs. Yes?'

Max von Bayer smiled. 'Crudely put, but that's about it. What could I do for them?'

'He's already got the job for you. You're being posted to Paris in charge of our operations against the so-called Resistance.'

'You mean de Gaulle's people?'

'Not only them but the English too.'

The call had come from the SD's headquarters at Prinz-Albrechtstrasse but the meeting was to be at a house in Moabit and an official car would call for him at his apartment off Unter den Linden.

He had heard all the gossip about Schellenberg, the one-time student of medicine and law at Bonn University. A man with a driving ambition and a good service record, and a man who was said to consider the Abwehr as a nest of traitors. Men who had feelers out to the enemy in Stockholm and Geneva. Schellenberg was not only a highly efficient administrator of the Security Service but had actual field experience of operations against the British in Holland.

'This report of yours, who ordered you to do it?'
  'My chief.'
  'The Admiral himself?'
  'Yes.'
  'What was the brief?'
  'To give my personal opinion on our capability to mount an espionage network in England.'
  'And a strong hint to make it critical and unfavourable.'
  'No, Standartenfuehrer. No hints of any kind.'
  'Did you have any assistance?'
  'No.'
  Schellenberg seemed to relax. 'You criticised your own organisation, the Abwehr. Why?'
  'They have nobody who could survive at this stage in England. No way of maintaining contact and nobody who would know how to avoid almost immediate exposure. It was tried at least twice. We heard no more from either officer.'
  'And what's wrong with the Gestapo?'
  'All their experience concerns Germany. And their personnel are entirely unsuitable.'
  'And my people, the Sicherheitsdienst?'
  Von Bayer shrugged. 'Your constitution requires that all such activities should be passed to the Gestapo and carried out by them. The SD has no executive powers. If you want something done you have to get the Gestapo to do it.' He paused. 'And if it suits them – they do it.'
  'Why do you think such restrictions apply?'
  'I think you already know, Standartenfuehrer.'
  'Maybe I do. But you tell me. Or are you scared to say it out loud?'
  'It certainly might give offence.'
  'Let it. That's the risk you take.'
  'The Gestapo is controlled by the Party alone. The SD is controlled by the government. That's why the SD is not allowed to involve itself in counter-espionage overseas or outside Germany.'
  'You mean the Party hierarchy don't trust us?'

'I mean they *do* trust Party organisations. They have all grown up politically together.'

'I see from your file that you are not a Party member. Why not?'

'Politics don't interest me apart from my work.'

'Doesn't promotion interest you?'

'Only if it helps us win this war.'

'Why? So that you can get back to your horses?'

Von Bayer smiled. 'That's my real life.'

'The record says you speak excellent English, what about your French?'

'A good working knowledge.'

For long moments Schellenberg was silent and then he said, 'I've arranged for you to be transferred to the SD for a specific task. You'll be posted to Paris.' He stood up. 'You'll be promoted to Sturmbannfuehrer and you'll be my liaison with the Paris office of the Gestapo with special responsibility for wiping out the Resistance. You will report directly to me if you don't get the co-operation you require.' He paused. 'I'll talk to you again next week.'

CHAPTER 11

Von Bayer had expected to find problems in his new posting in Paris but he was shocked at what he found. The SD detachment had a dozen or more offices in various districts of the city and its headquarters in Avenue Foch, and the Gestapo seemed to be mainly at 11, rue des Saussaies. The SD and the Gestapo had branches and sub-stations throughout the city with armed guards, garages, fleets of black cars and thousands of French informers at all levels of society. It was made clear to him on his first day that to complain or criticise anything back to Berlin would be considered as, in effect, a complaint against the Party. The Military Governor and the German embassy had the trappings of power but the SD and the Gestapo between them had the actual power.

There were over a hundred men employed on counter-Resistance operations but these included office staff and the signals men who operated the mobile radio direction-finder vans monitoring the air-waves for clandestine radio transmissions. The relationship between the SD and the Gestapo on the so-called anti-terrorist operations was good. The Gestapo's rough, ruthless methods didn't work well with patriots and they needed the SD's expertise and experience. A man or woman under torture would say what you wanted to hear and dead men ceased to be possible informants. The SD seemed to produce more reliable results.

The cellars of the Gestapo building had been converted into cells for prisoners and interrogation rooms. Von Bayer sat in on several interrogations of suspected Resistance people. In no case did their interrogations produce useful information, despite their brutality. It was too obvious to the prisoners that the Gestapo inquisitors had no knowledge of how the Resistance was organised. They were on what trained interrogators called 'fishing expeditions', hoping to break down the courage of a suspect man or woman.

At the end of three weeks von Bayer phoned Berlin and arranged a meeting with Schellenberg.

Schellenberg looked towards the windows which were covered with tape against bomb-blast and then he turned back to look at von Bayer.

'So what is it you want?'

'My own unit. Working with the SD and the Gestapo but entirely independent. Answerable only to you and anyone else you nominate.'

'How many people?'

'Four on research and records and ten on operations.'

'That's not many.'

'I want quality not numbers.'

'And what do I get if I agree?'

'Accurate details of the British and French Resistance organisations and an effective counter-operation.'

'Where?'

'A place of our own in Paris and maybe a place at Lyon.'

'How long to recruit these supermen?'

'I've made out a list of who I want.'

He pushed forward a typed list and Schellenberg glanced at it briefly and then pushed it aside. Finally he stood up.

'I'll write you a letter of authority for funds and personnel. It will be ready tomorrow morning.' He paused. 'How did you get here?'

'A bomber was coming back for service. The crew gave me a lift.'

As if no longer interested in von Bayer's transport, Schellenberg said quietly, 'You're a strange man, von Bayer. Not at all like your brother. Not even like your father.' He paused. 'I hope I'm not making a terrible mistake.'

Even in the short time he had been away there had been changes in Berlin. There were new gun emplacements on the top of the IG Farben headquarters in Parisenplatz and in the Zoological Gardens. And there were bombers over the city that night with searchlights probing the sky and the dull thud of explosions to the north of the city. He had gone to the Golden Horseshoe night-club with Siegfried after going to hear von Karajan conducting the Berlin Philharmonic.

They walked back in the black-out to Siegfried's apartment and as they had a last drink together Siegfried said, 'I'm glad you made the move over to the SD.'

'Why are you glad?'

'Two reasons. Firstly you were wasted at the Abwehr. And secondly their days are numbered. Himmler will see to that. Nobody trusts them any more.'

'Have you seen Father recently?'

'About three weeks ago.' He smiled. 'He spends all his time looking after those wretched horses of yours.'

'And Mama?'

Siegfried sighed. 'Very unhappy. She's afraid for you and me. She wasn't designed to cope with a war.'

'Who is, Siegfried, who is?'

Siegfried protested. 'Hitler has brought us from economic chaos to being the leaders of a new Europe. He deserves our support.'

'How do you think it will end?'

'Total victory. Why do you ask?'

'In the night-club it was obvious that people were tired of the war. Tired of rationing, tired of restrictions and tired of being bombed.'

'They aren't the people who will rule when it's all over.'

'Don't be so sure. It's much the same in France. All the worst characteristics of ordinary people begin to take over. Wives denouncing husbands as anti-German because they've found a new man. Black market, criminals and thugs making fortunes. Not a good foundation for the thousand-year Reich.'

Siegfried smiled. 'You're tired. Let's go to bed. And don't ever talk like this with anyone else. Not even with me.'

Schellenberg's authorisation had been like a magic wand. The Kommandantur had requisitioned the villa in Neuilly that he had asked for, and AMT I in the RSHA had collected together his list of names and dispatched them in less than a week to Paris.

For two days he told them what he wanted. They all spoke fluent French and they all had connections with France. He gave them his mental picture of typical types who were drawn to Resistance. He painted a picture of human beings rather than mortal enemies. And sent them off to their work.

Arrested suspects found themselves treated so sympathetically that what would have been formal interrogations were more like chats between people whose philosophies differed. Slowly over the weeks they built up a picture of SOE, its organisation and its personalities. Scant as the information was, it provided a background for their questioning of suspects. If you know what the offices at Baker Street look like and the names of several officers it made the questioning seem no more than comparing notes. There was no violence, and threats were barely implied rather than used openly. It was the first time that German intelligence had realised that there were two Resistance organisations operating out of London. SOE and de Gaulle's Free French who, like the Gestapo and the SD, were rivals rather than collaborators.

Building up a picture of his adversaries took weeks of concentrated efforts, but the most important result was that Max von Bayer realised that although the vast majority of the French were anti-German the various groups almost equally disliked one another, and their objectives were very different. The Communists wanted arms for open warfare against the Germans but analysis of the interrogation of the half-dozen captured SOE agents indicated sabotage and training as their intention and de Gaulle's people also had political objectives. Von Bayer concluded that SOE were the softest target and that at that stage there were few of them actually in France. He would concentrate on them, and on spreading the word amongst the general population that there were substantial rewards for those who informed on suspicious activities.

When they brought in the man who called himself Lafitte, von Bayer took over the interrogation himself. It was almost six months since he had been reported as acting suspiciously to the Gestapo detachment in Bordeaux who had interrogated him briefly before putting him in Fresnes prison until eventually he was handed over to von Bayer's unit. Arrested in the docks area without the appropriate passes and permits and without a satisfactory explanation for being in a precluded area under the control of the German navy he faced an inevitable death sentence. With the alternative that von Bayer now offered him of co-operating and living under house arrest instead of receiving a prison sentence, the offer was irresistible. Slowly, over two weeks' conversations, von Bayer built up a picture of how SOE operated. Cover names, details of training and locations provided a useful basis for future interrogations. When a prisoner realised that you knew all about the people who had sent him, there could seem little point in persisting with a poor cover-story. And SOE's assessment that the schoolteacher was not cut out for physical action had been correct. Lemaire was a patriot but patriots are not necessarily heroes.

CHAPTER 12

By the autumn of 1940 the Germans had achieved what they wanted.
Total control of France but a control that was wielded through
collaborating Frenchmen. Men who were already known to the
public. If those men accepted the Germans there was no justification
for anyone to be against them.

The German Propaganda Unit had moved into a building within
a couple of minutes' walk of Agence Presse Dijon, and Paul-Henri
dutifully attended their twice-weekly press conferences. He lived
lavishly now, always bundles of notes and the best table at the most
exclusive restaurants. But he still kept to the old apartment.

When Paulette asked him why he stayed he had just put down
the phone and he stood there by the small table moving an ash-tray
before he responded.

'It's my hiding place, my dear. Nobody here but you and me. No
Germans, no socialites, no intellectuals and no bastards working out
how to put a knife in my back.'

'Why should anyone do that?'

He pulled out the old wicker armchair with his foot and sat down
slowly, shifting the cushions to make room for himself. And as he
turned his head up to look at her she realised for the first time
how handsome he was. She had heard that he had a mistress, a
young girl barely out of the Lycée.

'You know, girl, I used to think I knew Paris and I knew France.
I was part of it.' He waved his hands around. 'OK. It was decadent
– but it was real. I knew who to trust, I knew who was on the
make. It was like a kind of sad musical comedy and I was one of
the cast.' He waved his hand and grimaced. 'But now – what have
we got? I don't know whether it's a tragedy or a farce. And there
certainly ain't no music.' He paused. 'I don't trust a soul.' He smiled.

'Except you. You're my proof that there once was a time when you could be French. Poor but happy – or at least content. Enthusiasm, ideas, drinking coffee with friends. Falling in love, humming a tune, standing and staring at the Seine.' He shook his head. 'I'm talking like an old, old man. But it sickens me. All those people on the make. Greedy, unprincipled, fawning on the Germans – not just going along with them as I do – but cultivating them, flattering them, working on them, never realising that the Germans see through them and despise them, all of them. They sleep with the wives and they hand out permits to the rich husbands and they're not fooled for a second.' He shrugged. 'I'm a grown man, nearly fifty and I don't know who I am or what I am.' He looked at her face and she saw tears in his eyes. 'And that's not good, my pretty daughter. That's not good.'

'Is there anything special that's upset you?'

'No.' He paused. 'When I write one of my pieces I make sure I know how it's going to end before I start writing. I think what troubles me is that right now I don't know how all this is going to end. Instinct tells me I won't like the ending.' He grinned and laughed. 'So I start it all like the fairy stories – "*il y avait une fois*" – once upon a time.' He looked at his watch. 'I must go. By the way I've got two tickets for Josephine Baker on Saturday – do you want them?'

She kissed him and said, 'Yes, please. Take care. And be a little bit happy.'

It was raining when they came out of the Casino de Paris and they hurried across the street to a small restaurant whose *patron* knew her father.

They were lucky, no rations cards given up, and fried eggs and bacon. She felt happy in the warmth and light and the steam on the windows, but Jacques seemed strangely subdued.

'Is anything the matter, *chéri*? You look a bit sad.'

He smiled. 'It was sad to see la Baker. Almost sedate, all that vitality gone. And that song always makes me feel sad.'

'You mean "*J'ai deux amours*"?'

'No. The other one – "*La petite Tonkinoise*".'

'But why – the girl in the song – she's happy – she says he calls her his little wife and that she's lively and charming – like a little bird that sings. How is that sad?'

'It's the last two lines that are sad.'

She hummed the tune, frowning and then said, 'I don't understand. She says despite all the others who look at him she's the one he loves best. What's sad about that.'

'She doesn't say that. She says that despite all the others she's the one who loves *him* best.'

Still frowning she said, '"*Mais c'est moi qui l'aime le mieux*". It's me who loves him best.'

He shook his head. 'The words are – "*mais c'est moi qu'il aime le mieux*". But it's me *he* loves the best.'

'So. What's sad about that?' She shrugged. 'He loves her the best.'

'She's black, a native and she sees him being ogled by all the French girls and she consoles herself that he loves her best. That's sad.' He sighed deeply. 'That's how I feel about us. All the other men flirting with you and you with them but when I'm alone I feel myself that I'm the one you love best.'

For several moments she was silent and then she said softly. 'Do you really think like that?'

He smiled warmly. 'Sometimes. When I'm low.'

'Finish your food and let's go home.'

For two days Paulette had been busy on research for her father and on the third day she phoned Jacques at his office to tell him that she had tickets for a concert that evening. There was no reply from him or his secretary. She tried again an hour later and her call was intercepted by the bank's telephone operator. A girl she knew from school.

'He's not here any more, Paulette. I thought you would know already.'

'What do you mean – any more. Where is he?'

The girl spoke in a whisper. 'I think they've taken him to the housing project at Drancy – by the airport at Le Bourget.'

'What's he doing there for God's sake?'

The line was cut and she felt the first stirrings of panic as she replaced the phone and went into her father's office. He looked up at her face.

'What's the matter. Are you all right?'

'Drancy. What's Drancy, Papa?'

'Sit down. Now what's it all about?'

She told him what had happened and he reached for the internal phone. He pressed a button, spoke a few words and put down the phone.

'I've asked Pierre to come in.'

Then the man was there. Tall and gaunt. He covered the police work in Paris.

'Drancy, Pierre, a housing project. What is it?'

'It's a camp for Jews being sent to Germany.'

'Who's in charge of it?'

'An old fool named Laurent is the Camp Commandant. Used to be a furniture salesman. Walks with a limp. Sold out to the Germans right from the start.'

'And who's his boss?'

Pierre shrugged. 'The Commissaire of Police, and *his* boss is some German at the Kommandantur. I don't know who.' He shrugged. 'Why d'you want to know all this?'

Paul-Henri told him and Pierre looked shocked.

'If you try to interfere with anything down there you'll be in real trouble, chief. They've got an anti-Jewish campaign going on German orders. They've been arresting Jews for the last two days.'

Fleury stood up looking at Paulette. 'You go home, my love. I'll be back with any news as soon as I can. Don't worry. I'll do all I can.'

He kissed the stricken face and reached for his hat as he hurried out of the office.

It was after midnight when he got back to the apartment, soaked to the skin from the rain. He walked over to the side-table and poured himself a neat whisky and drank it quickly. He wiped his mouth with the back of his hand. He closed his eyes and said, as if he were dictating a report, 'He was sent on a train to Germany yesterday. Him and all his family.' There were tears pouring down his cheeks. 'I tried, my love. I tried everything. I went out to the camp just to make sure he wasn't still there. My God. It's a terrible place. The Germans may have given the orders but by God it's Frenchmen who are carrying them out. I wouldn't have believed we could sink so low.'

She led him to his bedroom and tried to comfort him as he lay on the bed in his wet clothes drinking from the whisky bottle. She shed no tears, not even when she lay in her bed.

Four days later she took a train that would eventually get to Brantôme. She had drawn out all her money from her bank, had sold everything that was hers that was saleable and put her passport and press permit in an envelope. She also took a small velvet bag with eight gold coins in it wrapped in tissue paper.

Her father found the note leaning against the clock on the mantelpiece when he got home that night. He had bought her a small bottle of Chanel No.5 on the black market and he put it down on the table before he opened the envelope.

Dear Papa,
   Please forgive me. I know you will
understand. See you soon.
   All that's left of my love,

   P

CHAPTER 13

Fuller took his hold-all from the rack as the train pulled in to Lime Street, Liverpool. It was nearly two hours late. There had been an air raid on Crewe the previous night and workmen had to clear rubble off the lines before they could get through. There were no taxis in the station but he found one on the street outside. It wasn't far to the police station at the docks but it took fifteen minutes to thread their way through the bomb-damaged alleyways.

He showed his identity card to the Station Sergeant who looked at him with obvious interest.

'He's in cell number four. On his own like your people wanted. Been no trouble so far. I dunno where he's been but he looks a right mess.'

'Can you take me to where he is?'

'Come this way, sir. D'you want me to lock you in with him?'

'No. That won't be necessary. I'll be taking him away in about ten minutes. There's a car coming for me, perhaps you could let me know when it arrives.'

'Certainly, sir.'

The sergeant unlocked the cell door and opened it slowly and closed it behind Fuller as he stood inside the cell looking straight at the man sitting on the wooden bench, his head back against the wall and his eyes closed. He shook him awake, smiling as the man opened his eyes and looked at him.

'Welcome back. You look like you need a bath and some new clothes.'

'Jesus. Where am I?'

'Liverpool. Venice of the North.' He reached out and helped Harry Bailey stand up.

*   *   *

'Why did Lemaire go to Bordeaux?' Fuller asked.

'I warned him that security would be tight because of the German navy but he had friends there who lived in Bordeaux and actually worked for the Germans. He was sure they would help him.'

'The fool. Then what?'

'Then nothing. I never saw him again. I waited in Bergerac for two weeks. I tried the radio every day back to London but I got no response.'

'Using batteries or mains?'

'Both.'

'Go on.'

'I buried the radio in some woods and our friend in Bergerac got me onto an RAF escape line. It took three weeks to get down to Perpignan where they handed me over to one of the local guides. They'd already paid him but at the top of the mountains, right on the Spanish frontier, he wanted everything I'd got, money, compass, and my watch. The Spanish police picked me up and stuck me in a prison called Camp Miranda. I got a message out to the embassy . . .' He shrugged. '. . . and I expect you know the rest better than I do.'

'Do you think Lemaire will have talked?'

'He'd got lots of guts but yes – I'd think he would talk. His morale was low towards the end.'

'Why? You'd made some useful contacts.'

'He was shocked that so few French people cared about the Resistance. Wished it would stop annoying the Germans so that everybody could get on with their lives. He was too much the romantic. He wasn't a realist, he couldn't face the facts. To most Frenchmen he wasn't a hero, just a bloody nuisance.'

'What did you learn?'

Bailey smiled. 'A lot. A hell of a lot. How a network should really be run. What kind of people are needed. What back-up is necessary and better briefing before they go. More knowledge of the area they'll be operating in.'

'Could you write me out your views?'

'Sure.' He smiled. 'Criticisms and all?'

'Of course. That's why we risked sending you.'

Bailey laughed. 'The old army motto – time spent in reconnaissance is seldom wasted.'

*   *   *

They spent four days in a suite of rooms at a hotel in Manchester. Finally Fuller was satisfied and he said so.

'Satisfied about what?' Bailey said.

'You could have been caught by the Krauts and turned back on us. It's been tried before.'

'And what now?'

'We want to cash in on your experience. We want you to be an instructor at the Manor.'

'When can I go back to France?'

'Is that what you want? Haven't you had enough?'

'With a good team and proper back-up I'd go back tomorrow.'

Fuller had a pretty cottage facing on the bank of the Thames at Putney and it was there that he and Alistair Campbell had met. Fuller laid out a selection of bottles and glasses on a low coffee table and Alistair settled for a malt whisky.

'We've got two things to kick around, Tom. One is our friend Bailey, and the other is our operations in France. Which do we do first?'

'I think Bailey, if you agree.'

'OK. Are you entirely happy about him?'

'Yes. As near as anyone could be.'

'No question of him having had contact with any German intelligence outfit?'

'No, none. He waited for his partner and when it was obvious that he wasn't coming back he headed for home.'

'What happened to his partner?'

'We've no idea. I guess he got picked up. It was crazy to head into a high-security zone.'

'What good did Bailey do while he was there?'

'He's got two or three people he thinks he could rely on in the area between Bergerac and Périgueux.'

'That brings me into our second point for discussion.' He paused and then looked at Fuller's face as he spoke. 'I'd better say it frankly, Tom. No use beating around the bush. Agreed?'

'Of course.'

'Are you aware that we are sending people into German-occupied territory who are insufficiently trained, poorly supported and poorly briefed?'

There was a long silence before Fuller replied. 'Yes, I am aware of it, Alistair. All of it. And Bailey made the same point much more crudely.'

'They deserve better than we're giving them, my friend. Unless we do much better from now on we'd better recognise that we're sending brave young men on very dangerous missions with the odds stacked almost impossibly heavily against them.'

'I agree. Totally. I want to use Bailey's experience so that he can act as an instructor for all our people who have volunteered for France. Nobody can do it better. He's been there, he's seen what it's like and he's learned how a network should be built up and run.'

'One other thing, Tom. We need our own signals organisation. Better radio sets. Smaller, lighter and easier to use. And Bailey has been a prime example of what it's like with no working radio. If we can't communicate, an agent's wasting his time. We need to know what's going on. Daily, not just when the atmospherics allow it.'

'Could you take that over, Alistair? Get us a house and signals people and a decent budget?' He paused. 'I've got one point of my own I want to raise with you.'

Alistair Campbell looked surprised. 'Go ahead.'

'I've got a girl in Baker Street. She wants to be trained for a network.'

'How old?'

'Twenty-three.'

'Which country?'

'France. Virtually bilingual. And very bright.'

'Sounds perfect. Who is she?'

'Your Jenny.'

For a moment Alistair Campbell was silent, then he said, 'If she were not my daughter what would you have done?'

'I think I should have gone along with it.'

'Why?'

'Because she's got the basic things that an agent in the field needs. Perfect French, physically tough and mentally tough.'

'So don't ask me, Tom. She's a grown woman. She has to go her own way.' He paused. 'All I ask is that she is thoroughly trained before she goes.'

'She will be. And if in the end we think she's not right she won't go.'

CHAPTER 14

Christmas 1940 found most of Europe under snow. In Paris the real consequences of having lost the war were becoming more obvious. A bicycle cost more than a car had once cost, and, of course, on Sundays only Germans were allowed to drive cars anyway. The black market was by then no longer in the hands of amateurs and it didn't offer half a loaf for a kilo of potatoes. It was more likely to be five tons of copper with a truckload of Belgian tobacco thrown in as extra if the Germans ended up with the copper.

The petty exchanges of small items of food being exchanged for an antique necklace went on but they were the part of the black market that received the hardest treatment from the police. Twenty-five per cent of half a loaf was of no interest to a policeman who could make thousands of Francs informing on the really big deals to the Germans.

The miseries of occupation were beginning to be real and resented. When the Germans marched in in June it seemed that things might be bad for a couple of months until the British had surrendered. But despite the censorship people knew that the RAF had given the Luftwaffe a bloody nose. The invasion of England had been postponed. And among the generals and colonels at the Crillon it was well-known that Goering and Hitler were blaming one another for the débâcle of the defeat of the Luftwaffe over the rolling fields of Kent and Sussex. Operation 'Sealion', the invasion of England, had been abandoned before it had even been launched.

Paul-Henri Fleury spent Christmas Day with his estranged wife. Her German had gone back to Köln for two weeks' leave with his family and Louise was at a loose end. There was plenty of food at the apartment but they ate very little. Food wasn't a luxury yet for

79

either of them. They drank but they didn't get drunk and she asked him about his life. He knew all about hers. He didn't mention their daughter until she asked him what had happened. He told her and she said, 'Have you heard from her?'

'No. Not a word.'

'Where do you think she is?'

'I heard that she spent a couple of weeks at the cottage at Brantôme. After that . . .' he shrugged. '. . . who knows?'

'And if you knew you wouldn't tell me, would you? You wouldn't trust me.'

'That's true, my dear. That's how it is.'

She smiled and shrugged, seemingly unembarrassed. 'And you. I heard you had a young girl. Why aren't you with her?'

'She's with her parents for a few days.'

'You look much older, my dear. But just as handsome.'

He smiled, glad to be back on the party chit-chat. 'You look much younger and you'll always be beautiful.' He grinned and raised his glass. 'It's the bone structure that does it. You'll never look old.'

'What kind of life do you live these days?'

He shrugged. 'Just work and eat.'

'How do you get on with the Germans?'

He smiled. 'Much the same as you. Depends on the man. Some I genuinely like – the others, well I'm polite, but no more.'

'How will it all end, my dear?' She spoke softly as if they might be overheard. 'Tell me what you really think.'

'I genuinely don't know, Louise. I really don't. The Germans don't know either. They're holding their breath, waiting for something to happen. Something that pushes the scales one way or the other. What do your contacts say?'

She shrugged. 'The opinion of my contacts isn't worth a glass of water. They are having a wonderful time. They don't care about the war. To them it's all over.'

'No fears that all this might end?'

'No. None. They are here to stay. They are the masters, we are the slaves. If we can be of some use to them all well and good, but behind it all they despise us.'

'Do they say that openly?'

'Not at first but they are beginning to now.'

'Are these people soldiers?'

She laughed. 'They wear uniforms but they wouldn't know one end of a gun from the other.'

'And your German. Is he a real soldier?'

'Oh yes. He despises the others.'

'Does he think all this will last?'

'No. He's afraid.'

'Of what?'

'Is this off the record?'

'All of it is.'

'He says that Hitler is planning to attack the Russians. He says if that happens it is the beginning of the end for Germany.'

'I think he's right.'

'Have you heard this?'

He shook his head, smiling. 'No. You're better informed than I am.'

'They've taught me a lesson these people.'

'What was the lesson?'

She shook her head. 'I'll tell you some day.' She looked up at his face. 'Would you help her if she needed help?'

'Help who?'

'Don't pretend, my dear. We both know, don't we?'

'Yes. I'd help her.'

'Would you help me too?'

He smiled. 'You'll never need any help, my love.'

She said softly, 'If you ever need my help – just ask.'

'Let's change the subject, sweetie. We're getting far too serious. By the way I did an interview with your friend Charles Trenet last week. He said to give you his love.'

She beamed with pleasure. 'He's such a lovely man. I sang an impromptu duet with him at a prisoner-of-war charity concert last month.'

'What did you sing?'

'*Chanson des rues.*'

He had walked back to his empty apartment early the next morning. It was still dark and the snow crunched under his feet, reminding him of when he was a boy. That all seemed a long time ago. All those years to go from a happy-go-lucky innocence to a time when he had to talk in coded words to a woman he had once loved, about their daughter. Not even trusting each other enough to say out loud that they guessed all too well what she was doing. Maybe a little research would do no harm. Maybe a piece on the arrogant Frenchman who had fled the country, promoted himself from colonel to general overnight and proclaimed himself as the leader of La France Libre would provide a good excuse.

Max von Bayer spent Christmas with his parents and his father noticed without comment but with some disappointment that only once had his son gone down to the stables. And that was only because one of the mares had a new foal.

It was the first Christmas when the *Schloss* wasn't full of young people with parties every night. Siegfried was working at the OKW in Berlin and was due home for New Year. Despite the whiteness of the deep snow the days seemed silent and grey under the overcast skies. The old man had invited two young officers from the nearby hospital for the war-wounded to stay with the family for a few days. They were the only survivors of a bomber crew whose crippled plane had crash-landed in Normandy after a bombing raid on Fighter Command at Biggin Hill in Kent.

Count Otto had marvelled at their good spirits and their courage. With terrible wounds they plotted how they could get back onto flying duties. They were typical products of the Hitler regime. Tough, optimistic and full of courage, both in their early twenties. Sometimes it seemed that perhaps Hitler had got it right. Perhaps he was the one who had got it wrong, and beneath that vulgar appearance and the ruthless behaviour Hitler had merely taken that old German adage – '*Der Zweck heiligt der Mittel*' and the end really did justify the means. Siegfried was a shrewd, intelligent young man and he saw Hitler as the saviour of Germany, the man who had defeated the crippling inflation that not so long ago required a suitcase full of Marks to buy a loaf of bread. And the man who had swept aside the vicious Treaty of Versailles that required the defeated, poverty-stricken Germany to pay to the victorious allies more money than there was in the whole world. Maybe Hitler's frenzied little dance in the woods at Compiègne was forgivable after all. The French having to sit in the same railway carriage to sign the surrender as the Germans had sat in in 1918.

Why was it, then, that he knew so surely that despite all those facts he could never be part of it? Siegfried always said, with a smile, that it was because he was a snob. And an old-fashioned snob to boot. An old man who preferred Thomas Mann to the *Horst Wessel Lied*.

The snow had been swept away from both entrances to the Savoy, the Christmas tree in the foyer was even bigger than normal but there wasn't the usual glamorous view across the Thames to the south bank warehouses. The black-out had seen to that. But inside, the lights were as bright as ever. Boxing Night at the Savoy was already a great success. Carroll Gibbons was playing solos on the piano while the band refreshed themselves. All the regular girls were there. Jenny Campbell had her usual bevy of admirers. It was the mixture of her good looks and a lively outgoing personality that attracted them. Proposals of marriage were quietly side-stepped and less proper proposals were handled with a smile and raised eyebrows. Gradually her circle of men friends realised that Jenny Campbell was the greatest fun of all the party girls but the nearest you got to her was doing a quick-step on a dance floor. She was much liked by all the hotel and club band-leaders like Harry Roy, Roy Fox, and Bert Ambrose but her favourite was Carroll Gibbons. They liked her because she knew their music so well and was always smiling and cheerful.

She had no favourite but there were usually half a dozen young men who could always rely on her to make up a party for a night out. But that Christmas most of them were away in the forces.

From time to time she walked back to the table presided over by her father and mother to introduce some escort who was on leave. With a name like Campbell it wasn't surprising that most of them came from regiments like the Black Watch and the Gordon Highlanders. She didn't much like Guards officers, not even Scots Guards. She found them a little too sure of themselves.

Her actual escort that evening was a young lieutenant from the Rifle Brigade barracks at Winchester who she knew from before the war and was much loved because he had let her drive her MG around the circuit at Brooklands where he was training to be a racing driver. His name was Tommy Fowler and as he sat with her at her parents' table her father looked at the young man in his uniform. Red hair, blue eyes and the freckles that went with them, he looked far too young to be in uniform. So was his daughter and these days she wore the FANY uniform of the First Aid Nursing Yeomanry. But not tonight. She was wearing a black and white silk

83

dress that was her mother's and shoes with what she said were called Cuban heels. Her only jewellery was a gold wristwatch he had given her for her 21st birthday.

He had deliberately avoided asking Fuller how she was getting on at the Manor. When he visited their old home he noticed that although she had been told she could use her old bedroom, she had chosen to be with the rest of the recruits in what had been the stables. Seeing her now she seemed just as she had always been, intent on having a good time despite the war.

Major Bailey worked through Christmas. His outline for a new training programme had been agreed by Orchard House and there was much to be done. There were specialists to be recruited. Ex-Hong Kong policemen for unarmed combat, service marksmen for weapon-training, PE instructors for fitness training, map-reading experts, explosives experts, the list seemed never-ending. But most important of all was judging who would best survive in enemy-occupied France. His basic plans were being used by officers at other locations whose target countries covered much of Europe and some of the Middle and Far East.

He had two more months to weld together his training staff before the first recruits could start their training. It looked as if it would be mid-1941 before any of the new networks were operative.

Sometimes when he was over-tired he dreamt of Lemaire wobbling away on his cycle down the lane by the farm. Turning to wave to him as he disappeared behind some pollarded willows on the bank of the canal. When he was awake he wondered what had happened to Lemaire. He was a brave man, but stupid and obstinate, a bad combination. Bailey kept him in mind as the opposite of what he wanted an agent to be.

CHAPTER 15

They were sitting together at the wooden table and there was a cardboard model of a cluster of buildings on a plywood base at the far end of the table. A stencilled card said 'Camp Miranda'.

The Royal Victoria Patriotic School in Wandsworth was a grim cluster of buildings by any standards but it was the first stage of checking the background of any person wanting to enter the United Kingdom permanently in time of war. It made no difference what your nationality was. British subjects were as automatically suspect as any other nationality. It took many questions and a lot of research to be able to sort the sheep from the goats. Few mistakes were made. There were three possible outcomes to the process. You could be cleared completely, free to go and do whatever you wanted. You could be found wanting either on holes in your story or just the instincts of an experienced interrogator. In that case you were sent to a civilian detention camp. Then there was a group of uncertainty who didn't completely satisfy the process and they were released with restrictions on where they could live and what sort of work they could take up. This group had to report to their local police stations once a week. A few from this group were eventually upgraded and subject only to the same restrictions as any other citizen.

The girl was pale but very pretty with long black hair and big, heavy-lidded eyes. It was her third day of interrogation.

'Tell me about the man in Perpignan.'

She sighed at being asked the same questions again and again. 'He was in his fifties, short, stocky, black hair, very dark skin. I think he was a Catalan. He spoke French but with a very heavy Spanish accent.'

'Where did you first meet him?'

'At the butcher's shop. The butcher was part of the RAF escape chain. He put a card in his shop-window. The man came and was introduced to me.'

'Where did you talk together?'

'In my room over the shop.'

'And what did you agree with him?'

'One thousand francs to take me over the frontier at the top of the Pyrénées.'

'Where did you meet after that?'

'Usually at a restaurant called Le Lyonnais and other times down by the canal at Quai de Bourdan or Quai Nobel.'

'How long before you left with him?'

'Nine, ten days, I'm not sure.'

'Why the delay?'

She shrugged. 'He said it was the weather on the mountain or some problem with the police. He always had some excuse. I think he wanted me to panic so that he could squeeze more money out of me.'

'Did you panic?'

'No. I'm not the kind to panic. If he turned me over to the police the escape people would know. The least that would happen to him was that they'd never use him again. He'd lose a good income.'

'OK. You're at the top, on the frontier. What happens?'

'He asks for more money and I refuse. He curses me and I realised then that he thought I was a French-speaking English girl.' She shrugged. 'The usual flow of obscenities that men use to frighten one another.'

'Go on.'

'It's dark and it's very cold and he finally gives up and takes me to some rocks that are painted white. He tells me these mark the frontier. He says good luck and to wait until it gets light before I go on. I heard him clattering down over the stones and when everything was quiet I moved on in the dark. I must have gone about a hundred metres and suddenly a torch was flashed in my face. It was a Guardia Civil. He said I was under arrest. He drove me to the camp.' And she pointed to the cardboard model. 'You know the rest.'

'Show me again which cell you were in.'

She reached over and pointed to a cell window. 'I think it was that one. There was a tree facing the window.'

'What kind of tree?'

'God knows. I wouldn't know one tree from another.'

'Did it have fruit?'

'No.'

'Flowers?'

'No. Just leaves.'

'And the girl in the next cell, you think she was English?'

'She said she was, and she spoke perfect English. She said she had been brought in two days before but by a different guide.'

'Did she tell you her name?'

'Just that her name was Violette and she had been in touch with the American consul in Marseilles and somebody was going to contact her from the English embassy in Madrid.'

'Is that all she told you?'

'Yes. They moved her to a cell on the far side later that day.'

'Go on.'

'Two days later I was taken to the Camp Commandant's office and handed over to a civilian. He took me to a car and told me he was from the British embassy in Madrid. We slept that night at a small inn in some hills. I ate in my room. He wanted to sleep with me but I said no. We went on next day and got to the suburbs of Madrid. In a villa there I was handed over to another civilian and in talking to him it was obvious that he too thought I was English. And then it was obvious that they had rescued the wrong girl. They thought I was the other one.' She paused. 'Then they started interrogating me much like you have. Just on and on. When I told them I wanted to join the Free French and the Resistance they put me on a ship a week later.' She shrugged. 'And here I am.'

'Tell me. What made you decide to give up a good job and try to join the Resistance?'

She hesitated, but sounded very decisive when she said, 'It was something personal. I don't want to talk about it.'

'And you still want to join the Resistance?'

'Of course. That's why I'm here.'

'Is there anything you want? It'll take a couple of days for the committee to decide.'

'I'd like some make-up.'

'Make-up?' he said, frowning.

'Yes. Powder, lipstick, rouge. Maybe some perfume.'

'Ah yes. Of course. I'll see what the girls can do.'

The girl took off her earphones and shook her hair into place.
'What do you think?'
She shrugged. 'I'd say she's OK. Her story fits in with the other girl's scenario.'
'Who's interrogating her, the other one?'
'Lieutenant Harris. He's cleared her. He checked on her family and she's being released tomorrow.' She raised her eyebrows. 'Another one who wants to be interviewed by SOE.'
'My one wants the same. I think I'll pass her on to Orchard House.' He paused. 'You'd better tell Harris to warn his girl not to talk to her parents. Just tell them that several people helped her get back.'

CHAPTER 16

Bailey had picked out a dozen people for his training group. Three women, all young, and nine men. But he only planned to take seven or eight with him for his network.

So that they were usefully spending their time as he assembled his training schedule he sent them off to a combat course at the remote country house in Scotland, where they would be taught the skills they hoped never to have to use. How to kill silently, how to use certain nerve centres to paralyse an adversary, how to garrotte, how to use a knife and how to stalk a human quarry. They would learn how to survive in wild country, and about building shelters, hunting, trapping and fishing, edible and poisonous plants, natural medicine and first aid. For ten days they would live wild, alone or in pairs and finally in teams of four or five to test their tolerance in tough conditions. Tolerance was not judged to be an infinite quality. Survival of the fittest was imperative. But it was fitness in various forms, not solely physical fitness. Your radio operator may be the weakest physical link in the team but without him or her the existence of the rest of you was pointless.

He spent two days observing them on the survival course, watching their reactions and attention span. If you're bored by instruction about your survival you are likely to be both stupid and inattentive when you are being given your orders on an operation in the field.

They were sitting in a circle around the glowing embers of a wood fire listening to an ex-Canadian Mountie.

'I want to tell you some more about water. I've covered how to get water from plants . . .' he wagged a finger at them '. . . remember always what I said – milky sap is nearly always poisonous. So – other sources of water.' He paused. 'Get one thing firm in your minds – urine and sea water – never, never drink them. Both can produce

89

drinking water if distilled. But only when distilled. By the way, always melt ice rather than snow, ice produces more water faster for less heat.

'All fish contain drinkable fluid. Animal eyes contain water which can be extracted by sucking them. And remember – never waste animal blood – it's a valuable source of minerals.' He smiled. 'I'll stop for now – who's cooking the chow tonight?'

They were given forty-eight-hour leave passes and travel warrants at the end of the course and then had to report to what had been a scholastic college just outside Henley-on-Thames, where they did an intensive map-reading course using Ordnance Survey and Michelin large-scale tourist maps. The Michelin maps were not of the likely area of their operations.

At Orchard House the staff had been expanded and Fuller and Campbell were now the main links with the training centres. It was they who insisted on SOE having its own source of radio equipment to meet the needs of networks in the field. At that time SIS controlled the design and distribution of all radios for clandestine work and old rivalries meant that SOE had no priority and were dissatisfied with the arrangements.

Campbell discovered a fellow Scot, a Signals sergeant, whom he ear-marked as the likely founder of SOE's own Signals facility. Sergeant Black had a virtue that had been ignored by SIS, he listened attentively to what agents in the field told him they needed. Current sets were too large, required too much power from the mains and caused loud key-clicks in nearby domestic radios when they were transmitting. Campbell wore down the resistance from SIS by using his old Foreign Office contacts and Sergeant Black was posted to SOE.

But in mid-1941 the main problem was the same as it had always been. The recruitment and selection of suitable agents. Men who are capable of the dangerous work of sabotage tend to be tough, intelligent and prone to violence. They were seldom patient and methodical enough for the task of organising a resistance network. Harry Bailey was an exception and they kept a constant watch on his activities.

Expert printers and forgers had been recruited who could produce in hours perfect copies of documents including signatures of German and French officials who issued passes and permits for travel and work.

SOE were constantly criticised by SIS and others as being just a bunch of amateurs. They were, of course; no government in peace time has a need for hundreds of men and women whose sole purpose in life is to sabotage the means of travel and communication of some other country. But the amateurs of SOE worked long hours without complaint and did their best to bring order out of the initial chaos.

CHAPTER 17

They moved down to Beaulieu in the middle of the night and had been housed in a large house on the estate. The next morning they assembled for Bailey's first talk with them.

'You'll be glad to know that all the commando-type training is over. From now on you'll be learning how to do your job in enemy-occupied territory. You will be taught a wide variety of skills. How to use plastic explosive, how to blow up a bridge or building, the uniforms and organisations of the German *Abwehr*, the *Sicherheitsdienst* and the *Gestapo*.

'You will go on a lock-picking course with the Portsmouth Police and you'll do one more parachute jump at Ringway. You'll be shown how to use and maintain a number of foreign weapons and you will be taught how to evade surveillance.

'I shall talk to you about what it's really like doing an agent's job in France. Some background on French attitudes and politics. A run-down on General de Gaulle's organisation. Finally you will go through tough interrogation sequences and you will be told how we expect you to behave if you are caught, and how best to resist interrogation.

'Your evenings will be free and there will be cars going into Southampton every night.' He paused. 'I forgot one thing. You'll be taught how to repair cars and trucks and some more advanced first aid.' He looked at them, smiling. 'Get to know one another. You'll be split up into teams of four, if you have any preferences let me know. So. Any questions?'

There was the expected silence and as he dismissed them he was almost certain that the blonde girl with the long legs had winked at him. He checked afterwards on his list. He guessed she must be Campbell. Jennifer Helen Campbell.

* * *

They were in the locomotive sheds at Southampton and the man was pointing at parts of the locomotive.

'This here is the cross-head, the French call it *la tête de piston*.' He moved along the track a little. 'And this is the steam cylinder or the stuffing-box. In French it's *le cylindre* or *la boîte à étoupe*.' He straightened up. 'Always put the plastic on one side of an engine and then they can't cannibalise parts from one engine to repair another. So you've got seven places to go for and I'll be giving each one of you a diagram so you can remember the vital parts. Any questions?'

Bailey was sitting on the small table, swinging one leg, watching them as they wrote their reports on the counter-surveillance training they had done in Southampton that morning. He looked at his watch.

'Time's up. Jason, you collect the reports please.'

When the reports were on the table he said, 'Now you've had instruction every day on checking for booby-traps. After supper today I'll take you to a row of cottages. You'll go in one by one, on your own, and note where you think there are booby-traps. OK. Dismiss.'

It was still light when they finished taking their turns through the cottages. It was the last week in May and the trees made long shadows on the grass from the setting sun.

'Right. Anybody find more than ten? OK. How many?'

'Fourteen, sir.'

'Below ten but more than five?'

Slowly he took their numbers. Nobody had fewer than five suspected booby-trap sites.

'Well that's interesting my friends. For nearly four weeks you've been shown how to recognise a booby-trap and you've obviously learned well. However, it's easy to let things like these become and obsession.' He paused, smiling. 'I have to tell you that there were no booby-traps in any of the cottages. I just wanted you to get back to normal life again.' He paused again as he heard both laughter and complaints. 'And one more item. The Royal Navy sank the *Bismarck* yesterday.'

* * *

He was speaking on the telephone when she came in and he pointed to the chair facing him on the other side of the table. When he'd finished he turned to look at her. She really was very pretty and she obviously thought that the rules didn't apply to her.

'It's been reported to me that you and the other two girls have been leaving the unit every night and returning as late as 3 or 4 a.m. Is that so?'

She smiled. 'Not every night. But most nights.'

'When you were stopped the first time you were using one of our small vans, yes?'

'Yes.'

'And since then you've been using your own car.'

'Yes.'

'Where do you get the petrol coupons?'

'Mainly from boyfriends. Sometimes on the black market.'

'You think it's a good idea for a FANY officer to be trading on the black market?'

She shrugged and smiled. 'You gave us a talk on how to use the black market in France. Seems OK to me to use it here.'

'Why are you back so late?'

With not very well-conceived impatience she said, 'That's because the night-clubs don't close until late. It takes me an hour to get down here even with empty roads.'

'Why do you spend your free time in night-clubs may I ask?'

She laughed. 'Because they're good fun. My friends are there.'

'Your black market friends I suppose.'

'Oh no, they're all serving officers. The black market contact is local.'

For a moment he was at a loss for words. He had expected denials or even excuses but she sat there smiling and defiant. He was about to speak when she said, 'Can I speak?'

'Go ahead.'

'You know who my father is don't you?'

'What difference does that make?'

She leaned forward towards him and he saw the anger in her eyes.

'It makes a difference because you, Major Bailey, are a bloody snob. An inverted snob. You don't like me because my father is both a knight and well-off.' She banged her closed fist on the desk. 'My

95

father didn't get me into SOE. I volunteered. And while we're on it what's wrong with dancing at a night-club? Better than hanging around this place all night playing cards or dominoes.

His face impassive Bailey said, quietly, 'We'll leave it at that Officer Campbell.'

She stood up slowly and walked to the door where she stopped, opened her mouth to speak and then decided against it.

As he sat on his bunk later that evening his anger had subsided. He had made a fool of himself. He had treated her as if she were a soldier. But she wasn't, none of them were. They wouldn't have been any use to him if they had been. It was a lesson to be learned. She was right on all counts. He had disliked her because he had seen her as privileged. She *was* privileged but she hadn't abused what was just a fact of life. All the same he wasn't sure now that he wanted her in his network. She had the makings of a trouble-maker. A barrack-room lawyer.

June 1941 was a month of long hot days and Bailey had brought them outside for his talk.

'One thing you must always remember. Never use a house with children for a safe-house or even as a contact point. No matter how brave he might be for himself, any man is going to throw in the towel when his children are threatened.

'And while we are in this area let me tell you what is expected of you if you are caught. Don't try to out-smart them. Stick to your cover as long as you can. But when it's obvious that it won't work give your name, rank and number as required by the Hague Convention. You are all commissioned officers and registered as such. However, let's not kid ourselves. They won't recognise you as soldiers. They will claim you are saboteurs, you are not in uniform and therefore you have no protection under the Convention.

'Now all this could take several days or it could be just a couple of hours if they think you have information they want urgently.' He paused for long moments. 'And the information they want is, of course, the names of the members of your network and where they are. And if you are a radio operator, your frequencies, check-words and details of your code system.

'So we ask you to keep silent if you can so that the people in your network can get away to some place of safety. For how long should you try to keep silent? Twenty-four hours or what? So remember when one of your group is taken you get the hell out immediately, and if possible inform London on your next schedule. Any questions?'

Nobody spoke and Bailey said, 'OK. I'll ask the question. How long do I have to keep silent? How much is enough? Well each one of us has a different answer to that question. We ask you to think of your friends but we don't ask you to go beyond what your body and your conscience allow. Another point I want to raise is the break-off point. In ten days' time we shall move onto our actual operational details. Where we shall be, our roles, our objectives. If anyone feels that he or she is not suited for this work come and see me before the break-off point. Nobody will see you in an unfavourable light. On the contrary we shall admire you for thinking of the safety of your friends and colleagues.' He paused. 'Right. Tomorrow morning you will do the final run on the assault course and after lunch I'll give you the staff assessments of each team.'

He was woken at 3 a.m. the next morning by a call from London. The Germans had invaded the Soviet Union and there were German tank squadrons already outside Smolensk. This was going to make a huge difference to the outcome of the war. He almost decided to wake his team but it was a Sunday and they got an extra hour before first parade on Sundays. He tried to sleep but he couldn't. He dressed and walked out into the quiet summer darkness. There were the stirrings of birds in the woods behind the house and far away he heard the bark of a vixen. He wondered what difference the news would make to his operation. Would it make it even more necessary or make it a waste of time? He deliberately avoided bringing himself to any decision about which way he would prefer.

The mock interrogations had been realistic, with officers they didn't know dressed in German uniforms, the victim hauled out of bed in the middle of the night. The interrogations had been filmed with a concealed camera and the film had been developed and screened for Bailey the next day.

He set no great store by the individual reactions. They had shared no dangers as a team and after the initial shock they were aware that, despite the cold baths and the shouting, neither life nor limb was in real danger. The only good it did was to confirm his thoughts on the two who should be left behind.

Bailey had had the Michelin map 75 blown up until it filled the whole wall of the classroom and had gone over all he had learned about the area. He would be dropped first with whoever he took as his radio operator and would organise their reception after he had arranged safe-houses for them. He told them nothing of the local people who might be giving them shelter. He was going to interview each one of his squad separately, and during the rest of the interviews the others would have a refresher course on coding, de-coding and radio operation.

At the end of the week of individual interviews Bailey had expected to eliminate two of the men but one of his rejects had proved to be an exceptionally skilled radio operator. He decided to keep him in reserve. The other reject was to be taken on by the main training staff as an explosives and sabotage instructor. When someone had been through the training programme every effort was made to keep them inside SOE even if they were not suitable as agents. They knew too much that could endanger other people's lives.

He had chosen Paulette Fleury as his radio operator. She was not only a first-class operator but she had real knowledge of the area. His plan was that the two of them would go in first and the others would follow when he had established safe places for them to live and operate. They come in pairs at intervals so that they could be absorbed safely.

As the time approached for him to leave he spent his time em-phasising that the aggression they had been taught in their training was the essential ingredient for their success as a network. The self-reliance they had been taught would be tested to the full, so would their patience and their ability to cope with disappointment and still remain ready to snatch at any chance of harassing the enemy.

By then his antipathy to the Campbell girl had given way to respect for her courage and dedication. When she suggested that he and Paulette Fleury and Tony Ransome should go up to London for a last dinner at the Savoy he reluctantly agreed. Not that it was his idea of how to spend one of his last nights before dropping into enemy territory.

None of them was in uniform but Jenny Campbell seemed to know everybody. The staff were almost embarrassingly attentive and there was a constant flow of people from other tables coming over to chat with her. She introduced them all and Bailey was impressed that he and Tony Ransome were so easily accepted just because they were friends of hers. He found that he was enjoying himself.

She smiled as she asked him to dance with her and as she looked up at his face as they danced she said softly, 'Are you enjoying yourself a little bit?'

'A lot, actually. Your friends are such nice people.'

'Do you recognise what the band's playing?'

'Yes. I do.'

She sang softly, 'The last time I saw Paris, her heart was warm and gay. I heard the laughter of her heart in every street café . . .' She paused as she looked at his face. 'I hope all goes well for you. I'll be thinking about you. I think you're very brave to go on your own, just the two of you.'

'I've been there before. I know my way around. So does Paulette.'

'Are you scared?'

He shrugged. 'Not scared exactly – just crossing my fingers that the people I contacted there will actually support us as they promised to do.' He paused. 'And how about you? Are you scared?'

'Sometimes.' She laughed. 'Being dropped is bad enough, but going over to make a bloody nuisance of ourselves to the Germans seems kind of crazy.'

'Have you discussed it with your parents?'

'No. They don't need to know. It's nothing to do with them. This is me, not them.'

As they walked back to their table she held his hand but she was sure he didn't notice.

They drove back in her MG with the hood down and the moon was almost full, a golden October moon, the Hunter's moon. An SOE moon. Two days to go.

The last two days had been spent in briefing Paulette on what they would do when they were dropped and he showed her on the map roughly where it would be. There would obviously be no reception committee and it had been decided to take the risk of using the Fleurys' cottage at Brantôme for a few days while Bailey tried to contact Paul Cattoir on his estate just outside Bergerac. Paulette Fleury had given him a detailed description of the cottage and the name of a man in the town who she knew was a communist and whose son had been sent to Germany to work in a forced labour camp.

CHAPTER 18

The two of them had been checked over carefully by the ground dispatcher, clothes, teeth and documents. And they had watched as their leg containers were packed with various medical items and small packs of dried foods. Only Bailey was to be armed. A Luger that had been stripped down, reassembled, oiled and tested.

Fuller and Campbell came up from London to see them off. There was a Whitley bomber waiting on the runway, the slowest and most unwieldy of the RAF's available aircraft. But with extra tanks it had a range of almost 1000 miles. They had both made drops from Whitleys on their parachute course at Ringway.

The aircrew were awaiting 'met' clearance and final instructions that would keep them clear of bombers returning from a night raid on Dortmund.

Bailey sat in the Squadron Leader's office with Paulette. He saw her hand shaking as she drank a glass of water. There was a pile of magazines on the table, copies of *Blighty* and *Daily Mirror*s which had been kept for the cartoon character of Jane, the pretty blonde who was always having a bath or a shower. On top of this pile was a copy of *Picture Post*, its cover a photograph of Londoners clearing up the rubble of shops and houses after a Luftwaffe raid.

Then there was a bustle of activity as two men in RAF uniform pushed aside the black-out curtains and came inside. One was a flight lieutenant and the other a sergeant. They came over to the table.

'You OK chaps? We've had clearance if you're ready.'

Fuller and Campbell had been asked to wait by the huts but they walked with Bailey and the girl across the airstrip. The twin engines were already ticking over and after hurried handshakes they clambered up the short aluminium ladder into the body of the plane.

There were no seats, just metal boxes bolted to the floor of the aircraft with folded blankets for them to sit on. A weak light shone from an overhead fitting and Bailey looked at his watch. It was just before midnight, already half an hour behind schedule. Then he felt the lurch of the aircraft as it started its run, the whole aircraft shuddering as it gained speed. It seemed a long time before it was airborne and there was only the noise of the engines. They sat side by side, Bailey's arm around the girl's shoulders across the top of her parachute. They had been told that it would take two hours to get to the dropping zone and with the noise of the engines it was impossible to talk. And for the first time Bailey was having doubts about the operation. All the training and planning suddenly seemed to be stupid and misconceived. A game of make-believe that had come to a sudden end as they got into the plane. They would not be looking at maps and weaving hopes into a false reality in two hours' time. They would be dropping by parachute into another country. A country controlled by a ruthless, efficient enemy. They would be lucky to survive for an hour without being arrested. The Savoy and Carroll Gibbons seemed to have been in another world. Maybe he should lie low for a couple of days and then radio back to London to call the whole thing off. He closed his eyes for a moment to bring some relief to his mind and he slept for over an hour.

When he woke the doubts had gone. Other SOE networks were working successfully. They had losses but that was to be expected and anyway he had done it before and got back safely. He looked at the girl and she smiled back at him and gave him Churchill's V-sign. The sergeant came back with a Thermos of coffee and two tin mugs. He poured it for them expertly without spilling a drop and they drank it slowly. As he sipped it Bailey realised that they'd put in a drop of brandy to warm them up.

The pilot was going to use the River Dronne as a marker using the bridge at Brantôme if the moonlight was bright enough.

Half an hour later he saw the sergeant checking the clamps on the hatch and reaching up to look at the clip for their static lines with a torch. He turned towards them and put up both hands, fingers outspread to indicate that they should be ready in ten minutes. It seemed a long ten minutes. Then the plane banked and lost height as the sergeant came back and put his face close to them.

'Who's going first?'

Bailey pointed to his chest. 'Me.'

'Both of you come over with me. I'll hook you up and take off the cover. You watch for the red light. When I tap your shoulder you go. OK?'

Bailey nodded and the girl just shrugged. The sergeant hooked up both static lines and then pulled aside the cover with a rush of wind and cold air. Almost immediately the red light came on, the sergeant tapped his shoulder and just as he had done so many times in practice, he pushed his body forward into the rush of the slip-stream. For a moment he was on his back and then, as the weight of his leg canister took over he straightened a second before his canopy flared open so that he swung in a slow arc aware only of the moon in a cloudless sky. He looked down and saw sheep scattering as his shadow passed over them, the ground rushing up, the jar through his body and the instinctive forward roll to ease the impact. Still acting instinctively he unbuckled his harness and looked for the girl. She was swinging dangerously but she closed her legs as she came down the last hundred feet and disappeared in a cloud of silk canopy.

He ran across to her but she was already on her feet trying to collapse her parachute. He could see a wood over to the left and they ran with their parachutes only half collapsed to the edge of the trees. Panting, he dug a shallow hole with the digging tool and buried both the parachutes and the containers, covering them with dead leaves and dry bracken.

Still panting he looked at her face, pale in the moonlight, grinning as he said softly, 'We've done it, kid. We've done it.' He took a deep breath. 'We'd better try and find out where we are.' He looked up at the moon to work out their bearings and then pointed across the field. 'The river should be over there.'

She laughed softly. 'They won't have been that accurate.'

The walked eastwards for half an hour before they saw the river.

'The bridge should be down-river. Let's keep to the bank. We've got two hours before the curfew's lifted.' An hour later they saw the bridge and a huddle of cottages on the far side of the river.

'It's the wrong bridge, Harry. Those cottages are a village called Champagnac de Belair. But we're less than a couple of miles from the cottage if we cross the bridge and go through the village.'

'Let's go then.'

When they were almost across the bridge they froze as they saw a light come on in the nearest cottage and the sound of a dog barking. She said softly, 'What time is it?'

'Five a.m. local time.'

'That's probably a farm-worker. A shepherd.'

'Shall we risk it?'

'We have to go round two sides of that cottage, up the lane about a hundred metres and then turn right down another lane. Let me go first because if he stops me I can tell him I'm just down from Paris and my car's broken down. I know how to talk to these people. If it's OK I'll flash my torch at the corner of the cottage.' She paused. 'The dog probably heard the sheeps' bleating carried on the wind when we disturbed them.' She squeezed his arm. 'I'm off.'

Five minutes later the torch flashed briefly and he moved off slowly and cautiously. Ten minutes later she was waiting for him at the lane. They walked on silently and cautiously, birds stirring in the bushes as they passed by. It was twenty minutes before she pointed, whispering, 'There's the cottage.'

It was beginning to get light and he could see the cottage in the mist that was rising from the ground. Small, with whitewashed walls and blue shutters closed on the windows, a wooden porch over the front door.

'You don't think your father might be down here?'

'No. He hates the place. I'll see if I can get in. If we have to force a door or a window we'll do it on the kitchen at the back. Hold on till I flash my torch.'

It seemed a long time before he saw the flash of light from the darkness of the porch. The door to the cottage was open.

Inside, the cottage was more spacious than it looked from outside. A kitchen and scullery along the far end wall and the rest of the ground floor was open as living room and dining room combined, with an open stone hearth and a floor of terracotta tiles. Upstairs there were two bedrooms, one double, one single. And an old-fashioned bathroom. The furniture was simple but well made, typical furniture from country sales.

Paulette found a few things in a small refrigerator, cheese and biscuits. She was surprised. It meant that her father, or somebody, had been at the cottage recently.

Bailey found that the electricity was on in all the rooms and cold water ran freely from a tank somewhere in the attic. He found the well and the pump outside in a wooden shack with a collection of rusty tools and a can of petrol. There were two bundles of thick white candles and half a dozen cheap glass candlesticks.

Beside a couch in the living room there was a pile of magazines. The latest about a month old.

But the most valuable find was her long forgotten cycle in a shed at the far end of the garden.

When they had finished their inspection they sat at the kitchen table eating one of the special biscuits from their leg packs.

She looked at him. 'Would you like me to go and bring back the radio? It won't take long now I know where we are. It's easier for me. I've got my original travel permit in my own name.' She shrugged as she rehearsed her part. 'I'm just down here for a couple of days' leave from Paris.'

'Sure. And you just happen to have brought a suitcase transmitter with you. No. The first thing is your Commie friend – what's his name?'

'Louis. Louis Maurois.'

'You're sure he's safe?'

She shrugged. 'As sure as anyone can be.'

'Where's he live?'

'He's one of the butchers in Brantôme.'

'How long on the bike?'

'Fifteen, twenty minutes, each way.'

'OK. See if he'll let me use his phone. And try him out about helping us in the network.'

'OK.'

As he watched her wobble down the lane on the bicycle it reminded him of Lemaire riding off, full of enthusiasm, never to come back. He looked at his watch. It seemed incredible, it was only 9 a.m.

It was noon before she got back and he was relieved to see her. Her face was flushed from cycling and she was smiling as she propped the bike against the side of the porch.

'How did it go?'

'Fantastic. Let's go inside. I need to get my breath back.' She untied a box from the carrier. 'Food. All we need for a week.'

Inside she sat on the couch and he pulled up a chair from the table.

'He was fantastic, Harry. We can use his phone. He'll provide safe places – permanently or temporarily. With the shop he can get all kinds of food on the black market. He'll keep us supplied at minimum price. And best of all he'll do anything we want if it means damaging the Germans. He's got all sorts of contacts everywhere, here, Bergerac, Sarlat, Périgueux, and even in Bordeaux. You'll like him.'

'When can I meet him?'

'I said you would go down later this evening and make your phone call and then talk with him. He's got lots of ideas for sabotage.'

She stood up and started taking food out of the box. 'It's easy to find and you can use the bike.'

'Won't I be noticed on a lady's bike?'

She laughed. 'Don't make me laugh. There's a war on.'

CHAPTER 19

Louis Maurois was in his fifties, balding with grey hair and a strong face with the creases that came from the wear and tear of a hard life. Broad shoulders and a big muscular body, with the strong arms that come from carrying sides of beef from delivery vans to the back of his shop.

He was putting up the shutters when Bailey arrived, the butcher's big, rough hand closing round his as the blue eyes searched his face to check him out.

'Go through the shop to my living quarters. I'll be in when I've locked up.'

The rear of the shop was cool, and the furnishings were sparse and simple. There were silver cups and pewter tankards for various sporting achievements. The only picture on the walls was the photograph of a young man smiling at the camera as he squinted into the sun.

The butcher came bustling in, taking off his striped apron as he leaned back against the door to close it.

'I'll just call you chief, OK? Then no problems.'

'That's fine. Thank you for your help and the food.'

The butcher shook his head. 'I'll help anyone who wants to drive out those German bastards.'

'Tell me about your son.'

'Just picked up him and the others on the street. He'd gone before I even knew they'd taken him. I raised hell at the gendarmerie. They said he was a volunteer to work in Germany.' He trembled with anger as he thought about it again. 'There are going to be a lot of scores to settle before this is all over.' He paused. 'Can I ask *you* some questions, my friend?'

Bailey smiled and shrugged. 'Sure, but I can't guarantee to answer them.'

'You speak French like a Frenchman but you're English aren't you?'

'Yes.'

'Where did you learn your French?'

'I've spent a lot of time in France.'

'Doing what?'

'Just living.'

'Why do you risk your life doing this work?'

'Same as you. We've got to throw the Germans out of France.'

'OK. Let's talk about what I can do for you.'

'Can I phone to Bergerac first?'

'Of course.' He pointed to the old-fashioned phone. 'Help yourself.'

Paul Cattoir in Bergerac had seemed surprised to hear from him. They had to talk guardedly but it was obvious that Cattoir was still willing to co-operate.

Back with Maurois he had talked for over two hours. The butcher bought cattle and sheep from a wide area and also supplied meat to most of the small village butchers within a couple of hours' driving distance. He supplied meat to the German supply base at Nontron that in turn supplied meat to all German units of the SS and Wehrmacht in the Dordogne.

Maurois had suggestions for dozens of sabotage targets and had provided names of strategically placed people who could supply information about the local Germans. But eventually he looked at Bailey and said, 'You haven't asked me about my politics. Where do we stand on that?'

'I'm not interested in your politics, Louis. If you'll help us fight the Germans that's all that matters.'

Maurois wagged a thick finger. 'Don't take it for granted that all Frenchmen are on your side. There are plenty of collaborators and plenty more who just want a quiet life.'

'I know, my friend, I know.' Bailey paused. 'I've got some people dropping in shortly, could you put together a reception party?'

Maurois shrugged. 'Just tell me what you want and I'll do it.'

'I was going to make my base in Bergerac. What do you think about making it here instead?'

'How many you got coming?'

'Two drops of four. Two of them women.'

'What help have you got in Bergerac?'

'A big-scale farmer.'

Maurois smiled. 'Must be Paul Cattoir, yes?'

'D'you know him?'

'Of course. We do a lot of business together.'

'What do you think of him?'

'He's OK. Solid, reliable and well in with the Germans. They'd never suspect him. He's got property all over the region and lots of buildings on the estate apart from that mansion of his.' Maurois nodded. 'Go to Bergerac.'

'Anything against him?'

Maurois smiled. 'Only his politics.'

Bailey laughed softly. 'A nice balance to you.'

'Politics don't matter now but when the war is over it'll be everything. They'll all have been in the Resistance then.'

'Would you go with me to his place and talk it over?'

'Of course. When?'

'Tomorrow?'

'OK. I'll phone him to warn him to be around.'

'One more thing, Louis. I've got a radio buried in the woods and I want to move it to the cottage. It would help if I could have some transport.'

'When?'

'Is it possible to do it tonight? As soon as it's dark?'

'OK. I'll pick you up at the cottage.'

Paulette had rigged up an aerial and assembled the radio and checked its Morse key. The set was a Type 3 Mark 1 made by Marconi with a built-in Morse key.

London were keeping a twenty-four-hour monitoring until they received the first transmission. They had two separate crystals for emergency transmissions, one for daytime and one for night-time. Both of those frequencies were permanently monitored for all networks.

The code was an old one called the Playfair after its inventor and was highly secure as it was based on a memorised phrase, usually a nursery rhyme that was easy to remember. Bailey had opted for 'The last rose of summer'. The code's greatest advantage was that it was easy to use and left no compromising documents. His choice had led to much leg-pulling by the main signals reception unit.

Bailey's first message back to London reported only that they had landed safely and had established a safe-house and a reliable local contact. London had acknowledged contact and receipt of signal instantly but Paulette had been worried about the heavy load when using the Morse key that made their domestic lights dim and recover with each click of the key. That meant that she would have to transmit on the daylight frequency or at night by candlelight, otherwise it would be simple for a German detector van to identify the source of their signal. If they had been operating in a town, the neighbours' lights would have been affected too.

CHAPTER 20

Paul Cattoir looked more like a diplomat or a merchant banker than what he called himself – a farmer. That was because the four thousand acres of the estate had been in his family for over four generations. By any standards he was a rich man, but a rich man whose charm and generosity shielded him from the spite of the envious. His interests away from the responsibilities of the estate were music, art and history. He was tall with a sallow complexion but a handsome face. Solemn when he listened to other people's troubles but naturally optimistic when left in peace. He had married quite young but it had lasted only two years and the separation and divorce had been civilised and generous. From then on he had never had a close relationship with any woman. Rumours divided almost equally between him being a homosexual and a man who charmed dozens of young women into his bed. When those who knew him sought for a one-word description of the man the consensus was that he was '*un philosophe*'. That was how Bailey saw him, and he was slightly in awe of a man who combined such an elegant mind with such riches. Louis Maurois saw him simply as his idea of the perfect Frenchman. A cross between Joan of Arc and Maurice Chevalier.

There was frost on the fields as Cattoir walked them from one building to another. The vineyards produced a modest wine but the main income came from a mixture of arable, vegetables, milk, beef and sheep. A few hectares of lavender and tobacco kept up a local tradition but made no money. As Cattoir said – he wasn't a gambling man so he placed his bets across the board. But in wartime a farmer can't go wrong.

Bailey had told him of his plans and in the upstairs study Cattoir had listened patiently, glancing at Maurois to see his reaction from time to time. When Bailey was finished Cattoir said, 'You would be foolish to base your network in Brantôme. It's too small. Everybody knows everybody. All right if it was just the two of you but with a network as you describe it you would be exposed in a matter of weeks.'

'But it would save you being too deeply involved.'

'My dear man. I am involved already. Involved by birth. Involved by blood and history. Even if I wished it otherwise, and I do not, I have no choice.' Bailey opened his mouth to speak but Cattoir held up his hand. 'Believe it or not but those wretched Germans trust me. And I am useful. I stop them making ridiculous mistakes and I keep them happy in many ways.'

'But you have so much to lose.'

Paul Cattoir closed his eyes for a moment and his lips moved silently. Then he opened his eyes, smiling as he looked at the two of them.

'I may misquote it, my dear Englishman. He was after all your poet not ours – but he said it just as well for us today.

'He which hath no stomach to this their fight,
Let him depart; his passport shall be made
And crowns for convoy put into his purse:
We would not die in that man's company
That fears his fellowship to die with us.'

He hesitated and then went on.

'And gentlemen in England, now a-bed
Shall think themselves accursed they were not here,
And hold their manhoods cheap whiles any speaks
That fought with us upon Saint Crispin's day.'

Turning to look at Bailey, he smiled and said, 'So dear Englishman, do not fret for me. The risk for me is not to take the risk.'

'I'm very grateful to you, sir.'

'Let's get down to talking business.' Cattoir turned to Maurois. 'Can you stay the night, Louis?'

'Let me make a phone call, but yes. I'll stay.'

'And you, Englishman?'

'I'll be glad to stay if Louis could get a message to my colleague at the cottage.'

Maurois stood up. 'Leave it to me, chief.'

They had talked all night but even when Bailey was back at the cottage he couldn't sleep. He knew that he needed to rethink the whole of his network plan. There were too many people for the opportunities on the ground. At least for the first six months. He found a few sheets of dusty notepaper on a shelf and started writing out a report. A report for himself rather than for London. He needed more locals and he needed two radio operators, and an explosives expert and a network man in each of Brantôme, Périgueux, and Bergerac. And a reserve team of explosives man with a deputy. For his own HQ he needed a deputy, one of the radio operators, a sabotage expert and a courier. Finally he made out a list of his choices.

Bergerac HQ:	Bailey
	Jenny Campbell – radio
	Louis Maurois – deputy
Brantôme:	Tony Ransome
	Paulette Fleury
Périgueux:	Joe Parsons
	Violette Crowther
Reserve:	Roger Powers – sabotage
	James Long – sabotage

They were all virtually bilingual except Powers and Long who were fluent but with accents. He would have preferred to have Paulette Fleury as his radio operator but she knew the Brantôme area so well that it would be crazy to sacrifice the benefit. Only his HQ radio would be used, the second had to be in reserve or there would be confusion in London on the schedules.

When Paulette Fleury found him he was asleep with his head on the table. She woke him with a cup of black coffee and the news that in the morning schedule London wanted to know where they were. Just a map reference with digits and northings and southings reversed would be enough. He checked the maps, worked out the digits and gave it to her for the evening transmission.

He went down his list again and realised that Maurois with his business couldn't possibly be his deputy, he'd have to see what other local turned up. Paul Cattoir had made clear he'd do anything but he wasn't the kind of man who could organise the locals. He would be too much weight and they'd back off. And it would make Cattoir too vulnerable. Bailey didn't want the network to have any routine contact with Cattoir. It was not even necessary for them to know that he was involved in any way.

As things stood it would be only six of his team coming over. At least in the first stages. Although Fuller would probably transfer the others to some other network in formation.

And behind all this organising was the reason for it. The disruption, the sabotage. But that mustn't start too soon. They'd need to probe the German reactions first. Meantime they had routine tasks they could perform. Identify German units in the area, their supply lines and their functions. London were right, he'd have to be patient to be any use when it really mattered. Tomorrow he'd make out the list of supplies and equipment they would need.

After a week Bailey and Maurois had gone up to Cattoir's study and he'd poured them each a glass of wine while they made themselves comfortable in the leather armchairs. As he was handing Bailey his glass he said, 'Can you remember it all? I hope you haven't made notes.' He glanced at Maurois. 'Agreed Louis?'

Maurois smiled at Bailey. 'He knows that with your training you'll be more careful even than he is, he's just having a dig at me.'

Cattoir smiled. 'Very perceptive, Louis.' He paused and looked at Bailey. 'Do you want comments or just approval?' He noticed that Bailey hadn't touched his wine.

Bailey smiled back. 'Both.'

Cattoir sat down. 'Tell me about this planning the two of you have been up to.'

'Well in Bergerac you've already agreed that I can use one of your cottages with my cover as assistant estates manager and then Jenny Campbell can take over the stables and the breeding programme, yes?'

'Tell me, will you both be actually doing those jobs?'

'Of course. Let's say half our time.'

'Excellent.'

'There are two other men I'd like to house on the estate if it was necessary as a kind of reserve. Louis has found them good jobs that fit their experience. A job has been arranged for Roger Powers in the railway workshop as a welder and James Long we've fixed up at one of the hotels as a waiter. Both good sources of information. Could they be accommodated on the estate?'

'No problems.' He smiled. 'I could use them too.'

'In Brantôme Paulette Fleury will act as local reporter for the Bergerac paper and Tony Ransome will be a driver for Louis.' He paused. 'That just leaves Périgueux where we've fixed up Joe Parsons as assistant projectionist at the cinema. He studied film at college in Quebec. And Violette Crowther is a trained vet and will be a freelance.'

'I can use her and recommend her to plenty of others.' He smiled. 'Well done. You must be pleased.'

'Your contacts and Louis helped a lot.'

Cattoir looked at Maurois. 'Are you happy, Louis?'

'Yes.'

Bailey said, 'I want to spend at least two months establishing the network and finding suitable targets. They'll be impatient I know but they'll have plenty to do to establish themselves.'

'Then what?'

'Sabotage away from our three centres. Mainly in one area. Then moving on. If we do well then a wider spread on the same night. Bridges, buildings and then communications. No attacks on Germans for at least six months.'

'Why not?' Cattoir asked, but Bailey knew that he already knew the answer.

'When we start attacking Germans it's got to be more than just harassment. They'll revenge themselves on the locals. We don't want that unless it really serves a purpose.'

'What kind of purpose?'

'Something that contributes to throwing out the Germans.'

'How much help have you had from the locals?'

'A lot of help. Not necessarily involvement – but ready to supply information and turn a blind eye if they see anything odd going on.'

Cattoir nodded. 'I'm glad you're not one of these lunatics who think it's all a game. Ten-day heroes and then they're caught. A dozen civilians shot in reprisals and even more shipped off to concentration camps. Just remember there's a combined SD and Gestapo set-up in Bordeaux. They'll be putting out detachments. So keep good cut-outs between your main people and people who are mere informants or sympathisers.'

Bailey nodded. 'There's a rough code you should know about when we are forced to use the phone. If there are Germans at the place the response is "Fine, do come over", if it's clear the response is "We could meet next week maybe".'

'I'll remember that. Another glass, yes?'

They sat for another hour, talking about the war news and inevitably French politics.

It was Bailey who asked Maurois what had made him decide that he was a Communist.

Maurois shrugged. 'I was born a Communist. Always was, always will be.'

Cattoir smiled. 'Never ask Party members why they are Communists. Either you'll get a long boring lecture on Marx and Marxism or more likely a shrug, like good Louis, here. Most people don't know why they're Communists or even what Communism is. They just feel it's good for the soul, a kind of mental vitamin. Like old ladies think salt is good for the blood.' He grinned. 'Ask a Catholic why he's a Catholic and you'll get the same response. The Marxists have their dialectic and the Catholics have their creed, but neither of them live by their beliefs.' He smiled and raised his glass. 'Never mind, let's drink to the Red Army who are doing a hell of a lot better than anyone else in this crazy war.'

CHAPTER 21

London agreed his plan but two drops had been aborted. The first because a suitable plane was not available and the second because of weather conditions. Twice the reception parties had to be stood down and that had lowered local morale among Louis Maurois's volunteers.

Finally Bailey got a signal to say that the only possible date was December 20, was that convenient? He signalled back his agreement after checking with Maurois and Cattoir. The dropping zone was to be on Cattoir's estate and the team would be hidden in buildings scattered over the farm. Barns full of hay, derelict shepherd's huts and parts of the stables that still housed a dozen or so pedigree horses. The long wait was helped by hearing on BBC broadcasts that on the 7th the Japanese had bombed Pearl Harbor and by the following day Britain and the USA had both declared war on the Axis powers. It was an incredible end to 1941.

December 20, 1941 was a Saturday and Cattoir had organised the usual Christmas party for the estate servants and their families and friends at a hotel in the town. He made sure that the local police had been invited too. He had considered inviting a couple of senior German officials but decided that that would be going too far.

An hour before the plane was due they rehearsed the procedure. Three bicycle lamps in an inverted 'L' and Paulette with a torch to give the recognition signal – a dash and three dots for the letter B. There were a dozen carefully chosen helpers and they would be responsible for picking up the supply containers and transferring them to the piggery, and burying the parachutes in a shallow trench that had been dug at the edge of the woods.

It was bitterly cold but Cattoir had supplied them with three large Thermos flasks with hot beef soup and a dozen loaves of bread.

The sky was clear, a pale silver-blue and a moon that was barely visible in the mist that had risen across the fields. It was Bailey who heard the first hum of the plane's engines and Paulette who saw the plane glinting in the moonlight as it came from the northern edge of the woods. As Louis gave the signal the lights came on and they could see the moonlight reflected on the body of the plane. Then the bodies came out like a litter of puppies being born. One at a time, with only seconds between them; the waiting men ran towards them as they landed, helping them out of their harnesses, taking their hands and running with them to the woodcutter's cottage, another helper collecting the chutes, folding them and carrying them away to be buried. Only one figure lay prone. Joe Parsons had twisted his ankle on landing. Somebody crouched beside him until the others had left and then two men carried Parsons to a small van parked by the hut.

There was a log fire in the hut and kerosene lamps that threw crisp shadows on the walls and ceiling as the reception party handed out food and warm drinks. There was much subdued chatter as the usual relief and euphoria that came from a successful jump took over. When things had quietened down Bailey explained where they were and the basic security that was essential. They were to get some sleep and he'd brief them all in the afternoon. Then he'd see each one of them individually.

CHAPTER 22

There had been no network celebrations during Christmas. Paul Cattoir was in Paris for a week and Bailey wanted to make the point with the three groups that they were no longer to be in contact with one another, except in an emergency, without his permission.

Bailey and Jenny Campbell were in two small farm-workers' cottages. There were six in a terrace and the other cottages were empty. He spent two days before Christmas going over his instructions with each group and establishing the various channels of communication, and going over their cover stories now that they knew where they would be working. He was encouraged by their attitudes and their quiet confidence. Even though his previous mission in occupied France had been virtually useless they seemed to find some reassurance in the fact that he'd done it before. He was vaguely ashamed that he hadn't told them how ineffective he and poor Lemaire had been.

It was snowing on Christmas morning as Bailey walked past the two empty cottages to the one that Jenny Campbell had taken over. He knocked on the door and she called out for him to come in.

It was the first time he had seen her since he had briefed her and he was pleased to see that she was already dressed to go to the stables.

'How are things? Are you settled in OK?'

'It's fine. Let's have a coffee.'

As she busied herself making the coffee she said, 'When do I get to meet the handsome Paul Cattoir?'

'When he goes to the stables, I guess. Anyway, who said he was handsome?'

'I've seen pictures of him in *Horse and Hound*, he's quite famous for raising show horses. I think Daddy met him several times before the war.' She saw his face and grinned. 'Sorry, I mustn't talk about

Daddy, must I? Have to be a little Orphan Annie. There you are. No sugar till tomorrow.'

'How are things back at the Manor?'

She shrugged. 'Much the same.'

'And the Savoy?'

She laughed. 'I haven't been since I was there with you.'

'Why not?'

She shrugged. 'I wanted to remember it like it was that night.' Pausing, she said, 'It was the first time I'd ever seen you smile. And the first time I'd ever seen you looking relaxed and enjoying yourself.' She smiled. 'Or am I kidding myself?'

'No. I did enjoy it. It was like a different world.'

'Different in what way?'

'People who were enjoying themselves, happy. People who all knew one another and didn't take life too seriously.'

'Very perceptive, my dear. And how are things with you?'

'I've spent my time planning. I've been pretty busy.'

'I don't mean work, I mean you. How are you?'

He laughed. 'I don't know. I never think of myself that way.'

'You've been wasting your life, you know. You should have been falling head over heels in love with pretty girls, dancing, parties and fun and games.'

'I never had the money for those things.'

'Costs nothing to fall in love.'

He smiled. 'You're right. I'm a bit dull aren't I?'

'Far from it. You're exceptionally bright. Intelligent, perceptive and observant.'

'You're very kind – and you flatter me.'

'All the girls on the course thought you were the best of all the instructors.'

'But dull.'

'Maybe. Let's say too wrapped up in armour.' She smiled. 'Which, of course, made you even more desirable.' She stood up. 'Would you like to see the horses?'

He stood up too. 'No thanks. I've got things to do.' He paused. 'Tony Ransome will be bringing over your radio tomorrow morning. I shall need to contact London on tomorrow's evening schedule.'

'Have you been making contact OK?'

'No problems so far.'

'How about I cook us a beef casserole tonight?'

'Have you got meat?'

She grinned. 'Yep. He's taking me to a hop on Saturday night.'

He smiled. 'Is this Louis?'

'Of course. He's quite a lad for the girls is our Louis.'

'He's old enough to be your father.'

She laughed. 'So what? I've always fancied my old dad.'

CHAPTER 23

After a month of cautious work Bailey had been able to send back to London the locations of most of the German units in his area. In many cases he was able to identify the actual unit and its apparent function. Most of them were acting as guards on buildings and works that were producing goods for the German war effort.

Another month's work and he had sent back a long list locating what he considered to be prime sabotage targets. He asked if London wanted to suggest priorities. There was no response.

By the end of June Bailey was aware of impatience from his team at the apparent inaction and he was aware that he too sometimes felt a need to justify their existence.

It was Joe Parsons who provided him with an excuse to plan their first active operation.

They had met at a small café near the cathedral in Périgueux before Parsons had to go to the cinema for the evening performance.

'Do you have any problems with the owner?'

'No. I think he has his suspicions but he's an old man and a patriot. Keeps Pétain's poster on the wall by the cash desk but the other day I switched on the small radio he'd got in his office and it was already tuned to the BBC French Service. He's OK.'

'What kind of films do you show?'

'There's a newsreel every week called *Wochenschau* and a load of old German films. They've got a unit doing nothing but putting French subtitles on Kraut films. At the moment it's *Die Lustige Witwe*, the 'Merry Widow'. In a couple of weeks' time we're showing a ghastly anti-Semitic film called *Jew Suss*. It really is a stinker. It's on for two weeks, all tickets half-price.'

'Do the locals come for the German films?'

'Yes. There are no others. Mind you they're busy making French films. Propaganda films. Young Kraut superman from Rommel's panzers in North Africa comes back home on leave. Boy meets girl. Girl makes big sacrifice for the Fuehrer. Baby Kraut arrives in time to see his dad get Iron Cross from Rommel in desert ceremony. Fade on sand blowing across dead bodies. Cut to swastika on flag waving in the breeze. Fade out on any piece of Wagner that's available in the film library.' He paused, looking at Bailey whose eyes were closed. 'Are you listening to me, chief?'

'I'm thinking, Joe. This anti-Jewish film. How does it come to you?'

'There's a special delivery of all films from a Wehrmacht postal unit.'

'Where's the unit?'

'It's down your neck of the woods. Just outside Bergerac on the other side of the river. The south side. There's a road that goes to Castillonnès. About two kilometres out of town there's an air-strip that's used sometimes for VIPs and once a week a light plane brings pay for local units in the Dordogne, official post, personal post and our films from Berlin via Paris.'

'Tell me more. Does it come the same day every week?'

'Yes. Thursdays.'

'Same time every time?'

'Depends on the weather. And they sometimes don't bring me the films until the Friday. Same time, between six and seven in the evening. Motor-cycle and side-car. Wehrmacht camouflage colours.'

'Same fellow every week?'

'So far he is.'

'Have you seen the postal unit's place at the air-strip?'

'Only once.'

'What's it like?'

'Was a wooden hangar for road-digging and rolling machinery before the war. They've partitioned it up with plywood.'

'Where is your electricity supply – the mains junction?'

'Under a manhole cover in the street.' He looked at Bailey. 'What have you got in mind?'

Bailey shook his head. 'It's better for you not to know.'

Bailey checked with Maurois about the hangar at the air-strip and found that he supplied them with meat on a weekly basis. It was arranged that Tony Ransome would drive the van on the next delivery and do a recce of the place.

They met two days later down by the river. There were several anglers including a couple of German soldiers and they were within sight of the air-strip buildings.

'How many guards?'

'Only two. One on, one off. There's nothing there that would interest a criminal. The payrolls are sent out within an hour of arriving. The post is delivered by despatch riders on BMW motor-cycles. They even get the films over to the cinema the same day.'

'What are the guard's duties?'

Ransome shrugged. 'He just walks around. No checks, no discipline, smokes, has a glass of beer. That's about it.'

'No duty officer?'

'There's only one officer, a lieutenant, an old soldier serving out his time.' He looked at Bailey. 'You couldn't have a softer target.'

'Any dogs?'

'No,' he grinned. 'Half a dozen hens, that's all.'

'When do the posters go up for this anti-Jew film?'

'They went up today, ten days in advance because it's a big film. Paulette had to write a piece about it for the local rag. She was hopping mad. I had to calm her down.'

'Why was she so worked up?'

'Her fiancé in Paris was a Jew. The Germans took him and his whole family and shipped them off to a concentration camp.' He paused. 'That's why she came over to join us.'

'Why didn't she tell us?'

'Can't bear to talk about it.'

'But she told you.'

'I've got to know her. We're pretty close.'

For a few moments Bailey was silent, then he said, 'Thanks for the recce. I'd better get back.'

Bailey stood up, brushing grass from his trousers and casting a brief glance over his shoulder to the air-strip buildings before he moved off along the river bank to the bridge where Maurois was waiting for him with the truck.

It was a half-hour drive back to the estate and Maurois smiled as Bailey told him what he was planning.

He laughed as Bailey finished. 'They won't know who's responsible. No obvious people to round up or arrest.'

'Do you think they'll get the point?'

'Sure they will.'

'And the locals?'

'Oh they'll get it all right. They'll be scared but if nothing happens from the Boche they'll love it.'

'Do you see anything of Paulette?'

'I see her most days.'

'How is she?'

'Too many memories of that bloody cottage. I've offered to find her rooms but she won't move. Says she's at least got some roots where she is.'

'How does she get on with Tony Ransome?'

Maurois nodded. 'I thought you were working your way round to that.' He paused. 'She won't come to any harm with him. He cares about her and they're good company for one another. She's too pretty not to attract men and I wouldn't want one of the locals going for her. If they see she's already got a boyfriend they'll back off.'

As Maurois stopped the truck at the row of cottages he switched off the engine and looked at Bailey. 'What's worrying you, my friend?'

'Nothing.'

'Don't kid me, soldier. You've had a look in your eyes this last two weeks. I want to know what it's all about.'

Bailey sighed and looked at Maurois. 'It's all gone too easy, Louis. We need some action.'

'You've just planned some action.'

'That's just propaganda.'

'Like hell it is. You're throwing a brick into a hornets' nest and from now on they'll be waiting for the next move. That's what you should be thinking about.'

'I've got it all planned.'

'Tell me.'

'When we've done this first job I'll tell you.'

'You know, soldier, when a man builds a house he spends weeks on putting in the foundations that have to carry the building. That's what you've been doing since your people came. They're not in strange country now. They're ready for action but you've got to be patient. Especially you.'

Bailey sighed. 'Maybe. Anyway, thanks for the lift.'

Louis Maurois waited until Bailey had let himself into the cottage before he drove off. They could throw away months of good work and experience on one ill-timed, ill-planned act of frustration.

The posters advertising a two-week showing of the film *Jew Suss* went up on the Thursday evening. There were about twenty of them pasted to shop windows and nailed to trees. There would be a special first-night audience of local people, including the Mayor, invited by the German Town Commander.

On the Friday night they had been pasted over with a strip that said, '*Seulement pour Nazis*'. Two German soldiers were ordered to tear down the posters on the Saturday morning.

As the audience assembled for the special official screening of the film on Saturday evening there was widespread talk of the defacement of the posters and questions about who had been responsible. Nobody ventured to name names and there was ill-concealed delight on the part of some.

The performance started as normal with slides advertising local shops and tradespeople and then moved on to the German newsreel *Wochenschau*. The first item was an interview with a French army officer, an ex-POW, who claimed that he had been repatriated to France from England. He told of the torture he had undergone in England despite his wounds, to make him join de Gaulle's traitors and fight against his own countrymen. The second item was, the commentator coyly announced, news 'specially for the ladies'. It showed how women who painted their legs to look as if they were wearing silk-stockings could now buy a special pencil to draw a seam up the back of their legs. The last item showed Rommel's tanks massing in North Africa to drive the Desert Rats into the sea.

The feature film was introduced by a German civilian from Paris who claimed it as a masterpiece produced by the combined talents of German and French film makers. It was, he said, based on historical facts.

The lights went down and the curtains opened to show the title and credits against a background of medieval tapestry.

Ted Allbeury

L'Alliance
Cinématographique
Européenne
Présente
Le Juif Suss

It was well known that the film was a vicious piece of overt propaganda to excite anti-Semitism in its portrayal of the trial and hanging of a Jew.

As the credits gave way to the opening shots, close-ups of members of a court, the screen flickered and the sound groaned to a standstill. The cinema was in darkness and after a few moments there was an announcement from the stage that there would be a few moments' delay. After ten minutes sitting in total darkness there were shouts for the auditorium lights to go on. But there were no lights and people started to stir and then panic as they made their way in pitch darkness to the exits. There were appeals for calm from an unseen person but it was too late.

In the street people stood in small groups and watched as workmen lifted a manhole cover and shone torches down inside. The word quickly went around that the main electricity cable to the cinema and the nearby premises had been cut. It would take some hours before it was repaired.

Most people hurried to their houses but others went to the bars and restaurants to discuss the events of the evening. Word went around that the cable had been deliberately cut. Heads nodded knowingly but cautiously and for the first time the word 'sabotage' was whispered. Somebody had made fools of the Germans and the locals wondered what their reactions would be.

The next day the local Commandant announced that it was the work of vandals who had already been arrested, and the film would be shown only for a week as it was so much in demand elsewhere. During that week the cinema audience was never more than twenty. The episode was the talk of the town for a couple of weeks and the consensus of opinion was that at least it showed the Boche that they couldn't get away with everything.

But a week later the local paper had been ordered to devote the front page to the full text of the so-called Jewish Statutes introduced by the Germans that specified the genealogy that made you a Jew. A few days later a local tradesman put an ad in the paper to announce that despite his name, which was Klein, he was not a Jew but a life-long Catholic. When Paul Cattoir told Bailey that subsequently other cinemas in the area had been boycotted by the locals when the film had been shown Bailey was satisfied that it had been at least a kind of moral sabotage.

CHAPTER 24

Louis Maurois had brought two bottles of beer to the cottage and had been amazed when Bailey said that he didn't drink beer or any other alcohol.

'Not even wine?'

'No. Nothing.'

'But why for God's sake?'

'I never got a taste for it.'

Maurois shook his head. 'When this is all over I'm going to get you drunk.'

Bailey smiled. 'We'll see.' He paused. 'Did you bring the drawings?'

'Yes. And a couple of old photographs.'

He laid them on the kitchen table, pushing aside the glasses and plates. The photographs were faded sepia pictures of a deep embankment and the mouth of a tunnel.

'Tell me,' Maurois said, 'why Thiviers?'

'Because it's away from our area and there's no network operating up there. They won't be looking down here for reprisals.' He paused. 'And it's a junction for two lines.'

'I've got customers in Thiviers, what about them?'

'You've got customers all over, Louis, we've got to go somewhere. This is just a test operation to see how they react.'

'When?'

'June twenty-first.'

'Why then?'

'It's the anniversary of the surrender.'

'Is it now.' He was silent for a few moments. 'So why don't we do it on a bigger scale? All over the place so they get the point?'

'Then they'll know there's an organised resistance network in the area and they'll send in a Gestapo detachment.'

'They'll do that sooner or later anyway.'

'That's OK but I want it to be when London want us to really get moving and take bigger targets.'

'I don't understand.'

'There's got to be an invasion some day, Louis. That's when we can be most useful. I don't want us wiped out just because we lose our patience. It's not a game, my friend. It's a war, and when the invasion starts we'll be playing by the big boys' rules.'

'How long will that be?'

'I've no idea. A year, maybe eighteen months.'

'And in the meantime?'

'In the meantime we're just good law-abiding citizens. Going about our daily business with just enough action to remind us from time to time that we aren't just veterinary surgeons or cinema projectionists, or butchers or van drivers, welders and horse breeders.'

'By the way, Violette is doing a good job and she's got all the veterinary work she can handle.'

'So?'

'I think she's very lonely.'

'What makes you think that?'

Maurois shrugged. 'Just a feeling. She hasn't said anything but she looks kind of tense. Maybe she just needs a break. She's a bit too dedicated.' He laughed. 'Maybe she just needs a man.'

Bailey smiled. 'Do you want to sleep here tonight?'

'No. I've got an early start tomorrow.'

He was sitting in the late afternoon sunshine on an old oak bench outside the cottage and she was smoothing the coat of a chestnut gelding.

'How long since you've seen Violette?'

She straightened up, pushing aside her hair with the back of her hand. 'A couple of weeks, why?'

'How did she seem?'

She pursed her lips as she thought for a moment. 'Much as usual. She's been sending down a lot of useful information on the local Germans.' She grinned. 'She's the official vet for a couple of local German units who've got tracker dogs. She hears all the army gossip from them.'

'Louis thinks she's lonely.'

She laughed. 'Louis thinks all pretty girls are lonely. Just waiting for the right man.'

'How does she get on with Joe Parsons?'

'They don't see much of one another, but OK so far as I know.' She smiled. 'He's a bit too gung-ho for our Vi. A bit too rough and ready.'

Bailey took Roger Powers with him to do the recce on the railway tunnel. It was the first sabotage operation they had carried out and Powers' experience at the railway workshops and his explosives training were a real asset.

Powers had checked the train movements so that they could clamber down the embankment and check the track without being disturbed.

When they talked about it later, on the journey back to Bergerac, Bailey realised how little he had remembered of his explosives training.

'How long will they need to repair the damage?'

'If we can take out the actual junction of the two lines it'll take a month at least because the junctions are hand-built. If we only take out tracks they can have it working in a week. There's two other things we might do. Go back into the tunnel about half a mile and hit the track there and put a good charge near the top of the roof and try to cover the damage with rubble.'

Bailey had taken Powers from Bergerac and picked up Violette on the way. She would act as courier between them.

They left the small van down a lane where the signpost said Les Berges and cycled the rest of the way. Just two men and a girl on a picnic. A cane basket with bread and cheese and a couple of bottles of wine. And a metal box on one carrier with *plastique* and half a dozen pencil detonators all wrapped in clean table napkins, and two coils of thin wire underneath the false bottom of the box.

It had all been timed and rehearsed on the estate and Bailey sat alone as Roger Powers and Violette headed into the darkness of the tunnel.

It was a hot, sunny day and the embankment shielded Bailey from the breeze that higher up was moving the big white cumulus clouds slowly across the blue sky. It was quiet and peaceful and it would

133

be easy to lie back and doze, so he sat chewing a blade of grass from the bank beside him. There was some cover if they needed it. Blackberry bushes already loaded with green berries and some bright yellow bushes of broom. He tried to think of the French word for broom. It wasn't *balai*, that was a broom for sweeping. He consoled himself that most Frenchmen wouldn't know the word either.

They were half an hour in the tunnel and then Bailey and Violette moved to the top of the embankment while Powers worked on the junction of the track with the local line from Excideuil.

As she sat beside him she was leaning slightly forward, her knees bent and her head resting on her hands on her knees. She was very pretty. A gentle, calm face and a mane of black hair.

'How did it go in the tunnel?'

'It wasn't easy. The track was no problem but the walls of the tunnel are wet and slimey. The lever wasn't really enough, we needed a crowbar. But he packed it in tightly.'

'What time were the detonators set for?'

'Maximum six hours. It'll go some time after midnight.'

'Would you like to move down to Bergerac for a week or two?'

'Why?'

'Just for a change and a bit of company. You'd be with Jenny on the estate. I'll be there too.'

She looked away from him, her face cradled in her hands as she stared into the distance. It seemed a long time before she said softly, 'I miss them both, Jenny and Paulette.' She turned to look at his face. 'Just for a few weeks would be nice. I can work locally. Just until we have to do our stuff against the Germans.'

'The information you've collected for us is invaluable.'

She laughed softly. 'And I can solder radio wiring better than any of the others.'

'That too.'

They heard a stone rattle and Bailey turned to see Powers scrambling up the embankment. As Powers sat down alongside him Bailey reached for his hands and put them to his nose. Loosing them he reached for the half-empty bottle of wine.

'Hold your hands out, Roger.'

Powers held them out. 'Why, for God's sake?'

'Because they've got the smell of almonds from the *plastique*. If you were picked up with that smell on your hands they wouldn't bother to question you.'

Bailey watched Powers rub his hands with the wine and then wipe them on the grass.

The girl leaned back looking towards Bailey. 'I saw your radio file when I was doing my training. Did you ever see it?'

'No.'

'You know the bit that says, "Give description of subject's transmission characteristics when operating under stress". Do you know what it said?'

'No. Tell me.'

'It said this officer always transmits as if he's under stress.'

They all laughed and for a brief moment they weren't just about to blow up a railway tunnel in France but were back at Beaulieu just sitting in the sun and looking forward to the weekend. And he suddenly remembered that the French word for broom was *genêt*.

Bailey had given firm orders that nobody was to check that the sabotage had actually been successful. But by the Sunday evening Paulette had been telephoned anonymously at her office in the newspaper. The middle section of the tunnel had caved in completely and the line to the north would be out of action for at least two months. It was Paulette who reminded the caller that it was the anniversary of the signing of the document of surrender.

Violette moved in with Jenny a week later and she had her travel permit endorsed to cover her new area. Her reputation as a vet meant that she was in demand from the first day of her move.

London acknowledged the network's report without comment.

CHAPTER 25

They had eaten together and listened to the news on the BBC. The Germans had started an all-out attack on Stalingrad. And Rommel was assembling his forces for a massive drive against the Eighth Army with Cairo as its objective. It seemed as if September 1942 was going to be a month of decisions.

Bailey had gone with Jenny into the empty cottage and waited as she made her contact with London on the late schedule. She clattered down the wooden stairs half an hour later. There was only one signal from London.

'It's for you, Harry. Your personal code.'

As they walked back to his place there was a flash of summer lightning and seconds later the faraway rumble of thunder. The rain was lashing down as they went into the cottage.

She made coffee for them and stood watching him as he decoded the message that was 'for his eyes only'. When he had read the completed signal he walked into the kitchen and burned both pieces of paper in the sink and washed the ashes away. She saw his face as he turned, it was beginning to look drawn and the tension showed round his mouth and his eyes. She knew that she shouldn't ask him about the message but she hoped that he might confide in her. She desperately wanted to be somebody special to Harry Bailey.

She remembered what Violette had said – Violette thought he was handsome. But he wasn't. He was attractive but not handsome. She knew that for her what attracted her was that he was like her father. Very different backgrounds but they had both arrived at a similar pattern. You could trust them. Their word and their judgement. Genuinely modest and genuinely honest. Neither of them looked for other people's approval. Her mother's unstinting love and loyalty were her father's reward. But for Harry Bailey there was no such reward. The network took him for granted and carried out his orders without question. How did a man from his background become a leader of other men? It wasn't just his training. They had all had much the same training. She pushed the mug of coffee across the kitchen table towards him.

'Everything OK?'

He shrugged. 'I don't know.' He sighed. 'They want me to go back to London for a few days.'

'But why?'

'They say for discussions. They're sending a Lysander for me in two weeks' time.'

'Who'll be in command while you're away?'

'I don't know. I'll have to think about it.'

'They all respect Louis but they wouldn't accept him as leader.'

'It will have to be someone who's SOE. One of the network.'

'We've never done a reception for a Lysander.'

'Didn't you do a rehearsal on your course?'

She shrugged. 'A talk by an RAF pilot but not an actual pick-up.'

'We'll have to find a suitable strip and the rest is simple. They expect to be on the ground a maximum of three minutes.' He smiled. 'They'll bring some mail and personal things.'

'Can we send mail back?'

'Let's say – yes.'

'We'll miss you.'

He smiled. 'It'll be like a holiday for all of you. You can just relax and get on with your French lives.'

Bailey checked with Paul Cattoir that he would allow the reception air-strip to be on the estate. He agreed as he always did but Bailey was conscious again that Cattoir had much to lose if he were linked to any kind of resistance.

The night before the pick-up Bailey made a neat bundle of the mail to take back with him and spent the following morning with Louis and Cattoir. He had decided to leave Tony Ransome in charge while he was away. He was a good steady character and working for Louis with daily contact would give him the confidence to deal with any problems that came up. And because of his close relationship with

Paulette she would take over the radio contact with London.

The pick-up day was his birthday, a typically warm, misty autumn day and he had walked down to the lake by the orchard and leaned on the wooden rails of the small bridge watching the dragon-flies quivering over the water-lilies. He turned and watched her as she walked the horse down the slope towards him, patting its neck and talking to it as she guided it through the clumps of bracken and gorse. The breeze was blowing her long blonde hair and as she saw him she raised her arm, smiling as she waved to him.

She dismounted and tethered the horse to an old apple-tree at the edge of the orchard and then she walked towards him.

'Am I disturbing you?'

'No.'

'Happy birthday.'

She laughed as she saw the surprise on his face.

'How did you know?'

'Remember what you always used to say on the course – time spent in reconnaissance is seldom wasted.' She smiled. 'I had a sneaky look at your "P" File at Baker Street.' She shrugged and reached around to her back pocket taking out something wrapped in tissue paper. 'This is for you.'

He unwrapped it carefully, spreading the paper. It was an Omega wrist-watch and as he turned it over he turned it so that the light caught the word engraved on the back of the case. It said in script – *J'attendrai.* He looked at it for long moments and then looked at her face. She saw the tears at the edge of his eyes.

'It's very beautiful. How on earth did you find such a thing?'

She smiled. 'Paul Cattoir got it for me in Paris.' She paused. 'Put it on. Wear it all the time.'

He looked back at her. 'It was a very kind thought. I don't deserve it.'

'It's nothing to do with deserving.'

'So what is it?'

'Just a present. A sign of affection. From a girl to a man.'

He had walked beside her holding the horse's bridle as she rode back to the stables and he helped her water and feed the horses before they walked back together to his cottage.

'Do you feel like walking down to the woods?'

She shrugged. 'Why not? Have you heard from Louis about the reception party tonight?'

'Yes. It's all organised.'

As they walked through the woods she said, 'The last time we walked here there were bluebells as far as you could see.'

'Yes, I remember. You said that bluebells and daisies were your favourite flowers. Why daisies?'

'They are small and modest and most people see them as weeds to be mowed away on their lawns.' She smiled. 'Like the poem says – they waste their sweetness on the desert air.'

He stood still, facing her, his face close to hers and he said softly, 'How has it been for you out here? It's a long time. Two more months and it's been a year.'

'I worry that we aren't doing more damage to the Germans.'

'It's a time for building. Back home they will be planning for an invasion. Building up men and weapons, waiting for the right moment. The moment they land it will be our job to harass the Germans night and day. You won't have time for any doubts then. This is just the lull before the storm. We must use it so that when we get the signal from London we know exactly what we have to do. If we do anything now, blow up a bridge say, they can just repair it and hunt us down. Later on everything will count. But we must guard against wasting the time we've got now. Risking lives for very small prizes.' He paused. 'There are other networks who were impatient for action and results. They lasted less than two months.'

'What happened to them?'

'Some were killed "while resisting arrest" and the rest ended up in jail if they were lucky and extermination camps if they weren't.'

'Did you know them?'

'Some of them.'

'Do the others in our network know all this?'

'No. What's the point? We aren't going to fall into that trap.'

'How did the Germans get onto them?'

'In one case it was criminally careless radio procedures. In the other, it was a man who turned out to be a drunk and couldn't leave women alone. He was shot by a jealous husband and when they checked out the body they found coded and decoded messages. They rounded up the whole network inside ten days.'

She sighed and looked at him. 'Let's talk about something pleasant.' She smiled. 'Let's go back to my place and I'll play you one of my gramophone records.'

He smiled as he watched her turning the handle of an ancient portable gramophone.

'Where on earth did you get that thing?'

She laughed. 'I traded some horse liniment for it with the fellow who keeps that antique shop by the museum. It's in good order despite its age. The only problem is needles. I have to use gorse thorns.' She shrugged and smiled. 'Anyway listen to this. It's Charles Trenet. My favourite song.'

She lowered the tone-arm to the record and then turned, smiling to look at him, reaching out for his hand as she sang along with Trenet.

'J'ai ta main dans ma main, je joue avec tes doigts
j'ai mes yeux dans tes yeux, et partout l'on ne voit . . .'

She was laughing as she sang and when the record finished she leaned forward and kissed him before she stopped the machine.

'Not as good a send-off as the Savoy but the best I can do for the moment.'

Looking at her he said softly, 'I shall miss you.'

They had put an identification light at the lake on the far side of the estate as a guide and the field that had been cleared for the landing was in the middle of the grazing land.

It was one of Louis's men who first heard the Lysander as it circled the lake to fix the lights on the landing strip. When Bailey saw it he noticed the extra fuel tanks as the plane came in over the woods. It came down low following the standard landing pattern so that it faced the wind for take-off and he ran towards it with his canvas bag over his shoulder. The pilot threw out a bag as the plane came to a stop and turned to help Bailey clamber up the short ladder on the fuselage. Breathless, he slid his bag between his feet and pulled the sliding cockpit canopy closed.

The pilot warned him of turbulence through the head-set and there was lightning flickering in the clouds above them. By the time they were approaching the coast they were flying through heavy rain and the pilot told Bailey that he was putting down at RAF Tangmere instead of their original destination at Tempsford in Bedfordshire.

It was beginning to get light as they approached the Sussex coast and as the plane banked to come into the wind Bailey saw the faint glow of the sun across the patchwork of green fields as far as the Gothic spire of Chichester cathedral. It seemed a life-time ago when he did his infantry training there.

There was a staff car waiting for Bailey to take him to London and a message at the Station Commander's office with apologies from Fuller for not being able to meet him because of the last-minute change of venue.

He was driven up to London to the Dorchester Hotel where a room had been booked for him. There was a note for him in his room. There would be a meeting in Room 234 at the hotel at 0900 hours. Bailey looked at his watch. It was 3.15 a.m. He phoned down to Reception and booked a 7.30 a.m. wake-up call.

CHAPTER 26

He woke before the call came through and shaved and dressed and took a lift down to the ground floor. He didn't hand over his room key but walked out into Park Lane and waved down a taxi. It took several seconds for him to realise why the cab-driver was looking so puzzled. He'd been speaking to him in French. When he apologised and changed to English he asked for the driver to show him the places that had been destroyed by bombing.

The first thing the driver pointed out was that they had removed the bronze statue of Eros in Piccadilly Circus. There were potatoes and cabbages growing where there had once been beds of flowers in Hyde Park and there were soldiers guarding a sand-bagged hut and an anti-aircraft unit with a barrage balloon way above the trees. Near Hyde Park Corner there was an anti-aircraft gun and stacks of shells alongside it. There were few civilian cars but already people were coming out of the Underground Stations that were used as air-raid shelters at night, and many people on cycles with brief-cases strapped onto carriers and cross-bars. But it was in the City and the East End that he saw the real damage. Heaps of rubble that had once been shops and homes, signs warning of unexploded bombs and posters at Underground Stations and bus-stops asking 'Is your journey really necessary?'.

A few girls used a bright scarf or a pretty hat to give themselves a modest 'chic' but most people were drably dressed and their faces were pale like unbaked pastry. And suddenly Bailey felt isolated and depressed. And vaguely guilty. If you ignored the danger of their lives in France they lived better than these people here at home. His people had a sense of purpose but here the people looked like automatons, going about their duties, worn out with the routine monotony of their lives, their danger coming from the skies, random and indiscriminate.

Back at the hotel he bought a newspaper, the *Daily Express*. It was only four pages. There was a story that said that Oswald Mosley was going to be released from imprisonment on health grounds. Lord Beveridge was to write a report on how Britain should be changed after the war was won.

He went back to his room for the canvas bag that held the network's mail and his notes and then made his way to Room 234. It was Fuller who opened the door when he knocked. It was a warm welcome and Fuller led him over to a table in the centre of the room. There were two other men at the table and Fuller introduced them.

'Sir Alistair you know, and this is Henry Thomas from the Foreign Office. He's here as an observer.' Fuller pointed at a vacant chair. 'Make yourself comfortable,' he smiled. 'It's going to be a longish meeting I'm afraid.'

As Bailey sat down he opened his bag and took out a thick pile of envelopes tied with string. 'That's mail from my people.'

Fuller said, 'Ah yes. I'm afraid it has to be censored but it will be cleared tomorrow.' Fuller looked at Thomas. 'Perhaps you'd get it dealt with, Henry. Do it when we break for lunch.'

Thomas nodded and reached for the package pushing it to one side from the notepad in front of him.

Fuller looked across at the Foreign Office man. 'Before we get down to the real business, Thomas wants to raise a couple of points. Go ahead, will you, Mr Thomas.'

Bailey registered the lack of Christian name and took it as some kind of warning that Thomas was an outsider. SOE didn't usually go in for such formalities. The upper classes just called a friend by his name. You only used 'Mister' to those you distrusted or disliked.

Thomas folded his arms and leaned forward against the table. 'I hope you'll understand that my questions are not intended in any way as a criticism. Just a precautionary covering of what could be a problem at some time.'

He looked at Bailey but Bailey didn't respond. Thomas shrugged and went ahead. 'When looking through the notes on your original background vetting somebody noticed that you had been a member of the Left Book Club for almost two years.' He paused. 'Could you tell us about that?'

Bailey said, 'Of course, the books came monthly and cost two shillings and sixpence.'

Bailey saw the brief smile on Fuller's mouth as Thomas said, 'I mean your motives. Why did you join in the first place?'

'I came across a copy of the *New Statesman*, there was a thing in it about the club. I wrote off and eventually joined.'

'Where did you come across the *New Statesman* may I ask?'

'Of course. In the common room at school.' Bailey was smiling as he said it but Thomas was not amused. 'Were you a member of a union?'

'No.'

'Would you say you were left-wing?'

Bailey shrugged. 'Let's say I think we'll have to make changes when the war is over.'

'Tell me about Maurois. He seems to feature a lot in your reports.'

'He's a butcher in Brantôme. Hates the Germans because they shipped his son off to a labour camp. Travels all over my area. Tough, brave and loyal.'

'You forgot to mention something.'

'What?'

'That he's the leading Communist in the area.'

'His politics don't interest me.'

'But why not mention it?'

'I didn't mention the colour of his eyes or the kind of woman he goes for. It's none of my business.' Bailey paused. 'Nor yours either. How did you vote last time you voted?'

Thomas smiled. 'Don't be scared by my questions, Mr Bailey.'

'Mr Thomas – you couldn't scare me if you tried for a million years. I'm not scared of the Gestapo so don't kid yourself I could ever be scared of you.' Bailey looked across at Fuller. 'Let's get back to business. We're wasting valuable time.'

Fuller looked at Thomas. 'Have you finished?'

Thomas stood up slowly. 'I guess so.' He looked at Bailey. 'You might remember sometimes that there's more to winning a war than prancing around playing cowboys and Indians.'

After Thomas had left the room, Bailey looked at Fuller. 'What the hell was that all about? Was he really from the Foreign Office?'

Fuller glanced, half-smiling, towards Alistair Campbell who shrugged and then Fuller looked back to Bailey.

'A last spasm from SIS, MI6, who lose their control over SOE next week. Off the record – they've always hated our guts. They see themselves as professionals and us as amateurs.' He shrugged. 'It was poor thinking that linked us with them right from the start. But we've had a new remit from Lord Cadogan. That's one of the reasons we needed to see you.

'And whilst I wouldn't in any way support the crass attitude of a moron like Thomas, it's only fair to say that there are reasons for the rivalry and bad feelings. SIS is an intelligence-gathering organisation with its own people in France. Gathering information quietly and efficiently. We may contribute a little intelligence in the course of our work but our brief is sabotage and harassment. And sabotage and harassment cause vicious reaction from the Germans and that makes SIS's task harder than ever.' He smiled at Bailey. '*Tout comprendre*, and all that.'

Bailey frowned. 'Are they all like that specimen?'

'No. Of course not. But in a large organisation and in a war you'll get people who are paranoid about one thing or another.' He grinned. 'Anyway you're here and we love you.'

Bailey laughed and the tension was broken. But his resentment was still there. Despite Fuller's emollient words he felt an alien. He didn't belong here. He belonged in the Dordogne, where he thought naturally as a Frenchman thinks. But Fuller was speaking again, pulling his mind back into the room.

'Let me start by saying how impressed we all are with the way you have run your operation. We know it's not been easy keeping a team of people together when you can only concern yourself with preparation for future operations. But we're nearer the time when we here, and you and your network, can reap the rewards from your restraint.

'As I said we're now entirely free of our connection with SIS and our new brief extends our functions against the Germans. From now on it's not just sabotage but preparations for invasion. When and where I can't tell you, but the Dordogne is going to be a key area before too long for harassing German troop movements and organising civilian resistance.

'There's one other aspect we'd like you to cover. The RAF have gone over your lists of possible sabotage targets and are sufficiently impressed to want to consider some of these as bombing targets. We also need all the information you can get on German troops in your area. Who they are and what their function is.

'Finally we want you to receive and distribute arms, ammunition and explosives for the *maquis* in your area.' Fuller smiled. 'As you know, they are mainly Communist-organised and your man Louis Maurois would be an excellent liaison with them.' Fuller stopped and smiled. 'That's enough to be going on with. We'll talk about the details in the next couple of days. Now let's break for lunch.'

A waiter had brought a trolley of sandwiches and fruit up to the room and after they had eaten Fuller went off to make a phone call and Bailey was left alone with Alistair Campbell. They talked about the effect of the latest bombing of London and the Midlands and the German U-boats' all-too-successful campaign in the North Atlantic against the merchant ships. And then, rather diffidently, Campbell said, 'Can I ask you how she is?'

'She's fine. Fit and well and, as always, optimistic. She's my radio operator. Conscientious and efficient.'

'Homesick?'

Bailey smiled. 'I'm sure she misses you all but with her job at the stables and her work for me there's not much time for being homesick.' He paused. 'It's hard to explain but when that idiot Thomas was saying his piece I realised how much we lived in that world not this. London is just a place that takes our radio traffic and sends us orders from time to time.'

'Is there any mail for my wife and me?'

'Yes. That's the only mail from Jenny. She can't write to other people because there's nothing she can write about for security reasons.'

'Of course.' Campbell seemed to be choosing his words carefully as he went on. 'I'm not trying to defend that wretched man Thomas but both the FO and SIS are having a lot of problems at the moment because of the Communists.'

'Why?'

Campbell sighed. 'People are beginning to think that we are going to win the war. And this means that those Frenchmen who are politically inclined want to make sure that their party or their interests are seen as the liberators. De Gaulle wants, demands even, that he is recognised as the man who will take over France when it is liberated. But the greatest claim for power will be made by the French resistance, the *maquis*. And they are virtually controlled

by the Communists. We have to walk a diplomatic tightrope between the two contenders. Our official position is that it is nothing
to do with us. The French people must decide. All we are concerned with is liberating Europe. Thomas liaises between de Gaulle's
people and SIS. He's a natural right-winger and he sympathises with
their intention of stopping the Communists from taking over.' He
shrugged. 'And we, for our pains, must please everybody. You will
have to train and supply the *maquis* as part of your network's
function. But you've got to be careful not to get mixed up in the
politics.'

'I'm not interested in politics. All I want is to harass the Germans.'

'You'll be in a better position to do that now we have our new
remit. All your careful preparation is about to pay off.'

'Fuller said that my network was particularly strategically placed.
How does he make that out?'

'We have strong indications that quite soon the Germans will break
the agreement with Vichy and occupy the present un-Occupied Zone.
You'll get larger contingents of German troops in your area.'

'Why our area?'

'Because the Germans don't know where an invasion can be expected. From the north or from the south, the Mediterranean coast:
The Italians won't last very long now we've landed on the mainland.'
He paused. 'So the Germans will need to have a large contingent of
fighting troops, not just occupation troops, to be rushed up north
or down south. It will be your job to hinder them whichever way it
is.'

After the lunch break Fuller had brought back an RAF Wing Commander and they spent two hours looking at various targets, railways,
bridges and road junctions. Bailey was surprised to see that there were
already aerial photographs of a number of the places in the Dordogne
that they had in mind as bombing targets.

Another RAF officer joined them later to discuss arrangements
for the much more complex drops that would be necessary in the
future. Several dropping sites were discussed and it was obvious to
Harry Bailey that he would have to increase his reception facilities far
beyond what had been necessary so far. It was going to be a full-time
operation for dozens of men.

*   *   *

Sir Alistair had invited him to have dinner with him and his wife at the Savoy that evening but he'd asked that they should continue their meeting so that he could get back to the network.

It was past midnight when the meeting finally broke up. There was a good SOE moon in two days' time. The next day he would be shown new explosives, detonators, and weapons and meet two men who would be his to use with the *maquis*. One was a weapons and explosives expert and the other an infantry officer who had experience in training and leading resistance groups in Norway and Finland. Les Ames and Dickie Manson were young, energetic and eager to get on with their tasks and Bailey found them a refreshing change from the down-beat attitudes of most of the people he had met on this trip to London, who seemed as if they had had enough of the war. Not that those people wouldn't fight on. There was no doubt about that. But it was no longer a crusade to free the world for democracy. It was more like serving a long prison sentence for something they hadn't done.

He pushed aside the black-out curtains that covered the hotel entrance doors and walked out into Park Lane. It was nearly 1 a.m. and the all-clear had just gone but there were still guns firing tracers into the low clouds. There were people coming out of an air-raid shelter and a bunch of drunken American soldiers were staggering down the centre of the road waving to taxis who ignored them despite the dollars. They were more like occupation troops than allies. Even the Germans didn't behave like that. At Hyde Park Corner he could see the glow of a fire on the other side of the river, lighting up the underside of the clouds over Battersea Park. There were several ambulances at St George's Hospital across the square and he could see figures under blankets being carried inside on stretchers.

He turned and walked slowly back to the hotel. No matter what people like Thomas had to say there would have to be changes made. These people deserved a better life than the thirties had given them. He had asked Campbell about Thomas's background. Campbell had smiled and said, 'Eton and Magdalen, and his daddy owns a coalmine.'

They were treating him to a Lysander trip instead of a drop and he would land near Brantôme and Paulette Fleury would take him to the cottage for the night.

The morning of his flight was spent looking at lists of the explosives and weapons he would be receiving. Sten guns, Thompson sub-machine-guns, rifles and even Bren guns with case after case of ammunition. The explosives were all plastic with pencil detonators and grenades. Before he left for the airfield he was told that there would also be a couple of cases of mortars on a separate drop. He reckoned that it would take six or seven well co-ordinated drops to cover all the supplies, and that with winter weather prevailing it would need to be spaced over at least a couple of months. Les Ames would be a passenger on the Lysander with him.

He had lunch with Jenny's father in his room at the hotel and Alistair Campbell had handed him a locket with a thin gold chain and an opal in a gold heart-shaped setting, explaining that it had been bought in Paris and was a genuine French antique so there was no security problem. It was for Jenny from her mother. It was a piece she had always loved.

Fuller had collected a bundle of censored letters for the network and replacement crystals for both radios. A Humber staff car took Bailey and Fuller to the airfield at Tempsford where they were checked in by an RAF Police Sergeant attached to 138 Squadron.

Bailey went through the normal body check and his French clothes were released from the lockers. The BBC news on the Home Service announced that the Eighth Army was making progress in Italy and the Russians had retaken Kiev. It was the last week in November 1942.

The grass was white with frost as Bailey and Fuller followed the escorting RAF officer to the Lysander. Les Ames was already in the second cramped passenger seat. Bailey clattered up the short ladder with his canvas hold-all and slid down into the narrow space before pulling over the canopy. He leaned his head back and saw how clear the sky was. He closed his eyes and wondered what Louis and the reception party were doing at that moment. He smiled to himself. Louis was probably checking that his brandy flask was full. Jenny would be watching a casserole simmering on the old-fashioned cast-iron hob. Paulette was probably still at the office typing some local story of cats up trees being rescued by the fire brigade. Violette would be checking some farmer's flock of sheep. Locals always put the ram in with the flock on Armistice Day and two weeks later the ewes should all have that tell-tale blue paint mark on their rumps. Paul Cattoir would be entertaining a dozen local worthies and a couple of senior Germans. Subtly sowing doubts about the latest edict of the Vichy government or probing as to when they would all be able to celebrate the end of the war. Surely the so-called Allies would have to make a deal soon. And after they had gone he'd sit alone in his study listening to records of Erik Satie or, if his guests had been especially boring, it would be Fats Waller and Duke Ellington who soothed that complex mind.

As always with Lysander flights they came in low over the French coast and turned onto the long last leg of the journey. Once or twice they took avoiding action as searchlights swept the sky in the distant darkness. Another twenty minutes, maybe half an hour, and he would be back. Back again in that life that had become his real life.

The sky was still cloudless and the stars flickered brightly in the frosty atmosphere that covered the two countries as if to join them together. Churchill had offered the French dual nationality if they would go on fighting the Germans. A generous offer from a big-hearted man, from one country to another. The French had ignored it. They just wanted to surrender and get it over. He wondered how the French had ever got their reputation for being romantics. They had many virtues but they were all virtues of the mind, not the heart. Spontaneous, warm-hearted, generous gestures were not part of the vocabulary of French politicians.

He felt the plane losing altitude and the pilot warned him that he could see the reception party's lights, but he had to come round into the wind for landing. Minutes later they were bumping over the frozen tussocks of the field. The canopy back, his bag thrown out, the hurried scramble down the ladder, his hand reaching up to help Les Ames clamber down, the smiling face of Louis Maurois, the returning mail-bag thrown onto the plane, and then the pilot closed the hatch and the plane bumped forward, gaining speed, its port wing dipping dangerously as it took off. Despite Maurois's shouting in his ear to get to the hedges Bailey stood for a few moments watching the Lysander lift over the trees, a flash of moonlight reflected from the canopy as it banked to head northwards back home. For a fleeting moment he felt a pang of homesickness for that drabness he had so despised, then as Maurois tugged at his arm they ran together to the cluster of beech trees at the edge of the field.

CHAPTER 27

The landing had gone to plan and Louis had driven Bailey, Ames and Paulette back to the cottage. He was surprised to see Violette and Jenny there too. Jenny cooked a giant omelette and they sat down together at the kitchen table. After the coffee he handed out the mail to those who were there and it was then he learned why Violette was there. It was Louis who gave him the news.

'It looks like the Germans are moving into our area in force.'

'What makes you think that?'

It was Violette who spoke up. 'The day you left for London a team of four Gestapo officers and two senior Wehrmacht officers visited the mayor's office. They told him there would be German army units moving into the area and he would be required to order the sequestration of various buildings and houses to accommodate them. The two army officers had large-scale maps with places marked on them and the occupiers would be given twenty-four hours to get out. Their furniture and belongings would be left behind. Everything. They would be paid compensation on a weekly basis.

'Yesterday they set up check-points in Bergerac, Brantôme and Périgueux and they checked IDs and permits. A dozen or so people who weren't carrying papers were arrested and warned before they were released. They've put up posters everywhere stating that there is no longer a demarcation line. All France is now occupied.'

When Violette finished she sat looking at Bailey who was stirring his coffee. But he looked at Maurois. 'Anything else, Louis?'

'For God's sake, what more do you want?'

Bailey shrugged. 'London had warned me. It's happening all over France.'

'What else did they tell you?'

'There are a lot of things we've got to do. But they can wait for a couple of days until I've had a chance to do my rounds.'

CHAPTER 28

Louis had taken Bailey, Ames and Jenny back to Bergerac and Bailey had spent an hour with Cattoir telling him of the changes of emphasis for the network without mentioning the hints he had received regarding invasion. But Cattoir was quite capable of reading between the lines.

Bailey walked to the cottages with Jenny and as she made him breakfast in her kitchen he asked about the others in the network. He started with the other two girls.

'Tell me about Paulette. How's she managing?'

'Work or pleasure?'

'Both.'

'Well, Paulette's got it all worked out. She's got three very separate lives. Paulette, journalist. Paulette SOE and Paulette a very pretty French girl. Independent but lots of would-be lovers. Can look lost and vulnerable but in fact she's very tough.'

'You said would-be lovers. What about actual lovers?'

'None that you need worry about.'

'I want to know.'

'Why?'

'I'm thinking of promoting her.'

'She's totally committed and totally loyal, to both you and the network.' She smiled. 'I think she fancies you.'

'What about Violette?'

'Very much a loner. She's really absorbed in her work. She is a vet. That's her life.' She paused. 'She hasn't been well used in the network. She's been wasted because she doesn't push herself forward. She's committed but she feels she's not used. She thinks you don't rate her very highly.'

Bailey smiled. 'How would you use her?'

'As a courier when we get active. She has travel permits and genuine reasons for going anywhere she wants in the whole of the network area. Her own transport and contacts everywhere. She's a very competent vet. And her French veterinary qualifications are genuine. The Germans use her and she's got a lot of regular farmers as clients.'

'She always seems rather withdrawn to me.'

'She's just quiet, that's all.'

'Who did the encoding and transmitting when I was away?'

'I did.'

'Did you have any contact with Paul Cattoir?'

'He came down each day to see the horses. He always does that.'

'Did he mention any network things?'

'No. He asked me if I was OK. I said yes and that was all.'

'I've got something for you from your mother.'

She was instantly alive. 'Did you see her? How is she?'

'No, I didn't see her but I saw quite a lot of your father.'

He fished in his shirt pocket and gave her the small package. She opened it carefully and cried out as she saw her mother's gift. 'She shouldn't have. She loved it so much.' She smiled at him. 'I've always loved it too. It's the only piece of jewellery I've ever really liked.' She paused. 'Thanks for bringing it for me. Moma used to let me wear it on my birthdays when I was a little girl.'

He pulled out a chair and sat down at the table. 'Tell me about when you were a little girl.'

She sat stirring her cup of precious coffee, her long blonde hair down to her shoulders, her hands rough from her work but the nails still carefully manicured. Her lips were pursed and her eyebrows raised as she looked at him.

'I was thinking of those days while we were waiting for you to come in yesterday evening.' She shook her head slowly. 'I must have been a real pain in the neck. But they were always so supportive. They gave me confidence.'

'In what way were you a pain?'

'Constantly being thrown out of one school and another for disobedience, smoking – just defying the rules and any authority.'

'Were you unhappy at school?'

'I had to move school frequently because of Daddy's job. At home I was treated like an adult but at school it was all so petty and childish.

I couldn't stand it.' She laughed softly. 'I guess I've gone on being like that.'

'Do you feel like that about me giving you orders and telling you what to do?'

'No. Never. I believe in what we're doing and I admire how you do your job.'

'It's all going to change in the next few weeks. We've got so much to do.'

'Everybody's raring to go.'

Bailey's meeting with Louis Maurois had started cautiously.

'Do you know any of the local *maquis* people, Louis?'

Maurois shrugged his neutrality. 'Which people are you thinking about?'

'The kind of people who need weapons and explosives and an expert who can teach them how to use them.'

'What kind of weapons?'

'Rifles, pistols, sub-machine-guns, machine-guns, grenades – *plastique*, dynamite.'

'From your people in London?'

'Yes.'

The butcher was silent for long moments and then said, 'These people are mainly Communists – you realise that, don't you?'

'I don't care if they're Jehovah's Witnesses. If they're ready to fight the Germans I'll get them the weapons. But I need somebody to talk to them. To liaise with them.'

'You want me to do that?'

'As a first step, yes. But I still want you in my network. I need you, Louis, we've got a hell of a lot to do.'

'OK. I'll fix for you to meet the man. You met him once when I was arranging for your Roger Powers to get the job on the railway.'

'A tall guy with red hair?' Pierre something.'

'That's the one. He's an ex-army captain and two years in the Foreign Legion.'

'When can we meet him?'

'I'll get him up here tonight.'

'There'll be another SOE officer here you haven't met. The one who came back with me. Captain Ames.'

'What's he good at?'

'He's had a lot of experience with guerrilla groups. Training them and leading them.'

'Does he speak French?'

'Not too good but he'll be with the *maquis* out in the wilds. He won't have any outside contacts.'

'Be about eight when I get here.'

'Can you pick up Ames on the way? He's with Paulette at the cottage.

'OK.'

When Bailey heard the van pull up outside the cottage he opened the door and walked out. There were not only Louis and Ames and the railwayman, but four other men. Roughly dressed and unshaven and as he watched, the railwayman handed out rifles from the back of the van. Maurois was pointing into the darkness to show the men where to go to. For a moment he felt a flash of anger at outsiders taking things into their own hands. And then he realised that they had at least as much at stake as he did.

When the introductions had been made as they sat around the kitchen table Pierre Druon, the railwayman, told Bailey that he had over two hundred men out in the *maquis*, all of them ready to co-operate in fighting the Germans. Bailey told him of the supplies that would come from London as soon as Druon was ready to receive them. And Leslie Ames would be their adviser with Louis Maurois as the liaison with the network. Ames went over the supplies that would be coming and estimated roughly how many drops would be involved and how many men would be needed as receptions for the loads. Druon was obviously impressed but cautious. When Ames finished Druon looked at Bailey.

'There's no question of your people having control over my men. You know that don't you?'

'Yes. That's no problem.'

'You know we have liaison with Moscow on political matters?'

'That's up to you. So long as you help us throw out the Germans that's all we ask.'

'And when it's all over you don't claim it was your people who controlled us?'

'When France is liberated my friend it will be for the French people to decide who liberated them.'

'You don't take orders from de Gaulle do you?'

'No. He's got his own set-up. I don't know anything about it. Until it's over we'll co-operate any way you want. But no politics.'

Druon put out his big hand and Bailey took it. Neither of them spoke.

Louis said quietly, 'The Germans have put on a curfew. I've got a permit but I daren't risk being stopped with these others on board, can we bed down for the night in one of the empty cottages? We'll be gone as soon as it's light.'

'That's OK. Do you need some food?'

Louis laughed. 'I've got more food in the van than you've got, my friend.'

Paulette was the only member of the network whom it was safe to telephone. There was no phone at the cottage but she had constant calls at her office at the newspaper. People phoning about fires and burglaries, notices of weddings and funerals and the real or imagined scandals concerning local figures. But on the few occasions when Bailey phoned her he was always cautious in what he said. When he phoned her and said that he would like a delivery of meat that evening for guests the next day at the big house she knew what he meant.

She walked to the butcher's shop and spent some of her food ration on sausages and Maurois invited her into his living quarters through the bead curtains for a cup of coffee.

He looked at her with open admiration. 'You're far too beautiful for those idiots you go out with you know.'

'Cut it out, Louis.' She laughed. 'He wants to see you tonight at his place. He phoned me at the office.'

'For God's sake I was with him this morning. What now?'

'No idea. I'll have to contact him if you can't make it.'

'Tell me about little Violette. Why no man? What's wrong with her?'

'Is it OK for tonight?'

'You mean you and me?'

She laughed. 'You know what I mean.'

'Yes, it's OK. You like a piece of steak?'

'Yes, please.' She kissed him on the cheek and laughed as she wriggled away from his wandering hands.

As he wrapped the meat he said, 'This is courtesy of 22nd Panzer Regiment.'

Jenny had casseroled a rabbit for their evening meal when she knew that Louis would be joining them. Her radio schedule was at ten that evening and the short report was already encoded.

Louis was full of gossip about the scandals of Brantôme society and Bailey had seen that for Jenny, eager to know every detail, it was highly amusing.

When the meal was over Bailey outlined his plans.

'I want you to get your friend Druon to train four or five teams of his people for receiving arms drops. After the first couple of drops I don't want to be involved in the drops. Nor you. I'll arrange the drops with London, and Ames will take charge of the reception.

'I want your time to be spent with me. How many people do you reckon we have now whom we could safely count on?'

Louis shrugged. 'Count on for what – support or activity?'

'Both.'

'For support, over the whole area at least two hundred.'

'Support means what?'

'Messages, a safe-house for one night, information, that sort of thing.'

'And activity?'

'All the way. Sabotage, fighting – total commitment.'

'How many activists?'

'Seventy, eighty. A hundred once people see we mean business.'

'OK. Let's talk about business. Sabotage and destruction – one really big job once a month or a whole network of jobs on the same night all over our area? Which?'

Maurois looked impressed. 'My God,' he said quietly. 'You people really mean it this time, don't you?'

'I told you it was only a question of time, Louis.'

'And now really is the time?'

'Yes. I'm going to call a meeting here tomorrow night. All my network people and you, but not Ames. This is just family.' He paused. 'You get them here any way you can and I want you to assign five – six if it's possible – of the people you say will go all the way to each of the men – Tony Ransome, Joe Parsons, Roger Powers, James Long – and a group for yourself and me, we'll work together. OK?'

'That's fine but I can't believe it. After all this time it's really going to happen.'

'Two weeks for my guys to train their men while you and I plan what we're going to do.'

'And the girls?'

'Vi and Paulette will be couriers and a back-up for Jenny on the radio set.'

Maurois stood up slowly. 'You've got it all worked out, haven't you?'

'I've had a hell of a long time to think about it, my friend.'

Bailey held the meeting in what had been the cottage of the head gardener on the estate. It had started to snow and there was a log fire burning on the open stone hearth.

It was a long time since they had all met together and Louis had brought up two men from Druon's outfit to mount guard in the shadow of the pine trees alongside the cottage.

He had briefed them on what was going to happen and the new danger that came from having German army units right in the towns. All the old soldiers had been pulled back to Germany and the new men were well-trained fighting men. No longer concerned with maintaining good relations with the local people.

They would each have their own groups and Louis would go over their tasks with each one of them. They would have the Christmas period plus the first week of the New Year, 1944, to make them into effective units. Targets would be discussed with them after that time.

Bailey showed them large-scale maps of the network area and told them to absorb all they could. It was an offence under the occupation laws to possess any map and this would be the only time they would see full-scale maps. Rough sketch-maps of target areas would be available for operations but they would have to be destroyed later.

Their relief that the waiting was over was obvious and Bailey was relieved too. They could have been so settled in their lives that they were apprehensive about actual operations. But they were obviously ready to go when he gave the signal.

He left them to sleep the night in the shepherd's cottage and walked the short distance back to his place with Jenny. The snow crunched under their steps and was beginning to freeze but it was no longer snowing and the skies were clear.

As they approached the row of cottages they saw a car out-side Bailey's cottage. It was a black Lancia Aprillia and as Bailey put his hand on the bonnet it was still warm despite the freezing temperature.

As Bailey cautiously opened the door of the cottage and walked inside it was in darkness and as he turned the switch no light came on. Then he saw through the opening to the kitchen two candles on saucers flickering in the darkness. Cattoir was filling a small cup from a silver brandy flask. He looked up.

'Come in and close the door.'

'It is closed. What's going on?'

'I had some news and I took the liberty of removing your fuses and those in mam'selle's cottage too.'

For a moment Bailey was silent then he said, 'What was the news?'

'A pair of direction-finding vans moved into Bergerac this afternoon. Have you got a schedule with London tonight?'

'Yes but not for twenty minutes.'

'Thank God for that. I thought it would be better for you to give it a miss until the DF vans have left. I wasn't sure which cottage you used for transmitting.' He smiled. 'The fuses are here on the table. Would you like a brandy?'

'No thanks.'

'How about mam'selle?'

'Yes please.'

Bailey said quietly. 'Thank you, Paul. It would have been just the wrong time to get caught.'

Cattoir laughed. 'Anytime's the wrong time to get caught with your hand on a Morse-key, my friend.'

'Who told you about the vans?'

'I met the signals officer in charge of the vans in the Mayor's office. They're based in Bordeaux but they'll be covering the whole area. They'll be here for three days. I suggest one very short warning signal to London and no more until they've gone.'

'Did they suspect that there was clandestine radio traffic in this area?'

'Who knows? I had no intention of showing any interest in them.' He shrugged. 'I should think it's possible. There are always rumours about resistance activities. Collaborationists sometimes feel that it might do them some good if they make up some story of suspicious activities.' He screwed on the top of his flask. 'I'll tell you when they've gone. Take care both of you. *Soyez sage.*'

As January moved into February the seventh and last arms drop was not for the *maquis* but for the network. Although most of the load was explosives, detonators and fuses, for the first time there were mines, grenades, sub-machine-guns and ammunition. The canisters were hidden in two of the large barns on the estate, to be distributed when required.

CHAPTER 29

It was a very small group of family, close friends and estate workers who followed the simple coffin the short distance from the private church to the family vault. The flag that draped the old man's coffin was the old German flag, not the swastika of the Third Reich.

When the Gräfin died on a summer's day the old man was not expected to last through the winter. His much-loved wife was his last link with the days of dignity and hope, and once she had gone he no longer had a reason for living. His sons lived lives that were far removed from their family standards and upbringing. To them he was an old man who didn't recognise that the tide of history was turning against all those old ideas of how life in Europe should be based on good faith and sound values. He had witnessed what he saw as the destruction of his family so that he faced his end with one son a cripple and the other an officer in the Gestapo. He had died peacefully in his bed with the well-thumbed book he had been reading open on the coverlet. It was Thomas Mann's *Buddenbrooks*. The writer who had denounced the Nazis in an open letter to the University of Bonn. They had confiscated all his property while he was on a visit to Switzerland, and now he was visiting professor at Princeton University. A man who, like Graf Otto, was rather ashamed that he loved Wagner's music so much.

Siegfried von Bayer sat in the leather armchair with the stump of what remained of his right leg resting on a cushion on a stool. He was dressed in the uniform of a lieutenant-colonel of the General Staff, the Knight's Cross with Oak Leaves on the left breast of his tunic. He shifted uneasily in his chair as he poured himself another whisky from a crystal decanter.

He waved the glass towards his brother who was in civilian clothes, sprawled in the other armchair.

'Well, little brother, what will *you* remember him for?'

Max shrugged and Siegfried said sharply, 'Don't do that, you look like a bloody Frenchman.'

Ignoring his brother's comment Max von Bayer said, 'I'll remember him as a man with values. Who knew wrong from right and acted on it. A man who always encouraged me to try hard at everything I tackled.' He paused. 'And I'll remember a man who had enough love for all of us. And *you*?'

Siegfried shook his head irritably. 'He was OK. When do you go back?'

'Is your leg hurting you?'

'My leg, dear brother, is somewhere just outside Stalingrad. They tell me the pain's imaginary.'

'Why don't you call it a day? You've done enough.'

'I've got a colonel's posting to Rommel at Army Group "B". How about you?'

'Back to France. I'm moving my unit down south, either to Périgueux or Bordeaux.'

'Why there?' He smiled. 'Are they worried in Paris that the good life might be coming to an end.'

Max laughed. 'Let's say there have been a lot of requests for postings back to Berlin.'

'D'you think anything's going to happen?'

'Yes.'

'When?'

'Two or three months' time.'

'That makes it – let's see – March, April, May.'

'If it's coming it'll be about that time.'

'Where will it come?'

'Who knows. Could be from the south.'

'What makes you so sure that it's coming?'

'I'm not sure. But the resistance are moving more than normal. Whichever way they come the centre of France will be the vital area. That's why I'm moving down there. We need clear passage to move our troops north and south.'

'He made a mistake when he sent us into Russia. And the Japanese cut our throats when they bombed Pearl Harbor and brought in the Yanks.'

'You sound disillusioned. Are you?'

'I don't know. We've got the men and we've got good fighting generals but I think there's going to be a lot more men with only one leg when it's all over.'

Max stood up. 'It's time for bed. Do you want a hand?'

He reached for his crutches. 'No. I can manage. See you at breakfast. I'm going to finish the bottle.'

CHAPTER 30

The kitchen table had become the place for discussing and thinking, and Bailey was eating a thick slice of buttered toast. Butter courtesy of the estate's own herd with the compliments of the vet, Violette.

He was thinking about Joe Parsons and James Long. They tended to be seen as a pair merely because they were both Canadians. Parsons was twenty-six and Long was in his early forties. Both of them had French mothers but because of living in Quebec their French was heavily accented. Bailey reckoned that despite his age the older man was the tougher of the two. He had had several years on merchants ships but he wore his uniform at the hotel with considerable dignity. From time to time he served in the restaurant as a waiter and had been a useful source of information about the Germans who dined there.

Parsons had been an engineering student but had failed to finish his degree course at the university. Apparently besotted by some girl he decided that he needed to earn money if he was to persuade her to marry him. He had gone through several jobs, from car repairs to servicing cinema projection equipment. The old man at the cinema in Bergerac hadn't hesitated to hire him when Louis took him round, and the projection equipment had never been kept in such excellent order. So far he had played a very limited part in the network. Bailey wondered if he was ready to lead a team. If he performed well on the factory job he'd risk giving him a group of his own. He had no such doubts about Long. He was a natural leader but probably an erratic one.

The explosives factory was on the north side of the river on the edge of the town. There were eight sheds separated from each other in each direction by about fifty metres. Although it was common knowledge that the factory produced explosives, Bailey had no idea what type of explosives were involved. He had seen a copy of the factory's fire regulations but the security at night was very lax. At one time it had been two elderly men who acted as watchmen, but now a local artillery battery was providing two men and a sergeant to mount guard. But there was nothing that anyone would want to steal from the buildings and each guard took it in turn to patrol while the other played cards with the sergeant.

They cycled separately to Lamonzie St-Martin where Louis had arranged a safe-house for them for one night at a small farmhouse near the narrow river that was a tributary of the Dordogne itself.

Mid-afternoon Bailey cycled alone to the woods at the near side of the factory buildings. Using his binoculars he checked each of the buildings. They were wooden structures on a base of bricks and each had a large red fire extinguisher near the big double doors. He knew from Louis, through one of his contacts who worked at the factory, that the fire extinguishers had not been checked for at least six months. The fire precautions inside the building were strictly maintained but an attack from outside, a deliberate attempt at destroying the buildings, had not been considered.

He stayed for two hours memorising every detail of the layout and at 5 p.m. the double doors opened and the workers came out in small groups heading for a line of cycles chained and padlocked to a rough wrought-iron railing. According to Louis' informant there were eighty people working at the plant and whatever they produced was held in large, cylindrical, metal containers. He waited until the camouflaged army van brought the uniformed guards and then he left and cycled back to the farmhouse.

It was no longer a farm, just a smallholding that grew vegetables with a small orchard of ancient apple trees. It was run by a woman in her sixties whose husband had been killed in the fighting north of Paris as the Germans smashed their way through, almost unhindered, to the capital. She was a dour, silent woman who ignored them as they sat in her kitchen going over the plan again.

Bailey was aware of the tension in the others. Parsons talking too much, Long, silent, and seeming to ignore what was being said but yawning from time to time, a give-away of the inner tension. The man from Druon's *maquis* was there for the experience and was obviously amused by the strange French accents of the two Canadians.

The *plastique* and the detonators had been buried in the woods by Bailey two days earlier so that they were not carrying explosives if they were checked on their way to the site. A spade had been roped to the branch of an ancient oak tree.

They left the safe-house just before midnight and half an hour later they were digging up the explosives. Each took his two packets and settled in the bushes at the edge of the wood. As hoped and planned for there was no moon and the ominous dark clouds showed no movement in the windless sky. It was a ten-minute walk and a five-minute crawl and crouch across the rough land to the target. Bailey was going first and the others would go together so that Bailey would have completed his task and be able to supervise the others in case there were problems. None of them carried any identity papers, their pockets were empty except for a toothed knife to cut wires if detonators had to be linked.

His watch showed 00.15 when he stood up, nodded to the others and walked off into the darkness. It was the second week of March and the ground was frozen hard and he made good progress. As he saw the shadowy shapes of the two buildings that were his targets, he saw a match flare as the guard lit a cigarette. He was nearer than Bailey had expected. He tackled the further target first. It was a five-pound slab of *plastique* with a pencil time fuse. An L-type fuse that didn't use the usual acid bulb but was armed by withdrawing the pin with the tag. They were set for thirty minutes' delay.

He crawled to the nearer building and placed a similar charge and detonator flush against the wall and then moved away from the buildings back towards the woods. Roughly half-way back to the woods he stopped and crouched down, listening in the silence for a sign of Parsons or Long so that he could lead them back to where their cycles had been left in the woods.

He heard the hoot of an owl and the distant bark of a vixen and then the heavy breathing and hurried footsteps of a man. As he drew close he saw that it was Long who leaned over to speak to him. And then the whole area was lit up as brightly as a summer's day, a sheet of fire rising from one of the buildings in the back row. They heard shouts from the Germans and then all too clearly visible Parsons was running towards them. As Bailey raised himself up ready to run, Parsons shouted, 'It was short-timed.' Bailey heard the crack of a rifle and at the same moment Parsons fell to the ground. There were two massive explosions from the factory and then another and another. Bailey lifted Parsons onto his shoulders and with some help from Long got Parsons into the woods. As Parsons lay on his back there was enough light to show blood pouring from his shoulder. He was unconscious and Bailey tore off his jacket and shirt, tearing off one of the shirt-sleeves. Long said, 'He's bleeding. We'd better make him comfortable and come back for him when it's light.' Bailey looked at him angrily. 'It's never going to be lighter than it is right now. If we leave him they'll find him.' Awkwardly Bailey tied Parsons' hands together, slid them as if Parsons was embracing him, around his shoulders and eased him onto the crossbar of his cycle. As he turned to make a last look at the factory, it was an inferno with ground-shaking explosions every few minutes and there was grass burning, like after harvest time, on the land leading to the forest.

Twice he had to stop on the journey back to rearrange Parsons' inert body and to steady the unbalanced cycle. It took him nearly an hour to arrive breathless at the small-holding but Long was already there with saucepans of water simmering on the cast-iron hob.

As he pulled off Parsons' jacket he saw that the shirt was soaking wet with blood and Parsons groaned with pain as he pressed a hot pad of cloth to the ragged wound. He sent Long with a message to Cattoir for a doctor and when Long pointed out that there was another hour before the nightly curfew was lifted the look on Bailey's face sent him off into the darkness.

He had staunched the flow of blood and the old lady had given him a small bottle of brandy and by the time the doctor arrived Parsons was conscious. The doctor dressed the wound without asking any questions and left without comment or advice.

Not long after the doctor had left, Bailey heard the noise of a car making its way up the rutted path to the farmhouse. It was a small van and it stopped just short of the cottage and he saw a figure get out. It was a girl and then he saw with relief that it was Violette. Cattoir had told Jenny what had happened and sent Violette to bring Parsons back to the estate. They had loaded bales of straw in the back of the van to hide him on the short drive back to the estate.

After they had driven away Bailey cycled back to the road at the far side of the factory. The whole place had burnt to the ground. There were still flames flickering in the remains. There were two German staff cars parked there and several groups of people watching the two fire-engines spray the smouldering grass and bushes between the factory and the woods. A French police car drove up as Bailey cycled slowly past.

There were police checks on all the roads but when he showed his papers and they saw that he was employed by Paul Cattoir they waved him through. It took him over two hours before he was back at the estate.

They were sitting around the table talking after dinner. The deputy-mayor, an official from the Ministry of Agriculture at Vichy, and a couple of German officers. One from Bordeaux and the other from one of the new units in the town. The other guest sitting on Cattoir's right, the place of honour, was the one who mattered to Cattoir. He was the chief of police for the whole *département*.

The man from the Ministry had come to persuade Cattoir to put a few hundred hectares of the estate down to lavender or tobacco.

Cattoir shook his head. 'They take special skills that I don't have right now. Maybe when the war is over. All my staff are over-worked as it is.'

'But you are such a patron of tradition and these crops are part of the history of the district.'

Cattoir smiled and raised his glass. 'To tradition, my friends.' When they had drunk to his toast he turned to the locally-based German officer. 'I hear there was a fire at the nitro-cellulose factory. Was there much damage?'

'It was wiped out. It was burned to the ground. By the time the fire appliances arrived it was already too late.'

'Anybody hurt?'

'No. Fortunately not. But there was a rocket from Berlin for the officer commanding the unit that provided the guards.'

'Smoking on duty?'

The police chief shook his head and looked around the table. 'Not for any ears but yours.' He paused. 'It was terrorists.'

Cattoir frowned. 'You mean we have terrorists here in Bergerac? I can't believe it. How do you know it wasn't an accident?'

'We found signs of explosives.'

Cattoir shook his head. 'Is this the so-called *maquis*?'

'At this stage we don't have any more information than I have given you.'

The local German intervened. 'We have taken twenty hostages off the street today. Unless they provide us with information they will go to jail. All of them. Men, women and children.'

'But how could they know anything that your admirable police force don't know?'

The German spoke sharply. 'Because we have traitors among us. Frenchmen who prefer war to peace. They have lessons to learn and we shall teach them.'

Cattoir turned to the other German. 'Were you in Berlin last week, Herr Major?'

'I was. I had a very lucky escape. They came over in broad daylight at lunch-time. Over eight hundred United States bombers. The centre of Berlin is a heap of rubble.'

'But I was told that you shot down many of them.'

'About two hundred. But we lost planes too. And the damage to the city was unbelievable.'

Cattoir nodded. 'I think it was Field Marshal Rommel who said way back that this would be a war of attrition. It seems he was right.' He smiled. 'Let's change the subject. I heard that they were going to start producing that neat little Volkswagen next year. Is it true?'

It was past midnight when Cattoir watched his guests driving off into the night, and then he walked down the sloping gravel pathway to the cottages, and knocked on the door of Bailey's cottage.

Cattoir noticed the cards laid out on the kitchen table, a half-finished game of solitaire, and recognised it for what it was – therapy for a troubled mind. A revealing aspect of the man. Most men would have chosen drink or a woman but for this Englishman it had to be something solitary.

'I spoke to the doctor,' Cattoir said. 'It will be healed in three or four weeks. He'll end up with a shoulder that's not too well articulated, but nothing worse than that.' He paused. 'How did the charge go off prematurely?'

Bailey sighed deeply. 'I think someone pulled the tag too soon.' He shrugged. 'Who knows.'

'Louis spoke to me this afternoon because he couldn't contact you personally. He's found someone who used to be a projectionist and he'll cover for your man. Looks like five weeks' sick leave. Muscle strain.'

'I'm thinking of sending him back to London.'

'I shouldn't do that. Have you discussed that with Jenny?'

'No.'

'I should if I were you.' He moved on quickly. 'They've no idea who did it. They claim it was terrorists. But it's made them very uneasy. Good sabotage and good propaganda.' He smiled. 'The locals are sure it's de Gaulle's people.'

'And the hostages? We could try and release them.'

'No point. They would have nowhere to go. Be different if they were resistance people. Let it take its course. I'll do what I can.'

'Tell me about Parsons.'

'She looked up from her coffee cup, surprised. 'What about him?'

'I told Paul Cattoir that I was thinking of sending him back to London. He said I should talk to you before I decided.'

She smiled. 'I suppose he's thinking of Paulette's reaction.' She paused. 'They're very close.'

'What's that mean?'

'They're lovers.'

'I can hardly believe it.'

'Why not?'

'She's so sophisticated, so alive and he's – I don't know what . . .'

'And very handsome and very protective. He'd do anything for her.'

'Which one loves the other most?'

'I don't understand.'

'In a couple it's never really equal. One loves and the other is beloved.'

She laughed. 'What a nice, old-fashioned word – beloved. Maybe you're right. I'd never analysed it that way before.' She looked at him. 'You're quite a wise old bird in your funny way.' She paused. 'She'd be distressed if you sent him back.' She paused again. 'Why do you want to send him back?'

'He was careless about the detonator. We could all have been killed.'

'Long said you saved Joe's life getting him back to the farm-house.'

'What do you think of Long?'

She wrinkled her nose and pursed her lips. 'Not my kind of man.'

'Why not?'

'No idea. Just instinct.'

'Feminine intuition?'

'Yeah. You're grinning. You don't believe in it, do you?'

'I don't even know what it's supposed to be.'

'Like it says – it's intuition. All women have it. When a relationship is going wrong a woman knows from the first moment. She has little red lights flashing. Little warning bells ringing. It's not based on facts or anything she can prove. She just knows.'

'So what do you know about Long?'

'I told you – I don't know. I just wouldn't trust him.' She paused. 'No. That's going too far. Let's say I wouldn't *rely* on him.'

'You mean as a husband – or what?'

'Nothing as definite as that.' She shrugged and frowned. 'I can't explain. But that's how it is.'

'And are women always right?'

She laughed. 'Not always, but mostly they are.'

'You said you wouldn't rely on Long. Give me an example.'

'Look. It's simple. I'd expect Long to always do what he thought was best for him.'

'Not a team player?'

She burst out laughing. 'Oh, for God's sake. Yes, if you like.' She mocked his voice. 'I think he's not a team player.'

Bailey spent the rest of the day planning his next move and decided that it would be a more elaborate operation. An attempt to destroy seven or eight telephone exchanges all over the network's area from Périgueux to Brantôme and Bergerac. With possible additional targets in Mussidan, Ribérac and Coutras. And all on the same night. It would take at least three weeks of reconnaissance and planning and they would need to use some of their more committed local sympathisers.

CHAPTER 31

It took ten days to get the information they needed on the telephone exchanges and it was in the course of that reconnaissance that Bailey discovered that there was a special telephone exchange manned by the Germans that handled all telephone communications for the German forces in the Dordogne. It was based at Sarlat, a small town east of Bergerac, a little beyond what he had counted as being in his area. But it was too good a target to ignore. And Louis Maurois had friends and customers in the town.

He spent four days in Sarlat with Louis, staying at a house near the cathedral. The target was on the edge of the town and alongside the main road south to Bergerac and Bordeaux. Louis's contacts had found him a girl who was employed to clean the exchange and from her information he drew up a plan of the layout of the exchange. Although it used mains electricity it had two of its own generators which automatically came into action if the mains service was interrupted, which sometimes happened when there were thunderstorms in the area.

Bailey and Maurois talked for hours about how to destroy the Germans' exchange. It was a different operation from all the others. It was against soldiers, not civilians, and that meant they could expect resistance. A fire would be too slow-working and an external explosion might damage the structure but not the equipment. Slowly they were forced to accept that it would have to be an armed raid. They had one major advantage and that was surprise.

Bailey took them up the wooden ladder to the storage area in the barn where bales of last autumn's straw were stored for the stables. There was Louis, and Garin, Druon's man, and Tony Ransome from Brantôme.

Carefully they took the guns out of the oilskin wrappings placing them on four bales of straw that had been pushed together. There were two Thompson sub-machine-guns, ten Sten guns, six Lee-Enfield rifles and a Bren gun. There were wooden boxes of ammunition and four boxes of grenades.

When the guns were all in place Bailey looked from one to the other.

'You've all had some training on loading and handling these weapons. We shan't be needing the Bren on this mission. Garin and Tony, you take the Thompsons. You'll have no problem with those but load them carefully. Remember rim over rim.

'Louis, you and I will take Sten guns. Now I know they look rough and ready, as if they were made in a garage, and maybe they were, but they do their job. And all of you, when you're using a Sten remember that the magazine lips are rather fragile and if they're damaged they can cause stoppages.' He paused. 'One last thing, there's no safety fixed on the bolt and if you dropped a Sten on a hard floor it could fire a round at random.' He grinned. 'We can't afford to waste ammunition.'

Maurois looked at the others. 'I'll meet you, Garin and Tony at the shop by mid-afternoon on Saturday and I'll drive you up here so that we can leave for Sarlat as soon as curfew's lifted on Sunday morning.'

Bailey took over again. 'Now I want to go over the layout inside the building. There's a sketch of the interior on the grain-bin over there if you'll get it, Tony.'

They closed round Bailey as he pointed at the sketch.

'We go in here, the front door, after I've dealt with the guard outside. The equipment is all in banks with four seats facing it. We fire at the ceiling as we go in, a short burst, then, if they don't resist, you Tony and M'sieur Garin will tie them up and gag them. Arms behind and ankles crossed. Louis and I will smash up the equipment.'

Tony Ransome said, 'And if they resist?'

'Then we shoot them.'

'Have they got weapons?'

'The guard has a sub-machine-gun and as far as we know the squaddies inside just have hand-guns. Probably Walther PPKs or P38s. If any one of them goes for a gun, you shoot, OK?'

The others were silent but they nodded their agreement.

*   *   *

Bailey and Maurois drove to Sarlat with the guns, grenades and equipment later that day and left them in the workshop of one of Maurois's people.

On the Sunday they drove again to Sarlat with Tony Ransome and Garin. Late afternoon they went over the plan of attack again and Bailey emphasised that if there was no resistance there need be no bloodshed, but at the first sign of anyone going for a weapon they should shoot.

It had been a typical Dordogne April day. A day of sunshine with the tables and chairs already outside the cafés and restaurants, and families making a treat of the limited choice of food. But there was local beer for the men and a brave show of cutlets made from nuts and meat paste. It was still light at 7 p.m. and Bailey was aware of the tension that affected them all. For him was the recognition that for the first time it was not just a simple sabotage but an attack on a Wehrmacht installation and that Germans could be killed or wounded. And in Brantôme, Périgueux and Bergerac there would be other sabotage operations on telephone exchanges that made that day an open defiance of the Germans. It would be a humiliating blow for them and he wondered how they would react. And the fact that the Resistance could mount so many operations would mean a change of tactics by the Germans.

It was dark by nine o'clock and the streets of the small town were beginning to empty. In two hours the curfew would operate and people had things to be done to prepare for work the next day. At 10 p.m. they tied the canvas bags to the carriers of their cycles and headed down the main road towards the complex of the Lycée.

There was a deep ditch alongside the main road and they left the cycles in the ditch and moved up the slope of the ground until they could see the barbed-wire and the posts that fenced in the telephone exchange. Bailey crawled forward to the fence. He knew already that it was not electrified. Just five strands of standard barbed-wire nailed to thick wooden posts about two metres high. Slowly and carefully he clipped the bottom three strands and pulled them aside. Then he lay there looking at the building. There were two German army trucks parked outside and a civilian car alongside them. And there was no armed guard outside. The night shift had come on at 9 p.m. and would be in charge until they were relieved at 6 a.m. the next morning. The telephone and radio traffic they would be handling on a Sunday night would be quite heavy. Unit reports, troop movements, supplies requests and routine orders from Paris. Enough to keep them busy.

He made his way back to the others and they put on their woollen head-masks with holes for their eyes and a slit for the mouth. Bailey lifted his thumb and the others nodded and walked alongside him towards the building. At the door they stopped and they could hear music and voices and a guffaw of laughter. The noise and the light hit them as Bailey opened the door.

There were two men at the console, a man making coffee on a hob and two other men, one tuning a radio and the other combing his hair. Only one man noticed them and he was wearing headphones as he sat at the console. He turned and shouted to the others and one, a sergeant, reached for a rifle that was propped up against a wooden cupboard. Bailey's first shot took him in the chest. As he fell Bailey waved his Sten at the others, shouting to them to move over to the back wall with their hands in the air, Tony Ransome prodding them roughly to turn around and then guarding them as Garin tied their hands with wire, making them lie on the floor before he tied their feet together. And while this was going on Louis and Bailey were smashing the array of equipment mounted in the console. By the time the other two were stuffing gags into the Germans' mouths, Maurois and Bailey had finished their destruction of the console. The last thing they did was to cut through the mains cable. Then as the lights went out Bailey shouted to them to leave and they followed him out into the darkness.

They had to take their weapons with them as far as the junction at Beynac where the local priest had turned a blind eye to a grave being dug the previous day, in which the guns in their wrapping were now lowered and the earth loosely filled in to cover them. The rest of the grave would be filled in the next day and marked with a stone.

They cycled on, keeping off the main road where they could, and spent the night on the bank of the river just below St-Cyprien. While the others slept Bailey was restless, impatient to know how the other operations had gone, cursing himself for not staying back on the estate so that he was contactable by the others. He remembered something old Fuller had said: 'Sometimes a leader's most important function is just to be there. A point of reference.'

They set off singly the next morning at half-hour intervals, heading for Bergerac where one of Louis Maurois's delivery vans was waiting to take them to Brantôme. Maurois and Tony were based there and Bailey wanted to contact Paulette. Working at the newspaper she would know all that had happened at the other places. Louis had contacted her as soon as they arrived. It would be an hour before she could leave the office.

Tony Ransome had been sent out on a meat delivery as soon as they were at the shop and Garin had quietly headed back to his home.

It was mid-afternoon before Paulette arrived and walked through the bead curtains into the parlour where Louis and Bailey were waiting.

She put her handbag on the table. 'Well somebody must have done something right. There are no phones working anywhere and we're having to send out people on motor-cycles to find out what's going on.'

'Tell us what you know.'

'The telephone exchange here is destroyed completely, so is the one at Périgueux, and at least one other. I don't know where. The Germans are going crazy. Was it you two who put the Wehrmacht exchange out of action at Sarlat?'

Louis smiled. 'Maybe. Tell us about it.'

'The mayor of Sarlat, every town councillor, the police chief and about fifty other people are in jail all over the place. There's a rumour that a Boche was killed, and they're going to execute hostages unless they're told who was responsible. There are troops moving into the area from all over the *département*. Infantry, SS, tanks and signals people. It really is chaotic.'

'What's the public reaction?'

She shrugged. 'Mixed. Some delighted, some scared about what the Germans will do in revenge.' She looked at Bailey. 'What *will* they do?'

'I don't know. I suspect it will depend on what Paris want. They'll want to throw their weight about but they won't want to set the whole area against them.'

She pursed her lips. 'Was it worth it?'

Bailey said quietly. 'It's what we were sent here to do.'

* * *

Paul Cattoir listened to what Bailey had to tell him about the raid in Sarlat.

'You've moved into a new game now. You know that, don't you?'

'You mean shooting a German soldier?'

'No. I guess that's part of it. But you've moved from being a nuisance, an irritation, to being a danger and a challenge.'

'So?'

Cattoir smiled. 'So nothing. Don't be so tense. It had to happen, sooner or later.'

'London wanted us to move up a gear.'

'And what next?'

'I haven't anything specific in mind. Just general harassment.' He paused. 'What do you think the public reaction has been?'

'From what I've heard myself they can hardly believe it that somebody is challenging the Boche.' He smiled. 'They may be scared but they like it.'

'And civilian prisoners and hostages?'

Cattoir sighed. 'We should have made our sacrifices three years ago, and we might not have needed to make them now.' He paused. 'But you've made things tougher for yourselves now. There are German troops pouring into the area. Whether the British and the Americans come in from the north or the south, you've pulled a lot of fighting troops away from where they ought to be.'

'And you'll still support us?'

Cattoir stood up facing the Englishman. 'Don't ever doubt it, my friend. I wish I could do the things you are doing but I decided right from the start that I could be more use to you and to France by just providing you and your people with a cover and a background.'

'Maybe I don't say it often enough but I'm really grateful for the help you give us. I hope you're properly rewarded when it's all over.'

Cattoir laughed. 'You're very young, my friend. And very *naïf*. But it's nice to hear it.'

Cattoir put his hand lightly on Bailey's arm and walked with him to the door and with his hand on the big brass doorknob he turned to look at Bailey.

'Isn't it time you did something about young Jenny?'

'I don't understand.'

Cattoir shook his head slowly as if in disbelief. Then he said quietly, 'You really don't understand, do you?'

'I'm afraid not.'

'She hasn't slept for two days and two nights while you were away.' He paused. 'She loves you, Harry. Let her down lightly.'

CHAPTER 32

Paulette had built up a working relationship with most of the newspapers in the Dordogne and her own newspaper allowed her to use her office for her own business as well as reporting for them. This meant that for a couple of days she was handling the news of the network's attacks on the telephone exchanges almost to the exclusion of everything else.

And in those two days she learned a lot. At first she had tended to be critical of actions that had caused suffering to innocent people who had been taken as hostages by the Germans. But as the stories filtered through two things became obvious. The first was that the attacks had really disrupted the Germans' communications, and the second that the ruthlessness of the Germans was typical of them and their occupation of France. All their talk of non-interference and co-operation with a sovereign France was a myth. Just carefully thought-out, and skilfully applied, propaganda. Goebbels not Pétain.

She passed on everything to Maurois who had several meetings every day with Bailey. She had slept only a few hours a day in the last few days and on the Wednesday night she planned to wash her hair and go early to bed.

Outside the Paris black market soap had disappeared from the country but Louis had made up a substitute from boiled animal bones that he supplied to his most favoured lady friends. Paulette's ration was in a china pudding-bowl. Foul-smelling but effective and locally produced lavender-water would remove any unpleasant odours. Paulette had a large bottle of lavender-water from Jenny. It was produced on the estate.

She had washed her hair and rinsed it in the perfumed water and was reaching for the towel when she heard the car. It couldn't be Tony, he was staying at the shop for the night.

She twisted the towel around her head as she heard footsteps to the door. There was a pause but no knock and then she heard a key in the lock and she went cold with fear. The door wasn't locked and she held her breath as the knob turned, the door opened and the dark figure of a man stepped inside into the light. For a moment she thought she was going to faint and then he said quietly, 'What are you doing here, little girl?'

Then she was in his arms, her head on his shoulder as he held her tight. For long moments they just stood there and then she looked up at his face and said through her tears, 'Oh, Papa. It's lovely to see you again. I can't believe it.'

He smiled, and pointed to the kitchen table.

'Why don't we sit down. I've got two bottles of wine in my bag. Red or white?'

She smiled. 'Red for me.'

As they sat at the small table he said, 'I've wondered so many times about where you were and what you were doing. I drove down here once or twice just in case you were here.' He paused. 'Instinct tells me that I shouldn't ask you why you're here. Am I right?'

She nodded. 'I think it's maybe better you don't know.'

He smiled. 'That's the answer I expected.'

'Are you here on holiday?'

'No. Work.' He paused. 'There have been a lot of sudden resistance operations in this area. The Germans in Paris wanted me to come down and write a piece that would make the general public feel that such actions inevitably led to harsh reactions from the occupying power. Suggest that it would be unwise to shelter or assist resistance people.'

'They must be very worried to send you all the way down here just for that.'

'They are worried. They wanted me to assess what angle would persuade the population to see such acts as counter-productive.'

'I work for a newspaper and act as stringer for most of the other papers in the area.'

He smiled. 'Can I make an appointment to interview you?'

She smiled and shook her head. 'You should contact my editor but don't tell him that I'm your daughter. I use my own name but I have a different background.' She looked at him. 'You understand, don't you?'

He nodded. 'Of course. I'll keep well away from you. Would you like me to book into a hotel?'

'No.' She smiled. 'We can be old journalist friends from Paris. OK?'

'OK.'

'How long are you down here?'

'Three or four days if that's OK with you?'

'OK with me? This is *your* cottage. You're entitled to be here any time you want.'

'So are you, honey,' he said softly. 'How long have you been here?'

She shook her head and shrugged. 'How are things in Paris? How's Moma?'

'I haven't seen her for over a year. She's doing a singing tour in Germany right now.' He paused. 'The Germans are really cracking down on us these days. The easy days are over. They're not pretending any more.'

'Are you OK?'

He shrugged and sighed as he looked at her before he spoke, and then he said, 'I get by. I'm committed. I can't back out even if I wanted to.'

'You could stay here.'

He smiled as he shook his head. 'They'd come for me and that wouldn't be good for you.'

'I could move out.'

'No. Never. This is your safe-house. I'll do nothing to endanger you.' He paused. 'Or your friends.'

'I'll have to tell them you're here.'

'Does that mean trouble for you?'

'Of course not. They trust me.'

'Which bedroom do you use? I desperately need some sleep.'

'Your old bedroom isn't used. I use my old bedroom and my boyfriend sleeps on the couch.'

He smiled. 'Tell me about him.'

She shook her head. 'I can't. But you'll meet him.'

'What does he do?'

'He works at the butcher's shop in the town.'

'And . . . ?'

She stood up. 'I'll get the sheets for your bed.'

As he stood leaning against the door frame watching her make up his bed, he was aware that nothing had changed, everything had been left as it was. There was a framed photograph of the three of them on the beach at La Baule when she was about seven or eight. Smiling to the camera with the two front teeth missing that marked her age. A photograph of her in her communion dress, looking slightly solemn. There was a photo of Louise with Jean Sablon on the stage at the Palladium and, for some reason that he could no longer recall, a still from *The Gay Divorcee* with Fred Astaire in white tie and tails and Ginger Rogers with swirling skirts that showed off her lovely legs.

He wondered what Paulette's boyfriend was like and if it had helped her to put the grief of Jacques Lévy behind her, or at least into the background. It wasn't difficult to hazard a guess at what she was doing now. But she seemed too pretty and too alive to be involved in things like that. And too young. For a brief moment he wondered if there was anything he could do to help her, but he dismissed the thought. Her fellows would probably see him as the enemy, a collaborator. Which was true whichever way you looked at it. Not even a collaborator from conviction, or even just to survive, or save his own skin. A collaborator because it gave him a good life. Ah, well – *à chacun son goût.*

CHAPTER 33

She borrowed a car from Louis and drove up to Brantôme to talk to Bailey about her father. He seemed both casual and cautious about it.

'We ought to have expected it. Tell me about him. I read your background notes but I don't remember them.'

'What do you want to know?'

He smiled. 'Anything.'

'He's very charming, very well-informed and he's a journalist. Has his own press-agency in Paris. He and my mother separated a long time ago but they're still more or less friends. She's a singer.'

'If he's got his own press-agency and it's still operating he must be playing footsie with the Germans.'

'They use him a lot. He tolerates them.'

He shrugged. 'I suppose you could say the same about Paul Cattoir except that he works actively against them behind the scenes.' He paused. 'Bring him up. I'd like to meet him.'

'Thanks, Harry. I was scared you'd say I must cut off from him.'

'D'you like him?'

'Yes. We've always got on very well.'

'Did you tell him what you were doing?'

'No. But I'm sure he guessed. He's very shrewd.'

'Do you think he'd co-operate with us?'

She frowned and hesitated, and then said, 'I honestly don't know. But he detests the Germans and despises Vichy.'

Bailey laughed. 'Sounds a good combination to me.'

They had met up at the big house and Bailey was amused to see two natural charmers charming each other. Paul Cattoir and Paul-Henri

Fleury took to each other from the moment they shook hands. They chatted amiably for half an hour. They had many acquaintances in common in Paris and much scandal to reveal about most of them.

When the chat got around to Paul-Henri's contacts with the Germans he was open and frank. The pieces he wrote for them were their thinking not his. He was just a writer who, as he put it – 'cobbled the rubbish into some semblance of reality'.

Cattoir said, 'How do you get on with them personally?'

Paul-Henri shrugged. 'I loathe them, but there are two I like very much. One worked for the German press-agency in Washington before the war. He detests all politicians, German, French, the lot. He's well-read, intelligent and sophisticated in the true sense of the word. We are pretty frank with one another when we're on our own. The other is a younger man who concerns himself with the cinema, theatre and orchestras. Doesn't care what nationality the talent is, if there's talent there he'll help it along. Kind, gentle, a bit romantic, and barely recognises that there's a war going on.' He smiled. 'Uses my apartment for his assignations.'

Cattoir raised his eyebrows. 'Ashamed of his girlfriends?'

'They're not girlfriends.'

Cattoir smiled. 'Ah, I understand.'

Bailey looked faintly shocked, but Cattoir moved the conversation to other things.

'What are the Germans thinking at the moment?'

Paul-Henri shrugged. 'Those who really know what's going on are expecting an Allied invasion. A few think they've already lost the war. But they'll fight like tigers. All of them. Not for Adolf Hitler but for the Fatherland.'

'Where do they think the invasion will come from?'

'Most reckon it will be either around Calais or from the south, the Mediterranean.'

'And when do they think it will come?'

'All I can say is that they're pulling troops back from the Russian front to France right now.'

'And the French, what do they think?'

Fleury sighed. 'They lost hope a long time ago. They're too used to getting by from day to day. It's not very different from when the Boche first came in. They want to be free again but they don't want their lives to be disturbed. Their motto is "Life has to go on. Leave me in peace".'

Bailey said, 'What do *you* think will happen?'

Paul-Henri shrugged. 'The Germans have already lost the war but Europe is going to be torn apart until it's over.' He paused and said quietly. 'And I guess about half a million more are going to die in the process.'

'And what will you do?'

'God knows. I guess I'll end in prison as a collaborator.' He grinned as he patted his balding head. 'At least they won't shave my head.'

There was a silence for what seemed a long time and then Bailey said quietly, 'Would you collaborate with us?'

'In what way?'

'Just keep us informed about what the Germans are thinking.'

'And if I do, can I ask that you give special protection to my daughter?'

Bailey shook his head. 'All my people get all the protection that's possible. She's more than just a member of a network. She's special to all of us. We are all the same. We all trained together and we are all volunteers. Nobody forced us or even pressured us. The only real protection I could give to Paulette is to send her back to England. I can assure you she wouldn't go.'

Paul-Henri nodded. 'OK. That's fair enough. How can we communicate?'

'We'll work that out. I'd like you to meet the others so that they're not just names to you. You can just be a friend of Paul Cattoir from Paris.'

'Paulette told me she had a boyfriend. Is he one of your people?'

'Yes.'

'Tell me about him?'

Bailey smiled. 'She'll tell you once she knows you're one of us. Ask *her*.' He looked at Fleury and said softly, 'He's OK.'

Bailey realised that the information that Paul-Henri could give him was probably more valuable to London than all the harassment he was planning for the network against the Germans.

Every day for the four days that Fleury was in Brantôme they talked for hours into the night. Here was a man who spent all his time with Germans, both civilian and military, who knew what was in the minds of both Berlin and the German rulers of France and half of Europe. He was obviously accepted as one of the inner circle, trusted to write and paint a picture that translated their ruthlessness as for the good of France and their misdeeds as no more than the inevitable response to any form of resistance. Resistance being no more than lawlessness. And Paul-Henri was ready to keep him informed of what the Germans were thinking. Even ready to try and find out discreetly their views on specific things that London wanted to know. But Bailey realised too that the Frenchman's collaboration was not because of a commitment to the network or the Resistance but solely to protect his daughter. He would have to make that clear to London.

His first report back to London on the attacks on the telephone exchanges had been warmly received but with a warning to preserve his network intact for what they described as 'imminent events'. The warning had been coupled with further warnings that not even to his network must he indicate that he was aware that an invasion might be imminent. He understood what they meant, but he wondered if they realised that the whole of France thought an invasion was imminent. So did the Germans. All over Europe people speculated on where and when the landings would take place. Some with eager anticipation and others with dread, depending on how near or far they were likely to be from the fighting and destruction that was becoming inevitable.

CHAPTER 34

Siegfried and Max von Bayer picked their way slowly through the heaps of rubble that had once been the centre of Berlin. Siegfried was as mobile now with his new crutches as he had always been. He stopped and pointed with a crutch to the Gedächtnis Kirche at the far end of the Kufürstendamm. It looked like a broken tooth sticking up from the heaps of stone and bricks that had once been the beautiful shops and offices lining the wide expanse of Berlin's most famous street.

He looked at Max. 'It's hard to believe, Max. Goering said he'd change his name to Meyer if a bomb ever fell on Berlin. And now they don't bomb the centre any more because there's nothing left to destroy.' He shook his head as he looked at his brother. 'What the hell went wrong, Max? How did we come to this?' Max saw the tears on his brother's cheeks.

'Why are you in Berlin?'

'Rommel sent me to argue the case for reinforcements in France. And you? What are you doing here?'

'To attend a meeting about dealing with the Resistance.'

'The Resistance in France you mean?'

'No. There are Resistance groups everywhere, Norway, Denmark, Belgium, Holland . . .' he smiled, '. . . even in Italy.'

'Do you want to stay with me tonight at Otto's place?'

'OK. What's Otto doing these days?'

Siegfried sighed. 'He's dead. Was with SS Gross Deutschland Division outside Leningrad. I read a private report of what went on there. They killed over a million Russians, men, women and children, and they still had to retreat. Just left the dead unburied. The Russians aren't going to forget Leningrad and Kiev. They'll wipe us off the face of the earth if they get the chance.'

'Sounds like the reinforcements should be going to the East Front instead of to France.'

'Hitler's got to appease Rommel at Army Group "B" or he'll resign.'

'Would he really do that?'

'He wants Hitler to move over and let the Generals run the war. Says it's our only chance, and reckons Hitler's a shrewd politician but a disastrous failure as a military leader. Blames him for all that's going wrong.'

They were at the Brandenburg Gate and as they stopped for Siegfried to catch his breath the sirens sounded the warning of an imminent air raid.

'I'll see you tonight, Siegfried. About eight.'

'I'll be there. There's no windows left at Otto's place but it's boarded up and it's tolerable inside.' He paused. 'Watch your back, Max. There's a blitz going on against anyone with Abwehr connections. I've heard rumours that Canaris isn't long for this world.'

Max smiled wryly. 'I'm Gestapo now, Siegfried.'

'Doesn't matter. The connection's there. Like having a Jewish grandmother.'

The meeting was in an old house in Grunewald. It had been taken over when the previous owner, a rich Party member, moved out, having decided that it was the lake that the RAF and the Americans were using as a marker for their attacks on the city. Even at night the reflections of the moonlight on the water made it a bomb-aimer's delight. The house was, in fact, completely untouched by any bombs but the nearby trees of the forest had been burnt to the ground.

He was the first to arrive and as he stood at the big window the scene outside only emphasised his mood. The May sunshine and the blackened, burned-down trunks of the trees, thin branches spread out leafless like black lace, the lawns beautifully mown. He turned as he heard voices as the door opened. He recognised both men, Laufer and Kleist, both of them from the RSHA, the headquarters of all the intelligence and security organisations.

After a few moments of chat, Kleist pointed to a chair and von Bayer was aware that he was placed opposite the other two, as if there were an element of confrontation as well as a review of the current Resistance situation.

It was Kleist who seemed to be in charge, which seemed strange. Kleist was head of Special Investigations unless he'd recently been given new duties.

'Tell us about your present situation, von Bayer.'

Max noticed the 'von Bayer' too. He and Kleist had been on the same indoctrination course and knew each other well.

'I submitted a complete review of my department's activities a week ago, Herr Kleist.'

'I know. I've read it. Some people are worried that you seem to be having so little success in the centre of France. Is there any reason for that that you can offer?'

'I gave my assessment of the reasons in my report.'

It was Laufer who leaned forward as he said, 'Have you kept up your old connections with the Abwehr?'

Von Bayer stared back angrily at Laufer. 'If you've got some criticism to make, then make it. Don't try playing games with me.'

'Or what, von Bayer? What will you do?'

Von Bayer stood up and looked at Kleist. 'I shall put in a report on this waste of my time to Herr Schellenberg.'

Kleist shook his head slowly. 'Sit down, my friend. It was Schellenberg who ordered us to check you out.'

Von Bayer sat down slowly. 'I don't believe you. And to answer your question I don't even know who are the Abwehr men in Paris. No doubt they don't trust me any more than you do now that I am Gestapo. What else do you want to know?' He was still looking at Kleist, deliberately ignoring Laufer.

Kleist smiled. 'Don't get worked up, Max. Everybody goes under the microscope from time to time. Even rumours have to be checked out.'

Von Bayer noticed the change to 'Max'.

'So carry on checking.'

'Let's change the subject. Your people did well in Paris but since you've moved to Bordeaux it's been a total flop. Why is that?'

'Are you really interested?'

'Of course.'

'First of all in big cities like Paris we found it easy to recruit informers who gave us leads to Resistance networks. But in the rural areas people stick together. Secondly the people we are up against in the Dordogne are obviously well-trained and they operate in very small groups who are trained to be secure. It will take us longer to penetrate these groups but once we get a lead we'll be as successful as we were in Paris.'

'How do you get on with your brother?'

'My brother?' He sounded surprised. 'We don't see much of one another. He's with Rommel, concerned with military matters.'

'We've heard that he's saying that we're going to lose the war. Do you share his views?'

For long moments von Bayer looked at Kleist and then, barely concealing his anger, he said, 'My brother lost a leg fighting on the Ost Front while you were sitting on your fat arse here in Berlin.' He smashed his fist on the table. 'How dare you criticise my brother.' He stood up. 'I've had enough of this shit. If you want to talk with me arrange it with Schellenberg in writing.'

Kleist called out to him as he headed for the door but von Bayer ignored whatever he said. He was still shaking with anger as he got in his official car and told the driver to take him back to Berlin.

He had left his gear at Otto's place and he collected it and ordered the driver to take him out to Tempelhof. There was a plane taking spares to the naval base at Bordeaux in the early hours of the morning and after he had arranged to go as a passenger he slept in the Luftwaffe officers' mess in an armchair until they woke him for his flight.

He was the only passenger on the flight and they had put a pile of blankets for him to sit on between large wooden crates marked Kriegsmarine. As the plane droned on its way through the night he wondered if he should warn Siegfried about what Kleist had said. Siegfried was Graf Siegfried von Bayer now, the head of the family and a respected soldier who had lost his leg on active service. The bastards owed him more respect than making derogatory remarks about his patriotism. And why the reference to his own earlier service with the Abwehr?

It had been a mistake setting up a new HQ in Périgueux. Bergerac was the real centre of activity in the Dordogne *département*. He'd send somebody down there to requisition a house for them. Not in the town but somewhere just outside. He tried to remember the date and couldn't even remember what day of the week it was but worked out that it must be somewhere in the third week of May. Berlin had said that there was an abnormal amount of clandestine radio activity. He would move a couple of DF vans permanently down to Bergerac. Increased activity could well be part of the preparations for a landing. He had a considerable amount of information about SOE in London now. Names and methods. In the Paris area his unit had captured and interrogated dozens of Resistance people. Two had changed sides, a few had talked, but only after physical pressure and that seldom yielded anything reliable. They just told you what they thought you wanted to hear. He even had a photograph of one of the SOE training places, a mansion somewhere in Surrey. He had sent an official request to the Air Ministry in Berlin to treat it as a bombing target.

He had arranged for one of his own vehicles to pick him up at the airfield and drive him up to Périgueux. It was a long journey and he slept all the way except for two road checks by local SS detachments.

A week later his unit was in an old house just outside Bergerac and von Bayer was going through his usual routine of making himself known to the French officials in the town and the commanders of the various German units stationed in the area. None showed any inclination to co-operate, not even the Germans, but from the Mayor's secretary he got the names of the most influential Frenchmen in the area. It was obvious that the man he needed to meet first was the man Paul Cattoir, who was apparently the largest landowner, well-educated and cosmopolitan, and wealthy. Most important he had been hospitable to many of the local German officials and military commanders.

It had been an excellent first meeting, Cattoir had been both friendly and helpful, obviously a patriot but not a bigot and seemingly not anti-German. They had kept to mainly neutral topics like the problems of running a large estate in times of war and the necessity to provide employment and foodstuffs for the locality.

He had been taken down to the lake which had recently been restocked with carp and trout and it was as they were walking back to the house that von Bayer saw the girl on horseback who rode past them down the bridle path at the edge of the woods. He stopped and watched her for a moment and turned to the Frenchman.

'A real horsewoman that one. You still have horses?'

'We have kept a stallion and half a dozen mares to maintain our breeding line.'

Von Bayer frowned. 'You know I felt I'd seen that face – the girl – before.' He laughed. 'Very pretty, probably looks like some film actress. A bit like Renate Muller.' He smiled. 'I used to ride for the German equestrian team before this wretched war.'

'Did you now. Do you miss the riding?'

Von Bayer sighed. 'I never think about it. Neither the time nor the opportunity I'm afraid.'

'You're welcome to take out a horse any time you want. Just give me a call.'

'That's very kind of you but I'm going to be very busy.'

As they walked on towards the house Cattoir said, 'You're not my idea of a Gestapo officer. How did it happen?'

Von Bayer smiled. 'I think some of my colleagues also find me not their idea of a Gestapo officer. I was originally Abwehr but got transferred.'

'You knew the old admiral did you?'

'Canaris? Yes, I knew him.'

'What's he like?'

Von Bayer stopped, thinking, then he said, 'A gentleman, an old-fashioned gentleman – rather like my father. He doesn't fit well into today's world.' He smiled. 'You'd have liked him.'

'I hope you're not going to be too hard on my countrymen who can't accept being occupied by a foreign army.'

Von Bayer looked at him quizzically. 'We each have to fight for our own countries. We don't blame the French, we blame the British. They were offered the chance of a settlement and they refused. It's the British who are trying to stir up trouble now in France.'

'Are they really so much involved?'

'They are totally involved. They are the instigators. They supply the weapons and explosives and the people who call themselves the Resistance. To us Germans they are terrorists and have to be treated as such.'

'Sounds grim.'

'Yes,' he said slowly, 'I'm afraid it is just that.' He put out his hand and as the Frenchman responded von Bayer said, 'I hope you don't mind if I keep in touch. I think your wise counsel could be very valuable to both sides of the . . .' he was going to say conflict but changed it to '. . . the equation.'

They were interrupted by the sound of galloping hooves as the horse and rider rode back along the edge of the woods towards the stables.

'My God, she really can ride, that girl. Exceptional.' Spontaneously he waved to the rider but she didn't respond.

Cattoir said quietly, 'I don't think she saw you.'

When Von Bayer had driven off, Cattoir walked slowly to the stables. She was brushing down the horse and looked over to him, smiling. 'She's going to be a winner you know, Paul. She's terrific.'

'Did you notice that the man who was with me waved to you?'

'Yes, but Harry told me that some German was due to see you this morning. I guessed the chap with you was the Kraut, so I ignored the wave.'

'He said you were a marvellous rider.'

'What the hell does he know about good riding?'

'He rode for the German equestrian team before the war.'

'What was his name?'

'Von Bayer.'

'You mean Max von Bayer?'

'Yes.'

'My God. Did he recognise me?'

'No. Said he vaguely remembered your face but thought it reminded him of some German film-star.' He paused. 'How well did you know him?'

'Our families were old friends. We spent holidays with them. He was a very good rider. A nice chap all round. I rode against him several times.'

'I'll warn you if he's coming here again so that you can keep out of the way.'

'Is he likely to be around?'

'Yes.'

'Who was the film-star I reminded him of?'

'Renate Muller.'

'Never heard of her. Was she pretty?'

'Yes. Very pretty and you do have a resemblance. She was in a film called *Sunshine Susie*.' He laughed. 'Even sounds like you.'

'Have you listened to the BBC French service in the last few days?'

'No. Why?'

'There are a hell of a lot of the network messages every day. A lot more than usual.'

'What do you think that means?'

'Don't act dumb. You know as well as I do what it means. It's going to be any day in the next couple of weeks.'

'And then?'

'And then the gloves will be off. No more playing around like we have been doing, but the real thing.'

Cattoir looked at her face and then said quietly, 'You're quite an Amazon aren't you?'

'I came here to do a job. To throw the Germans out.'

'Why should you care so much about France?'

'I always did care and when the Germans marched down the Champs-Elysées I cried my eyes out. It was like jackboots trampling down a bed of flowers.'

He leaned forward and kissed her forehead. 'We French will remember you all when it's over. What a celebration we shall have.' He grinned. 'We might even get Harry to drink champagne without pulling a face.'

CHAPTER 35

London were obviously excited by the brief report Bailey had sent through of his talk with Paul-Henri Fleury and had asked for detailed information to be sent on the emergency daytime transmission schedules. DF vans seldom operated in daylight hours because clandestine operators knew that a dark signal path increased the power of a small transmitter. But Scorpio network's radio sets were both powerful enough for daytime transmission and using non-standard frequencies. Bailey decided that as the transmissions would be long it would be safer to transmit from Louis' premises in the town rather than from the estate.

Paulette, Jenny and Bailey himself coded out the long report. Paulette and Jenny were going to take turns transmitting so that the speed could be kept up, and they had abbreviated words wherever possible. Bailey worked most of the night to reduce the number of characters but they estimated it would take fifteen minutes to transmit. They notified London of the problem but London insisted they go ahead the next day.

A simple wire aerial had been run up to the dusty attic above the butcher's shop and in Louis' bedroom the transmitter and the text were on a baize-covered card-table. A single frame of a 35mm film giving the emergency schedules lay on a white card. The crystal had already been changed to one of the emergency frequencies.

London acknowledged immediately and they started the transmission. Despite their calculations Bailey timed it at seventeen minutes. Far in excess of what a secure transmission should be.

He and Louis spent the afternoon discussing plans for the network's operations if there was a landing. They also took the basic precaution, using Louis' vast network of helpers, to allocate alternative safe-houses so that they could be used if any of the Scorpio group was captured in circumstances that might mean he would succumb to pressure from his captors. The various sub-groups were now so well separated that it seemed they could be considered as being independent. Only Bailey, Louis and Jenny knew everything that was going on. He had only vague reports of how Les Ames was getting on with the *maquis*, but he knew that there could well come a time when he needed their help.

Louis drove Bailey and Jenny back to Bergerac where he had deliveries to make that would take a couple of hours before he could take them back to the estate, and Jenny took Bailey to her favourite place in the town, the square between the Rue du Grand Moulin and the Rue de la Mirpe. There was a café there and Jenny was known to the patron through Louis and they sat with an incredible plate of *gâteaux* and pot of real coffee.

The sun was warm on their backs and she watched his face as he ate a cream bun. No longer a Resistance leader but a small boy hogging away at a plate of cakes. When he saw her smiling he said, 'What are you smiling at?'

'You.'

'Why?'

'I was thinking of something my mother once said – "You can always trust a man who loves cream cakes".'

'Why did she think that?'

'I don't know. Maybe it was a joke. And of course Daddy loved cream cakes.'

'Do you think about them much?'

'Only when I'm lonely.'

He paused in his eating. 'When do you get lonely?'

She shrugged. 'When you're away and I don't know what's happening to you.'

He reached out with one hand and put it on hers where it rested on the table, and she looked at him fondly as she said, 'Do you ever get lonely?'

He nodded, slowly. 'Yes.'

'When?'

'Most of the time.'

'But why?'

He shrugged. 'Wondering what the hell I'm doing here. Wondering why people put their lives in my hands. Wondering what's going to happen to us all.'

She was silent for a long time. It was so different from how she had seen him. So sure of himself, so dedicated to his mission. So calm when things went wrong. She was about to speak when he said, 'Are you ever happy?'

'Yes.'

'When?'

'When I'm with you. Like now.'

He was silent as he poured more coffee into their cups and as he put down the pot he looked at her face, and said softly, 'It's only you that keeps me sane.'

'How? How do I help?'

'When I think of you you're always smiling or laughing and I feel back in the real world again.'

'And when do you think of me?'

He smiled. 'Does it matter?'

'It does to me.'

'Why?'

For a moment she was silent and then she said, 'For the oldest reason of all – I love you, Harry Bailey. I think I always have.'

'What kind of love do you mean?'

She shrugged. 'Just plain old-fashioned love. Happy when I'm with you, sad when I'm not. Hoping against hope that one day you might love me.' She smiled. 'Even *like* me would do to be going on with.'

He looked down at his coffee cup and he didn't look up as he said, 'D'you remember when we went that last night to the Savoy?'

'Of course I do.'

He looked up at her face. 'I loved you then for bothering to invite me and I've loved you ever since.'

She smiled and squeezed his hand. 'You could have fooled me.'

He sighed. 'I didn't want to take advantage of our situation. You seemed to be from such a different background from mine. I didn't want to risk not having you around by making a false move.' He paused. 'As time went by, like I said, it was my only pleasure – being with you.'

'And now? Do we have to go back to the old scenario?'

'Not if you don't want to.'

'I don't, my love. I don't.' She leaned forward across the table and kissed his mouth, and it only stopped when Louis's voice said amiably, '*Bon voyage et bonne chance, mes enfants.*'

Jenny looked up at him, laughing. 'Go away, you horrible man.'

They listened on the old Phonola radio to the news on the BBC's French service as they ate, and then they listened to the messages. That long litany of seemingly meaningless phrases, the messages to the Resistance in France. They had been warned a week before to listen carefully for the next three weeks.

And then they heard it. '*Bonsoir, le Scorpion – où sont les neiges d'antan.*' It was their message. The invasion had started.

They tuned to Paris but there was only news of the Allies being held up in the advance in Italy, and Hamburg and Berlin were both covering the record production of tanks and aircraft with brief comments on the low morale of Londoners who were starving and homeless.

Bailey switched off the radio. 'They must be already on their way. I can't believe it. It really is happening.'

She looked subdued as she said, 'A day to remember, Harry. You and me and company for tomorrow's breakfast. I wonder where they'll land.'

'How long before our next radio schedule?'

Jenny looked at her watch. 'Two hours. Might be something on that.'

'No. They wouldn't risk it being intercepted.' He paused. 'Shall I tell Cattoir?'

'He deserves to know after all he's done for us.'

'Let's go up together and tell him.'

It was a warm night, the night of June 5, 1944, and they stood at the bottom of the flight of wide stone steps that led up to the entrance of the *manoir*. There were searchlights probing the darkness over the town, but there was no sound of aircraft.

She shivered as she said, 'Do you think they know already?'

'I'm sure they don't. Wherever they land they'll have to hit those beaches running and there will be a lot of diversions.'

Paul Cattoir took them to his small private room and when he had closed the door he turned to look at them. 'You look excited, you two. Tell me the good news. Stop looking so smug and pleased with yourselves and tell me when it's going to be.'

Jenny looked up at Harry Bailey and then back to Cattoir. 'It's not just us, Paul, they're on the way. They've probably started coming ashore by now. We thought you ought to know.'

'There's nothing on the news. I've been tuning around.'

Bailey said quietly, 'It's happening, Paul. It really is.'

'How do you know?'

'A coded message on the BBC World Service. About an hour ago.'

'Sit down.' Cattoir waved them to a leather couch and sat down himself, looking from one to the other. 'Forgive me. It's hard to take in. I've thought of this moment a hundred times. Cracking open the champagne. Drinks all round.' He paused. 'And now it's happened I feel deflated, like a pricked balloon.' He sighed. 'Is it general knowledge now? Do the others know?'

Bailey said, 'No. But my people will know. They'll have heard the message tonight.'

Cattoir stood up, pacing slowly around the room, then turning to look at them, smiling at Jenny. 'And now, dear Jenny, no more sighs and no more tears when our hero has to ride off into the sunset from time to time.'

She laughed. 'I shall want more respect from you in future, my friend.'

He poured them the champagne before they left and she and Cattoir had smiled as they watched Harry Bailey take one brief sip before putting his glass aside.

When he was alone Cattoir turned on his radio. There were few stations broadcasting in the early hours of the morning. There were brief news bulletins on Radio Stockholm's overseas service but no mention of an Allied landing. The BBC's World Service gave details of the Allies having taken Rome the previous day but nothing more.

It was beginning to get light as Bailey and Jenny walked back to the cottages.

CHAPTER 36

Fremde Heere (West), Foreign Armies (West), was a highly special-
ised unit attached for administrative convenience to the HQ of Army
Group B and on the night of June 5, 1944 it was going to be put to
the final test.

For over a year it had been responsible for monitoring the day-
to-day operations of the Allied forces being built up for an invasion.
It monitored the British and American frequencies day and night to
give details of every unit, its location and function and its operations.
Its expert and dedicated staff knew more about the overall situation
than some Allied divisional commanders knew.

At 4 a.m. Siegfried von Bayer stood watching their activity with the
officer commanding *Fremde Heere (West)*, Oberst Fromm. Fromm
was a career officer, a graduate of Magdalen College, Oxford and
Göttingen University. He not only spoke fluent English but had
kept up his friendship with many of his contemporaries at Oxford,
especially those who went on to careers in the services. He understood
the British, their characters and their idiosyncrasies and he had
researched the backgrounds of all the senior British officers as part
of his grooming as commanding officer of *Fremde Heere (West)*.

A large-scale map of England showing the whole of the southern
counties and East Anglia covered one long wall, and a dozen
assistants were continuously moving the markers and flags on the
map to update the display as more and more information came in.
Forty coding experts were decoding the signals traffic of the Allied
forces assembled for the invasion.

Back in his private office Fromm poured a drink for himself and for
von Bayer. He smiled as he held up his glass. 'To the next seventy-two
hours.'

'Why seventy-two?'

'The Generals say that if we don't throw them back into the Channel in seventy-two hours we have lost the war.'

'Do you agree with them?'

Fromm smiled. 'I've been able to load the dice a little our way.'

'How?'

'There are fourteen Allied divisions on our situation map outside that don't exist.'

'I don't understand.'

'The Allies set up special signals to create all the radio traffic of an operational division. Twenty men instead of many thousands.'

'You mean they're just deception units?'

'Yes.'

'So why mark them up on the map if they're not real?'

Fromm topped up their glasses and looked at von Bayer. 'Hitler was taking away unit after unit from France and shoving them into the East Front. But as the Allies built up their invasion forces he had to respond and bring forces back. My mythical divisions had a military job to do.'

'How did you know they were phoney divisions?'

Fromm shrugged. 'I know the men who were supposed to be in charge. I knew them well. After about four months' being taken in I realised they were playing games.'

'Give me an example.'

Fromm thought for a moment and then said, 'There was a division that was supposed to be infantry units from Northumberland and the Scottish borders. The supposed commander was an old friend of mine. Brigade of Guards and totally unsuitable to command rough northerners. Apart from that he was an artillery man with no infantry experience. It made me wonder, and as I checked all their radio traffic I realised it was artificial. So I started looking at *all* the divisions.'

'Did our generals know you were covering up and deceiving Hitler and the other Nazis?'

Fromm said, 'I never asked them. I guess I'll find out sooner or later. If they knew they turned a blind eye.' He smiled. 'We got troops and supplies that we wouldn't have got otherwise.'

'My God, if they ever find out they'd shoot you.'

Fromm smiled. 'If I was lucky. How can they find out? Only I and the British know what was done.' He laughed. 'I could have been just fooled by the clever tactics of the enemy.'

Fromm looked at the clock on the wall. 'Hitler said they would do the shortest journey – across to Calais. I'd bet on further down the coast – say Normandy.'

'Why do you think that?'

'The RAF has been dropping supplies to the Resistance around Calais and knowing them I'd guess that was another bit of deception. And if it was Calais they'd have landed by now.'

The phone rang and Fromm picked it up, listening intently for several minutes. When he hung up he looked across at von Bayer.

'They've already landed. Cherbourg. Over a thousand ships, air superiority, estimated attack forces of well over a hundred thousand men.'

'I'd better get back to my people.'

Fromm was already heading for the map on the operations room wall.

Outside there were dozens of searchlights probing each section of the sky, and in the distance the roar and thud of heavy artillery, and von Bayer shook his head in disbelief as the dawn sky thundered with the continuous roar of aircraft engines.

Bailey had brought over Paulette to cover the emergency schedules with Jenny all day but the traffic from London was sparse with no special instructions and no mention of a landing. But in Bergerac people had phoned anyone they knew in Paris and the Channel coast and there was no doubt that the Allies had landed. And where there were doubts they were dispelled after that night's bulletins from BBC World Service. But there had been no details of where the landing had taken place or the size of the forces involved.

The late-night schedule with London was short and explicit. All their efforts must be concentrated on preventing German troop movements to the north. Maximum disruption of rail, road and telephone communications. Identification of German units, location and movements extremely valuable.

Paul Cattoir had obtained documents allowing travel in the *département* of Dordogne for both Bailey and Jenny. The *autorisation de circuler* document was issued from the *sous-préfecture* in Bergerac and stamped and counter-signed by the German Town Commander. Cattoir had good supplies of petrol and diesel for the farm machinery and Louis had been able to buy an old Renault for Bailey from the widow of one of the local antique dealers. It meant that they would no longer be so dependent on Louis for transport.

The three of them, Jenny, Bailey and Louis, spent a couple of hours wandering around the town listening to people talking, trying to assess people's reaction to the news of the invasion. The reactions were mixed, relief that it was happening far from their town, a fear of what the Germans locally would do, and with many people, a relief that at last the Germans might be thrown out of France, even totally defeated. Even so soon there had been guarded talk of the revenge that would be taken on local collaborators.

In the afternoon they spent an hour with Joe Parsons and Violette in Périgueux. Bailey warned them of the new orders from London. There would be no problem for Violette. She was a free-lance and self-employed. She could take whatever time off she needed but Joe's job at the cinema meant that his nights were fully occupied. He would have to feign illness so that he could take nights off whenever it was necessary. Louis had a doctor who would give him the necessary medical certificates. Meanwhile they were to prepare plans to attack at least four strategic targets in the Périgueux area. He could only give them a week for their planning.

CHAPTER 37

She had gone up to the big house to ask Paul Cattoir if he would monitor all the BBC's news bulletins as they would be too busy to do it continuously. As ever, he was only too ready to help.

'There's a plateful of chicken sandwiches in the kitchen, how about you join me?'

She smiled. 'Thanks. I will.'

As they sat munching the sandwiches and sipping claret in fine glasses, he looked across the table at her.

'How are you getting on with him?'

'With whom?'

'Don't play games, little girl. You know who I mean.'

She smiled. 'Much the same as ever but I think it's given him some kind of assurance that somebody actually loves him.'

'I told you long ago that he loved you. Why d'you take so long?'

'To do what?'

Cattoir shrugged. 'You know exactly what I mean. Why did you take so long to tell him how you felt?'

'Firstly I wasn't sure you were right and secondly I didn't want to risk damaging our working relationship.'

Cattoir smiled. 'You women tell such terrible lies. You knew he loved you, didn't you?'

She smiled back. 'I thought it was possible.'

'Have you slept with him yet?'

'Technically, yes.'

Cattoir stopped his hand on the way to his mouth and slowly put his glass back on the table. 'Technically? How the hell do you do that?'

She shrugged. 'We slept in the same bed but we didn't have sex which is what you really meant, isn't it?'

He nodded slowly. 'Yes. That's what I meant.' He saw the pain in her eyes and said softly, 'It doesn't surprise me.' He paused. 'But you must see it as a compliment.'

'Tell me more.'

For several moments Cattoir was silent, and then he said, 'Have you ever talked to him about his background? His parents and so on?'

'No.'

'I've had odd chats with him about his life before SOE. There are lots of inhibitions there. Rather romantic inhibitions in many ways. Talk to him about France and you can see and hear the restraints falling away. I asked him once whether his mother kissed him on the cheek, the forehead or the mouth when he was a child.' He paused. 'It was rather sad. She'd never kissed him, ever. But he was quite sure she loved him. Kissing was nothing. It proved nothing. It was what you did that was love.

'They were good, honest working-class people. Caring people. But they didn't understand this bright child who became a teacher. It was outside their expectations, their circle of knowledge. And as far as he was concerned life was for working and achieving. For surviving, not for enjoyment. He had never mixed with people who saw life differently until he met you.' He looked at her face and said softly, 'He may not be an eager kisser but I can tell you this – he'd lay down his life for you without a second's thought.' He paused. 'Anyway, why do you love *him*?'

'I don't really know. I've never analysed it.' She shrugged. 'I just love him. He's a kind of rock for me. Safe, and utterly reliable.'

'Fair enough. And remember, my love, that in the next few months a lot of people's lives are going to depend on that young man, his courage and his judgement. Not just your network but people fighting up in Normandy who don't even know you all exist. If you can hinder the Germans from transferring troops and armour up North it could be decisive.'

'I'll do my best, Paul.' She paused. 'You like him, don't you?'

Cattoir nodded. 'He's one of my favourite men.' He stood up. 'You'd better get back. Take care.'

He watched her as she walked from the room and then moved over to the window, looking down as she walked slowly down the wide stone steps and then turned on to the pathway that led down to the cottages, her slight figure moving into the shadows cast by the poplars. He was glad that she wasn't his daughter, and he wondered what France had done to warrant such devotion from foreigners. More devotion than most French people had so far displayed. He had once asked Bailey how much he was paid and he obviously had no idea. In France, like the others, he lived frugally from the SOE funds that London had provided for them. Cattoir loved France himself, *les philosophes*, the countryside and the country people and that was why he took risks in giving them help and cover. But he knew in his heart that if he were caught his name, his status and his money could probably mean some kind of deal could be done. And if he was not caught, then, when the war was over, he would be a local hero, but if Bailey and the others survived they would just go back to their old lives. A medal maybe and then back to earning a living. He shook his head as if to get rid of his thoughts. The least he could do was to go on supporting them.

Paulette had a phone call from her father that was made to seem just an exchange of basic information between two well-informed journalists. He told her that in all northern France there was not only a strict curfew but a ban on all use of vehicles and cycles and the sale of alcohol. Restaurants and places of entertainment were closed and in some areas, just to the rear of the actual fighting, civilians were not allowed out of doors during the day. As for Paris, the authorities and population had been warned that similar restrictions would apply if the public did not remain calm and co-operative. He dictated his report so that he could be quoted and asked if there had been any signs of civilian or resistance disturbance in the Dordogne. She had been able to say truthfully that life had gone on much the same.

When she asked him how the Normandy fighting was going, he said it was classified information.

When Bailey sent brief details of his intended attack on the central station and railway workshops at Périgueux there was a response on the next schedule.

London wanted the bridge taken out at Boulazac just south of the town and the bridge at Chancelade, rather than the station and workshops.

When Bailey studied the map with Louis, London's analysis made sense. Not only would the track and the bridges be destroyed but the destruction of the bridge at Chancelade would block off the alternative feeder line from Bordeaux.

The problem was that Bailey and his people had no experience of blowing up a structure as massive as a bridge. Railway trucks and buildings they could tackle confidently but not a civil engineering structure. Captain Les Ames was the only one who could show them how to destroy a bridge. It took two days for Louis to get Ames back from the *maquis* and Ames and Louis had taken another day to do a recce of both bridges.

They met Bailey at Louis's place the next day by when Ames had drawn sketches of both bridges.

Ames was quite sure what they had to do. 'There's no point in putting a charge at the centre of the bridge. They could get it going in a week that way, just putting a rough and ready joint over the gap. We've got to bring down both ends. That would take them at least a month to provide even a temporary crossing.' He paused and looked at them both. 'And you're going to need a lot of explosives to do the job. And the real stuff. *Plastique* won't do it. We're talking dynamite here. Have you got any?'

Bailey shook his head. 'No. Have you?'

'Yeah. But how long before you could replace it?'

'I'll check with London.'

'And I need more ammunition reserves. For Stens and the Bren guns. A couple more Brens if possible.'

Bailey smiled. 'You drive a hard bargain, my friend.'

'I'm going to need it, chief. We'll be harassing fighting soldiers before long.'

London had responded on an extra schedule that night. The drop was agreed and it would be made in two days' time. He was to give details of the drop zone. He made it for the meadows between the woods on the estate, a site they had used before.

Because of the heavy load there were twenty men and two trucks assembled for the drop. And Bailey stood alongside Jenny who was to give the shout for the lights to go on.

There was some cloud despite the fine weather and quite a strong wind coming up from the coast and Bailey was checking his watch every couple of minutes despite knowing from long experience that drops could easily be up to twenty minutes over time if conditions of weather or air defences meant making a diversion.

They heard the bomber in the still night air and Jenny signalled for the lights. Then they could see the plane a couple of miles away. A big bomber. And then there was a shout as it came in low and slow over the woods. One of the engines was on fire but the parachutes with their loads were already falling. Dozens of them, right on target.

Bailey could see the flames spreading from the engine cowling, flickering along the leading edge of the starboard wing. The plane roared overhead, the glow from the fire lighting up the faces of the men running to the cylinders. Bailey stood transfixed. He knew little about planes but he knew that that plane was not going to make it back to its base wherever that was. They heard the next day that the plane had gone down in the sea just after it had left the coast a few miles north of Bordeaux. It had been hit again by anti-aircraft fire before it got to Bordeaux and was obviously out of control. There had been no survivors.

Jenny sat with Bailey for most of the night as he played game after game of solitaire and listened to a Glen Miller concert from some Swedish station. They slept for barely two hours before he left to check the supplies with Louis and Les Ames. After some discussion Ames agreed to place the charges on both bridges himself, provided Bailey could give him four men. He asked Louis if it were possible to steal an SNCF official truck so that they could look like railway employees.

Roger Powers, working at the railway in Brantôme, had made a clay impression of the two keys that locked the double doors of the workshop's garage. There were five trucks and two vans locked in the garage and they were all reliable, ready for emergencies and always full of petrol. No guard was ever mounted on the garage.

It was almost 11 p.m. before it was dark and the van and the team were in the orchard of a farm in the village. Boulazac was just a huddle of farm cottages, half a mile from the nearest built-up area of Périgueux.

The charges had been tied with sisal and wrapped in newspapers, the detonators already in place but the timers not set. The dusk turned very quickly into night at that time of the year but there was a curfew from midnight and they wanted to be back at the farm before then.

Roger Powers drove the truck so that if they should be checked he could use the railway jargon to authenticate the use of the truck and its crew.

The bridge was part of a sharp left turn of the railway track over the main road and as they turned the corner Louis, who was sitting in front with Powers, said suddenly, 'Christ, there's a guard. Slow down and pull up.'

They had been travelling without lights and as they stopped they could see the silhouette of the guard on the bridge pacing slowly up and down beside the railway track. Bailey and Louis knew instinctively what they had to do. They went their separate ways, each scrambling quietly and carefully up his side of the embankment.

It was Louis who lit a cigarette at the top and the guard shouted to him, walking towards him, rifle pointed towards him.

'Halt.'

Louis did a fair imitation of a slightly tipsy farm-worker on his way home. Smiling and swaying as the soldier approached him. The man spoke a mixture of German and bad French and Louis pretended not to understand but he reached in his jacket pocket and pulled out his various ID papers. As he looked over the guard's shoulder Louis could see Bailey only a few yards from the man.

The guard carefully placed his rifle leaning against the wall of the bridge and fumbling in his pocket brought out a torch and shone it on the papers. And as he studied the documents Bailey was on him, his hands around the German's head. One hand across his mouth, the other at his windpipe. With his knee in the German's back he lifted him off his feet, his legs thrashing wildly then slowly hanging loosely, his body jerking once or twice, and with his windpipe crushed Bailey released him and he and Louis rolled the body into the shadows cast by the low wall. By the time they had scrambled back down to the truck, the charges were laid at both ends of the bridge. But Bailey told them to put an extra half-hour on the fuses in case there was trouble at the bridge at Chancelade.

At Chancelade there was no guard and they had planted the charges and set the timers in just over fifteen minutes. And there was nothing on the road back to Boulazac.

They sat in the warm night in the small orchard at the farmhouse so that they could listen out for the explosives. They heard the two separate explosions from the Chancelade bridge at 1 a.m.

followed almost immediately by the sudden thunderous crack of the explosions only a mile away.

Lights went on in two or three of the cottages but they were soon extinguished. It was getting light when the first Wehrmacht trucks and vans came up the road from Bergerac. It was a Sunday morning and it had taken time to check what had happened and to organise the engineers, and Bailey's van with its SNCF markings wasn't stopped on its journey back midday.

Bailey slept the rest of the day after he had put a brief message for Jenny to encode and transmit on the early-evening radio schedule.

It was Louis who woke him with a cup of coffee, grinning as he said indignantly, 'Can't make deliveries north of Périgueux, some stupid bastard has blown up the bridges. No trains for at least six weeks, they say, and the road's closed for two weeks.'

'Tell me.'

'Both ends went on both bridges and the whole structure came down on the road. They've got every digger for miles down there.' He paused, wagging a finger. 'A lesson to learn. Next time we leave a long delay charge that waits until the Krauts are doing the rubble shifting and then they go up too.'

Bailey smiled, relieved at the news. 'You're a barbarian, my friend.'

'I'm trying. I'm trying.'

Paulette was waiting for them at Louis' shop and trying to hide her agitation as she told them that James Long had been picked up by the Milice, the special French police who carried out the Germans' punitive orders against civilians.

'When did they pick him up?' Bailey said calmly.

'This morning. They were rounding up men who looked younger than thirty-five. They're being shipped to Germany to work in factories.'

'How many others did they take?'

'About twenty. They just seemed to go at random for men sitting in cafés and restaurants. They picked up two other men at Long's hotel. Another waiter and a cook.'

'Where are they now?

'They put some in the jail and when that was full they put the rest in the waiting room at the station.'

'D'you know where Jimmy Long is?'

'No.'

'OK. Go back to your office and see if you can find out. Louis will have a word with the hotel manager.'

Louis said, 'Leave it to me. I know the *patron*. We're old friends. I'll phone him.'

Louis was back in five minutes.

'He's been moved with six others to the station.' He paused. 'The Germans couldn't have done anything more stupid at this time. The town's seething with anger. There have been delegations from the mayor, the priest and God knows who, protesting. But the Germans won't budge.' He smiled. 'How about we make a few friends?'

It was quite a time before Bailey replied. 'OK. When?'

'Tonight. I'll find out what I can about the guards.'

Bailey nodded. 'I'll be back this afternoon. I'll need to have a look at the station beforehand.'

'There are two guards. One on, one off. But there's a detachment of a dozen from their regiment who are billeted at the bakery. If we fired shots they could be there in minutes.'

Louis shrugged. 'So we do one each. Where are they posted?'

'One sits on a bench by the door of the waiting-room. The other patrols the station platform. The one on the bench is officially resting but most of the time he sleeps. Two hours on, two hours off. They change at 10 p.m. and midnight.'

'What weapons have they got?'

'They've both got MP44 machine pistols with night-sights.'

'We're going to need somebody else. Somebody who can do something to distract them. Throw a brick or something.'

'What do we do with the people inside?'

Louis shrugged. 'Let them go. It's up to them what they do. Long can stay at my place for a few days. They just picked men off the streets, they won't have any idea who the hell they are.'

'What time shall we do it?'

'Just before curfew so that there are still people in the streets.' He paused. 'Can we get a key to the waiting-room door?'

Louis smiled. 'My foot's all we'll need, pal.' He sighed. 'What do we use on the guards?'

'Hands, wire, knives, or anything else that does it quietly.'

*   *   *

It was only a five-minute walk from the butcher's shop to the station. The lights were just going on in the shops and restaurants. The round-up of the men by the Germans meant that there were fewer people on the streets than they had expected and there were more German soldiers wandering around than usual. Some of them were with girls and some of them were obviously drunk.

Bailey had decided that there was no point in them having a third man. They could create a diversion themselves easily enough.

They crossed the railway track and crouched down in the bushes looking across at the station buildings. There was a dim light over the ticket office that showed that the platform had been cleared except for a luggage trolley across the double doors of the waiting room. The two guards were standing together talking and one of them laughed. A few minutes later one of them moved to the bench and carefully laid his automatic on the bench beside him so that he could light a cigarette.

It was ten minutes before the off-duty guard swung his legs up on to the bench and peeled off his jacket, folding it to support his head as he leaned back, the sling of his gun looped loosely over one foot.

In the far distance in the direction of Bordeaux they saw the sudden probing and weaving of searchlights in the night sky and Bailey prayed that there wouldn't be an air-raid warning which would mean both guards would be alert and watchful.

They waited another ten minutes and went back down the line and crossed the track in the darkness. Bailey whispered to Louis to take the guard on the bench. As they got to the end of the platform Bailey held up three fingers. He would give Louis three minutes to skirt the buildings and get to the other end of the platform.

Exactly on time Bailey edged himself on to the platform and crawled along in the shadow cast by the canopy. He was only three feet away from the guard when he saw Louis at the other end. The guard turned his head in that direction and slid the sling of his automatic from his shoulder. Bailey heard the man's gasp as he flung himself on him, the wire pulled quickly round his throat, the tags pulled tight until they crossed, the clatter of the gun falling to the platform as the guard's hands scrabbled at his throat. Bailey inched the wire loop tighter and tighter and was fleetingly aware of Louis towering over the man on the bench, one hand on the man's face and a knife flashing in the other hand. Then his man's body collapsed and he smelt the stench as his bowels voided and Bailey let him slowly to the ground. A swift check with two fingers to where a pulse should have been and he moved to where Louis was kicking open the waiting-room door. There was no light inside and they told the men they were free and to find somewhere safe for the night.

There were actually ten men in the waiting room and one man led the way out, hugging Louis as he went past. In the light from the bulb over the door, Bailey saw that there was blood all over Louis's shirt. He gave him his jacket and they walked off together down the steps to the station and headed back for the shop. Jimmy Long followed behind them but turned off into the side-road where he lived. There were still a few people hurrying back to their homes before curfew and the cafés and restaurants were taking in the tables and chairs from the pavements and locking up for the night. Paulette and Joe Parsons were waiting for them at the shop. Bailey saw Louis wash the big butcher's jointing knife under the tap and put it back with a dozen other tools of his trade. They played cards all night until the tensions went and they could sleep.

Paulette came back from her office just before noon. It was mixed news. None of the men had been caught and the public were both surprised and pleased that the Resistance was capable of carrying out such an operation. One bold spirit, the chemist, had hung out a French tricolour over his balcony and had been taken into custody on German orders by the police. He had been released an hour later because he was the only qualified pharmacist in that part of the town. And he had the only stock of the drugs that local doctors prescribed.

There was a rumour that the mayor was to be arrested along with the chief of police. But there were apparently legal problems in both cases and the Germans always went by the rules.

The bad news was that 13th Panzer Division had been ordered north from their base in the south. They would probably be passing through the area in ten days' time.

Bailey drove back to the cottage in mid-afternoon. There had been the scheduled contacts with London but no messages.

As he sat drinking coffee in Jenny's kitchen they heard on the BBC French Service that the Allies had captured Cherbourg and were heading for Caen. There had been a light shower in the afternoon and the grass was still wet as they strolled their regular evening route to the woods. It seemed strange that there were no hedges dividing the fields as there would be at home in England but there were long swaths of daisies and field poppies at the edge of the woods. And only a few yards inside was a sea of bluebells and a cock-pheasant flew up in front of them.

She slid her arm around his waist. 'I love these woods. It's like being in a church or a cathedral. Long shafts of sunlight and deep shadows from the trees.' She smiled up at him. 'When I come down here on my own when you're not around, I can pretend I'm with you because nobody else comes down here. It's just ours.' She stopped, turning to look at his face. 'Do you ever think about me when you're away?'

'I think about you all the time. Not *think* perhaps, you're just there in the background. I wonder what you're doing and how it will all turn out for us.'

'How long will it be before it's over?'

'Quite a long time. It isn't just a question of throwing the Germans out of France and we all go back to square one. Our people will want to go on into Germany so that they can't ever do all this again. They'll fight like tigers to defend their own country. They're good fighting men but they must be running down their resources of armour and planes – and men.'

'Will you try and stop them coming up from the south?'

'We could never stop them. All we can do is hold them up. London's message said that holding them up for a week was the equivalent of an extra division for us.'

'Paul Cattoir asked us both to dinner tonight. Shall we go?'

'What time?'

'He said about eight. Just the three of us.'

'Do you want to go?'

She smiled. 'Yes, please.'

'OK. Let's go.'

They sat together at one end of the long mahogany dining table, the French windows wide open to the evening sunshine.

It was Jenny who turned the conversation away from breeding lines and show-jumping.

'What do you think it will be like after the war, Paul?'

'Where?'

'Here, in France.'

Cattoir leaned back in his chair, closing his eyes as he spoke. 'Six months of head-shaving young women who slept with or actually loved, some German soldier.' He shrugged. 'Everyone will claim to have been in the Resistance.' He paused, and then went on, 'The politicians will play musical chairs but most of them will survive. Still in politics and full of *patriotisme*.'

'But at least France and England will have become real Allies.'

'What makes you think that?'

'Because the English and the Americans will have liberated France. The French will never forget that.'

Cattoir opened his eyes and leaned forward, his elbows on the table. He looked at Jenny's face.

'You make me feel so old, my dear.'

She frowned. 'Why? How?'

'The French will not love you or the Americans for liberating them.' He paused. 'I think it was Oscar Wilde who said "I can't understand why that fellow hates me so much – I've never done him a good turn." From the moment de Gaulle takes over, France will be more self-centred even than before. After a year they won't agree that they were liberated by anyone but themselves. And they won't want to be reminded that they surrendered, almost without a fight. If you expect gratitude, then you'll be disappointed.'

'I can't believe it, Paul. If I believed that I wouldn't be here. This country is like a second home for me. For all my family.'

Cattoir said quietly, 'Some of us will remember. And some of us will be grateful. They're the ones who matter.'

'Who will they be, Paul? The ones who remember.'

'Ordinary people. Like the ones you meet here in Bergerac and Brantôme. People without influence. People who have to go on strike to get a fair deal. They'll remember.' He smiled. 'Always remember that despite our reputation, we French are not romantic. Charm we may have, but we live by heads not hearts.'

CHAPTER 38

London's transmissions the next day were longer than usual and more specific. They now had information from other sources that two Panzer Divisions, not one, were under alert to move north at short notice. The message went on to say that at least one division, if not both, would travel by rail as far as Poitiers to save wear and tear on their tracks and transporters. London wanted maximum rail disruption at Périgueux and Brive, and, if possible, bridge demolition on all exit roads from Limoges. London would appreciate any information on the Panzer Divisions' progress as soon as they started their journeys from Toulouse and Tarbes.

When Bailey studied the maps with Louis it became obvious that they would have to change their tactics. Destroying the railway tracks and the road bridges would have to be left to the last moment, when the Panzers were no more than about twenty miles from Périgueux and Brive. If the targets were blown earlier then the Germans could try to find alternative routes. Either way they would be delayed, but if they were committed to their routes it would take weeks to detrain two tank divisions and use the roads to get to alternative rail routes. And if the main roads were blown outside Limoges the delays would be substantial.

Louis was concerned that the *maquis* should be included in the network plans and, if feasible, used to attack the Germans when they were halted and vulnerable. All this meant that several groups under network people would have to be assigned different targets, there was no time for their usual carefully planned operations. And all the explosives would have to be in place ready to be detonated some time later. That meant risking that the charges could be discovered on routine checks or by accident. It was going to stretch the network's reserves to the limit and it would be impossible to control it in detail.

Bailey hoped that his training and security would prove to have been sufficiently instilled in them. They would all have to find cover stories for absences from their jobs. Paulette and Jenny would be manning the radios and he himself had no problem, but alibis could cause problems for the others. Even Louis with his own business to organise would have problems.

For the rest of the day Bailey and Louis argued out the best way to use the members of the network and the targets allotted to them. And that night they checked the explosives and detonators that were hidden deep in the woods. They were going to need Ames to advise them on the size of the charges once the targets had been specified. Paulette would only be the reserve radio-operator and she had a car and a phone and all the permits she needed. All of them genuine, so that she could act as his courier as well. Roger Powers with his railway know-how could do the recces with Louis and Ames.

James Long was provided with the necessary travel permits to make the journey down south to see what he could find out about the two Panzer Divisions. He sent back a report to Bailey that in fact only one division had tanks, the other was a Panzer Grenadier formation equipped with assault guns instead of tanks. Long stayed until he saw the start of the loading of the tanks and the assault guns which went on day and night with searchlights after dark, and then he came back to Bergerac. The Germans were obviously desperate to get the troops up to the fighting area.

Although Caen had been taken, the German defensive ring outside the city had not been broken and already General Montgomery was being criticised for not having broken through. Even after an over-whelming air bombardment on July 19 there was no deep penetration. The Germans were holding on doggedly, but were desperate for reinforcements to make up for their heavy losses in armour and anti-tank guns.

The day following the massive bombardment the news came through of the failed assassinaton attempt on the Fuehrer and by the evening of the same day phone calls to Rommel's HQ from Berlin gave news of senior army officers being arrested as suspects; rumour had it that some had already been shot.

Siegfried von Bayer was at the HQ of Panzer Lehr where they were facing an American attack on their forces south of St-Lô which they had been driven out of the previous day. The temporary HQ was in the shell of a bombed house about five miles from the actual front line. He was looking at a map with Oberst Haller who was now in charge of the unit's operational planning. When the staff car pulled into the drive he noticed it briefly and glanced at the two men who got out of the car. He wondered why civilians should be so near the front. Maybe they were French officials, coming, as they often did, to plead for the fighting to cease in their area. But a few minutes later they climbed over the rubble that covered the ground in front of the small hole in the wall that gave access to the room.

It was Haller who straightened up and said to the older man, 'Civilians are not allowed in this area. You'll have to leave. If you want Army HQ it's back down the road about forty kilometres.'

The man said, 'Rhode, Gestapo Berlin. I'm looking for Graf Siegfried von Bayer. I'm told he's on your staff.'

'Why do you want him? He's on the staff of Army Group B.'

Von Bayer walked over to the two civilians. 'I'm von Bayer. Show me your identifications.'

The man shook his head. 'Siegfried von Bayer, you are under arrest.'

'You must be mad. Show me your documents.'

The other man said, 'You're being arrested on the personal orders of Commissioner Goebbels.'

Oberst Haller had had enough. 'If you two don't piss off I'll have my men arrest you.'

The older man reached in his pocket and took out a folded sheet of paper and handed it to Haller.

'Before you go too far, colonel, I suggest you read this.'

Haller took it and unfolded it slowly. It was written on the official notepaper of the *Geheime Staats Polizei* at Prinz-Albrechtstrasse, Berlin.

It was a typed note ordering the immediate arrest of Graf Oberst-Leutnant Siegfried von Bayer as an enemy of the state. And it was signed by Josef Goebbels, Reichskommisar for total mobilisation of all resources for war. It was dated July 21, 1944. He handed it to von Bayer and looked at the Gestapo man. 'When was Goebbels given this new appointment?'

'Yesterday, from the Fuehrer personally.'

'And you think that this piece of paper entitles you to arrest a senior officer of the Wehrmacht? A man who lost a leg on the Russian front and was given the Knight's Cross by Hitler himself?'

The Gestapo man smiled. 'Our cells are full of generals, colonel. Guilty men, all of them.'

Von Bayer said angrily, 'Guilty of what?'

'Attempted assassination of the Fuehrer. Men ready to do a deal with our enemies. Men who say that we have lost the war.' The man shrugged. 'You can say your piece when you get back to Berlin, Herr Graf.' He paused as the sounds of shelling grew nearer. 'Let's go. It's a long drive to Paris.'

'What can I take with me?'

'A blanket and your razor.'

'I'll want to make phone calls when we get to Paris.'

The man shrugged. 'We'll see.'

'My belongings are back at Army Group. I need to go back there to pick them up.'

The man shook his head. 'Forget it, there's no time for any diversions.'

'I suppose I'm allowed to take my crutches?'

'Don't be smart, my friend. Save your wit for the People's Court.'

Siegfried von Bayer sat in the back of the car as it made its tortuous way along bombed roads to Argentan, the night sky lit by distant fires as villages burned. There was an air raid even as they reached Dreux where they were stopped by the *Feld Polizei* who were guiding troops up the road northwards. As they got onto the final stretch of road to Paris he lay back and closed his eyes. He was at a military air-strip just outside Paris when they woke him and bundled him into a Junkers 88.

In the dim light inside the plane he made out the seated figures of half a dozen men in naval and army uniforms that were torn and stained. Several had bruises and blood on their faces, their eyes closed and their jaws slack with fatigue.

It was almost an hour before they took off and after several stops it took two hours before they landed at a Luftwaffe air-strip just outside Berlin.

They were loaded with other prisoners onto a bus and driven towards the city. An elderly admiral whispered to him, 'They've got Canaris and Feld-Marschall von Witzleben. I heard they've made over seven thousand arrests. Rommel and von Kluge have committed suicide and that old fool von Stulpnagel tried to shoot himself in the head and somebody else had to finish him off. It's a bloody nightmare.' He shook his head in disbelief. 'Music by Wagner.'

And then the old man began to cry.

Hearing about von Stulpnagel's abortive suicide attempt made Siegfried think of Max. Von Stulpnagel had been the military governor of France. And with his connections to Canaris Max could be suspect too. Legality and morals had finally been swept away. You didn't have to have done or said anything. Accusation was enough in itself.

For this special occasion the People's Court was held in the great hall of the Berlin Supreme Court, Dr Freisler, known as 'the hanging judge', presiding. All the trials were to be filmed on Goebbels' orders.

Despite the invective and screamed insults of the presiding judge the accused, one by one, faced him and his fury with all the dignity they could muster. The cameras panned continuously from pale, drawn faces to the judge's blood-red robe and the large swastika flags draped behind the dais. The accused were portrayed as a small, aristocratic clique, out of touch with ordinary people.

It seldom took more than fifteen minutes from the routine accusation to the inevitable – 'Accused, the People's Court sentences you to death by hanging.'

Siegfried von Bayer was held in Tegel prison but was there for less than two weeks. Despite his angry demands he was given no lawyer, and received no visits or communications from the outside world. Beaten daily by guards who had no idea of what he was accused nor the purpose of the beatings, he closed his mind on the world, expecting neither justice nor mercy. He tried many times to trace in his mind what had been the fatal step that had brought him to this fate but he found no clues. It was meaningless. All of it.

He spent his days in his filthy underwear and even when he was taken to the court he was not allowed to wear his uniform. No attempt was made to hide his bruised face and arms and he was taken straight from the court to the execution chamber, an echoing single-storey building that stank of urine, excreta and disinfectant. It was unfurnished apart from a black curtain that only half-concealed the guillotine that was generally used for executions. But the court had decided that none of the prisoners would be 'awarded the privilege' of execution. They would all be hung by crude strangulation. Hitler had personally ordered that 'they must all be hanged like cattle', and that all the hangings should be filmed so that he could watch them later, twisting and jerking in the agonies of death. The film showed that Siegfried von Bayer died from strangulation, hanging by a length of piano-wire around his neck.

The guard at the gate leaned inside the car and asked for her ID card. When he'd checked it he waved her towards the house. It was an old house, its stone golden in the sunshine where it wasn't covered in wistaria or Virginia creeper. They kept the guard dogs in what had once been the stables.

She stopped the car by the wooden doors and got out with her black bag of veterinary drugs and instruments in her hand. As she walked towards the stables a young man came out, his fair hair lifting in the breeze. He was wearing a pale blue shirt and a pair of slacks. He never wore uniform if he could avoid it.

He was smiling as he put out his hand.

'You got my message, then, Fräulein Vi?'

'Yes. What's the problem?'

'It's my dog, Offa, something's wrong with one of his back legs. I thought you'd better see it.'

'Is he one of the guard dogs?'

'Yes. The black and gold one. I've got him inside.'

For a long time her hands traced the dog's bone structure on his quarters and then she made him walk the dog back and forth, watching its gait. Finally she stood up.

'It's not good news, Karl.'

'Tell me.'

'It's a breeding fault. Have you got his pedigree?'

She took the leash as he walked over to a small table with files in a cardboard box. He came back with the pedigree and looked it over carefully.

She pointed at one of the names in the column of grand-sires.

'That's where it started, Karl.'

'What is it?'

'It's called hip-dysplasia, a malformation in the hip joint. It's a common feature in German Shepherds.'

'What can we do about it?'

'Nothing, I'm afraid. It just slowly deteriorates.'

'Is it painful?'

'Not at this stage but it will become painful in time until he can't stand any more.'

'But that grand-sire was a Kripo *Sieger* before the war.'

'I know. I've seen pictures of him. He was a beauty, so is this one. This one has perfect shape and the right temperament.' She shrugged. 'But it's a breed fault and the grand-sire should never have been used for breeding.'

'Are you going to tell the sergeant about this?'

'Why not?'

'He'll say he's got to be put down.' His eyes were on her face as he said quietly, 'He was always my dog.'

'So keep him as a pet.'

He shook his head. 'They wouldn't allow me to have a faulty dog on the premises in case there was an accidental mating. He's very strict, the sergeant.'

For long moments she looked at his stricken face. He was such a gentle boy, always polite to her when she came to check the guard dogs and the officer's horse.

'How about I talk to the sergeant and ask if I can have him. He'd be OK with me.'

She smiled as she saw the relief on his face.

'Could I see him sometimes? Take him for a walk or something?'

'Why not?'

He clapped his hands like a child, grinning and reaching down to pat the dog. 'Do I have to come too? He'll be more impressed by you.'

She laughed. 'You're a coward.'

He grinned. 'You're right, I am.'

The elderly sergeant who was in charge of the guard dogs at 'Les Lavandes' was no problem. She was welcome to the dog in return for reduced charges on her monthly veterinary bill.

Karl Hoffman came with the dog in the back of her car so that he could explain the commands that the highly trained dog was used to. She had taken them both back to her rooms over the bookshop and loaded the small refrigerator with the meat for the dog that Karl had smuggled from the kennels.

When they had put the dog through his commands, she had made them a cup of ersatz coffee and they sat at the kitchen table talking about German Shepherd bloodlines and the breeding standards of the *Sieger Verein*. He was easy to talk to and she learned from him that he came from a small village near the Dutch border at Venlo. His father was a farm labourer but was now in a factory in Essen.

He was a shy boy and he blushed as he said, 'Have you got a boyfriend?'

She shrugged. 'Several friends who are men but, no, I don't have a boyfriend.'

'Why not?'

'I guess I'm too busy.'

He smiled at her. 'Could I take you to the cinema on Saturday?'

For a moment she hesitated and then she said quietly, 'I don't think so.'

'Is that because I'm a German?'

'No.'

'Then why not?'

'Because you're a German *soldier*, occupying a country that doesn't belong to you.'

'Other French girls go out with German soldiers.'

'Tell me something. What do those people up at the house do? Some of them seem to be civilians.'

He looked embarrassed. 'They're security people. We aren't supposed to talk about it but most people seem to know.' He shrugged. 'They're Gestapo. We moved here from Bordeaux.'

She looked at his face for a long time. 'You don't look like my idea of a Gestapo man.'

He laughed softly. 'I'm not. I'm just a dog-handler. They're mostly quite ordinary men.'

'Ordinary men don't torture people, Karl.'

He shrugged. 'They just do their jobs. It's just the war.'

'What are you going to do after the war?'

'I don't know.' He shrugged. 'Just work.'

'And if you lose the war?'

He sighed. 'I guess I'll be dead.'

'What's the film on Saturday night?'

'It's *The Merry Widow*. It's in Agfacolor.' His face was suddenly serious. 'I wouldn't be wearing my uniform.'

'OK. What time?'

'I'll call for you at seven if that's convenient.'

'That'll be fine.'

When he had left she sat there thinking about what she had just done. Maybe it would be useful having a contact at the Gestapo place. But she knew that that wasn't why she had done it. She guessed he was the same age as she was but he was like a child. Eager to please. She reached down to pat the dog lying beside her. It licked her hand. He was rather like the dog. Working for a ruthless organisation but untouched by what went on. He was obviously both shy and lonely and she felt protective towards him. And he was an attractive young man with those blue eyes, fair hair and the rather girlish face.

When von Bayer rang Paul Cattoir to ask for a meeting, Cattoir suggested that he came up for dinner. Cattoir warned Jenny to keep out of the way and not to exercise any of the horses.

Cattoir's elderly housekeeper had prepared a meal of salads and cold meats and fresh fruit and left them to help themselves.

As Cattoir poured the wine he said, 'How are things with you?'

'That's what I wanted to talk to you about.'

Cattoir nodded. 'Go ahead – help yourself to food while we talk.'

'I need your advice.'

'About what?'

'About how to deal with the Resistance in this area.'

Cattoir raised his eyebrows and half-smiled as he reached for his glass. 'I hardly think I'm the right person to do that. Do you?'

'It could save making costly mistakes. Costly to French people that is.'

'Tell me more.'

'Paris have complained of our lack of success since we moved into the area from Bordeaux. They want me to use more forceful pressures.'

'Like what?'

'Hostages, physical and psychological pressures.' He sighed. 'In my experience that never works. Your prisoners end up talking but they just say anything they think you want to hear. They probably know nothing about the *maquis* or the Resistance – and we spend days chasing false trails.'

'So what advice do you want from me?'

'Tell me how to stop the sabotage in the Dordogne.'

It was several minutes before Cattoir responded, and then he said quietly, 'What do you know about the people concerned?'

'Very little. I know about the structure and methods of SOE, Special Operations Executive, but it doesn't help.'

'How did you get that information?'

'We arrested a man in the Bordeaux area a long time ago. A Frenchman named Lemaire. He was SOE. Our Bordeaux office were a bit rough with him and in the end he talked. But as I say – it doesn't help me right now. It's academic.'

'Where is he now this Lemaire fellow?'

'He's in a labour camp in Germany.' Von Bayer shrugged. 'He could have succumbed to the conditions. I just don't know.'

'You mean he's dead.'

'It's very likely.'

'Despite the fact that he told you all he could.'

'I'm afraid so. Once a prisoner has talked he's of no further use to the organisation.'

'What about the Hague Convention on prisoners of war?'

'They're not POWs. They are not in uniform and we classify them as terrorists. They have no legal status.'

'And you want me, if I know of such people, to tell you who they are?'

'Not exactly.'

'So what have you got in mind?'

'That you could use your influence to arrange a truce.'

'Do you think you're still going to win the war?'

'The war with France is long over. We are just fighting the English and the Americans.'

'And the Russians.'

'Yes,' von Bayer said, reluctantly.

'Will you carry out your orders from Paris if there is no truce?'

'I'll have no choice.'

'All you would do is put the whole population on the side of the Resistance. And when you've lost the war, as you surely will, you and your people would be tried as war criminals.'

'What makes you think we'll lose the war?'

'You lost it when you attacked the Soviet Union. And the final step was when your allies, the Japanese, bombed Pearl Harbor. Both acts of treachery.' He paused. 'I met your father before the war at one of the jumping competitions. He seemed a very wise man to me. Why don't you ask his advice? My advice would be tainted, anyway. I'm a Frenchman.'

'My father's dead.'

'I'm sorry to hear that. Didn't you have an elder brother?'

'He was executed for treason a couple of weeks ago. He lost a leg on the East Front. He was a colonel with the Knight's Cross. They claimed he had said that we had lost the war. They hung him from a beam with wire round his neck.' He reached into his tunic and took out an envelope. 'Read that.'

Cattoir slid out the sheet of paper and unfolded it. It was some sort of official letter. A bill of some kind. He looked at von Bayer. 'I'm afraid my German is too primitive to read it. What is it? It looks like a bill.'

'It *is* a bill. A bill from the Ministry of Justice in Berlin. I got it yesterday. It's a bill for five hundred and twenty Reichsmarks, The cost of my brother's execution. Not his burial – his execution. I phoned the Ministry as soon as I got it and asked them what would happen if I refused to pay. The quite senior official told me that if I didn't pay it within one month, my home and the estate would be seized. He also told me that I was lucky to be a Gestapo officer or I'd have shared the same fate as my brother.'

'Was your brother part of the July 20 plot?'

'In no way. He did think we were losing the war but that was never said in public and was merely his opinion as a soldier. He was a colonel on the General Staff.'

'It's a sad story, my friend. But your people have been doing this to hundreds of thousands of Jews since you voted the Nazis into power.'

For a few moments von Bayer looked across the table at the Frenchman's face.

'I've been a fool, haven't I? I thought you would understand.'

233

'I do understand, my friend. I just don't intend helping you. That's all.' He paused. 'And you aren't a fool, far from it. But you've got one basic problem.'

'What's that?'

'You're a German, and you're in France. And you're here by killing French people, not by invitation.'

'You must be very sure of yourself to talk to me so frankly.' Von Bayer stood up. 'I guess this is the last time I'll see you. Thank you for your past hospitality and I hope I haven't offended you by what I asked.'

'Colonel von Bayer. I quite like you. You're a nice young man. I just don't like what you and your countrymen have done to my country and the rest of Europe. I hope when your country is occupied that we don't behave in the same way.'

He walked with von Bayer to the door and watched him walk down the steps, get into his car and drive away.

For a moment he wondered if it had been all that wise to antagonise the German. Maybe he should have pretended to go along with him. But he had paid a hard price to have some influence on how the Germans behaved in the area and he was sick of the duplicity. But he had better warn Bailey and Louis Maurois.

As Max von Bayer drove back to 'Les Lavandes' he was angry that he had left himself open to humiliation by the Frenchman. Maybe Paris was right and it was time to face the facts. These people in the Resistance were there to ensure an Allied victory. Not just the liberation of their country, but the defeat of Germany. Germany would be occupied and every country in Europe would wreak its revenge on the Germans. From now on he would show no mercy in the war against these arrogant French peasants. If they wanted to play at terrorism, so be it.

CHAPTER 39

Even with only two days available for reconnaissance it became clear that the network had to shift its influence. The maps alone made it obvious that if they could take out rail and road communications at four towns they could severely delay the German reinforcements from the south. The four vital towns were Périgueux and Brive to the south and Limoges and Angoulême to the north. These four towns made a square of roughly four equal sides that sat across all rail and road communication to the German armies fighting the grim defensive battles in Normandy.

A member of the network was assigned to each target area and supported by untrained men from the *maquis*. Ames was to have a supervising role to oversee all four operations and liaise on the network's behalf with his friends in the *maquis*. It was Ames who insisted that timers were not reliable or accurate enough and that trailing wires operated personally were the only way of ensuring a reasonable chance of success.

When Cattoir told Harry Bailey of von Bayer's visit and conversation, Bailey was too occupied to spend much time considering the possible repercussions.

Two days after the charges had been laid at a dozen different locations, news came through that the Panzer Grenadier Division was now loaded and ready to leave. It started its long journey in the early hours of the next morning. When London had been notified, a message came back giving details of the armour involved. They were GIIs, heavily armoured self-propelled weapons for infantry support. Petrol-driven engines with a single 7.5 cm gun. They were not capable of destroying tanks but were otherwise very effective. They had problems when depressing their guns below horizontal and would therefore be vulnerable when mounted on rolling stock. Information indicated that they were support troops for the ongoing battles in Brittany.

It looked as if Brive would be the most important point. If they could stop the train it would be impossible to move on until the track had been repaired. With such heavy loads a temporary repair would not be enough. Bailey decided that he would join the local group to watch what happened. It looked as if the Germans were aiming to spend the night in Brive. The charges were laid just south of Brive itself at a village called Noailles and Bailey got there at midday. He was to meet Ames and Louis at a cottage near the railway track.

When he got there Bailey was surprised to see that there were at least fifty men being harangued by Louis with demonstrations by Les Ames. He had not been asked about the *maquis* taking part in the operation and he walked across to Louis.

'What's all this about, Louis?'

'If the train is stopped, they'll be vulnerable and we want to take advantage of the surprise and confusion.'

'There's a four-man crew to each vehicle and they'll be armed and well able to defend themselves.'

Louis shrugged. 'So when we've killed a few we'll fade away. It's all been planned. Don't worry. We've got two hours at least to get in place.'

Bailey resented the fact that he had not been asked. Not even consulted. But he recognised that Louis's plan would certainly be another hazard for the Germans. He said nothing but walked with Ames and Louis to where the charges had been placed.

Ames explained. 'Because this is a key target. If we could do a real big job here the other places wouldn't matter. They'd never get there by road or rail. So we've doubled the charges and brought along major weapons for Louis's men.'

'Who else is here from the network?'

'Just Jimmy Long. He'll give the signal to press the buttons.'

'What kind of signal?'

'A red flare.'

'And who'll give the signal to open fire with the weapons?'

'Louis.'

Bailey nodded. 'Ask him to come over.'

Louis arrived, wiping the sweat from his face. 'What is it, chief?'

'When do you plan to open fire?'

'As soon as the train goes up.'

'What if they send a forward patrol up the road ahead of them. Motor-cycles or a personnel carrier?'

Louis was silent for a moment. 'You're right. I'd have to let them through.'

'Would your men hold back or would they just be trigger happy with a soft target?'

'I'll talk to them again. I'll warn them.'

'I'm going to stay and watch what happens.'

'Where do you want to be?'

'Somewhere camouflaged on the embankment but well ahead of where the charges are. I'll use my field glasses.'

'Let's walk up there now and pick a spot so I'll know where you are.'

'OK. Let's go.'

Bailey lay in a fold on the slope of the embankment. It gave him a straight view down the track and was well camouflaged behind a clump of ferns and foxgloves. The train was not due for half an hour and had stopped at Cressensac for the locomotive to take on more water.

He craned his neck to look up at the sky. It was a typical July sky. Clear of clouds, and as his eyes came down to the track he could see the heat shimmering above the rails and sleepers.

The more he thought about the *maquis* intervention, the more angry he felt. He had seen it as an almost no-risk operation. Just three or four of them watching what happened, then fading away at the edge of the field. Back to the cottage and then the drive along the main road to Périgueux and down to Bergerac the next morning. Paulette would be able to let him know what had happened.

He wondered what Jenny was doing. She would cover the night schedules to London but she'd have no news for them. He wondered for a moment if the RAF couldn't bomb the other targets. But they would probably reckon it was too dangerous and maybe uneconomical. Not worth a bomber being shot down when a handful of men on the ground could do the job just as well.

Then he heard the sound of a vehicle on the road on the far side and a few moments later he saw the black SS uniform of the man on the BMW motor-cycle and his companion in the side-car smoking a cigarette. It was six or seven minutes until they disappeared round the bend in the embankment. He lifted his binoculars as he thought he heard the noise of a train. He saw the plume of smoke first and then the hazy outline of a massive locomotive. The charges had been laid by a heap of gravel and sand used in the winter against slipping wheels and for a moment Bailey thought the locomotive had passed the charge. Then it clearly had passed but as he focussed the glasses he saw a huge flash and almost as if in slow motion there was a cluster of flat-tops and armoured vehicles hanging in the air, rolling over slowly and crashing to the ground. There were two more explosions but he could see nothing because of the clouds of dust and steam and smoke. There was one more explosion that sent a rush of wind past his hiding place and the stench of hot metal and burning oil. Suddenly everything was quiet except for the distant shouts and screams of men and a flare from a burning petrol container.

There were several minutes of silence and then he heard the 'thunking' noise of a Bren recoil and the clatter of several Stens. Half a dozen explosions that could have come from rocket launchers. He heard a whistle blow and then the heavy thud of the German 7.5s. He could hear them whistling overhead and crashing into the woods because they were firing too high.

It was time to leave and he scrambled along the contour of the fold in the embankment until he got to the bridge. As he crossed the field crouching he saw the motor-cycle and side-car patrol heading back toward the train. It was getting dark when he saw the farmhouse where they were to meet up again.

They made him a sandwich and he sat in the cosy kitchen wondering what had happened to the *maquis* men. The more he thought about it, the more convinced he was that it was totally unnecessary. Just bravado. He understood all too well their frustration and impatience but it was a leader's job to prevent his men from taking risks when there were no prizes.

Bailey dozed fitfully in an old armchair but when nobody appeared and it was getting light he decided to head back through the woods to see what was going on at the derailment. By the time he got to the impact area of the German 7.5s he saw that the trees were stripped of branches and leaves and many had been broken in half with their roots torn up from the ground. And as he stood there with his binoculars he saw that the Germans had put out a protective line of SS men armed with sub-machine-guns patrolling the top of the embankment. He was too far away and too badly placed to see anything of the train. There were no signs of Louis's men or Louis himself.

When he got back to the farmhouse, Louis was there, his clothes in tatters and a dirty bandage around his left wrist. He was lying on a mattress, asleep in a small back room.

It was mid-afternoon when Louis came to and struggled to sit up, cursing as he used his injured wrist. He sighed and rubbed his face with his hands before he looked up at Bailey with bloodshot eyes.

'How much did you see?'

Bailey shrugged. 'Very little. Just heard the explosions and saw a couple of light tanks flying around.' He paused. 'What happened?'

Louis shook his head and stood up slowly. 'We need to get the hell out from here. They've put on a twenty-four-hour curfew. They'll shoot anyone on sight anywhere. We'll have to wait until it's dark.'

'How?'

'Christ knows? I'll have to work something out.'

'Tell me what happened.'

'The locomotive, the tender and the first five flats are just a tangle of twisted metal. It's going to take them a minimum of two weeks to clear the scrap and repair the line. I'd say three weeks would be more realistic.'

'And your *maquis* operation?'

'Four dead Germans including an officer. About a dozen injured. On our side three wounded, two dead. And one of the dead was your man Long.'

'What happened to him?'

'He was hit in the head by two rounds from a machine-gun.'

'Where's his body?'

'In the woods with the other casualty.' He paused. 'We can't bury them in a church for a few months. They'll have informers checking out funerals.'

'Where is he?'

'There's a blacksmith's forge half a mile down the lane. He's there.' Louis paused. 'He's not a pleasant sight, chief. Leave the arrangements to me.'

'Let's go. You lead the way.'

They made their way along the ditches and hedges to the forge and Louis led Bailey round the back to where bags of charcoal were stored.

Bailey stood looking at Jimmy Long's body. 'How did it happen?'

'One of my men, my *maquis* men, got drenched in petrol and it went on fire, Long was going to pull him back up the embankment. It was just two rounds rapid.'

'Where's your man?'

Louis shook his head. 'There's nothing left. He was burnt to a cinder. We dug a shallow grave in the woods but we'll have to leave him there. He couldn't be moved again. He's coming to pieces already.'

'Was he local?'

'He was from Sarlat. No wife, thank God. Lived with his mother. She's very confused. She won't realise he's gone. We'll look after her.'

Bailey looked back at Long's body. His face was unrecognisable. One shot had taken out one side of his throat and the other had smashed the top half of his head. The open skull was a mass of blood and grey-blue brain. Bailey looked around and saw a neatly folded empty bag that had held new potatoes. He laid it carefully over Long's face and Louis noticed him touch Long's hand before he turned away.

The twenty-four-hour curfew was lifted after two days and it took a further whole day before Bailey could safely contact Cattoir and through him, Violette. The blacksmith had a horse that was badly shod as an excuse for Violette's journey if she was stopped by the Germans.

When Violette arrived Bailey was in the woods trying to check the state of the work on the train. She had brought Jenny with her and Louis and one of his men had helped them get Long's body into the back of the small van. It was covered with loose straw to the roof of the van. Bailey went back in Louis's van.

They buried Long in the woods on the estate, just Bailey, Louis and Jenny, and when Louis had left they walked together towards the cottages. Most of the way she was silent and then she slid her arm in his and said, 'Would you mind if we went to the stables?'

He saw the tears on her cheeks as she looked up at him. 'Of course.' He put his hands on her shoulders and turned her to him. 'What's the matter?'

'I'll never forget what he looked like. It haunts me. I told you I thought he'd always look out for himself. I feel so ashamed.'

'What you said was just an off-the-cuff comment. Forget it. I'm sorry you had to see him like that. But there was no way we could get professional help. The whole area is swarming with SS troops.'

In the stable she stroked the horses, resting her head on their necks, gently rubbing their soft muzzles.

When they eventually left she said, 'I needed to be with something alive and beautiful.'

She made them an omelette for their evening meal and Cattoir had sent a servant with a bottle of wine for them.

Bailey poured himself a glass of milk and left the wine. As Jenny sipped her wine she looked across the table at him.

'You seem very down, my love. Is it because of Jimmy Long?'

He sighed and shrugged. 'That doesn't help. Our first fatal casualty. But it's not just that. I don't know what it is.'

'But the operation was a real success, wasn't it?'

'Yes. But I didn't like Louis bringing in his *maquis* friends without consulting me.'

'Would you have agreed if he'd asked?'

'No. It was irrelevant. An unnecessary complication.'

'Anything else worrying you?'

'Like I said, I don't really know. We've been waiting so long to go into action and now we've got the all clear it all seems rather pointless. The real war is up north.'

'You'd better read last night's message from London.'

'Did you report the operation?'

'Yes. Paulette gave me what she knew. They're very pleased.'

'What did Paulette find out?'

'They won't be able to use the line for at least three weeks. The locomotive, five flat trucks and six of their eight tanks completely destroyed.'

'What's the local feeling?'

'Angry about the curfew until it was lifted. Pleased, but aware that their fate is being decided in Brittany and Normandy, where the news is pretty good by the way.' She shrugged. 'The locals put it down to the *maquis*.'

'Fair enough. Can you get me London's message?'

'I'll have to get it from the stables. I've moved the radio there.'

'OK.'

The message was brief. There was a new set of targets. They wanted the network to sabotage the whole telephone system to cut off communications with Paris and the northern areas of France. It was urgent. The attacks were to include any air-strips used by the Germans and any aircraft based there. Sabotaging military vehicles and installations where possible. He walked to the kitchen sink and burnt it, watching the paper blacken to a cinder and disintegrate before he washed it away down the sink. For some unknown reason his mind went to Lemaire. There was little that was useful that he could have told the Gestapo but it was a sad ending to a journey that had started with such patriotic enthusiasm for defeating the Germans. He wouldn't have held out for long. Not that he was a coward. He was just an ordinary man who ought never to have been sent on such a mission.

'Have you acknowledged this?'

'Yes. On the return schedule yesterday.' She paused as she looked at him. 'You look as if you need a month in Nice.' She smiled. 'Let's go to bed. It's getting late.'

'You know . . .' he said, shaking his head, '. . . I'm almost too tired to even speak.'

CHAPTER 40

Bernd Kraus was an old Gestapo hand who had earned his reputation for ruthless brutality on the Eastern Front, savagely repressing
the groups of resisters who stayed behind as the Russian forces
retreated before the onslaught of the SS and the Wehrmacht. He
hung his victim's bodies from the gaunt trees of overrun villages
and when there were more bodies than standing trees the corpses
were left for the pathetic survivors to bury after he and his unit had
moved on. Feared and despised by even the Wehrmacht, Bernd Kraus
and his Einsatzgruppe 92 knew all about how to deal with resistance
groups and their passive supporters.

When his car drew up at 'Les Lavandes' he hurried up the steps,
pushing aside the guard at the door and marching through to von
Bayer's office, slamming the door open and standing there, hands
on hips.

'You must be von Bayer.'

'Who are you?' von Bayer looked angrily at the man filling the
narrow doorway.

'Kraus. Bernd Kraus. Oberfuehrer Kraus. I'm taking over. You
will be staying on as my deputy provided you make yourself useful.'

Von Bayer reached for the telephone.

'You're wasting your time, my friend.' He waved a hand. 'Phone
Berlin if you want.' He reached in his jacket pocket and took out a
sheet of paper. 'These are my orders.'

Von Bayer reached out for the sheet and read it carefully. It was
on Schellenberg's own official letter-heading. Brigadier Kraus was to
take over immediate control of all operations against terrorists from
Poitiers to Bordeaux. Von Bayer would remain to hand over his unit
with the post of deputy for such time as it was deemed necessary by

Oberfuehrer Kraus. It was signed by Schellenberg himself and headed 'To all German commanders and officials'.

When von Bayer handed back the paper he said quietly, 'Let me know how I can help you.'

'Find yourself another desk in another office and then find offices for the two men in my car. After that, come back here and brief me on what's going on.'

Von Bayer walked alone in the garden while Kraus interviewed each of the men in his new command. There had been angry criticisms from Berlin about the attack on the railway and the Panzer Grenadier Division and obviously Kraus had been sent to teach the civil population a lesson. All the talk of correctness and co-operation with the French was obviously over. The Allies were pushing ahead on all the sectors in the north and now Berlin were going to treat the locals as they had treated the civilian population of the Ukraine when the Wehrmacht were fighting their way towards Moscow and Leningrad. There was nothing he could do about it. If he complained or argued against it he would be treated as an enemy of the State and end his days as Siegfried had ended his. His father's Germany was long gone, and now his Germany was on the way out. Knight's Crosses but no knights.

Louis had brought one of his men who was a telephone engineer to the meeting and he made it clear how difficult it was going to be.

'There are over sixty manned telephone exchanges and about twenty repeater exchanges. And you shouldn't ignore the cutting of telephone wires and the poles that support them.'

Bailey nodded. 'Can you give Louis the actual locations of the exchanges?'

'I've done that already. And I've given him the location of a dozen or so electricity sub-stations that would each take out several telephone exchanges at the same time.'

'If we took out all the electricity sub-stations, how many telephone exchanges would we put out of action?'

The man thought for a moment. 'Between seventy and eighty per cent.'

Bailey looked at Louis. 'We'd need fewer teams and get quicker results but have we got enough explosives?

Louis nodded. 'I'd need to check with Ames about the size of the charges but I'd think we've got more than enough.'

'Will you do that, Louis, and see me tomorrow with Ames about making up these teams and allocating targets.' Bailey turned to the other man. 'Are these sub-stations guarded?'

'No. They've always reckoned there was nobody to guard against.'

Bailey stood up. 'Tomorrow, here, about six, OK?'

'OK by me, chief.'

Bailey called them back and asked the telephone man, 'How many repair teams do you have?'

'There's only one team who could deal with anything more than a minor fault. I expect the Germans would send in teams but if they were heavy charges it would be two weeks to clear the rubble and even basic replacement telephone equipment would have to come from Germany.'

'How long before they worked again?'

'At least three months if they got priority and the German troops would have to use radio while they were waiting. Only basic stuff and it would have to be in Morse code.'

Bailey nodded. 'Thanks.'

After several meetings with Louis and Ames it was decided that it would double or treble the value of the operations against the telephone system if they could all take place at roughly the same time, so that any repair facilities would be stretched to breaking point.

Bailey gave them a week for reconnaissance and planning, but this time he was determined not to be involved. He wanted to oversee all the operations and be available to solve any problems.

Jenny, Vi and Paulette had been warned that the operation was taking place the following day and advised to stay near their bases in case there was a twenty-four-hour curfew applied after the operation by the Germans.

On the day of the operation Vi was due to spend the evening at the cinema with Karl but she decided that she'd give him a meal at home and send him off early.

He looked worried when she opened the door of her rooms to him and when he was inside he seemed ill at ease.

'What's the matter? You look scared or something.'

'I can't stay to take you to the cinema tonight. I'm real sorry.'

'That's OK. We'll go some other time. How about a coffee before you go.'

'I'll have to be quick. There's a panic on at the house.'

She poured the boiling water onto the coffee grains and then passed him his cup. 'There you are. Let it cool a bit.' She brushed the hair from her face with the back of her hand. 'What's it mean – a panic?'

'We've got a new boss. He's a real bastard. And they got one of the terrorists this afternoon.'

'Really? What's his name?'

'It isn't a fellow, it's a girl.'

'Who is she?'

'I don't know her name but she works for the newspaper in Brantôme.'

For a moment Violette thought she was going to faint and she took a deep breath and sat down at the small table. 'But I thought you were only concerned with the dogs.'

'I am but I had to go with three of our people and search a cottage with a dog.' He smiled. 'It was old Bruno. He found a radio up in the attic under the floorboards.'

Her heart beating, she said, 'That sounds serious.'

'It is. They're interrogating her now. Trying to get the names of the others she works with.'

'What if she doesn't tell them?'

He shrugged. 'She'll tell them all right. They're real savages when they get a suspect.'

'Where is she?'

'At the house.'

'Shall I see you tomorrow?'

He smiled. 'I was going to ask you that. But I can't be sure. We might be confined to the house. Where will you be?'

'I'll be here all day doing my paper-work.'

He stood up. 'I'd better go. Thanks for the coffee and I'm sorry about tonight and the cinema.'

'That's OK, Karl.' She paused. 'Maybe I'll see you tomorrow.'

As she closed the door behind him, she stumbled over to the table and sat down, bending over, her head between her knees like they had taught her on the course to get the blood back to her head and stop her from passing out.

When she felt better she looked at her watch. It was 8 p.m. and at that moment she heard the explosion, and the pictures on the wall rattled. The tele-exchange phone was nearly half a mile away and it must have been a huge explosion.

She washed up as she tried to work out what to do. Obviously the first thing was to warn Bailey. She would have to ignore his orders to stay at home. And then, as if to underline it, she heard a loudspeaker van and a man's voice in bad French announcing that there was an immediate curfew until further notice. There would be a one-hour break for shopping at noon and any group of more than two persons together would be immediately arrested. But the more difficulties there were the more certain she was that she must contact Harry Bailey no matter what the risks.

She sat at the kitchen table trying to collect her thoughts. Her first thought was to get to the hotel and phone Cattoir and then she remembered that Jimmy Long was no longer at the hotel. Jimmy Long was dead. Joe Parsons was at the cinema but the cinema would have been closed by the curfew. She couldn't remember where the nearest public telephone was but she was almost sure that it was inside the post office. That wouldn't be opened until 7 a.m. the next day. And then she realised that there would be no phones still working. Her van was in the alleyway beside the house but there was no way she could get past the German patrols. And it was then she remembered her old cycle that she used for getting down farm-tracks that were impossible for the van. It was in the back of the van tied loosely with rope to where the canvas top was looped under metal hasps to the metal body of the van. What excuse could she give if a patrol did catch her. If she made up some spurious story of an emergency they could easily check on it and the time they took would make it far too long, apart from being under suspicion. She tried hard not to think of Paulette and what might be happening to her. She'd use the bike and cycle up to the manor house no matter what the risks were.

It was 10 p.m. before it was dark and she let herself out of the side door in the alley and quietly undid the leather straps that held the flaps together at the back of the truck. Inside she untied the rope that held the cycle and pushing aside the van's back flaps she lowered the cycle to the cobbled street.

The quickest route was to go due north up Avenue Pasteur but the avenue was a main road and there would certainly be patrols and road blocks, so she used the side-roads parallel to the main road. She was well clear of the town before she saw any Germans but they were standing on the bank of the river while two of them checked a boat moored to a post, its anchor-chain rattling as it swung in the wind. She walked the bike for half a mile and then she took a left-hand turn up a lane beside a row of cottages. She made her way along rutted paths alongside fields of lavender and orchards of old-established apple trees.

Twice she had to stop to rest but after two hours of dogged progress she was at the foot of the hill that led to the manor house. Just once she lay in the ditch as she saw car headlights coming down the hill but after that everything was silence apart from the rustle of small animals and birds as she went past.

As she got to the wrought-iron gates she was relieved to see that they were open. Too exhausted to push the cycle up the long drive, she abandoned it and went on foot past a summer-house and a small pond with ducks angry at being disturbed.

At the foot of the steps up to the big house she decided to go directly to the cottages where she had stayed with Jenny a few months earlier. Standing in front of Jenny's door she was trembling as she raised her hand to knock on the door.

She heard Jenny's voice say, 'Who is it?'

'It's me, Jenny. Vi.'

She heard footsteps on the tiled floor and then the door opened. She saw Jenny's face in the dim light of a candle. 'Come in.'

With the door closed Jenny looked at her. 'What are you doing up here at this hour?'

'They've got Paulette, Jenny. The Gestapo have got her. I came to tell Harry.'

'He's in Brantôme. There's a curfew everywhere, he obviously couldn't get back. Sit down. You look terrible. Are you sure about this or is it just a rumour?'

'I'm sure.'

'How did you find out about it?'

'I was going to the cinema tonight with the German boy I told you about. The one who works for them looking after the dogs.'

'What did he tell you?'

'Said he couldn't make it tonight. There was a panic on at the Gestapo house. They'd caught a terrorist this afternoon. A woman. He didn't know her name but she worked for a newspaper in Brantôme and they'd searched the cottage where she lived and found a radio under the floorboards in the attic.'

Jenny closed her eyes. 'My God. What the hell shall we do. I'd better go and tell Paul Cattoir. Get yourself something to eat while I'm away.'

She was already on her way as she moved towards the kitchen.

Paul Cattoir in a silk dressing-gown stood quietly listening as she told him what had happened.

'Where have they got her?'

'At the house they took over, "Les Lavandes".'

For long moments Cattoir stood there thinking and then he said, 'I know where Harry is staying. I can phone him there but I'll have to disguise the message. Say she's ill or something. You're shivering, I'll get a blanket for you.'

When he had draped the tartan blanket about her shoulders, he walked over to the phone. But the line was dead. He turned to look at Jenny. 'They obviously did a good job. The phones here are dead too.' He paused. 'Look. You go back to Vi and both of you get some sleep. Meantime I'll see if I can sort something out. Don't worry. I'll deal with it.'

It was 7 a.m. when Cattoir went to the cottage. Both girls were already dressed and waiting.

'I've got a travel permit for a meeting with the Mayor of Brantôme. Just me and my driver.' He pointed at Jenny. 'That'll be you, my dear. I hope to God our friend is where I think he is.'

As expected, Bailey was at Louis's place. Louis arrived a few minutes later. He had been talking to the German Town Commander about a permit to deliver meat to his customers.

They all sat in the kitchen as Jenny told Bailey what they knew.

249

'Am I right in thinking you knew she had this German boyfriend?'

'Yes.'

'Why didn't you tell me.'

'I didn't think it was important.'

'Not important that she had contact with a German who worked for the Gestapo?'

'But he gave her the information for God's sake. We shouldn't have known what had happened if it wasn't for him. She had other boyfriends too.'

'It didn't strike you that if I had known we might have been able to find out things about the Gestapo people from this fellow?'

'He just looks after the wretched dogs, Harry. That's all.'

'But you decided I didn't need to know?'

She shrugged. 'I guess so.'

'That was stupid.'

'Why?'

'Because it's what you don't know about somebody that gets you killed.'

Cattoir took a deep breath before he intervened. 'What do you think we should do?' he said quietly.

Jenny said, 'We ought to try and contact her father.'

Bailey shrugged. 'With no telephones that's impossible.' He turned to Jenny. 'How much does Vi know about the Gestapo set-up at "Les Lavandes"?'

'Not much. It was a very casual relationship.'

Bailey looked at Louis. 'Could we put together enough men to take it over?'

Louis shook his head. 'By the time I'd got them together and planned something it would be too late.' He paused. 'If she's going to talk, she'll have talked by now.'

Bailey looked at Jenny. 'What do you think? Will she talk?'

'I'd stake my life on it. She'll never talk.'

Bailey nodded. 'If she had talked they would already have picked us up. Some of us, anyway.'

Louis said, 'The Boche have given me a permit to deliver meat to all German units I deal with regularly. Let me do a quick run round and see what I can find out. The Gestapo place isn't one of my customers but I'll see if they need any meat for themselves or the dogs. I'll come straight back here and let you know what I've found out, if anything.' Louis stood up. 'I think we'd all best stay here in my place until we've sorted out the situation.'

As Louis got to the door that led to the back yard, Bailey got up and walked out with him, putting his hand on Louis' arm, turning him so that they faced each other.

'You realise what you're doing, Louis?'

Louis nodded and said quietly, 'Yes. I know.'

'If Paulette has talked, your name and all about you will be on their list. You're risking your life.'

'I know that, my friend.' He paused. 'But if I come back in one piece it will be Paulette who deserves the medal, not me. Go back to the others. Even Paul Cattoir looks depressed. Make him think.'

It was two hours before Louis came back and it wasn't good news.

'It's like a fortress. They've got soldiers from an anti-aircraft unit guarding the place. They've got massive guns and barbed wire around the house itself. I was told to get the hell out of it. They didn't want any meat and they didn't want me or any visitor.' He shrugged. 'Given time we could still put together a force to take the place but it would take a week to ten days to get it together.'

Cattoir looked at Louis. 'Could you ask your telephone friend where the nearest town is that has telephones working?'

'I can tell you that. You'd have to go as far north as Poitiers and the Germans are not issuing travel permits for journeys beyond Angoulême and Limoges.'

'Is the mayor still functioning?'

'More or less.'

'I'll go and see him.' Cattoir stood up. 'I'll be right back.'

Bailey said, 'What have you got in mind?'

'I'll get to a telephone and speak to her father. He's more or less a collaborator. He can use his influence.'

Bailey shook his head. 'They won't interfere with the Gestapo no matter what influence he has.'

Cattoir shrugged. 'Maybe you're right. But there's nothing else constructive we can do.'

Cattoir was away for no more than twenty minutes but he had his *permis de conduire* signed by both the mayor and the German Town Commandant.

He ate a sandwich, drank a glass of wine and walked with Bailey to his car.

As he opened the car door he turned to look at Harry Bailey. 'It's a terrible blow but you mustn't stop doing your work. Even if it's only blowing up telephone poles, do it. Keep their minds occupied. I guess it will be two days at least before I'm back.'

Cattoir was stopped seven times before he got to Poitiers around midnight. He took a room at a small hotel and dialled Paul-Henri Fleury's number in Paris on the public phone in the hotel lobby.

He was not at the press agency but they gave him Fleury's home number. He answered straight away.

'Fleury.'

'My name's Cattoir. We met at my house some months ago. Do you remember me?'

'Of course.'

'It's your daughter. She's in trouble. I think you should come down here.'

'What kind of trouble? Is she pregnant or what?'

'Life or death trouble. I can't say more. Your phone might be monitored.'

'To hell with that. Just tell me what's the matter.'

Cattoir told him and there was a long silence at the other end and then Paul-Henri said, 'I'll come down right away.'

'Meet me first. I'm in Poitiers because the phones are out all over our area. How long will you be? I'll wait for you.'

'I need time to contact my friends here, my German friends. Could you wait until mid-afternoon?' He paused. 'Are you sure she's with the people you mentioned?'

'Quite sure.'

'How long have they had her?'

'About thirty-six hours.'

Cattoir heard the deep sigh at the other end of the line.

'I'll see you tomorrow.' Paul-Henri's voice was very flat.

It was nearly 4 p.m. when Paul-Henri arrived in a Citroën and Cattoir took him up to his room.

Cattoir pointed to a chair and perched himself on the edge of the bed.

'How did your German friends respond?'

'I asked them to intervene but the bastards wouldn't do more than give me a letter.' He reached in his jacket pocket and passed an unsealed envelope to Cattoir. 'Read it.'

It was on the official paper of the Paris Kommandantur, *Presse Stelle*.

TO WHOM IT MAY CONCERN

The bearer, Paul-Henri Fleury, should be given all possible assistance by both military and civilian authorities. He is a much valued journalist who has an excellent record of co-operation with the above authority.

Signed: Wilhelm Strauss. Senior Press Officer.

It was dated with that day's date. Cattoir handed it back to Fleury.

'That's as good as you could expect, my friend.'

He saw the anger on Fleury's face. 'Is it hell. They owe me, the bastards. They could have picked up the phone and ordered her release.'

'Nobody tells the Gestapo what to do. You know that as well as I do. And nobody is going to order the Gestapo to release a suspected resistance worker.'

Fleury's voice was shrill with rage. 'I've never asked them a single favour and by God I've used any talent I have on their behalf since the day the bastards arrived.' He saw the look that Cattoir couldn't hide. 'You think I deserve this don't you? Well what about Paulette?' She's not a collaborator for God's sake.' For a few moments Fleury was silent. The he said, 'I'm sorry. Thank you for getting in touch with me. It was a shock. I've dreaded this happening but everything seemed so under control. So well organised.'

'What are you going to do?'

'I'm going down to Brantôme and demand they release her.'

Cattoir nodded without comment and then he said, 'The journey will be easier if you follow behind me. Between us we've at least got enough influence to get past a road-block.'

Fleury stood up unsteadily. 'Thanks.'

*　　*　　*

They drove through the darkness and were stopped by several patrols. There had been some obstruction once they got back into the curfew area but they had eventually been let through.

The sun was coming up when Cattoir stopped just outside Brantôme. He walked back to Fleury's car and bent down to speak to him.

'Have a rest here and there is a place for lorry drivers about two kilometres down the road. We can have a sandwich and a drink and you can get cleaned up.' When he saw Fleury's hands trembling as he clutched the steering wheel of his car he said, 'Let's sit in the field and watch the sun come up.'

Fleury was asleep only moments after he lay back in the grass with its swath of red field-poppies and Cattoir tried to collect his thoughts. There had been no choice but to contact her father. But he felt certain that nothing would persuade the Gestapo to release Paulette. Maybe if they hadn't found the radio there would have been a slim chance. He wondered how the Germans had got on to her. According to the mayor there was a new man in charge of the Gestapo but he wondered if the man who had visited his house, von Bayer, was still there. Maybe some deal could be done with him. Bailey had run the network very effectively. Good security, no silly games of cowboys and Indians. But once the Allies were fighting their way to Paris the pressure had been irresistible. They did what they were there to do. And they'd done it well. But the Germans were bound to react ruthlessly, tormented by sabotage and humiliated in front of a population that hated them. He guessed that in two or three months there would be no Germans in the Dordogne. If only the network could survive for that time. It was like two lines being drawn on a graph, waiting to see where the lines crossed. But Bailey wasn't the kind of man who would hold off on the network's harassment of the Germans no matter what the cost. Bailey and Louis were a pair. Very different in many ways but born leaders and with the same determination to throw the Germans out of France. And a year after it was all over nobody would remember who the hell they were.

He looked at his watch and then at Fleury who was still asleep. It was time to get on their way. The Germans had had her for nearly three days now and every hour counted. He woke Fleury and ten minutes later they were at the café. All they could offer was a bowl of fruit and a glass of milk. An hour later they were at Louis' place drinking real coffee. As they talked Cattoir realised that Fleury was too agitated and worked up to be able to deal calmly with the Germans.

'Would you like me to come with you to the Gestapo place?'

Fleury shook his head dismissively. 'No. I'll go alone.' He looked at his watch and then back at Cattoir. 'How do I get there?'

Cattoir found one of Louis' blank delivery notes and sketched out the route to 'Les Lavandes'. Fleury studied it and then slipped it into his pocket. As he stood up Cattoir saw the desolation on the man's face and suddenly he had an idea.

'Sit down a moment, I've had an idea.'

When Fleury was sitting, Cattoir said, 'It shouldn't be just you. It ought to be a delegation. You, her father, me, an influential local man with contacts in Berlin as well as Paris. And the mayor.'

'Why should the mayor speak up for Paulette and risk his standing with the Germans?'

Cattoir smiled. 'Because he knows that if he doesn't he won't get a single vote at the next election. I'll see to that. And he's a very ambitious man.' He stood up. 'I'll be back as soon as I can.'

Cattoir's meeting with the mayor had been brief and to the point but the fear of losing his sinecure was even greater than his fear of facing the Germans, and the three of them set off in Cattoir's car to 'Les Lavandes'.

The beautiful house was swathed in bougainvillea, the sunlight glinting on the leaded windows and several large, terracotta urns planted with geraniums, were spaced along the patio. The barbed wire and the guards looked even more barbarian than Cattoir had imagined they would be.

A sergeant stood at the narrow gap in the wire, a sub-machine-gun cradled along one arm. In rough French he said, 'Nobody permitted to enter.'

Without comment Fleury handed him the official letter which the German read slowly and carefully. Then he looked at Fleury, pointing at the letter.

'Are you this man?'

'Yes.' And Fleury nodded.

For a moment the sergeant hesitated and then waved to a man in SS uniform and shouted for him to get one of the officers.

The three of them waited without speaking and then a man came out of the house and walked slowly over to the guard and the three visitors.

It was von Bayer and he nodded to Cattoir as he took the letter from the sergeant. He read it carefully and then looked at Cattoir.

'What is this all about, Monsieur?'

'I understand that you have detained a Mademoiselle Fleury. This gentleman is her father. And this other gentleman is the Mayor of Brantôme. We require an explanation of why Mademoiselle Fleury is detained. And I am here as the senior French citizen in this area.'

Von Bayer shook his head slowly. 'I am no longer the commander of this unit. Oberfuehrer Kraus is now in command. It is he you will have to talk to.'

Cattoir said quietly, 'I think it would be wise for the Oberfuehrer to see us, Herr Oberst.'

Von Bayer looked away for a moment towards the rolling fields that surrounded the house. Then he spoke to the guard who stood aside and waved them through the opening in the wire.

Von Bayer said quietly, 'Follow me.'

Inside the entrance-hall he signalled for them to wait and knocked on a door at the far end of a narrow corridor.

They waited for ten minutes before von Bayer came out and signalled to them to join him. He held the door open and a man sitting at a desk looked them over as von Bayer closed the door and joined them.

The man at the desk had draped his uniform jacket over the back of his chair and his rolled up sleeves showed his hairy, muscular arms. He was in his fifties and Cattoir guessed that he was probably recruited into the Gestapo from the Kriminalpolizei. He was obviously physically strong, with the jowls and flab that wrestlers often developed. His eyes were grey and hard and his voice was loud and harsh as he pointed at the letter on his desk.

'What's this shit all about? Which one of you is Fleury?'

Fleury said, 'I'm Fleury. I understand you have arrested my daughter. I should like to know what offence you allege she has committed.'

'And who are you?' The German said to the mayor.

'My name is Jean-Paul Roux. I am the elected mayor of Brantôme.'

Kraus turned to von Bayer. 'Show this fool out.'

When von Bayer hesitated for a moment Kraus smashed his fist on the table. 'Now. Get him out of my sight.'

When von Bayer came back Kraus leaned forward, elbows on the table as he looked at Fleury.

'Listen – you're treading on very thin ice here. I have no need to explain what my people do to anybody. I *am* the law. No Frenchman, no German even, can question my actions.' He paused. 'If I did not know that you are permanently in Paris I would arrest you too as a possible accessory to your daughter's criminal actions.'

'What criminal actions?' Fleury burst out angrily.

'Don't shout at me, my friend. Your daughter is held as a terrorist. Working for Germany's enemies. We have her radio transmitter which she used to receive her orders from London. She is an accomplice of people who have murdered our soldiers and attacked our troops and communications. And if you are contacted by any of her fellow-terrorists tell them from me that they will be shown no mercy.'

'Where is my daughter? Can I speak to her?'

'Your daughter is on her way to a labour camp in Germany, my friend.'

'Which labour camp?'

'That's a matter for Berlin.' He grinned. 'Once we've squeezed them dry I don't care which garbage bag they put them in.' He paused and pointed a stubby finger at Fleury. 'As for you, if you're not out of this area in forty-eight hours I'll have you arrested.'

Fleury was trembling with anger as he said, 'There's a German word that describes you perfectly – *Arschloch*.'

Cattoir put a restraining hand on Fleury's arm and turned to von Bayer. He said very quietly and slowly, 'I shall not forget this episode Graf von Bayer. When it is all over it will be accounted for. Believe me. You and your companions are having your little day now but your turn will come. I'll see to that.'

He led Fleury to the door and von Bayer followed them. As he accompanied them down the path to the gap in the wire von Bayer whispered to Cattoir, 'I'll come up and talk to you this evening. Will you be there?'

Cattoir nodded but didn't speak, his arm around Fleury's shoulders as they walked to the car. Nobody spoke as Cattoir drove them back to Louis's place.

Fleury declined the offer of a meal at Louis's place and said that he would drive straight back to Paris to see if any of his friends there could find out where Paulette had been sent.

Cattoir told Bailey and Louis what had happened at the Gestapo house and then drove back to the manor house with Bailey.

They sat together later in Cattoir's study, as the light began to fade and it was Cattoir who said aloud what Bailey had been thinking.

'They obviously didn't break her?'

Bailey nodded, 'I agree. But why are you so sure?'

'Because that bastard would have us all by now if she did.' He paused. 'Stop thinking about it. There's nothing you can do.'

'D'you think Fleury can do anything?'

'No. The people in Paris have got their backs to the wall. I heard from a contact of mine in Paris that all those Krauts who can wangle a posting back in Germany are heading there fast. I listened to the BBC news last night. They'll be in Paris in three to four weeks. The suspicion in Paris is that Hitler has already issued orders that if they have to evacuate Paris the city must be razed to the ground as a lesson to the French.'

Bailey sighed and stood up. 'I'd better see how Jenny is doing.'

Von Bayer came late in the evening and Cattoir was cold but polite as he showed him into the sitting room. When von Bayer was seated, Cattoir offered him a glass of wine which the German sipped cautiously before he spoke.

'I apologise, Monsieur Cattoir for the exhibition today and for the reason for your visit.'

Cattoir looked at him coldly. 'Did they really send her to a labour camp or did they torture the girl and kill her?'

'She was brutally treated but she wasn't killed. But the camp she was sent to is an extermination camp.'

'Where is it?'

'In Poland. Oświęcim. Auschwitz in German. She was in a bad state when they sent her away.' He sighed deeply. 'She may not have lived to see the camp.' He paused. 'This would not have happened if you had accepted my offer of a sort of truce. The destruction of the train and then the telephone system was too much for Berlin to stomach. I accept my share of the blame for what my fellow German has done. It disgusts me.'

'How did they get on to her?'

'The phones in her newspaper office were monitored. They picked her up the night before you destroyed the system.'

'Not me, von Bayer. I'm not a hero. But I'm sure you didn't come here just to apologise.'

'That's true. I've got a problem. I'd like your advice.'

'Go on.'

'I don't know if you know that my brother who was a career officer, a senior officer on Rommel's and Model's staff, was executed after the bomb plot against Adolf Hitler.'

'Yes, you told me yourself. *Was* he part of the plot?'

'No. He knew nothing about it. But in his official capacity he had criticised Hitler's handling of military matters. It's been a well-kept secret that Rommel himself was given the choice of public disgrace or suicide. He chose suicide at his home. All he had done was to criticise the handling of the war.' He sighed. 'I went back to my home to deal with my brother's ashes and to sign various papers.' He looked at Cattoir. 'While I was there I looked through some of my old show-jumping magazines and trophies, and I saw a photograph of a girl I knew in the old days. Our families were good friends.' He paused. 'I realised then that I'd seen her here the first time I visited you. She was riding a horse in the woods. I thought I knew her face but I couldn't place her. Her name was Jenny Campbell and she was in the British junior jumping team. I was in the German team at the same time. She's been many times to my home, and I've been to hers.' He paused and looked at Cattoir's face. 'What do I do about her?'

For long moments Cattoir was silent, and then he said, 'What are you thinking of doing?'

'She's in the Resistance, isn't she?'

'Tell me about Paulette. Paulette Fleury. How did they treat her, your Gestapo colleagues?'

Von Bayer shrugged. 'Badly, I'm afraid. They were desperate to make her talk so that they could round up the others.'

'What part did you play in this?'

'I had to interpret because nobody else could speak French fluently. I protested but I have no standing any longer with those people.'

'Why stay with them? Why not apply for a transfer?'

'My orders were to stay. I'm a German officer and an order is an order. In any case if I asked for a transfer I would probably be arrested as an enemy of the State. Just like my brother Siegfried. They have long and spiteful memories, the Nazis.'

'You didn't answer my question. What do you want to do about the girl you think you recognised?'

'You know as well as I do what I should do.'

'Say it. Say it out loud.'

'I should have her arrested and questioned. I know for certain that she is English not French. If she is innocent why is she here in France pretending to be French?' Von Bayer seemed embarrassed by what he said. 'I thought maybe you could persuade her to move away from here. I could get her permits and documents to cover a move.'

'And if she refuses?'

'I should feel I had done all I could to protect her and that she would have to take her chance with the others.'

'But you wouldn't betray her to your Gestapo friends?'

'How could I do that? We were children together. We loved horses and riding. Our parents were good friends. We spent Christmases together.'

'But now she's an enemy.'

Von Bayer shook his head. 'She's not my enemy any more than I am her enemy. We just happen to be on different sides in a war that was made by other people. It seems almost fated that even our rôles in a war should be almost the same. She liked Germany and I liked England.' He shrugged his despair. 'We're just people.'

Cattoir sat looking at von Bayer. To the Frenchman the German epitomised the total stupidity of the war. A decent man whose life had been distorted by others. A man whose incoherent words still illuminated the truth.

'It's *Max* von Bayer isn't it?'

Von Bayer nodded. 'Yes.'

'Well, my friend Max. You and I share some secrets that would do both of us, and some other people, a lot of harm.' He paused and leaned forward. 'So. I suggest we both hold on to our secrets. And with a bit of luck we might all survive this wretched war. I respect your honesty and your integrity in talking to me. I won't forget it and I shall bear it in mind no matter what happens from now on with our respective colleagues. We are like two people who've been badly cast in a film. You belong with your horses, and I belong . . .' he smiled, '. . . with my books and music and other pursuits of a non-committed dilettante.' He paused and held out his hand. 'Agreed?'

Von Bayer reached out and took Cattoir's hand in both of his. 'Agreed.' He paused. 'You're not as old as he was but you remind me of my father. He could never understand why a whole nation could let a handful of men decide that there would be a war. He used to quote Schiller – "*Mit der Dummheit kaempfen Goetter selbst vergebens*" – against stupidity the gods themselves struggle in vain.' Von Bayer stood up, looking at his watch and then at Cattoir. 'I'd better go. You know where I am if you needed to contact me.'

Cattoir stood at the window in his bedroom, the curtains pulled aside so that he could look out towards Bergerac. There were no lights because of the black-out but there were searchlights and tracers from anti-aircraft batteries between Bergerac and Bordeaux. He wasn't sure that he should tell Bailey about his meeting with von Bayer. He needed to think about it. But there was a word that von Bayer used that stuck in his mind. He'd said 'if you *needed* to contact me' not 'if you *wanted* to contact me.' It was surely a hint that he would be willing to help if he could.

CHAPTER 41

In the next few days the Gestapo had arrested five or six people, none of them part of the network, but they had been interrogated brutally for even for smallest clue as to who the Resistance people were. When nothing was revealed because nothing was known, some of them were released but at least three were designated as enemies of the state and sent to labour camps as a lesson to the population who were now openly hostile to all the Germans in the area and particularly the Gestapo.

On Tuesday, August 15, the Allied 7th Army landed on the French Mediterranean coast between Nice and Toulon. And on the same day Violette was stopped in her van on the main road from Bergerac to Ribérac. She was on a quite innocent journey to a farm at a small cluster of cottages called La Garde where they had a cow due to calve.

The patrol was four men and an officer. The officer was in a black uniform with Gestapo insignia. As he looked through Violette's permits and identity documents, one of the soldiers stood grinning in at the cab window. He said something in German and she shook her head to indicate that she didn't understand him. He laughed and reached in the open window and closed his hand round her left breast. Without thinking she hit him across the face with the back of her hand. He roared in anger, flung open the door and dragged her out. She fell on to her knees on to the road and a hand grabbed her hair, dragging her along on her back. She screamed for help and she heard them laughing. Hands lifted her up, and she was thrown into the back of a truck. There were two of them in the back of the truck as it bounced along the country road, and as she struggled to sit up a boot smashed into her ribs and she fell back, faint from the pain and only half-conscious.

When she came to she was sitting on a chair, her hands tied behind the chair back and her legs knotted to the chair legs. The big man who was slapping her face as he shouted at her was asking her in almost unrecognisable French what she was doing driving without a permit and with forged identity documents. He kept calling her a terrorist, asking who her friends were who attacked German soldiers. Where did she live? Why did she have drugs in her vehicle.

As the hours went by she lost all sense of time. Two or three different men interrogated her. But remembering her training she said nothing.

The next day it was obvious that they had found something that convinced them that she really was a terrorist. They talked about traces of blood on the wooden floor of her van and they mentioned the names of SOE people in London and at Beaulieu. One day she was left completely alone except for a guard who brought her a bottle of water and a bowl of some sort of soup. She guessed by then that she was at the Gestapo house and several times she had heard the throaty barking of German Shepherds. She wondered if Karl knew that she was there and if he might help her in some way. But she knew in her heart that there would be no help.

The Wehrmacht had rigged up a telephone service for its own use but the first call received by Oberfuehrer Kraus wasn't good news. That day, August 20, Resistance forces had taken over Toulouse and set fire to the oil refinery at Douai.

When he went down the stairs to the basement where they had built makeshift cells for the flow of prisoners he checked them one by one, leaving the girl till last. There were six prisoners at the house and four in the cells at the police-station. All he had got from them was a dozen or so names, none of which had been even vaguely useful. But the girl was different. He was sure she was part of the local resistance. They'd made her scream but she hadn't said a word. If she hadn't been trained she'd have said something just to stop the pain. A pack of lies maybe, but something.

He stood looking at her lying on the three planks that had been put together as a bed. Her face was swollen and there was dried blood from her nose in a trail down to her neck. She was half naked and one knee was swollen out of shape and there were weals across her · stomach and thighs. He shook her roughly by the shoulders but she was still unconscious, and even her groan of pain was barely audible.

As he walked back up to his office he decided to phone Paris. Let them decide.

None of the men he knew in Paris was available to take his call and when he had insisted on somebody making a decision he had been told to let all the prisoners go. To destroy all his local records and if he really thought the girl was important she should be sent up to Paris immediately.

Bailey was walking through the market with Jenny when a small boy told him that Louis wanted to speak to him urgently at the shop.

Louis was in the kitchen at the back and he waved to them to sit down.

'They've got Vi. They've had her for five days.'

'How do you know?'

'She hadn't collected the scraps for her dog and I took them to her place. There was a young German there and the place had been searched and wrecked. I practically strangled him to find out what had happened. He said he'd given her a dog. A German Shepherd. He looked after the dogs at the Gestapo place. When he found out that they'd got Vi, he'd waited for a chance to take the dog back. He said he was a friend of hers.'

'Did he say what had happened to her?'

Louis nodded. 'Yes. They beat her up.'

'We must get her out, Louis. No matter what it takes. How many men can you get together in a couple of hours?'

'She's not here now. They took her to Paris during the night and they've released the other prisoners.'

'If they've taken her to Paris it means either that she's talking and they want to interrogate her there or it means she hasn't talked but they're sure she's worth the time of top operators.'

'The BBC news said that Marseille had been taken and so had Melun, which is only half an hour or so south of Paris. They should be taking Paris in the next two or three days.'

Bailey looked at Jenny. 'We must get back so we can contact London and see if our forward troops can do anything to find her.' He turned to Louis. 'She'll be at Gestapo HQ in Paris or in Fresnes prison. Have you got people in Paris who could do something?'

'I've got no way to contact them. No telephone, no radio link and the Germans are still holding out between here and Orléans. . They're not letting anyone through.'

Bailey nodded. 'OK. I'll try and keep in touch.' He turned to Jenny. 'Let's go.'

Bailey wrote out and encoded a long report and request for assistance in Paris and asked for additional schedules. At least six schedules every twenty-four hours. London had agreed and had asked for reports on local civilian morale and current disposition of any German troops.

In the north town after town was falling to the remorseless advance of Allied troops and in Paris the German Military Governor and General Speidel, commander of all German forces in France, were negotiating secretly with the Swedish Consul-General, Raoul Nordling, for a compromise that would mean if the planned Resistance uprising in Paris did not take place, the city would not be destroyed despite Hitler's personal orders.

The French 2nd Armoured Division was fighting its way towards the city and sustaining heavy losses of men and tanks as it advanced against the German defences, until finally on August 25 in the left-luggage office of the Gare Montparnasse General Choltitz surrendered the city intact to the Allies despite Hitler's orders. It was hard to realise that despite the taking of Paris the war in the rest of France was still being waged with the desperate ferocity of a Wehrmacht and SS that was just beginning to realise that the fighting wasn't going to end at the French frontier. The tanks and the artillery were heading for the Fatherland. After years of easy conquest it didn't seem credible that it might be their turn now to be the losers.

On August 26 General de Gaulle marched with units of the French Army and the Resistance down the Champs-Elysées. But outside Paris the Allied advance ground to a halt for want of fuel.

There had been virtually no survivors from the SOE networks in and around Paris. The intensified efforts of the Gestapo had been largely successful in wiping them out.

It was the intelligence officer from the FFI, Forces Françaises de l'Intérieur, who had scoured the Paris prisons and Gestapo quarters for signs of Resistance survivors and it was he who found Violette in a solitary cell in Fresnes prison. There was one sure but sorry way to pick out Gestapo victims. They always bore signs of torture and beatings.

By August 29 the intelligence officer, Gaston Tapier, had traced seven members of the Resistance and two 'possibles'. It was the girl who was the problem. The doctor from the FFI had diagnosed at least two broken ribs, severe bruising on both legs, face and neck, severe dehydration and almost certain internal injuries in the area of the abdomen and skull. The girl had been fed intravenously all through the first night and the coma seemed to have been broken when she opened her eyes for a few moments at midday. A nurse had stayed with her continuously and she had called the doctor when the girl opened her eyes and tried to move her body in the early evening. By the next day there was considerable improvement in the girl's condition. The doctor would not let her be moved to hospital until she was capable of describing what had happened in case moving her caused internal bleeding.

There had been no prison records kept during the week before the German surrender because the prison staff were in a state of panic, fearing that they might be classed as collaborators. Which of course they were.

When Tapier sat with the girl he was sure she could now at least hear his questions. He was very gentle in his questioning but the girl would turn her head away whenever he spoke. He had tried to get her to nod or shake her head in response to his questions but she didn't respond in any way.

It was the doctor who provided the first tentative clue. He pointed out to Tapier that although several of her teeth had been broken there were three teeth with established fillings. And all these fillings were English-style fillings. He pointed out also that SOE had been notified of this give-away and fillings of SOE operatives had been subsequently changed to continental-style fillings. This meant that if she was English and SOE she must have been in France for about three years. Why not check with the British on missing SOE women.

Only two names came back. One was Violette Crowther, cover-name Violette Rémy. Arrested in Brantôme by Gestapo and believed transferred to Fresnes prison in Paris. SOE London were ready to send somebody who knew the person if it was thought necessary. The missing woman had an appendix scar seven years old and a heart-shaped birthmark under her left armpit.

The young woman in the cell corresponded on both counts with the identification. SOE London were notified immediately and Dickie

Fuller was in Paris the next day. Up to the time when he stood looking down on the rag-doll that was called Violette Crowther, code-name Rémy, he had seen the Germans as ruthless opponents but he hadn't hated them. But he hated them then, not just as Germans but as men who could do such things to a young woman. Gaston Tapier had noticed the tears on the older man's face. But he shed no tears himself. He had seen many other bodies like that. And it wasn't always Germans who had done it. He sympathised with the Englishman and envied him the kind of war that had left him so innocent. A planner, not a doer.

When Bailey had decoded London's message asking him to arrange a landing for a Lysander to pick up Jenny in two days' time, he had pointed out that that would leave him without a radio operator. London responded that a relief operator would be sent on the Lysander. Irritated that his existing problems were being made worse by London, he asked what his function would be in the changed circumstances, both locally and in the Allied drive to the German frontier. London obviously recognised his aggravation and listed new responsibilities. The Gestapo units were to be kept under surveillance and when the situation allowed he was to arrest all of them in conjunction with the local police. London also wanted daily reports on local morale and reaction to the likely end of the fighting in France. But London pointed out that the Germans were still defending Caen and along most of the Seine.

The arrangements for the landing were simple now that the Germans were beginning to lose their grip on the area but Jenny had been in tears at having to leave him on his own. The new radio operator was a Frenchman called Albert Louissier, a Seychellois who had long experience in clandestine radio communications. Cheerful and willing, he settled in quickly and efficiently. But Bailey still resented London's removal of Jenny without any explanation at a time when the network was beginning to fall apart.

With the Luftwaffe no longer capable of patrolling the skies of Kent and Sussex, the Lysander landed at RAF Tangmere without any problems. She walked across the runway with the pilot and then across the grass that was wet with dew. It was getting light and she could see the silhouette of the cluster of buildings.

The pilot said, 'There's somebody from SOE waiting for you in the Officers' Mess.'

'Who is it?'

The pilot smiled. 'They never tell us people's names. I don't even know your name.'

He leaned forward and opened a door, pushing aside the black-out curtain inside and for a moment the bright lights were too much for her eyes. Then she saw him standing by the table, smiling, and she was a little girl again.

'Daddy.' His arms went round her, holding her tight, one hand stroking her hair as she rested her head on his shoulder. He lifted her chin. 'You look very thin, my dear. How was the flight?'

She laughed. 'I've no idea. I slept most of the way.' She paused. 'I can smell the sea.'

'It's only a mile away.'

'Where is this?'

'RAF Tangmere. Just outside Chichester.' He paused. 'I've got a car and driver, are you up to the ride back to London?'

She laughed. 'Of course I am.'

As they drove past the guard-room he said, 'How's Harry?'

'He's rather down. I hated leaving him. Why have I been recalled?'

'But he's been doing so well. Why down?'

'Well . . .'

He cut her off and pointed briefly to the driver. 'Let's save it till you're home.'

She shrugged. 'OK. Where shall I be staying?'

'At home. At the flat.'

'God. I am tired, you know.'

He put his arm round her. 'Just snuggle up and sleep. I'll wake you up when we go past the Savoy.'

She laughed softly and closed her eyes. As she slept he looked at her face. She was still as pretty as ever but there were dark shadows under her eyes and he noticed that she was wearing a ring on the third finger of her left hand. She didn't go in for jewellery and he wondered if it was significant. It seemed incredible that a few hours ago she had been standing in some field in France waiting for the plane. Not his daughter but the radio operator of an SOE network that was being hunted down by the Gestapo.

As they came over Waterloo Bridge and turned into the Strand he stroked her face and she jumped away, startled. '*Qu'est ce qu'il y a?*' She didn't seem to recognise him and then she relaxed. 'Sorry. I didn't know what was happening.'

He nodded. 'We're just getting to your old stamping-ground.' And a minute later they passed the Savoy. She laughed softly and waved her hand.

They had breakfast at the Dorchester and as they drank their coffee he said, 'I've got a rather unpleasant task for you. We had a meeting about it and the doctors said that maybe you could help.'

'What is it?' She said quickly. 'Is it Moma?'

'No. It's a friend of yours, Violette Crowther.'

She was stunned. 'But the Gestapo have got her. They sent her to Paris for interrogation.'

'I know. But the Free French found her. In Fresnes prison.'

'Oh, my God. How marvellous.'

'I'm afraid not. She has been beaten up badly. Bones broken, internal injuries and so on. And she's in a state of trauma. She won't talk to anyone. Dickie Fuller went over to Paris to see her but it didn't help. The doctors said that someone like you might be able to help. She's obviously had a terrible time and we want to help her recover.' He paused. 'Will you help?'

'Of course I will. Where is she?'

'She's in St Thomas's in a private room being artificially fed and medicated. She sleeps a lot but she wakes up from time to time. But she doesn't respond to anything or anybody.'

'Let me freshen up at the flat and then I'll go and see her.'

'That's fine. There's just one more thing.'

'What's that?'

'Don't ask about our house.'

'Why not?'

He sighed. 'It was hit by a V2 about two weeks ago. It's mostly just a heap of rubble. It upset your Ma a lot.'

'I bet it did. It upsets me too.'

'It's just a building, sweetie. Just a building. The government will have to pay for it to be rebuilt.'

'So when can I see Vi?'

'Now, if you want.'

'OK. Let's go.'

*   *   *

The doctor recommended that she saw Violette alone and her father had gone to his office.

She stood with the doctor outside the door of the room.

'It's difficult to help her much at the moment. Touching her seems to bring on immediate signs of stress.'

'What's actually wrong physically?'

'Two broken ribs. Double fractures. A dozen or so burns. Looks like cigarette burns. Heavy bruising on her torso, face and legs. Both little-fingers broken. And her mouth is a hell of a mess. Looks like she sustained a blow on the upper jaw with a hard object. Four teeth missing and the others are broken. We'll have to reconstruct the whole mouth.'

'And what do you want me to do?'

'Sit with her. Talk to her about pleasant things.' He shrugged. 'Just see how she responds.'

She took a deep breath. 'Let's hope I can do some good.'

'You may be a bit shocked by her appearance. Have you ever seen dead or severely injured people before?'

She looked at him amazed and then realised he had no idea what her work was or even what had caused Vi's state. He hadn't been told as a matter of security. To him she was a badly injured patient with psychological problems.

'Yes, I have, doctor.' She put her hand on the doorknob. 'Shall I go in?'

'Yes, do. There's a bell-push by the bedside table. Ring if you need anything and ring for a nurse when you need a break or you're leaving. I'd be grateful if you can see me when you do leave, no matter what time it is. I'm on call round the clock. Rhys Jones.' He paused. 'By the way. She may have been sexually assaulted but we don't know for sure.' He nodded. 'Just a possibility to bear in mind.'

The room was all white, walls, floor-tiles and ceiling and the midday sun cast deep, sharp shadows across the bed from the stands that were arranged around the head of the bed. There were tubes and wires taped all over the body on the bed and she burst into tears as she looked at the sorry figure under the clean white sheets.

She quietly pulled up the chair beside the bed and reached out to touch the hand with its plastered fingers. She was almost certain she heard a sigh from the inert figure on the bed. Then she talked

271

quietly, in French, of the streets in Bergerac and Brantôme, watching Vi's bruised face as she talked. Several times in the course of the afternoon Vi had opened her eyes and slightly turned her head towards Jenny, but that was all.

It was 8 p.m. when she spoke to the doctor who seemed surprised and encouraged that there had been any response so soon.

She took a taxi back to the flat and it seemed strange to feel loved and cared for again. She knew that Harry Bailey both loved and cared for her, but their life together was too disjointed and complex for it to have any effect. In the field it was better that way. Any other way could magnify their actual vulnerability.

Helen Campbell had been warned not to ask about Jenny's life in the Resistance or about the reason for her visit, so they talked about clothes coupons, food coupons, and petrol coupons. And her mother's job at the Forces Club in Piccadilly Circus. It reminded her of scenes in one of those Ralph Lynn and Tom Wells farces at the Aldwych.

As she lay in bed that night she thought about Vi and her own mother. Her mother cut off from any real news about her and now looking much older than she had expected. Hesitant as she talked and all that self-assurance gone. And poor Vi lying there with all her senses closed to the world. And that abused body, a heart-breaking reminder of what SOE and the war were really about. For the first time she realised why Harry Bailey had found it so hard to relax and so hard to smile. She wondered if he even knew that Vi had been found and why she had been recalled to London.

It was on the third day that the change came. She had taken her portable gramophone and some records to the hospital and she'd played some Tino Rossi and some Charles Trenet records. It was when Charles Trenet was singing '*Il pleut dans ma chambre*' that Vi stirred and tried to sit up. Her eyes still seemed focused on something far away but she turned her head slowly to look at Jenny. And then she spoke haltingly and her voice was slurred. 'I feel funny. I can't see properly. Who is it?'

'It's me – Jenny.' And she was crying as she leaned over to kiss Vi. 'Oh Vi, oh Vi, I'm so glad.'

POSTSCRIPT

CHAPTER 42

To most fighting soldiers, British, American, German and Russian, the war was never going to end. It was too much to imagine how it would end. And when the end came it was after a week of shocks and destruction that were a kind of madness, a nightmare that defied belief, tragedy and destruction on a scale that was too much to absorb.

On Monday, April 30 Hitler and Eva Braun committed suicide in the Fuehrerbunker beneath the Reichs Chancellery in Berlin. On Wednesday, May 2 Stalin's Order of the Day No.359 said: 'Troops of the 1st Byelorussian Front, commanded by Marshal Zhukov . . . have today, May 2, completely captured Berlin . . . hotbed of German aggression.' And on May 4 in a tent on Lüneberg Heath, Admiral von Friedeburg and General Kunzel signed the surrender of all German forces in NW Germany, Holland and Denmark.

And suddenly there was a silence all over Europe while victors and losers tried to absorb what had happened. German cities were now just heaps of rubble and the stench of decomposing bodies hung like a grim mist over everywhere. It was a time that was going to be hard to forget, and even harder to remember.

Oberfuehrer Kraus had deserted with several others in Paris and Max von Bayer had been transferred to a Panzer Division defending Köln and was taken prisoner two days before Germany surrendered. He was taken with thousands of other prisoners to a camp ten miles outside the city. He was held for a year in the POW camp and after several interrogations and investigations of his wartime background, he was tried as a war criminal at one of the minor courts. A character reference from a Frenchman, Paul Cattoir, was favourable enough for him to be found not guilty. He returned to his father's estate but lacked his father's devotion to history and custom. He left the running of the estate to a manager and spent his time on building up the stables and blood-lines again. He was not loved or genuinely respected by the staff, many of whom had been there when he was a boy. It seemed that even Germans were afraid of Gestapo officers, even ex-Gestapo officers, and opinions were all too obviously divided as to whether poor Siegfried was a hero or a traitor. Now you could buy a Knight's Cross, even with oak leaves, for a carton of cigarettes.

As the years went by public memories faded, he was appointed manager of the West German Equestrian team. But when the team was due to compete in England the front page of a London newspaper had a headline that said: 'Gestapo man leads German come-back', and von Bayer resigned his honorary appointment.

In his private life he was much sought after by the daughters of wealthy Americans and a little less wealthy Frenchmen, and he rather enjoyed the social round. His name was linked, in the gossip columns, with various attractive young women and eventually he married a Hungarian girl. A talented, lively actress from the Städtische Bühne in Hildesheim. They had two daughters and without realising it, or intending it, the Graf von Bayer was making his family a small enclave, a duty-free zone from the rest of the world.

When Paul-Henri Fleury stood on the office balcony watching General de Gaulle walking down the Champs-Elysées with his Free French soldiers and their retinue of fighters from the *maquis* and the FFI, it was all too reminiscent of the years before when the marchers wore field-grey uniforms, and looked like real soldiers, not a mob whose minds were already eager for revenge.

After two weeks of seeing women having their heads shaved and men being beaten up in the streets with crowds shouting obscenities, he knew it was time for him to move out.

The wind was blowing the few receding strands of Louis' hair as he got out of his car and walked up the stone steps to the manor house. Cattoir was talking on the phone in the hallway and he smiled and waved to Louis, pointing to the open door of the sitting room. But Louis ignored the sign and waited until Cattoir hung up the phone.

Cattoir walked over to him, his smile changing to a frown. 'What's wrong?'

Louis handed him a piece of paper and Cattoir looked at it. Written in ink were the words: 'Tell Cattoir'. And there were marks where the paper had been pinned to something.

Cattoir still frowning, looked at Louis. 'What is it, Louis? I don't understand. What does it mean, "Tell Cattoir"?'

'Some kids were looking for apples and they went to the small orchard at Paulette's cottage. They found a body hanging from one of the trees. It had this pinned to the jacket.' He paused. 'The police came to me because they knew I knew Paulette. I went up there with the police. It was Paulette's father.'

'Good God.' He was silent for long moments and then he said, 'Why this paper?'

'He only knew you and me. But he didn't know my name. He guessed somebody would have to identify him. I've spoken to the priest but he won't bury a suicide on consecrated ground.'

Softly, Cattoir said, 'The bloody old hypocrite.' He paused. 'We'll bury him here in the family plot and we'll put up a headstone for him and Paulette. Is there any other family?'

'I think there's a mother. A singer. A collaborator. They hadn't been in touch since she left the father. I should forget her.'

'Speak to old Masson for me. Get him to lay out the body and fix up a coffin and bring him up here.'

Louis nodded. 'We're the only two left here who know what went on.' He sighed deeply. 'I sometimes wonder if it really did happen.'

Cattoir smiled. 'I hear it's certain you'll be the new mayor.'

'Not till next month. And then I'll make the bloody town start working again.'

'I heard that the President will be touring the area next month. Shaking hands and giving out medals. I've been in touch with Harry Bailey and Jenny. They said they'd come over, for old times' sake.'

The President's stop in Bergerac was planned for an hour. It was a crisp autumn day with bright sunshine and the President had waved away the local dignitaries. It was just himself and an equerry with the purple velvet cushion and the container with the medals in their leather cases.

There were three lines of men, a dozen in each column and ample space between for the President to carry out his inspection. Slowly he moved along the lines, exchanging a few words with each man, handing him his Cross of the Liberation and moving on. Cattoir, Louis, Jenny and Bailey were the last in the back row. Cattoir got his few words and a *Chevalier de la Légion d'honneur*. And then the President walked past the other three. No handshake, no decoration and no chat. It was a spiteful man's way to show his hatred for the English and for Communists.

Cattoir sent his decoration back to the Elysée Palace with an angry letter and Louis Maurois was elected mayor two weeks later with an overwhelming majority over his Gaullist rival.

The war had been over for a year before Vi was released from hospital and she went back home to work part-time in her stepfather's veterinary practice. But more and more often she went back to see her mother's elderly relatives on the small farm in France. And eventually she gave up the struggle. She was not at home in England although she liked the people. Her home was France and that was where she wanted to be.

With her accumulated back-pay and her service gratuity she had enough money to buy a place in France. She had no doubts about where she wanted to be and she spent a month looking for a place in Brantôme. It took another month to conclude the formalities. The property was on three floors and the part at street level already had a tenant installed with a small business in artists' materials. There was a separate door and stairs to the two upper floors and one floor was enough for her accommodation and a small-animal surgery. The third floor was one large area with a polished wooden floor and big windows. She kept it in reserve. She wasn't sure what for but the decision fitted her prudent nature.

She saw a lot of Paul Cattoir both as a client and as a friend and with his recommendation and her old contacts she made a good living and lived well. She ate out most days and entertained regularly. Just two or three friends or a family.

Louis threw a party for her thirtieth birthday at the hotel. And that was where she met Pierre Daudet.

Daudet was thirty-five and an artist and quite unlike Violette Crowther. He undoubtedly had a talent for landscapes in an Impressionist style. Somewhere between Alfred Sisley and Camille Pissarro. He always laughed at such comparisons for he was a modest man but his paintings sold readily and he lived a happy, carefree life.

They fell in love at first sight and neither they nor anyone else could explain what caused the instant recognition of a soul-mate. And interested observers wondered whether the man would turn the rather earnest young woman into a bohemian or the young woman bring the rather feckless artist nearer to earth. In fact, they both stayed much the same and entirely happy with the other's characteristics.

They married six months after that first meeting and the church was packed with friends and acquaintances. It was a happy day.

Daudet knew from Louis that Vi had been involved with the Resistance during the war but that was all he knew. Vi herself had never mentioned anything about it.

When the shop tenant moved out, they turned the shop into a gallery for Pierre's work. It was about this time when he started painting pictures of domestic interiors with people. He portrayed realistically the daily life of ordinary French people, usually with some sort of vague moral message. The first Paris review described them sarcastically as 'even more banal than a Norman Rockwell *Saturday Evening Post* cover'. It wasn't an inaccurate description and the price of a Pierre Daudet interior trebled in months. And a condescending and disparaging review from some Parisian Berenson was enough to ensure support from everywhere outside the capital, and when the paintings were of French rural life it was *lèse-majesté* indeed.

They had talked about whether or not to have children. Vi was strongly against it. Her experiences during the war were warning enough about the pressures that could be put on you because you loved a child. Pierre went along with her reasoning. He was not a natural-born father. He had sisters and brothers and he sometimes had second thoughts when he saw how delighted his nephews and nieces were to spend time with Tante Vi. And how easily she dealt with the small children as if they were puppies or kittens, patting and stroking as she doled out sugar lumps and sweets. But life wasn't all sugar lumps and sweeties.

CHAPTER 43

When the war in France was over and the Allies were fighting in Germany itself, Harry Bailey made his way back. He left from Bordeaux in a Royal Navy destroyer and landed several days later in Portsmouth, where he was met by Dickie Fuller and driven back to London.

There had been things to clear up and a visit to his parents in Birmingham. They deserved some explanation of why his letters had been so few. Before SOE agents were dropped in occupied or enemy territories they had to write before they left a dozen or so letters to their nearest and dearest. Letters that said nothing about where they were or what they were doing. The address was a Post Office Box that was controlled by SOE who also despatched the letters from the agent from time to time at their discretion. Bailey's letters had not been enough to cover his long time in France. They also censored the mail to the agent.

Dickie Fuller told him why Jenny had been recalled and about what had happened to Vi.

Bailey's first call the next day was to the hospital to see Vi. She was still very ill but the doctors were dealing with the damage piece by piece and they said that although she would always have problems with movement and posture, she would otherwise be able to live a normal life.

Sir Alistair had collected him from the hospital and taken him to the Reform for breakfast. As he poured the coffee Sir Alistair said, 'My daughter can't wait to see you. You've certainly made a conquest there. Makes you sound like a cross between Sir Galahad and Mahatma Gandhi.'

Bailey laughed. 'Doesn't sound too good a combination to me.'

'Well it is so far as Jenny is concerned.' He paused. 'And the very sincere thanks of my wife and me that you looked after her so well.' He put up his hand as he saw Bailey open his mouth to speak. 'I know, I know. You looked after them all very well. I wish every network had been as sensibly run.' He shrugged. 'Ah well. It's over now, thank God. Any idea what you want to do when you're released?'

'I haven't given it a thought, sir.'

'Well, there's time enough. I think you'll be held back for at least a year. I understand that they're thinking of sending you to Germany to collect all the information you can of Germans who misbehaved with SOE prisoners.'

Bailey shrugged. 'I'll do whatever I'm asked to do.' He smiled. 'I'd like to see Jenny as soon as it's possible.'

'She's staying with us at the flat. The family seat is a heap of rubble from a V2. I'm not sure that we shall want to go back even when it's been rebuilt.' He paused and smiled. 'I hope you don't mind but I've booked a table at the Savoy tonight for the four of us.'

Bailey laughed. 'She'll love that.'

And she did love it. Bailey in his barathea uniform and his major's crowns, and her in a gown that had to be hurriedly taken in that afternoon because she had lost weight. A few people came to their table to exchange pleasantries with Sir Alistair and Lady Campbell. They were introduced to the younger couple but the acknowledgements were perfunctory. There was no string of young men coming over to claim a dance but it was a pleasant evening. Bailey had been given a small flat near SOE headquarters in Baker Street.

When the Japanese surrendered on September 2, 1945 it was more a news item rather than a cause for the wild celebrations of VE day.

Harry Bailey and Jennifer Helen Campbell were married at Chelsea Registrar's Office on November 20, 1945 and rented a flat in King's Road, Chelsea. Four furnished rooms at what they felt was an extortionate rent of £7 a week plus rates.

By the end of November the old rivalry between MI6 and SOE culminated in the almost complete destruction by SIS of SOE's records. By then Harry Bailey had been transferred back into the Intelligence Corps and Jenny was working in the Foreign Office as assistant in one of the legal departments helping to clean up the affairs of the Free French in London.

Bailey was given a temporary posting as an observer at the Peace

Commission in Paris. Nobody told him what he was supposed to observe and nobody asked for his help or advice. At least nobody official did, but several American journalists plied him for his views on life in post-war Paris. One of them, Al Goldsmith, asked him to write a piece for his press agency and paid him four times what he earned in a week for one hour's work.

A week later Al Goldsmith phoned him and they met for coffee in Montmartre.

As the waiter put down the tray, Goldsmith paid him as he carried on talking to Bailey.

'I know it's Harry but do they call you Hal, Hank, Harold or what?'

Bailey laughed. 'It's just Harry.'

'How long you got to stay in the army, Harry?'

'I'm not sure. A few more months anyway.' He paused. 'Why are you asking?'

'The features guy at the agency, back in New York, was crazy about that piece you did about life today in Paris. It's been syndicated in thirty newspapers including the *Washington Post* and the *New York Times*. They want more.'

Bailey smiled. 'Officially I'm not allowed to write anything for publication while I'm still a serving officer.'

'They've got a proposition. They want a weekly piece from you. Not just about Paris, not even just about France. They think there's going to be a demand for news about the people of Europe.' He grinned. 'They've even got a title for it. "Letter from Europe". I'm authorised to do a deal right now. The money's good, you'd have a three-year contract with all the usual benefits. Travel and subsistence costs and no editorial interference.'

Bailey frowned. 'But why me? I wrote what I saw about ordinary people. No politics, no statistics. It was just like a letter to a friend back home.'

Goldsmith jabbed his arm with a finger. 'That's it, fellow. That's just what they want.'

'But anyone could do that.'

'You're crazy, man. You've got things, two things that others haven't got.'

'Tell me.'

'First, you're a trained observer of people, you understand small lives. And secondly, you can write.' He paused. 'We could give you a written offer of employment if that would help you get out of the army.' He finished off his drink. 'Are you interested?'

'Of course I am. I'm flattered. Are you sure they're right about all this? Me particularly?'

Goldsmith grinned. 'Those are hard old boys back in New York. They've been at it for years. They know what will sell. And I can assure you they ain't asking you for the sake of your blue eyes, pal.' He signalled for another drink and then looked at Bailey. 'So what do we do?'

'I'll say yes provided I can talk to my wife about it. She's due here tomorrow morning. And I'll check when the army will release me. I don't see any problem.' He smiled. 'Tell me about pay and conditions and all the rest of it.'

She came running towards him, hair flying and arms outstretched, oblivious of the other passengers on the platform. He took her to a café near the station for croissants and coffee. She listened intently as he told her about the American's proposition.

'Was that the piece you sent about *concierges* and postmen and little old ladies who made beautiful cocktail dresses in an afternoon?'

He laughed. 'Yes. That's the one. What did you think of it?'

'I thought it was wonderful. Made me wish I was with you in Paris.'

'So what do you think? Fifty pounds a week and all expenses paid. A decent apartment, travel and travel expenses.'

'Where would we live?'

'Anywhere we like, so long as it makes easy travel to cover Europe down to Spain and Greece.'

'Where do you think?' She paused. 'But not in Germany.'

'I can do Germany in weekly visits. They don't want an insider's view. They want an outside eye. It seems a bit unadventurous but I thought London was as good as anywhere as our base.'

'My parents would like that. They're scared that I could be going away again.' She paused and looked at him. 'Are you sure you don't want to stay on in the army? It seems to suit you.'

'I guess it does. But even a major-general doesn't get fifty quid a week and all expenses paid.'

She shrugged. 'So let's do it. If you're sure you want to.'

*   *   *

Six weeks later Bailey was out of the army but they kept on the same modest flat in King's Road. Bailey had made research trips to Rome, Berlin, Athens and frequent trips to France in the first year of his new job. He still found it almost incredible that he could earn good money just writing about people and places. But he realised that Americans had a kind of nostalgia for Europe. The generosity of the Marshall Plan that provided the funds to rebuild a battered Europe was matched by a yearning to get back to the old days before the war when Europe was 'going back home' for an older generation and the place Americans loved to visit. America too had its post-war problems and it was interesting to read how Europe was coping with the same problems. And Bailey's pieces were essentially about small people, not the famous.

When they heard from Vi that she was going back to Brantôme they were able to tell her of Jenny's pregnancy. And on September 3, 1948 Pauline was born and named after Paulette. By then Harry Bailey was an established writer and there was talk of publishing an anthology of a selection of his pieces with an introduction by Eleanor Roosevelt.

They spent a week with Cattoir in October and he gave a dinner for them and Louis and Violette. Bailey noticed that they didn't speak at all of old times but kept to what had happened subsequently. It was Cattoir who brought up the subject of de Gaulle. He looked first at Louis and then at Bailey.

'Have you both recovered from that ghastly ceremony with the President?'

Louis shrugged. 'A tall man – but a small man. If you won't shake hands with a Resistance man because he is a Communist then you insult the whole *maquis*. It didn't go unnoticed.' He turned to Bailey. 'What did you think, Harry?'

Bailey smiled. 'He came to London as a colonel, turned himself into a general overnight and demanded from his hosts money, assistance, understanding and respect.' He smiled. 'He got everything he asked for except respect. He was grateful for nothing and came back hating the English and Americans with a hate that bordered on mania. There's a lesson to be learned from that man of course.'

'Tell us the lesson,' Cattoir said quietly.

'I find it frightening that one man or a small group of men,

Russians, Germans, French or whoever, can decide the fate of millions of people who have no say in the matter. Can decide that just to demonstrate their power they can cause the deaths of millions of people who don't even know what it's all about.' He paused. 'I find that obscene.'

'But they got there by a democratic vote,' Cattoir said, but he was smiling as he said it.

'That's rubbish, Paul, and you know it. Stalin, Hitler and de Gaulle had no brief from their people to start wars.'

Louis said, 'It was the Nazis who started the war, my friend.'

Bailey shook his head. 'What you just said is part of the problem. If somebody wants to insult somebody or a group of people these days they call them Nazis or Fascists. A Nazi is or was just a member of the NSDAP, the German National Socialist Workers Party. Most of them joined the Party because they'd lose their jobs if they didn't. I've met Party members who were ordinary, sensible people who wouldn't hurt a fly. But technically they were Nazis. Or if they were Italians, they were Fascists.

'We generalise too much. The German people have suffered just as much from the war as any other country. You, Louis, will say they deserve it because they started the war. Not true. A handful of power-crazy men ordered the attack on Poland. Nobody voted for that. Ordinary people don't vote for their fathers, husbands, brothers and sons to be killed.'

Cattoir smiled. 'You're an idealist, Harry. And I admire you for it. It's better than being a cynic like Louis and me.'

Vi said quietly, 'What do you think about the people who shaved the heads of women who'd had some sort of relationship with Germans?'

When nobody else responded Cattoir said, 'It was barbaric but it was understandable.' And Cattoir half-smiled as he saw Jenny's hand close round Vi's hand.

Jenny said quickly, 'How is it understandable? I can remember Marie-Claire at the library, she was terribly in love with that young German – Günther – or whatever his name was. And he was in love with her. Are they supposed to hate one another because a bastard like Hitler decides to invade France? People are just people. You're only French or English or German because that's where you were born.'

Cattoir smiled lovingly at Jenny. 'Well said, my love. But cast your mind back to Romeo and Juliet – the Montagues and the Capulets. As I'm sure Shakespeare will have said, "twas ever thus".'

When the others had left, Harry Bailey asked Jenny if she'd like to walk down to the cottages that had once been their home. She seemed rather subdued and she shook her head. 'No. I don't want to see them. You go if you want to.' He'd left it at that but wondered what had brought on his wife's mood.

It was three years later that they went back for Vi's wedding. They had stayed again with Cattoir who now had substantial financial interests in a French and an Italian film company.

It was the day after the wedding when Jenny and Bailey and Cattoir were sitting on the patio in the sunshine on the south side of the house.

The conversation turned to Vi and her husband and Cattoir told them of the difference their marriage had made to both their lives.

'She was rather serious, you know, and being with Daudet has helped her a lot. He cares for her very much but he's got a sunnier disposition than hers. But there will be problems of course. Bound to be.'

Jenny half-closed her eyes against the sun. 'What makes you say that?'

'You don't really recover, ever, from what the Germans did to her. You can put on a show. You can look outwardly normal. But you're not. Daudet talked with me about what went on in those days. Wanted to know what happened. I asked him why he was asking and he said that sometimes she had nightmares and woke up screaming and for several days she couldn't, or wouldn't, speak. Just shook her head or nodded. And after a few days she would be back to normal.'

Jenny said, 'Did you tell him what went on way back?'

'Some of it. Not all of it. But enough to make him understand.' He paused and smiled. 'To change the subject for a moment. I'm getting married next spring. Will you both come over? And the little girl of course. Put it in your diaries for May 6.'

Jenny beamed, clapping her hands with pleasure and excitement. 'Who is she, Paul? Tell us about her. Come on.'

'She's Italian, not a *contessa*, and she's very very beautiful. It's a terrible case of cradle-snatching. She's only twenty-six but I love her very much.'

'Have you got a photograph?'

Cattoir grinned, reaching into his pocket. 'By pure chance, I have.' He handed a black and white photograph to her and Bailey leaned over to look at it too.

Jenny looked up at Cattoir. 'Paul, she's so beautiful. Those eyes and that face. Where did you meet her and how long have you known her?'

Cattoir laughed. 'How female those two questions are. One from a friend, the other from a mother.' He smiled. 'We've known each other for just over a year. And we met at Cinecitta in Rome where she was an advisor on a film I've put money into called *La Dolce Vita*.'

'She should be in the film, Paul. She looks not just beautiful but serene.'

'What a lovely word, my dear. And so right.' He laughed. 'I must remember that.'

CHAPTER 44

Although Harry Bailey still wrote his weekly piece for the agency he was now well-enough known to be asked to write other things. He wrote copy for a couple of advertising agencies and wrote a treatment and script for a film that was never produced because of disagreement among the potential backers. But it got his name known as a competent writer of film-scripts. His first script to be filmed was a modern version of Romeo and Juliet set in Naples after the war. Girl's father a Fascist and boy's father a Communist. It was seeing the dailies of this that made Cattoir phone him. He wanted him to come to Rome to discuss making the film version of a novel that Cattoir had bought the rights to. It was a book about life in France during the German occupation based on a Resistance network in Clermont-Ferrand.

After Bailey had read the book they would discuss the film.

'It's got problems, Paul.'

'Tell me.'

'Points of view. It uses somebody looking in but not involved. We could make that a journalist, a woman maybe. And a lot of people are doing thrillers based on the Resistance at the moment. One at Pinewood and at least a couple in Hollywood. Big budgets too.'

'I know about the others but they're all phoney. Nothing but non-stop action – the Germans always losing out – half the budgets spent on big bangs and buildings going up in flames.' He laughed. 'They've been buying up film clips of the landings. It's crazy. Let them get on with it. What I want is the real thing. The network is only part of it. The daily life of the people in the area is what matters. The network is the focus, but it's the people who matter.' He paused. 'And no stars, just good credible actors. So it would all depend on your script.'

'Do you want to talk to other writers first, before you decide?'

'I have done, dear boy. Four or five, all very bankable but they couldn't do it in a million years. Not what I want. And if I can't do it my way I shan't do it at all. So – do you want it?'

Bailey smiled. 'Of course I do.'

'When can you start?'

'We've got a new arrival expected in two weeks' time. I could start in a month if that's OK?'

'Congratulations. And how is the lovely Jenny?'

'She's fine. Gets a bit dull for her these days.' He shrugged. 'I've been thinking of getting a nanny so that she could find some interesting job that would occupy her mind a bit.'

For a few moments Cattoir was silent, then he said, 'When I think of Jenny I think of somebody very youthful, full of charm, very romantic . . .' he smiled, '. . . in the worst sort of way. Gay, happy-go-lucky and very innocent in the best kind of way.' He paused. 'Why on earth did you choose her for your network?'

Bailey shrugged. 'Bilingual French, independent, courage and willingness.'

Cattoir nodded but didn't look convinced. 'It's the solid ones like you and Louis who survive. In the end the romantic enthusiasts can't face up to reality. I don't know why.' He shrugged. 'You need a touch of cynicism.'

'Depending on the new baby, perhaps we could meet in London to go over the script. When I've done a treatment.'

'What a good idea.'

The second baby was born on time and was another girl, Victoria. Pauline was five years old in the same week but was not the slightest bit jealous of the newcomer. Some said she took after her father, others said it was more her grandfather.

The film treatment had been accepted with enthusiasm, so had the script. But it took a dozen versions to arrive at the final script.

CHAPTER 45

———————

Nanny Freeman not only had excellent references but she was one of those quiet amiable Scots who got her own way without raising her voice. She had a lovely Perth accent and chose her words carefully. Harry and Jenny took to her and trusted her immediately. The girls loved her too.

Bailey's work had increased so much that he had to rent a small office in Soho and employ a secretary. She typed his handwritten work, dealt with his mail and looked after his finances.

When the intercom buzzed he picked up the receiver.

'Yes?'

'It's Lady Helen on the line for you.'

'Put her through.'

'Is that you, Harry?'

'It is.'

'I wondered if I could pop round and take ten minutes of your time?'

'Why don't you and Alistair come over for dinner tonight?'

'That's very kind of you but I wanted to speak just to you.'

'Fine. You know where I am. Come round. I'll tell Jean to get the kettle on.'

When he'd hung up he looked around the small room where he worked at a small teak and tubular steel table. By the window was a trestle table covered with piles of scripts and manuscripts. The wall was shelved from top to bottom with books. He tidied up a bit and moved the visitors' chair nearer to his desk and turned the photograph of Jenny and the girls so that Helen could see it.

* * *

She kissed his cheek, slowly peeled off her gloves and loosened the fur collar of her coat as she sat down. They did the weather and the coming election until his girl had brought in the tray with the tea things. Then, as she carefully stirred her tea, she turned to look at him.

'Is there anything the matter with you and Jenny, Harry?'

He looked surprised. 'Not that I know of. Has she said there is?'

'No. Not a word.'

'So what's worrying you?'

'There's something wrong with her, Harry. And I don't know what it is.'

'In what way wrong?'

'She seems unsettled. As if her mind's on something far away. When we chat she isn't there somehow. There's a kind of melancholy.' She waved her hand. 'I'm probably just an old fool. But I've always known her so well and she seems to have drawn away.' She shrugged. 'I wondered if you and she weren't seeing eye to eye.' Her voice quavered as she smiled. 'Maybe it's I who've changed.'

'Nothing I know of, *Maman*. She's happy with Nanny Freeman, and the girls are OK. Maybe now that Pauline has started school she's missing her a bit, or feeling a bit left out.' He smiled. 'Anyway, I'll keep an eye on her. Changing the subject I hear that the mansion will be ready for your return in a few weeks' time. Are you looking forward to that?'

'Not really, Harry. It reminds me too much of the old days. Everything's changed.' She shrugged. 'After all, it's just a building. Moving back won't bring it all back again.' She stood up. 'Anyway, I must get on my way. Thanks for listening to me.' She smiled. 'Too vivid an imagination – that's my trouble.'

He walked with her to the street door, kissed her and waved down a taxi, opening the door and giving the address to the driver.

As he walked back to his office he thought about what she had said. He hadn't noticed any change in Jenny but maybe that was because he was with her every day and the change had been gradual. The only upset he could remember was when he had had the final confirmation that Paulette had been executed by a firing-squad not at Auschwitz but at Ravensbrück in the last weeks of the war. She had cried for days – that was only to be expected. They were close friends. But that letter had arrived nearly a year ago. Yet Lady Helen Campbell wasn't a panic merchant and he'd have to keep an eye on Jenny.

It was almost two months later that they were at the Savoy as guests of her mother and father who were entertaining some acquaintance from the Foreign Office and his wife.

The other guests were a strange couple. A rather loud-mouthed man in his fifties and a much younger and attractive new wife. He had been at the British Embassy in Washington for the whole of the war. His wife was American and he was obviously intent on impressing her with his close acquaintance with the White House and its inhabitants. Bailey was never quite sure how the conversation had got on to the OSS, the Office of Strategic Services that had been modelled on SOE. According to the man it was the OSS who had run the Resistance in France. Swirling his brandy he looked at Sir Alistair.

'Of course our people, SOE, were bloody useless. Swanning around the Riviera and living like lords off the fat of the land. Useless. A total waste of time.'

Bailey saw only the brief flash of a light reflected on her glass as she did it but he saw the wine dripping down the man's face as Jenny stood up and screamed, 'You bastard. You bastard.' And then her chair overturned and she was hurrying away. He followed her and as he left he heard Sir Alistair say, 'I'm afraid you asked for that, my daughter served in the Resistance with SOE.'

'I say. I'm sorry old chap. Had no idea . . .'

He waited for her at the ladies room and got her coat from the cloakroom. She swept out, pale and chin up and he kissed her mouth as he put her coat around her shoulders, walking her with his arm around her shoulders down the short road to the Strand.

He walked her in silence down to Trafalgar Square and they stood at the junction with Northumberland Avenue. He stopped, looked behind him and then across at the lights on the fountain and Landseer's stone lions in the Square.

She turned to look at him, tears still flowing down her upturned face. 'But the bastard was right, Harry. It *was* all a waste of time, and lives. A ghastly game.'

He kissed her forehead and turned her round to look behind them.

'D'you see that shop?'

'You mean the barber's shop?'

'Yes.'

'What about it?'

'That's where I was recruited into the I. Corps.'

'You mean you were recruited in a barber's shop?'

'Yeah.' He laughed and she laughed too. 'Let's go sweetie.'

He waved down a taxi and by the time they were home she seemed more relaxed.

He phoned her parents and apologised, but her father was on her side. 'The man was a bore. Should have been the soup not half a glass of decent Burgundy.'

When he got back to their small sitting room he poured them both a whisky.

'Ice or water?'

'Neither. Just the whisky.'

As he handed it to her she sipped it and then looked up at him. She patted the settee beside her. 'Sit down for a moment.' She sighed. 'Was Daddy annoyed?'

'Not with you, sweetie. But angry with the man.'

She looked down at her glass. 'I can't bear to think of Paulette alone in that ghastly concentration camp. And being taken out one morning to be shot. And the things they did to Vi. And Jimmy Long burned to death.' She looked up at his face. 'It wasn't just Germans who did all that. It was men. How could men do such things to helpless people?' She paused for a moment and then she said quietly. 'I can't stop thinking about them. I think about it all every day.'

'I've got to go to Rome for two or three days next week. How about you come with me?'

Her face lit up. 'Oh yes. I'd love that.'

The trip to Rome had been a great success. Cattoir had been in a party-giving mood and she had thoroughly enjoyed the few days.

It was a Saturday and no secretary so he answered the phone himself.

'Bailey.'

'Is that you, Harry?' The caller spoke in French and he replied in French.

'Yes. Who is it?'

'It's Vi, Harry. I'd like to talk to you.'

'Where are you?'

'In London.'

'Great. Come to dinner. Is your husband with you?'

'He's in London with me. We've been here for a month but I'd like to see you alone, not at your home.'

'Of course. What's the problem?'

'When can I see you?'

'Now, if you want.'

He took her to an Italian café in Frith Street and ordered a cappuccino for her and black coffee for himself.

'Why haven't you been to see us before in the month you've been here?'

'I've seen Jenny several times and that's why I wanted to talk to you.' She paused and looked at him. 'Did you know she's seeing a psychiatrist?'

'No. Are you sure?'

'I'm quite sure. That's why I came over to London.'

'I don't understand.'

'He contacted me and said she had problems and that it might help if she could talk with me.'

'About what?'

'About the days in the network.'

'Good God. Who is this psychiatrist?'

She opened her handbag, took out a card and slid it across the table. Bailey read it but he didn't recognise the name. He looked back at Vi.

'Why hasn't she told me about this?'

'She says you're too sane to understand.' She paused. 'He gives her drugs to keep her stable. Too many, too often, in my opinion. But I'm a vet, not a doctor.'

'How long has she been seeing this man?'

'About three months.'

'I'd better see him.' He paused. 'Is he doing her any good d'you think?'

'I don't think so. That's why I wanted to tell you.'

'Thanks.'

'Don't tell her that I've told you or she won't confide in me any more.'

'Why do you think she's got like this?'

She shrugged. 'She had lived a very sheltered life before the war. Just a little bit spoiled too. Very much the bright spark, the party girl. Show-jumping, dancing at the Dorchester or the Savoy.' She paused. 'A very attractive, very bright young creature.

'Then going into SOE. The training absorbed, but still a bit of a lark. Impetuous, disliking restrictions, always ready to defy authority – you for instance.

'And then the grim reality of the network. Competent, brave and totally loyal: To the network at first and then to you. This rock of a man, totally reliable, cool and calm. Then suddenly it's all over. You marry your hero and have two babies – and that's it. No qualifications, no manor house, no show-jumping. Just a nice lazy life. So then you have plenty of time to think. And what do you think about? You think about your old friends, some of whom didn't come back.' She put her hand across the table on his. 'She showed me a book you'd brought back for her after one of your visits to London. A book of poems, and you'd written some lines of a poem on the fly-leaf. Do you remember it?'

'Yes. It was a poem by Leigh Hunt.'

'Say it to me.'

He smiled and thought for a moment and then said softly,

'Jenny kissed me when we met,
Jumping from the chair she sat in;
Time, you thief, who love to get
Sweets into your list, put that in!
Say I'm weary, say I'm sad,
Say that health and wealth have missed me:
Say I'm growing old, but add
Jenny kissed me.'

She smiled. 'When she was whisked back to London it was the only thing she took with her. She told me it had taught her a lesson.'

'What lesson was that?'

'It was not a lesson about the poem but about you. That romance wasn't about a laughing girl, dancing the night away at the Savoy, but a man who people saw as tough, ruthless and impersonal who loved in a quiet way. She said you were like those candles you can't blow out.

'So where are we? A brave man comes back to the responsibilities of marriage and building a career, and a very brave girl whose blood still ran with adrenalin comes back to a pleasant but rather dull routine, and nowhere for her adrenalin to go. But full of sad memories of times past.'

'So what do I do about it?'

She shook her head. 'I've thought about it constantly. I honestly don't know what you should do.' She paused. 'There's only one piece of advice I can give you, my dear. Don't let her know that I've spoken to you about all this. She'd die of shame.'

The pretty receptionist showed him into the office. It was large and furnished with Swedish teak and chrome and the man sitting at the desk was young and expensively dressed. He smiled and pointed at the visitor's chair.

'And how can I help you . . .' he glanced at Bailey's card '. . . Mr Bailey?'

'I came to ask you about my wife.'

The young man shook his head and waved his hand as if he were cleaning a window.

'It's a golden rule, old chap. I only deal direct with the patient, they have to come to me under their own steam.' He smiled an unsmiling smile. 'Can cause endless problems with one spouse eager to establish that the other is mentally unbalanced.' He stood up, unwinding slowly.

Bailey didn't move. 'My wife is already a patient of yours.'

The man sat down slowly. 'Bailey. I don't remember a Bailey.'

'Maybe she used her maiden name, Campbell.'

'Ah yes. Jennifer Campbell.' He shook his head. 'But I still can't discuss a patient with a third party.'

'I'm her husband, not a third party, and I want to know what's the matter with her.'

'Are you familiar with her background?'

'Of course I am.'

'So what do you think her problem is?'

'I've no idea.'

'I can hardly believe that, Mr Bailey.'

'I don't give a damn what you believe. If you don't tell me what I want to know I shall find her another doctor.'

'That would be a great mistake.'

'Why?'

'Did your wife tell you about her sessions with me?'

'No.'

'So how do you know about them?'

'That's my business. And now I know I want to know what treatment she is getting and if it's suitable for her.'

'You would put in jeopardy the small progress she has made so far.'

'That's a risk I'm prepared to take unless you tell me what is going on.'

'What, exactly, is it that you want to know?'

'I want to know, first, what you think her problem is.'

'I don't *think*, Mr Bailey. I know exactly what her problem is.' He paused. 'Your wife has a guilt complex a mile wide.'

'Guilt about what?'

'Oh come, come, Mr Bailey. A man you know is burnt to death. A close friend, a girl, is executed in a concentration camp and your closest girlfriend is beaten up and made into a semi-cripple for the rest of her life. But you yourself come back to a pleasant life with no harm done.' He paused. 'No wonder she's got a guilt complex. In my opinion she *should* feel guilty.'

'That's how you read her situation?'

'Precisely.'

Bailey stood up. 'You won't be seeing any more of her. You're a sick man. It's you who needs treatment.'

He phoned Vi at her hotel and told her about his meeting with the psychiatrist and she agreed that he would have to talk to Jenny despite breaking her confidence with Jenny. The problem was that although he knew the man she had been consulting was totally unsuitable, he had no idea about what he could do to really help her. He decided that before he took any action he ought to speak to her parents.

They both sat in silence as he told them what had happened. Her father was obviously shocked, almost disbelieving that she needed help. But her mother was calmer and he suspected that she had already sensed that something was wrong when she came to see him at his office.

'What do you think should be done?' she said.

'I think I must find her another, more perceptive, psychiatrist. I can't just cut that man off without suggesting somebody who might be able to help her. But I'm not sure how she'll react. She may resent what I've done.'

Lady Helen shook her head. 'She won't resent it, Harry. She's got great faith in you.' She paused and looked at her husband. 'What about Tim Winters?'

'He gave up practising five years ago.'

'But he'd do it for you. Phone him now. He'd do it for your daughter.'

Sir Alistair went to the phone in the hall and it was ten minutes before he came back.

'If she'll phone him herself he's willing to see if he can help her.' He looked at Bailey. 'He'd do his best for her. He says it's not uncommon amongst women who were agents. But he thinks it will only be time that resolves the problem rather than anything he can do. But he's a good man, and at least he'll be sympathetic.'

The girls were already in bed when he got home and after he'd kissed them both goodnight he came downstairs and poured a whisky for himself and a sherry for Jenny. As he handed her the glass he sat down beside her on the couch. He held up his glass.

'Cheers.'

'Vi phoned me and told me she'd talked to you and that you'd seen the doctor.'

'She was worried sick about you.' He paused. 'The man you were seeing would never be able to help you, sweetie. I talked to your parents and your father has an old friend, a first-class psychiatrist. He's retired but he's ready to see you if you'd like to talk to him. He knows the background and is definitely sympathetic.'

'What did my parents say?'

'They were sympathetic too.'

For a few moments she was silent. 'There's no point in me seeing anybody. They can't help me. Nobody can. Not unless they could somehow wipe out my memory.'

'They could maybe help you see it from a different perspective. You did everything that could be expected of you. If anyone was to blame for any of the things that happened it was me.'

She smiled and shook her head. 'You carried out your orders, my dear. You took every precaution to protect us all. It's not about blame or responsibility.'

'What is it then?'

She shrugged. 'Just memories and thoughts that I can't forget.' She shook her head. 'Nothing can change what happened. And it wasn't just Vi and Paulette. It was all of us. We thought we were fighting the Germans. We did. But it made no difference. It was a waste of courage and a waste of lives.'

He kissed her cheek and said softly, 'I love you so much, Jenny dear. We'll talk again tomorrow.'

It was beginning to rain as he paid off the cab and looked up at the flat. There were lights on everywhere. He was later than usual and at the top of the stairs he called out for Jenny as he took off his coat. It was Nanny Freeman who answered his call. She seemed uneasy.

'Madam's not back yet, sir.'

'Where was she going?'

'She didn't say.'

'What time did she leave?'

'About midday, sir.'

'I think we'll go out for dinner tonight. I'll book us a table at Giorgio's.'

Nanny Freeman stood there looking worried and he said, 'What's the matter. You look worried.'

She almost whispered as she said, 'She took a bag, sir. And she'd had several drinks. I think she was crying as she went downstairs. I've been very worried. I put the girls to bed and they're asleep.'

'OK, Nanny. Leave it to me.'

He phoned Vi's hotel but she and her husband had checked out the previous evening. They had said they were going home.

Her parents hadn't seen her for several days and although they were obviously worried about her they had no suggestions as to where she might have gone. They didn't think he should report her missing to the police so soon. They were sure that she would contact him in a day or so when she had calmed down.

On the third day he phoned Vi in Brantôme. She had heard nothing from Jenny. And it gradually dawned on him that she had made no new friends back in England and the friends she had had in the network she never saw. But for better or worse they were the only friends she had.

In desperation he went to see her father's old friend.

He was a kindly man but he said, 'It's terribly frowned on to discuss somebody's mental state with someone else, no matter how well-meaning they may be. But now she's gone missing you'd better fill me in on the background and see if we can make some sense out of it.'

It had seemed a rambling, disjointed description of their lives in France and the man had asked questions from time to time to keep him talking. Finally he said, 'When you went back to Bergerac for this parade for de Gaulle did she seem to want to go back to look at places where you had been?'

'No. When I suggested we had a look at the cottages where we lived she said she didn't want to.'

Tim Winters looked at his watch. 'We've been talking for nearly two hours about her days in the network. A couple more questions.' He paused. 'Were you, yourself, happy in your work there?'

Bailey shrugged. 'I was too occupied to be either happy or unhappy. There were too many people dependent on me to take my eye off the ball.'

'Was Jenny happy?'

Bailey thought for a moment. 'Yes. I think she was happy. In a kind of way.'

'She had a vital role, a fulfilling role?'

'Yes. She was my closest colleague.' He paused. 'Why do you ask about being happy? There was a war on.'

Winters smiled. 'Four times when you talked to me you needed to describe something that happened. And in each of those times you mentioned the weather. It was always sunny. But there must have been snow and rain as well.'

Bailey smiled. 'I think it was just that we both loved France, the country and the people. I guess enthusiasts see things through the proverbial rose-tinted glasses.'

'And if you felt that way about it she, with her outgoing personality, would have felt the same affection.'

301

'Yes. I'm sure she did.'

'But it all ended in a kind of dead-beat way. Some disappointments, some disillusion?'

'Not for me. I expected that that's how it would be.'

'Would she have expected it to be that way too?'

'I guess not.'

Winters smiled. 'So it's back to Bergerac. I think that's where she will go. Like Proust – *à la recherche du temps perdu* – eager to go back to what reminds her of those days when all was hope and endeavour. She was risking her life every day she was there – and in the end there wasn't a prize. She realises that it wasn't worth the risks. And a stupid man tells her that she should feel guilty because she wasn't beaten up or killed. She told you herself that it haunts her. She can't stop thinking about it.' He sighed. 'That's where you'd better start looking for her. That's where she'll be.'

'Are you sure of all this?'

'No. Of course I'm not sure. But everything you've told me points that way.'

'But why go there. What good would it do her?'

'She isn't looking for that.'

'What's she looking for then?'

'She's just putting back the clock.'

He took the early flight to Bordeaux and hired a car at the airport.

'They all helped me – Vi, Louis and Paul Cattoir. She'd booked in at a local hotel and Louis told me that the patron had told him that she'd been drinking heavily. But she hadn't been seen at the hotel for two days.' He sighed. 'And I suddenly realised where she might be. And that's where we found her body, at the place in the woods where the bluebells grew. She'd taken a bottle-full of pills. There was no note or anything . . .' As his voice faltered he stopped for a moment and took a deep breath and he heard Victoria say, 'Don't talk about it any more, Daddy. We understand. We really do.'

He looked from one to the other and said, 'I've told you all this because you'll hear it, some day – totally distorted. She didn't die of drink or drugs. She died because she'd been in the war. What had happened to Violette and Paulette was more than she could bear.'

For a moment they were silent and then Pauline said quietly, 'What happened in the end to Violette?'

He was terribly tempted to make the point by telling her the truth. That Violette was the woman at the Special Forces Club that she'd described as 'that old bag'. But you don't do that to people you love.

'She's still around,' he said.